2204 Hunter Lane

Publisher's Note: This is a work of fiction. Any resemblance to actual events, or persons, living or dead, is entirely coincidental. Names, characters, places and incidents are either the product of the author's imagination or are used for the purpose of this fiction tale.

Cover Design: Marie-France Leger

ISBN Paperback: 9798426293311

For more information, updates, and/or teasers, follow @mariefranceleger on Instagram.com or @maariefraance on TikTok.

~~Author Playlist~~

Animal I Have Become – Three Days Grace

Back to Me – Of Mice and Men

The Big Bang – Rock Mafia

Do I Wanna Know? – Arctic Monkeys

End of Me – A Day to Remember

Enter Sandman – Metallica

Go Fuck Yourself – Two Feet

I found – Amber Run

The Wall – Patrick Reza

Without You – Breaking Benjamin

Memories – We Came As Romans

My Understandings – Of Mice and Men

One Night Only – The Struts

Red Flag – Billy Talent

Paralyzer – Finger Eleven

Porn Star Dancing – My Darkest Days

Break My Baby – Kaleo

Can You Feel My Heart – Bring Me the Horizon

To all those who forget to live while they're still alive...
You matter.

This story is inspired by true events.

TW: Drunk driving, alcohol abuse, loss of a loved one, mental health/insecurity, body image and toxic family dynamic.

2204
Hunter Lane

Marie-France Leger

Chapter One
Marley

"*Will you just fucking listen to me?*"

I didn't. I ignored every single slimy bullshit comment that waste of a man had to say. Besides, I had more pressing issues to attend to. Like the fact I had absolutely nothing anymore. No home, no family, and no man who could lie about being unfaithful. *AMEN to that.*

"Ha-ha." My own thoughts brought a chuckle out of me. That, or my insanity was slowly creeping in. *One of two things.*

"What?" Todd scowled, eyes blazing and ready for a fight. "Just fucking laughing now are we? This look like a joking matter to you, Marley?"

He took a heavy step towards me but I held out a hand and met his eyes. "Back the fuck up, Todd."

Surprisingly, he did. *If only he knew what loyalty meant.*

"Let me pack in peace."

Todd kept his jaw locked and looked me up and down, evident disgust cemented all over his features.

I let him stare in silence as I continued to rummage through drawers and throw whatever the hell I could get my shaky hands on into the black luggage I took with me from New York.

It's crazy how life can change in just a year. How you can go from being a promising marketing executive to getting cold feet and running away with a no-good man to Nebraska. *Nebraska* of all places in the world. I lived in the Big Apple, surrounded by award winning artists, athletes, lights that could blind you and buildings that were crafted by world renowned architects.

Now I'm moving out of this one bedroom apartment in Lincoln because the man I trusted with my heart decided to step on it with a red stiletto that belonged to his ex-girlfriend. You know, stupid me for believing his reasonings for coming back to this place. I thought he was charming at first. He grew up here and was only in New York for a bachelor trip. One drunken night out led me to him, led him to me, and led us to fifteen tequila shots and a full night of sloppy sex and instant *"I love you's."*

And yet, I assumed he was the best freaking thing to happen to me. It was like all the stars had magically aligned and I thought wow, this 5'9 hunk of flesh is going to be my husband one day. Well screw marriage. *Especially if it's with him.*

"Can you just leave?" I finally released with pure exasperation. "Like, go fuck your ex or something. I don't care. I don't want to see you. I don't want to hear your voice, and I sure as shit don't want you staring at me with that disgusted expression when I should be looking at *you* that way."

"I didn't fuck my ex."

"No she just fucked you, right?" I raked my fingers through my long brown hair and shook my head. "I don't understand guys like you, Todd. You still had a thing for your ex? Fine. You wanted to move back to be with her? Even better. But what I don't understand is why you took it upon yourself to string me along for a year while screwing around behind my back."

Tears filled in my waterline, but I refused to let them fall. I didn't want to let him see how much pain he put me through, I *couldn't* let him see it.

He yanked his eyes away from my face and for a split second, I thought I could see a smidge of remorse. But when his eyes returned to meet mine, it was clear he felt nothing but shame in himself for getting caught.

"It wasn't like I planned for this to happen, baby, you got to know that."

"No? So every time you went out looking for a *"job"* you just happened to stick your dick inside your ex on the way?"

He zipped his lips immediately, unable to deny what he'd been doing for the past few months.

The shittiest part about all of it was that he didn't even have the decency to tell me. I literally had to find out right before one of his "outings" to meet her while he was in the shower. His phone was going crazy so I turned it over to check who was spamming him and found myself staring at a set of boobs and copious sexts.

So naturally, I was in a blind rage and went down a rabbit hole reading every single text, snapchat, and DM from the past few months. I think it's safe to say that I saw everything he'd seen while fucking her, only I witnessed it through photos.

"Where are you going to go?" He asked sharply.

I raised my eyebrows in realization that I was officially played. Badly. And the man I fell in love with was no longer there. Maybe I fell in love with someone I thought he was, someone I wished he could be. And that drive for a happy future with someone who could take care of me was clouding the reality of it all. *The reality that he was just like everyone else and I was incapable of finding something substantial.*

My eyes fell on the massive luggage of spilling clothes, skincare and books as I took in a deep breath before pressing it down and zipping it up.

I didn't answer his stupid question. I didn't look at his stupid face with his stupid facial hair and snake-green eyes.

The muscles in my arms flexed as I lifted the luggage off the bed and wheeled it with me towards the door, but he grabbed my hand as I shoved past him.

"I still care about you, Mar. I want to know you'll be okay."

I practically spit in his face, but the saliva settled at the back of my throat. "As long as I'm away from you, I'll be the happiest girl on this planet."

Flashing a saccharine smile, I stepped into my white boots and scanned my apartment for the last time. Everything felt out of place now that I knew the truth of Todd's infidelity. All the happy memories in this place were tainted. All the late nights binging Big Mouth and drinking wine didn't exist. Not in the way that I remembered those memories.

I shut the door without even looking at Todd, fully aware that I would be crying about him once I'd reached my destination. But where did I want to go? What the hell would I do now? My family practically shunned me out of their life the second I gave up my executive position to move to Nebraska with Todd. "You ruined the family name," is what my mom said to me the last time we spoke. "How could you be so stupid? Think for once in your life, Marley" my dad followed suit. I guess I deserved it. I was an idiot. And this decision ruined my life.

I stepped into my 2016 Malibu and locked the door, inhaling the leftover scent of Todd's cologne clutching to the passenger seat. Anger began to boil in my insides as I took out my perfume and sprayed it all over the lining, erasing any trace of Todd that remained in my car. Luckily I just bought it so he didn't have any of his stupid shit anywhere, so that was a –

"Marley, wait!" I turned to see Todd running out of the apartment complex, waving his arms like a maniac.

And I pressed the gas. I pressed the gas like my life depended on it. Because at this point, that was all my life depended on.

Chapter Two
Hunter

"C'mon Hunt, done already?"

Josh slammed his hand on the wooden table, calling over the busty blonde who purposely chose our table to serve.

She was a sweet girl, Addison I think her name was. I'd seen her around a lot at this bar, *probably cause she works here dumb ass.*

Fucking shit, lots of lights. Tons.

I blinked away from the manic commotion in the middle of the dance floor and attempted to zero in on Addison; black long sleeve, tight as a condom. Her tits jumpin' about, and about, and about.

"Another round, boys?" She winked, pursing her lips at me.

"You already know, baby." Josh wrapped a flimsy arm around my shoulder, pinching my collarbone. "Hunt, Coors or Bud?"

"Uh..." *Man, I need some goddamn water.* "Can I get a cup of ice, Addison?"

I think she frowned at me. I don't know. Too many fuckin' lights.

"It's Britt, Hunter. But of course you don't remember that."

Huh?

Josh leaned back into the seat next to me, chuckling under his breath. He shot me a look that said, *"you're on your own, man"* as he took a swig of his beer, downing it in one gulp.

I turned my attention back to Addi – I mean, *Britt*, as she crossed her arms and glared into my fuckin' soul.

"Were you that drunk when we hooked up, Hunter? Or was I just that underwhelming?"

I stared at her blankly. Absolutely no recollection of us getting together crossed my mind.

"Seriously?" She spat. "Nothing?"

I rubbed the stubble across my jaw and averted eye contact, trying to figure out how I would get myself out of this mess.

"Can I uh," I licked my bottom lip, tasting broken skin and dried blood. "Can I get that cup of ice, please?"

Josh howled in laughter before covering his eyes and turning away from me completely. *Definitely was not the right thing to say. Nah. But my fucking tongue feels like sandpaper and I'm tired as fuck and I'm not in the mood to have this fight. I'm not in the mood to do fucking anything but get home and pass out.*

Britt snorted and uncrossed her arms, looking me up and down before grabbing a glass of water from another server's tray and throwing it in my face.

I closed my eyes, letting the cool water soak into my eyelashes, falling down to my neck and coating my flushed skin. *Feels like a damn nice bath.*

With pride, she stomped off and escaped into the kitchen.

"Well," Josh said, still laughing and shit, "looks like we aren't gettin' another round."

I took out my wallet and threw a twenty on the table, running my fingers through my wet hair before grabbing my coat.

"I don't know her, man."

"Nah, but she knows you." He smirked.

We walked back to my truck in silence, the booming sound of classic rock fading into the distance as I reached my driver door.

"You sure?" Josh asked, making his way to the passenger side.

I rolled my eyes, unlocking the truck and sliding in. "You really goin' to ask me that each time?"

He shrugged. "Yep. Maybe one day you won't fight me off."

I held up the middle finger and planted my ass on the seat. *God I love my truck.* I sat there for a few minutes, closing my eyes and leaning into the headrest. *So warm and fucking drama-free. No Addisons or Britts or whatever.*

After a few minutes I brought the engine to life and took off into the direction of my house. Yeah, probably not the best idea to drive, but this was my adrenaline rush. No one could take this away from me. I'd done it countless times and I still had my life so, no harm no foul. Besides, my house was just eight minutes away from Cid's Pub. *Easy.*

"You really don't remember her, man?" Josh asked, glancing over at me.

I grunted and turned away. "Not a clue in hell."

"Pfft." He placed two hands on the dash to stretch out his arms. "You'll remember tomorrow."

"Hopefully not."

Josh cleared his throat, tapping the window glass. "Feelin' okay, Hunt?"

Grinning, I rolled down my window and let the icy air smack my face. "Just peachy."

It was moments like this where time stilled and the only thing that mattered was my damn self. No problems, no loss, no pain. Alcohol was on my side, masking my sadness, freezing my thoughts. Just me, only me. I was good. *I'm good.* I was alive, and I was happy. And nothing could hurt me. *Everything's good. I'm alive and I'm -*

"... and I know you don't want to talk about your mom but –"

Josh's words snapped me back into reality real fucking quick. I bit down hard on my bottom teeth and clenched my fist. "What are you going on about?"

"Dude –"

"No. Shut the fuck up. Just shut the fuck up and keep quiet."

And he did just that. No more follow up comments. No protests. Nothing. Good man.

After a few minutes we pulled into my driveway and I inhaled a deep breath. "You stayin' over?"

"Nah," he shook his head, "Beth's going to pick me up."

"Hm," I smirked. "Things heatin' up between you two?"

But Josh didn't respond. Instead, he stared out the window and rested his chin on his knuckles.

Ah, fuck. *Alright, about time you fess up, Hunter.* "I didn't mean to snap earlier, man. I'm sorry."

Josh didn't understand, not even a little. But I was done with this night and the last thing I wanted to do was talk about my mom. He knew that it was a sore subject, yeah. Didn't excuse me being an asshole, though.

Josh looked over at me and shook his head. "I'm just worried about you, Hunt. You been drinkin' yourself to oblivion every night since" – he paused and sucked in a breath.

"Look man, I'm happy to be here. You've been my best friend since we were kids and that's why I'm sayin' this. Talk to someone. Talk it out, do somethin'."

Who does he think I am? "I do things."

His phone lit up and he snagged it before I could get a read.

"Beth's pullin' up. I got to go."

I nodded and stepped out of the truck, barely holding myself upright as I tapped the hood.

"Same time tomorrow night?" I called after Josh as he moved down my driveway.

He kept walking and shot a thumbs up before disappearing into Beth's car and driving off.

He seemed happy. They'd been hookin' up for a few months now and as far as I knew it, he hadn't slept with anyone else. Not that I cared who my best friend shagged but it was good to see some loyalty around these parts.

Maybe one day I'll trust someone enough to call them at midnight to come get my drunk ass. But until that day comes, my bottle of Jack will keep me company.

Chapter Three
Marley

How the hell I ended up stranded on the side of a dark backroad in Nebraska was beyond me. I just drove and drove, convinced that Todd had superspeed and was zooming behind me.

You know how some people pretend to be chased by zombies to run faster on a treadmill? Yeah, well, I truly believed I was being chased by Todd. That's how foggy and exhausted my brain was. And I guess I manifested it into my car because my tire was now flat, and my phone was dead because stupid me forgot my freaking charger trying to keep myself together and run out of the apartment.

"Ugh, just *kill me!*" I yelled into the onyx sky.

And the stars laughed at me, every single one of them. But I didn't care. I needed to yell. I needed to cry. I needed to do something because I couldn't just stand here in the cold October air and wait for my death. *Well,*

*I could. But I would rather die peacefully than at the
hands of a crazy masked murderer.*

I developed a good routine of pacing outside my
car, *my new car* might I add, for a few minutes then
proceeded to retreat back into the drivers seat and cry. I
cried my heart and soul out. Whatever water was left
swimming in my body came out through my eyes and
stamped my cheeks in a coat of mascara and sadness.

How did I ruin my life this badly? I mean, I've
seen movies about how sad, depressed women went
A.W.O.L and changed their entire life, ended up
meeting a sexy business man and became a millionaire
all within six months.

But me? Of course I wasn't that lucky. My
brother was a shark on Wall Street, raking in over six-
figures a year by simply breathing in the direction of the
right person. My parents adored him, of course they did.
He was everything they wanted him to be and he did it
happily.

Not Marley Matthews. Nope. I was the black
sheep of the family I suppose, tainting the Matthews
lineage for future generations to come.

I never meant for any of this to happen. I never
wanted to be the rebellious kid who preferred going to
parties over burying my nose in a book. As much as I
wanted to be in good graces with my parents, I was
never going to turn into Adam.

Sometimes I wish I turned out like my brother.
He kept to himself, graduated Columbia with a summa

cum laude in finance and got married to a successful chef at an expensive restaurant in Manhattan.

He was my parents' little angel even though he was three years older than me. It was never a competition between us because I wasn't even in the races, not to Harlow and Mike.

I remember how happy they were when I finally graduated from NYU with a marketing degree – even happier when I copped a paid internship position at BH&Y for marketing. Don't even get me started on the sheer heart attack I thought they'd had when I landed a secure placement as a permanent marketing assistant.

And then I messed it up.

I messed it up by meeting Todd Sherman on a random Friday night at SixFiveFour downtown NY and moving my dumb ass to Nebraska.

Naturally the question that plagued my mind for the entirety of my four hour drive was if I could go back. *Should I even want to.* But that was not an option.

My parents were already under the impression that their only daughter was a lost cause, a mess of a woman and an embarrassment to the Matthews name. If they heard about my split from the one man who forced me out of my near-successful life in New York, they'd laugh in my direction before slamming the door in my face.

I stepped out of my car and began circling the perimeter of the road as I pulled my thin, baby blue cardigan around me tightly. My jacket was buried somewhere in the thick of clothes stuffed into my luggage and truthfully, the cold air soothed my insanity. Almost like a last *hoorah!* for being such an idiot.

It was in my period of pacing that I noticed a bright light across a field in the distance. I squinted a little harder and made out the silhouette of a barn and a farmhouse.

"Oh my God," I laughed, my breath clouding as it escaped my mouth. "This is how I die."

Like every single bad horror movie I'd ever seen, the idea of me finding help was definitely slim. But what the hell was I going to do? Todd and I had been living off of his previous lottery winnings and my grandparents' inheritance was running thin. *Like I said, I didn't think anything through.*

Sure I could maybe afford a few weeks at a hotel but then what? Was I staying in Nebraska? Hell no. There was nothing for me here, nothing. But then again, what was there for me in New York? Did I even like it there? Was this even –

A cold gust of wind chilled my spine and I shivered, rubbing my hands all down my arms to create a warm friction but that did absolutely nothing.

I jogged back to my car and placed my keys in the ignition, checking how much gas I had left. But of course, continuing on my lucky streak, I had none. I probably could've made it another thirty seconds before my car shut down entirely.

And yup! My tire was flat and I had no spare. Even if I did, I had no idea how to change it. *This is truly my karma. I find out my boyfriend has been cheating on me for months and now I'm stranded in the middle of butt-fuck Nebraska, in the dead of night, with no cellphone and a flat. God... You really do hate me don't you?*

My eyes zeroed in on the distant farmhouse once more. The feathered sounds of cicadas and frog croaks floated through the air, accompanied by crickets and my own heavy breathing.

The house seemed bigger than most abandoned, petrifying homes they depicted in scary movies. It was almost... welcoming? Homey? *Maybe I really am losing it.*

Before my mind could warn me against any potential danger, my feet carried me in the direction of the farmhouse as I marched through a field of mud and hay, my white boots submerging in brown swamp.

So what if I die? What life am I living right now? A failure, a nuisance to the people who were supposed to love me through the bad and the ugly. I got nothing to lose.

I walked for minutes. Time dragged on slow, but my heartbeat was frantic. I couldn't stop thinking about how I, a twenty-three year old girl, messed up so badly I ended up in a different state hundreds of miles away from everything I worked towards.

All my life I sought out a purpose. I thought I
was born for a reason, and I would die being
memorable. What a hefty expectation to have. Because
sometimes, you make choices your heart thinks is right
and your mind doesn't. But as the romanticized saying
goes, *"follow your heart."* What a load of bullshit. All my
heart did was cast me out of my family, my city, my
future, *everything*.

And slowly, my exhaustion turned the
atmosphere into a blur. My movements. My breathing.
All the thoughts in my brain swiveling together like
weeds. The sound of crunching hay. The blinding
flashlight that grew closer and closer to me. Oh shit –

"Who the fuck are you?" A voice sounded at the
cock of a shotgun. "What in the hell?"

My heart stilled, my hands immediately flying up
into the air as I surrendered. "I – I'm just – My car! The
tire's flat and I don't have a spare and I just – I need
help? Help! Do *not* shoot holy shit, please."

*I was totally joking about the dying thing. I didn't
want to die. But nope, nope I am going to die right now.
At the hands of a crazy farmer who has a bloody shotgun.
A SHOTGUN.*

A low laugh invaded the open air as the dark
silhouette of the shotgun lowered and the flashlight
dimmed a radical amount.

"Payton!" A husky voice called, causing me to
flinch at the weight in his tone.

A moment of silence passed before a sweet voice called back through the light of the farmhouse window. "Yah, Dex?"

Southern twang. Charming.

The flashlight shone in my eyes once more, brighter than before. I raised my hand to block the beam, squinting through my fingers.

"Get out here!" The voice, who I assumed belonged to this Dex character, responded.

"I ain't cleanin' no cow shit, Dex! That's your job to do!" She hollered.

I still hadn't gotten a clear view of anyone's appearance and I wasn't sure I wanted to. Dex, whoever this man was, was one move away from killing me and the other individual standing behind him remained mute. Though, through the dimness of the night, I could make out a twinkle of his eyes observing.

Crap. "I'm not –" *How the hell do I even say this?* "I'm not dangerous or anything. You can search me, I have no weapons, I –"

"You're trespassin' on private property, miss. I don't give a rat's ass what kind of excuse you done been conjuring up, as long as you're off my field in thirty seconds."

This is a nightmare. "Sir I don't want to be here anymore than you want me here but I have a flat tire and I have no gas and I'm not from here and –"

"Oh, goodness!" A middle-aged woman with short blonde hair and a curvy build jogged down the white porch stairs, alerting the motion sensor lights. She wore a friendly expression, dressed in a white apron that covered a blue dress and beige sneakers.

I took a step back as she approached and she froze in her step, scanning me up and down with a tentative expression. My eyes quickly switched to the burly man in front of me as this woman clutched his forearm. *My murderer.*

He had to be over 6'5 with brown hair and a rugged beard to match. His red plaid shirt was undone a few buttons, revealing a beer belly and a hairy chest. *A true sight for sore eyes.*

But the guy standing behind him... he looked nothing like Dex, at least not from what I could see. He was a tad shorter, but only by a few inches with blonde hair and a coat of scruff. Even though half of his face was being shielded by Dex's shadow, I could still make out the sparkle of his crystal blue eyes boring into me.

"She's freezin' Hunter, give her your coat." The woman spoke, nudging at the man behind her.

Hunter.

"She should've dressed for the weather, then." Hunter's voice was raspy and low, much like Dex's. I could sense a hint of amusement in his response, though he didn't smile. He didn't move.

Good God, I'm dead.

Gentle fingers wrapped around my wrist as Payton led me towards the porch steps of the farmhouse. We passed a white sign with black lettering stuck in the ground before the stairs: 2204.

"Come on deary, let's get you warmed up inside."

Is this a red flag? Am I walking into my death? I don't feel particularly threatened? Then again, I'm clearly not good at assessing situations. If I was, I would've figured out months ago that Todd was cheating on me. I wouldn't have left my job in New York. I would still have a family to turn to, friends I didn't abandon all for my stupid relationship. I'd still be me. Now... who the hell am I? And what the hell am I doing on these people's property?

"Payton." A sharp tone sounded behind me. Dex's voice.

But Payton just kept walking until she opened the screen door of the farmhouse and nudged me inside. Warmth immediately engulfed me, pressing through my pores and making me feel human. Heat fought against my growing hypothermia as Payton guided me into the kitchen before I could even have a look around the walkway.

The scent of cinnamon filled my nostrils as I scanned the dozens of cheesy quote frames hung all over the exposed brick walls. Their kitchen looked like something out of a hallmark movie, where the main character decided she wanted to reinvent her posh lifestyle and move into a cottage-core themed home... and I wasn't mad at it.

I wouldn't call myself a material girl by any means. Of course I love my possessions, but I never overindulged in things I didn't need. Besides books, *that was the exception.*

A dark wooden table sat in the corner of the kitchen with two small benches on either side of it. All of the cooking utensils were exposed, hanging on a rack to the side of the oven while a series of bulbs strung from the top of the ceiling. It was cute. It was very cute.

"Sit, please. Can I make ya a coffee?" Payton offered, rummaging through cabinets.

"It's okay, really –"

"Silly me not thinkin'. It's late an' I'm offerin' you a coffee." She shook her head, flashing me a sweet smile before she opened another cabinet and pulled out a white jar. "I'll make a tea."

I smiled and nodded in appreciation as she placed a kettle over the stove, patting down her apron before sitting across from me on the bench.

"You cold?" She asked, reaching underneath the table to a basket of blankets. "Here," she stood up again and draped a scratchy, wool cloth around my shoulders. "That should do ya."

Once again, I smiled in thanks. "I'm sorry for the trouble, um..."

"Payton," she sat down and folded her hands over the placemat. "Just call me Payton, deary."

It was now, in the clear light that I could truly see the sweetness of this woman. Mind you I still

remained careful, I mean, Ted Bundy was charismatic
and charming yet killed over thirty women so.

But there was no... *edge* to this woman
whatsoever. She was a bit taller than me, though many
people were at my whopping 5'3 height and the evident
stains on her apron indicated that she loved to cook.
Judging from the cinnamon scent in the air I could tell
she had baked something today, maybe even a few
hours ago. *Do serial killers like to bake? I wouldn't rule it
out but I wouldn't peg it as their primary hobby.*

"Want to tell me how ya ended up in our field at
–" Payton glanced at the oven clock, "one-thirteen in the
mornin', little lady?"

*Nope. But I had to. Question is, how much was
acceptable to say?*

"I..." *How do I even start this?* "My name is
Marley, by the way. Just to, you know, get names out
there and stuff."

"Nice name, kid. Now answer the question." Dex
said walking into the kitchen with heavy breaths, the
blonde guy, *Hunter,* following suit.

Dex took his spot next to Payton on the bench,
tossing his shotgun on the table while Hunter stood
back, leaning against the kitchen wall with arms
crossed.

I swallowed hard, glancing back and forth
between the two intimidating men and the literal shot
gun inches away from my fingers.

"Um..." *Shit I'm turning red. Oh my God.*

"Did you forget how to speak, or?" Hunter chided, eyeing me like a hawk.

"Hunter, please." Payton scolded, returning her attention back to me.

He rolled his eyes but followed his mom's orders. Well, I mean, I assumed that Payton was his mom. They had the same blue eyes and blonde hair, though there were still some obvious differences.

"Sorry. I'm honestly just a bit overwhelmed and nervous." I admitted. *That's an understatement.*

Payton lovingly placed a hand over mine and pressed her thin lips into a small smile. "Don't be nervous, hun. None of us bite." She glanced at Dex. "Well, maybe this one but that's after hours."

Oh.

Dex softened his gaze at her and shook his head, returning her smile.

"Get on with it then, I'm losing my patience." Hunter scoffed, rubbing his jaw in agitation.

Holy asshole, Jesus.

Payton swung her head to face him. "Hunter, get some rest, will ya? You're still drunk."

"I'm good right here," he countered.

Before they bickered some more, I lowered the blanket over my shoulders and cleared my throat.

"I moved here last year to live with my boyf – *ex*, boyfriend," I corrected. "I um, found out a few hours ago that he'd been cheating on me so I packed whatever I could get my hands on and just drove off.

"My car got a flat in front of your lot, and I don't have any gas or charge in my phone..." I trailed off. I sounded pathetic, *I am pathetic. Admitting my problems to a bunch of strangers, two of which would've probably shot me had Payton not intervened.*

"Listen, I was just hoping that –"

"What? You think we're some bed and breakfast?" Hunter interrupted.

I blanched. "No, not at all –"

"What then? Think we're gon' solve all your issues like it's our cross to bear? Like it's any of our damn business?"

Dex stood up and pointed to the doorway. "Out."

Hunter scoffed and turned on his heel, disappearing behind the walkway and slamming the front door. A few moments later, the sound of an engine roared from the open window and headlights flashed and faded as Hunter drove off into the night.

Dex sat down and Payton smiled apologetically, both of them seemingly calm at the fact Hunter was literally driving drunk. Or supposedly drunk. Whatever the hell he was on.

"He ain't a bad kid." Was all Dex said before kissing Payton's temple and leaving through the same walkway.

The kettle screamed from the stove, infiltrating whatever active thoughts were bouncing in my brain from the last few minutes of chaos.

"I'm sorry about him." Payton shook her head, her expression pensive as she fiddled with her fingers. "He's been through a lot."

So *have I and I'm not a living, breathing douchebag.*

"I understand." *Yeah, that's a better thing to say.* "And I'm sorry for the trouble I caused. If you can set me up with a taxi number or something I can just get a hotel and come back for my car in the morning."

Honestly, I'd feel a lot safer that way anyway. I don't know what the hell I did to piss Hunter off but if he came back and I was still here, Christ, I think he'd shoot me on the spot no questions asked. *This guy was rogue.*

Payton waved me off and slid out of the bench, grabbing hold of the kettle and two mugs. "Nonsense deary, stay the night. We got a spare room in the basement and Dex will look at your car in the mornin'."

My heart practically exploded in my chest. This lady was truly an angel. If only my own mother was like this. *If only.*

She opened the fridge and pulled out a baking tray of cinnamon rolls, slicing one and handing it to me on a white plate. *I knew it.*

"I can warm it up for you if you'd like? Two seconds in the oven should do the trick."

I almost broke my neck shaking my head so many times. "No, please this is more than enough."

She smiled contently, pushing the plate further in my direction. "Alright, eat up then and I'll get your room ready."

"Payton," *it smells so good.* "Thank you for the offer, but it's too much. I've been at your home for under an hour and already drove your son away and inconvenienced your husband beyond belief."

Her cheeks flushed. "Oh, Hunter's not my –" But she stopped herself and nodded quickly. "Right well, eat. No discussion. Like I said, car will be fixed in the mornin' and I'll get some hot towels for you."

Before I could protest any further, she sped out of the kitchen and turned the corner, leaving me alone with the acceptance that I was staying here whether I liked it or not.

Holy crap. How did this become my life?

Chapter Four
Hunter

Probably shouldn't have gotten on the road but to hell with it. I had a couple solid hours to control my buzz so I knew I was able.

My mind wandered the entire drive to Cid's Pub, thinking about that girl that showed up on our property. I don't know why the fuck my dad ordered me out when all I was trying to do was get the answers they sure as shit weren't going to get.

Why they wanted to help that chick out was beyond me. Honestly, not even sure my dad wanted to but Payton on the other hand. God, that woman loved to play house. Trying to build this perfect family, pick up all the pieces that broke the second my mom met the grave.

Tears burned in my waterline but I wouldn't let them fall. I needed to be as far away from the house as possible, away from any distressing situations or dramatics.

And yet, the smallest part of me wondered what her story was. I saw what she was wearing and she didn't look like any of the girls 'round here. She had that polished look about her; blue cardigan, pearls, gold earrings and shit. Someone who thought she'd be better than the rest of us; someone who thought a random family would solve all her problems. Yeah, that's exactly what she expected and Payton was out here gifting her that on a silver platter. *Not me, can't be bothered.*

I pulled into Cid's and parked my truck next to an old Buick, locked it and headed inside with one single mission.

And there she was. All 5'7 of her; still sexy, still serving and still fuming.

Britt noticed me standing at the bar and rolled her eyes, cashing out a customer before making her way towards me.

"What are you doin' back here, Hunter?" She snarled, though her tone was less witchy, more bitchy.

Makes for a better challenge. "I wanted to apologize for earlier, sweetheart."

She crossed her arms, pushing her tits up a little more and clicked her tongue. "I'm waiting."

I chuckled, raking my hair back before leaning on one of the stools, making me eye level with her chest.

"C'mere, baby."

And that she did. Her fingers laced around the nape of my neck before she checked our surroundings and pulled me closer to her tits. I caged her in my arms, my hands slipping down the arch of her back as I took in the scent of her flowery perfume.

"I'm off in ten, wait for me."

"Yes ma'am." I smirked, respecting her wishes.

She grinned and released my hold, running back to the kitchen with kicking heels and a hop in her goddamn step.

I admired her ass one last time before bouncing the back of my fist against the bar to order a Jack and Coke.

The smooth whisky coated my throat, going down like water. This is exactly what I needed, every damn day of my fucking life, this is what I wanted.

No problems, no pain, no memories. *I'm good. I'm alive. I'm here.*

I ordered a couple of tequila shots before the bar closed and the familiar buzz of sweet serenity returned to me, the drunk settling into my conscious and relieving me from all the unwanted thoughts.

"Ready to go, Hunter?" The sugared sound of Britt's voice caressed me as she leaned onto my lap and planted a wet kiss on my neck.

I threw back the rest of the liquor, planting my hand firm on her ass before sliding a five to the bartender and stepping out of the pub.

"Your place or mine?" She asked, pawing at my jacket like a kitten.

"Don't care, I'm drivin' though."

I could already see the worry in her eyes without even meeting them. Well, she wanted all of me and this was the condition.

She matched my pace but released my arm. "Are you sure about that, Hunter? You had a lot to drink."

I continued to walk to my truck, allowing the alcohol to properly consume me before I posed the question. "You live far?"

"About fifteen minutes."

"Alright then," I tapped the hood of my truck and unlocked it. "My place."

I could see the hesitation boiling inside of her, but I knew what I was doing. I'd driven down this road so many times, and I never died. I knew it like the back of my hand. Could be the darkest knight and I'd survive. Could be blindfolded and I'd come out unscathed. I was fucking untouchable. *Some people weren't that lucky.*

Before she rounded the truck I grabbed Britt and pulled her towards me, pressing my lips to hers in a gentle motion. If I could ease her fret then I'd do it, cause God only knows I needed to feel something tonight.

Her body melted into mine like jelly. She slid her tongue into my mouth with deep desire, biting down on my bottom lip. At the taste of blood, my adrenaline spiked and I felt my dick hardening beneath my jeans. My fingers traced her curves, outlining her silhouette as she grew hungrier for me.

This is nice. This feels good. I like this. I like this. This is normal. This is hot. I like this.

We made out for a few more minutes before I needed to catch my own breath, guiding her inside the truck and shutting the door.

"Easy does it, baby."

Once I got situated in the drivers seat, I leaned over and grabbed her seatbelt, clicking it in place and planting one last kiss on her lips before pulling out of the parking lot.

"Aren't you a gentleman?" She cooed, running her fingers up and down my thigh before they settled atop my groin.

"Safety first, darlin'." I winked, and reversed my truck, heading in the direction of my place.

The irony in that sentence was hilarious.

Safety first, darlin', ha. Says the drunk driving with a fucking death wish.

Chapter Five
Marley

I was hoping that the bed would've been hard as rock, or the pillows weren't fluffed or I don't know, an infestation of bed bugs. *Anything* to make me hate it and provide a reason to sleep in my car so I wouldn't burden these people any more than I already have.

But nope. The bed Payton set up for me may have been the most comfortable thing I'd ever laid on in my entire life.

After I had finished eating the cinnamon roll, I sat at the kitchen table for a few minutes before Dex approached me and asked if I wanted any help taking in my luggage. Of course I fought it, but I guess Payton gave him a stern talking to and convinced him to be nice just for the night, even though he would've rather swallowed nails.

I tried to say thank you, but he grumbled in response and deposited my luggage like it was a newspaper before slamming the basement door and retreating up the stairs.

I couldn't believe I accepted the offer, but Payton was so persistent I felt rude refusing. Me, who they owed nothing to, who literally disturbed them in the dead of night, and here I was lounging in their space like it was my own. *Do I seriously have any humanity left?*

Regardless of how I felt, there was nothing I could do now. I was locked in the privacy of their basement and all I craved was rest.

I took a quick look around and relaxed, inhaling a mix of wood and ash emanating from the lit fireplace against the middle wall. There was a small loveseat positioned next to it with a marble side table that held a candle and some matches.

A bookshelf was positioned in the corner of the wall with only a few novels on war and hunting, while the rest of the shelves were occupied by boat figurines. *Huh, cute.*

I placed my luggage next to the bed and pulled out some silk pyjama shorts, a tank top and some clean underwear.

My next order of business was upping the battery in my phone. Payton kindly lent me a charger for the night and I just about kissed the ground she walked on. *I owe that woman my life.*

The shower was calling my name as I slid the power cord into the wall outlet and made my way to the bathroom, peeling off my clothes and hopping into the tub.

I pressed my back against the tiles, absorbing the heat and steam of the warm water kissing my skin. After the night I had, this was everything and more.

It was in this one moment of serenity that the intrusive thoughts crept in, disturbing my peace and forcing me to deal with the severity of my decisions.

After tonight, where will I go? What will I do? I have nothing to come back to. My parents hate me, my friends think I abandoned them, what was left? I was always going to be a fuck-up in everyone's eyes, so why not prove them right?

Tears dripped down my cheeks, and I didn't have the energy to stop them from falling. A sob escaped my throat as I sat down in the shower, drawing my knees to my chest.

This was my life now. A runaway. A disaster. Too scared to face my family. No one to turn to, to talk to, to be around. I was in the middle of fucking Nebraska with nothing. Absolutely. Fucking. Nothing.

I remained frozen in a ball until the hot water began to prune my skin. I knew that my life was in shambles, but the last thing I wanted was to look like a dried-out grape.

After turning off the shower knob, I wrapped myself in a towel, wiping the fog off the mirror to really look at myself for the first time in hours.

My long dark hair cascaded down one side of my neck, exposing the small music note tattoo on my right collarbone.

I grazed my fingers over it and smiled, returning to the happy memory of me at eighteen getting it with my brother after our piano recital. We beat out the entire competition and won first place for our duet at the Oxville Center of Arts.

Almost immediately after, we decided to celebrate by getting matching tattoos, cracking open a bottle of red and splitting a large pizza.

I chuckled but it was sad. I was sad. Tears found my eyes again, blurring my vision. Back when I was close with Adam, we would do everything together. He knew how hard our parents were on us, but he was a pro at staying in their good graces.

Me, I was a pro at pissing them off. I think he felt sorry for me. Maybe he still does. I wouldn't know. I haven't talked to him since I left New York, and he never tried reaching out. *I guess that says a lot about our relationship now, doesn't it?*

I shook away the sadness and glanced at the set of brown eyes staring back at me, almost unrecognizable.

There was a time where I thought my features were endearing, beautiful, kind. I thought my brown eyes delivered warmth and safeness, only now they were hollow and empty, filled with dread and pain. God, I envied those who felt nothing. *Only I could never feel nothing. This world loved to punish me.*

I crawled into bed and found the courage to finally check my phone, scrolling through dozens of missed calls and unopened texts from the devil himself.

9.02pm – Todd: Marley, where are you?

10.06pm – Todd: You can't fucking do this to us! Get home right now and we can talk about this.

11.13pm – Todd: You're such a lunatic. Fuck you.

11.14pm – Todd: I'm throwing out your bathrobe. You left it in here. Peace whore.

12.12am – Todd: I'm sorry, baby, I didn't mean that. Come back. We'll talk about this.

I wish I was fazed, but honestly, I wasn't. Todd never spoke down to me in our relationship, but there were a lot of things he had done that I was clearly unaware of. His immaturity just kept shining through and I was sick of it.

I'm sure the pain of losing who I thought was my other half would hit me soon, but I was soaking in the numbness that accompanied this situation. *I'll deal with it eventually.*

After skipping all the other messages and deleting our conversation, I danced over a contact name that I hadn't pressed in a year: Adam Matthews.

My fingers hovered over the text I wanted to send him, contemplating if it was even worth it.

2.41am – Marley: Hey, Adam It's Marley. I miss you.

Delete. Delete. Delete.

2:43am – Marley: Adam, can we talk?

Delete.

2:46am – Marley: What happened to us?

Delete. Exit. Fuck this. I can't do this. I can't.

I shut off my phone and turned to face the wall, shaking relentlessly. There were so many things I wanted to say, numerous apologies I needed to make and yet, I couldn't do it. I couldn't even send a text to my own freaking brother.

Tiredness forced my eyelids shut as my mind wandered to the only place that felt permanent comfort.

My loneliness.

The morning sunrays cascaded like lasers through the small basement window as I stretched out my arms in disbelief.

My phone read: 10:55am

Shit, shit, shit. What am I still doing here?

I leapt out of bed, brushed my teeth and threw on a knit sweater and jean combo. The clothes in my suitcase were pretty much packed and ready to go so all I needed to do was thank Payton and head out to see if Dex actually fixed my car.

After a few moments of hesitation, I found the courage to climb the basement stairs and rounded the walkway to the kitchen.

Quiet voices sounded on the other side of the wall, halting my steps before entering. I could make out Payton's tone in deep conversation with a man. *Dex, I think?*

"I told you, baby, you can work with us on the farm." Dex said.

He spoke so softly and sweet with her, almost as if his voice didn't belong to a scary, gigantic lumberjack.

"Dex, I said it once and I'll say it again. I ain't shovelling cow shit for a living."

"You won't be –"

"Our business can still survive. I know it can. We just need to find ourselves a hire that can bring the life back into it."

Payton sounded defeated yet determined. I wished more than anything that whatever she was struggling with I could help. She had done so much for me already, it pained me to see her go through, well, whatever it was she was going through.

"Cramer can't work on the ads?" Dex asked.

"Don't be dumb, Dex. Cramer's a hands on kid. Got no creative eye to him, not a bit."

The familiar roar of my Malibu engine sounded from outside the side door at the back of the house. It was probably best that I left them to their conversation in the meantime while I checked on my car. After all, that was my only ticket out of here.

The side exit led me to a dirt pathway next to a massive open garage and a table of tools. As I approached, the scent of gasoline flooded my nostrils, causing me to wince. Smack dab in the center of it all was my beautiful Malibu alive and well. *At least one of us was thriving.*

I jumped at the sound of clamoring tools as Hunter emerged from the back of my car. His blonde hair was wet and pushed back from his face, curling over his ears. He wore a grey long sleeve that clung to his frame like second skin, highlighting tight, broad muscles that could be in a copy of Men's Health magazine. *Don't stare. Don't stare.*

Those crystal blue eyes finally found mine and I realized a second too late. *Shit.*

"Mornin'." He sniffed, rubbing an oil-stained hand over his nose. "Tire's changed and gas is at full tank."

Well, at least he didn't seem like he wanted to bite my head off anymore. That's a good sign. Maybe he cooled off on his drunken night adventure. *Don't jinx it, Mar.*

I walked towards the Malibu and pet its front. "It looks great, thank you."

He turned his back to me and said nothing, placing all the tools he used back onto the table.

Oookay.

"How'd you get it off the road?"

A few seconds passed before he decided to respond. "We pushed it."

We. So Dex did help.

I walked around the side of the car to meet him, fishing for my wallet in my back pocket. "How much do I owe you?"

He looked up at me in confusion, furrowing his brows. "Huh?"

"The car," I took out two twenties and a couple of ones. "I don't have a lot right now but I can drive to the bank to get the rest of it and –"

"I'm goin' to stop you right there." He said, placing a hand out in front of him.

I swallowed back my words as he took a step towards me, his tall frame towering over mine with intimidation.

"This isn't tit for tat. I'm doin' my family a favour cause they felt like they needed to help you. The second I take your money, it means I owe you a service. And I can assure you, sweetheart, your service is the last thing I owe."

His cold words sliced me in half, freezing me in place as he went about organizing his tools as if I was a ghost he couldn't see.

In the marketing industry, you meet a lot of players whose sole purpose is to rise to the top. My parents were the harshest, most critical people I'd ever known. My brother introduced me to some of the most foul personalities on Wall Street and yet, I'd never met someone as rude as the man standing before me.

I must've stood with a gaping mouth for five minutes before I finally took in a breath. "What the fuck is your problem?"

He paid me no mind as he grumbled in response. "Don't got one."

I crossed my arms in frustration, watching him completely disregard my presence as he wiped away oil residue from wrenches and screwdrivers and whatever the hell else.

Before I could open my mouth, he waved a dismissive hand at me and stole a glance. "Darlin', I had a long night and I'm really not in the mood. So if you're going to argue with someone, head down the road, pop onto fourth street, and beef with a homeless woman named Dolly. She loves to start fights. Even better at keepin' up with 'em."

It was then that I noticed a small, plum bruise on the side of his neck. As my vision focused on it, I realized it wasn't a bruise at all. It was a freakin' hickey. *Ha-ha, long night indeed. Asshole.*

"I'm sure jeopardizing society as a drunk driver constitutes as a long night, but that's entirely your own reckless behaviour and you have no right to take it out on me. You don't even fucking know me."

He dropped a tool down onto the table and let out a sarcastic laugh, throwing a look of daggers my way.

"Don't I, though?" He inched forward, his chest rising with each heavy breath. "Let me take a wild guess.

Big city rich girl, fell for the wrong guy, doesn't know how to deal with her problems cause mommy and daddy aren't around to solve them no more."

I - "Stop." My heart hammered in my chest, leaving me breathless with anger.

"Now how the hell you ended up in Nebraska is beyond me, but truthfully, I could give less of a fuck." He closed his distance, clenching his jaw as his eyes scanned my face.

"I fixed your car. Now run along Bambi, back to the land of rainbows and happy endings."

My fingernails dug so deep into my palm I winced in pain. But it was good. I needed a distraction from my anger. I needed to feel something that wasn't the predatory urge to rip his head off and feed it to alligators.

The gall on this man. I couldn't grasp how someone so disrespectful lived in the same space as Payton. She was so kind and nurturing and Dex, as scary as he was, just seemed like a protective father. No bad blood there, just doing his duties.

But this grade A asshole was a walking, talking, piece of shit. And I was not about to let him win. I'd dealt with so many horrible men in the past, and I was done tolerating it.

Screw that. If Hunter wanted me to go so bad, he was in for a rude awakening. Because I heard Payton was in desperate need of a creative eye to help her with her business, and I think I knew just the person.

Like I said, w*hat is left to lose?*

Chapter Six
Hunter

After Bambi stomped off into the house, I felt like I could finally fucking breathe.

Christ, that girl had only been around for twelve hours and she already gave me the biggest damn migraine of the 21st century.

Yeah, I was being a dick. A mega one at that. But I was right in saying that she owed me nothing, and I owed her even less.

I wasn't raised in no sugar cookie land, surrounded by wealth and opportunity like her. Where you could walk up and down the sidewalk of a Hollywood town and get scouted by some cad movie producer. Nah, that wasn't my life and I'm fucking glad for it.

Call me a piece of shit, but I was the realest motherfucker out there. And I wasn't about to bend over backwards for a big city brunette with pleading puppy dog eyes.

Whatever, she'll be outta my hair in a few hours.

I finished rehoming all of my tools and wiped the sweat off my brow, admiring the white Malibu in front of me. Nice ride, no maintenance. She probably didn't even realize her car needed a fucking oil change. *Well, not anymore. I had some extra time to spare.*

I was never a sedan type of person, didn't think I had the personality for it and frankly, my Ram 1500 was my goddamn baby - wouldn't switch it out for the world. But as far as cars went, Bambi's Malibu was a solid choice.

The smaller desk in the corner of the garage was my safe space. When I wasn't helping my dad out on the farm, I sat my ass down at this table and worked on building my boat figurines.

Call me a loser, but I loved that shit. Back when I was a kid, my mom n' dad would take me sailing at Rivertown Bay, and I'd sit in our tiny boat no bigger than a raft and watch the massive ships float on by.

I asked my mom, my beautiful, *breathing* mom at the time if I could sail a boat as big as theirs one day.

She smiled at me with her ice blue eyes and nodded. "Of course, baby. No tide is ever too great for a captain of the sea."

I remember being filled with pride and poked at her. "Then where's my sailor hat?"

She ripped out a piece of cartridge paper from her sketch book and began folding it this way and that.

At the end, she had crafted a tiny little boat hat for me and plopped it on my head.

"There ya go, Hunt. The greatest little sailor I ever did know."

I forced the memory out of my head, controlling my staggered breaths as a single tear slid down my cheek. The paper boat hat was nailed to the grid board next to my work station, containing all the bottled up happiness I could no longer feel. *It should've been me, Mom. It should've been fuckin' me.*

Fifteen minutes of quiet figurine painting passed when my phone started to buzz. *It better be my dad letting me know that Bambi was ready to grab her car and ride off into the sunset.*

But when I checked the caller ID, it read: JOSH BAXTER.

I let it ring for a couple more seconds, finishing off a final stroke before answering with a grunt. "Yeah?"

"Down for a hike, man?" Josh suggested, accompanied by a soft woman's giggle in the background.

I placed the phone on speaker and continued to paint the stern of my ship a bright yellow. "Didn't you get enough exercise this mornin'?"

He chuckled in response. "I say I used my mouth a lot more than my legs this time."

That same woman's laugh echoed through the phone and I could place it as Beth's.

"That you did, mister." She said.

Yeah, alright, fuck this. "I'm hanging up."

"No, wait – Hunt. Let's go hiking, man. I think we could both use some fresh air, don't ya?"

"I'm outside." I replied, flatly.

"I meant some movement."

"I walk around plenty."

Just one more final coat on this bad boy and the stern will match the rudder –

"Hunter!" Josh blared, causing me to tip my paintbrush into the transom area of the boat, staining it with a bright yellow streak.

I inhaled a deep breath before dropping the paintbrush all together and pushing out my chair.

"If I come will you quit botherin' me till tonight?" I snapped.

I could feel the motherfucker smiling through the phone. "Promise."

"Be there in twenty." I hung up and placed my paintbrush in a cup of water, stirring the remnants of acrylic out of the bristles.

I took one last look at the white Malibu that belonged to Bambi and shook my head. *You better be gone by the time I get back.*

Chapter Seven
Marley

As soon as I entered the house, I ran straight to the basement and cried. Like a freaking toddler who got their applesauce taken away, I bawled my eyes out.

Yes I had a plan in place, but I also needed to regain my composure because Lord knows I needed all the strength right about now.

Why the hell I even cared about what this stranger in the middle of Nebraska thought of me was ludicrous. And yet, I did. I did because a part of me liked the feeling of home that this family provided. This smidgen of normalcy that I didn't experience in the big time rush of New York.

Growing up, my parents would never let Adam and I eat any junk food. My mom put us on a strict Paleo diet plan where carbs were forbidden and sugar was a cardinal sin.

I remember when I was in my mid-teens, I asked her if she was training me to be a model because I couldn't fathom all the restrictions. And you know what this woman said to me? "You're *my* daughter, and that comes with responsibilities. One day when you get into the working world, you can use those pretty features to your advantage. Isn't that right, Mike?"

My heart practically split in two when my dad agreed. He literally agreed to my own mother objectifying his daughter like she was some slab of meat to be sold on the market.

But the worst part was, I soaked in all of it. I relished in it. I thought I was this perfect little princess on Castle Hill and everyone loved me. I'd hookup with the hottest guys, get invited to the best parties, throw bitchy glares at shy kids in the halls. *I became my mom.*

When I moved out for school, I started binge eating on sweets and processed foods just to rebel against her. Kind of like a fat brag: *'HA, you can't control my life anymore'*. But instead, I gained twenty pounds and developed an eating disorder which threw me into a ghastly depression.

I skipped out on all our family parties because I was so ashamed of my loss of self and what they'd say, which in turn made my family's opinion of me even worse.

A few months before I met Todd, I'd finally picked myself up off the ground and began training again. I limited my sugar intake to just once or twice a week, *and thank God for Payton's cinnamon roll last night because I freaking needed that,* and started eating whole foods.

I was a good mix of lean and strong, thanks to all my yoga and cycling classes, but that didn't mean my mom's scrutiny went away. She'd still pick apart my eating habits and comment on any fine lines on my face. To me, I was her Barbie doll gone rogue. To my dad, I was a failed waste of potential.

Maybe that's why I was so messed up in the head. *Imagine being petrified of sweets? The best creation on Earth?* It was stupid! I hated eating bland food every day, but I forced it to be my preferred palette.

God, thinking about it now... I really didn't have time to find myself. Instead, I was just chasing the shadow of a girl my parents created.

Maybe that's why I never felt like I was good enough for anyone. For all of my shitty boyfriends who treated me like dirt, for all of the jobs I couldn't keep, the friends I'd lose to pointless drama.

They were the problem. *They* made me this way. *But who the hell am I when I'm alone?*

I sought out validation from people who didn't like me. I gave second chances to people who didn't deserve it. I turned a blind eye to manipulation because I mistook it for affection.

Honestly, I thought if I could please the people who hurt me, turn their opinions around, then I won. I won them over and I was useful. Because often times, people branded others based off their own insecurities. And I sure as hell didn't want to be someone's painful reminder of what they hated.

Maybe that's why Hunter got under my skin. He didn't even give me a chance, didn't want to. He was rude, disrespectful, intimidating... an absolute wrecking ball. And yet here I was all the same, thinking about those shark blue eyes and wondering why they looked so sad.

Maybe it was just my delusional belief that I could change people, or fix them for that matter. There had to be something wrong with him. I mean, a person couldn't just act so aloof and cold without a back story. Payton had even said he'd been through a lot. *But what was a lot?*

God, screw it. You know what? I didn't have time to think about some asshat who hated my guts, despite whatever the hell he went through. No, I was going to help Payton. I needed a distraction, something to keep my mind off my crumbling life. I needed *anything*.

After wiping the grey smudge underneath my eyes, I reapplied another light coat of mascara and gathered myself, climbing the stairs to the walkway.

Faint voices of her and Dex chatting floated from the kitchen, but only about mundane things like the news and harvest season. *I guess now's a good time.*

I knocked on the door frame lightly, smiling as they noticed me come in.

"Good morning," I released.

Payton grinned brightly but Dex paid me no mind, taking one last swig of coffee before clearing his throat.

"Car keys are out back with Hunter." He mumbled under his breath.

"Uh, yeah, I already spoke with him." *And I wish I hadn't.*

"Coffee, deary?" Payton asked, already moving towards the cupboard to grab me a mug.

"Please, thank you."

Dex slid out of the bench as the wooden floor creaked beneath his boots. He dumped the remnants of coffee down the sink before giving Payton a swift kiss on the head and pushing past me to get outside.

What the hell was with the guys of this family? I mean, at least Dex didn't outright berate me with his words but he still treated me like some freaking parasite that crawled out of a wormhole.

Whatever. I wasn't here for them. "Payton, I was hoping to talk to you about something."

"Anythin', you got it. How much cream?" She responded, stirring in some sweetener.

"Hm..." *None, none, none.* "Two tablespoons?"

She nodded and brought the mug to the table, waving me over before taking a slurp from her own cup.

"Did ya sleep okay?" She asked, rounding her blonde hair into a low bun.

I wrapped my hand around the mug, lifting it to my lips. "So well," I sipped, allowing the rich liquid to soothe my throat. "I wanted to thank you for everything you've done for me, Payton."

"Oh, it was absolutely no bother hun. You've gots to lean on people from time to time, and you can't be sorry for nothin'."

That brought a smile out of me. "Well I'm sorry that your husband and son – *Hunter*," I corrected myself, "hate my guts. I'm sure you had to hear about it a lot this morning."

She snickered but it wasn't a happy laugh at all. If I didn't know any better, I would've placed some sadness in her tone.

"Dex, yah, tons. He wasn't too keen 'bout a stranger showin' up at our place, eatin' our food and all that but he's an easy tree to cut. Hunter on the other hand –" she shook her head, taking a sip of her coffee. "He's out most nights. Can't talk to someone who ain't around."

I wanted to ask where he went, why she always looked so upset when his name came up. But it wasn't my business. I didn't know the kind of relationship they had, how they were even related, *if* they even were. She kept saying that he wasn't her son, but they lived together so they must've been family or something? No? *Forget it.*

"Anyways, what'd you wan' talk about sweet pea?" That sprightly visage came back and it eased my nerves.

Okay. Here goes nothing. "Right, um. So I sort of overheard a conversation between you and Dex this morning..."

I glanced at her quickly, assuming anger would've been written on her face but she wore no sour expression, so I continued.

"I heard that you have a business that's maybe not performing as well as you'd want it to..."

Again, she just sat there listening to me attentively, so I let out an exhale.

"Okay, I'm just going to come out and ask. Do you need any help at all with advertising? I have a degree in marketing and back in New York I was in line to get a promotion so I think I'm pretty good at what I do and I just wanted to repay you for –"

Her sweet laugh filled the air as she placed a soft hand over my fingertips, joy in her face. "Marley you talk a mile a minute, don't ya?"

Marley. I liked that. I liked the way she said my name and addressed me like I had one to begin with. Unlike the men of the family who probably erased my name from their memory the second they heard it.

"Sorry, I just don't want you to think I have zero credentials or I'm not qualified. I am, I promise. I can really help you grow your business if that's what you're looking for."

Payton furrowed her eyebrows in confusion, a glint of amusement in her features. "This ain't –" she laughed, "oh hun, this ain't no interview, you got nothin' to prove to me. I just, I guess I just wan' know why you're offerin'?"

That was the biggest question of the hour, wasn't it? Why was I so hell bent on helping Payton out when I barely knew her. Why did I feel such a strong connection to this house, this family, when I should be driving three thousand miles in the opposite direction of this place.

"I don't..." *Are you really going to admit this, Marley?"* "I don't have anything else." *Shit, I guess you are.*

She scooted her chair closer to me upon admission and squeezed my fingers.

"I'm going to be honest, Payton, I really messed up my life. I... I had a lot going for me in New York, but I threw it all away for some guy, upped and left everything behind to move here and screwed around for a year until I figured out he was cheating on me.

"A whole year... I had no direction, just living off inheritance money and lottery winnings and – anything, *anything* we could get our hands on. I try not to regret it, you know? The way my life turned out. I mean, if I truly loved my life to begin with I don't think I would've left it behind."

That was the first time I ever admitted that out loud. The first time I truly didn't blame the world for shoving me in a pile of shit. It's like my brain didn't even register my admission, like it wanted to come out for so long but only to someone who genuinely cared to hear it.

I didn't know why I trusted the woman sitting before me, but I did. I did so much that I dropped a tsunami of sentiments and feelings and vulnerability that I hadn't even coped with myself.

"I'm sorry, Payton, I –"

She pulled me into a tight hug, silencing my overthinking and spiralling thoughts. Her warm embraced caressed me as I wrapped my arms around her in response.

When she pulled back, a glossy sheen swept over her eyes. "Two things I've learned about you, deary. One, you apologize a ton, and two, you talk and talk and talk."

I laughed and shrugged, biting down on my lip. "I just never really open up like that."

"Well, I'm glad ya did. We all got our baggage, Marley. Some we think we can carry and others that just pull us right back down until we can't get up no more."

"I don't want to go back to my family in New York," I sighed. *Not like I can.*

"Then don't," she suggested. "But how's about you come with me to The Square and we can visit P&D's hardware shop."

Uh... okay? Ha-ha. She stood up, pushing the bench in place and taking both our mugs to the sink. There was a jolly bounce in her that made me giggle.

As much as I loved to see her happy, I questioned why the hell she asked me to go to a hardware store in the midst of my emotional word vomit.

"P&D's hardware?" I asked Payton.

She grabbed her purse off the counter and jiggled a set of car keys, beaming from ear to ear. "Yah, deary. Just got a new hire named Marley and I'd like to show her the ropes."

Chapter Eight
Hunter

"Glad you came out, Hunt?"

"Yeah," I replied, scrunching up the sleeves of my black thermal. "Race you up the hill?"

Before he could answer, I booked passed him, trekking up the dirt slope with long strides. This was one of my favourite fucking things in the world. Beating Josh in races sure, but hiking out on the plains was unlike anything else.

When I was training for track in high school, my mom took me out here every morning to practice my endurance. She always loved to run, but I didn't. I ran for her, with her, and that's why I tried out for track. Dad was always working and I wanted an excuse to hangout with my parents.

Now I spent more than enough time with my dad in silence, and the only way I'd see my mom was by driving seventy-five down the backroad with a beer in one hand and whisky in the other.

Aurora, Nebraska was a damn small town and besides my dad and Payton, all I really had was Josh. An old buddy of mine, Carter, got scouted to play baseball in Boston and my family dog Baxter passed away a couple years back so yeah, all who was left to keep me company were the mains.

Being real though, I didn't mind it; a small circle was better than a crowded one with no room to breathe and less room to grow. *My mom taught me that.*

I sprinted up the slope until I reached the top, looking down over the green plains absorbing the sunlight. Looked like a goddamn dream. *Fuck, if I could bottle this view and drink it every night I'd be as sober as a priest.*

Josh's sluggish breathing sounded behind me as he approached, holding his appendix with a sweaty palm.

"Christ Hunt, for a guy who drinks every night you got the stamina of a stallion."

"It's my fuel, what can I say."

He placed his opposite slimy hand on my shoulder, wiping the perspiration off his brow.

"Off." I nudged him away. *Man I hate being touched unless it's on my terms.*

Instead of listening, he slapped the side of my face and hopped back, chuckling while battling his exhaustion.

I pounced on him, knocking my fist against his ribs before fully tackling him to the ground.

"I'll throw you off the fuckin' cliff in a burlap sack, don't think I won't?"

"I give up, I give up!"

I eased my grip on his shirt and stood up, extending a helping hand. When he grabbed hold, I let him slip, laughing raucously.

"That's for touchin' me against my will."

He grumbled in annoyance and stood up on his own, shooting me an irritated sneer.

"You let girls touch you all the time."

"Yeah," I shrugged, "then they suck my dick. Want to suck my dick, Josh?"

He let out a snicker and dusted off his sweats. "What I *want* is some fucking ice cream. What'd ya say, Hunt? Let's hit up Blu's?"

"Kind of defeats the purpose of our hike, man."

He smirked, slapping my shoulder before shooting a playful grin my way. "Not if we run there."

"Got to admit, I come up with the best ideas." Josh chided, mauling his double fudge ice cream cone. "First the hike, now the ice cream. Should I choose the bar tonight or d'you wan' go back to Cid's?"

We made our way out of Blu's ice cream parlor and began our walk to my truck. I parked in The Square even though the hiking trails had free accommodation just to get some extra steps in.

"Cid's." I responded, shovelling a scoop of cookie dough into my mouth.

Josh smirked. "Goin' to see our girl Britt? Or what'd you call her that night. *Addison?*"

I rolled my eyes. "It's half price rum on Thursdays man, can't beat it."

"Uh huh, so how did last night go with her?"

It was then that I noticed Payton walking up to P&D's, the store she owned with my dad. But she wasn't alone. She was with fucking Bambi.

"Did you remember it this time?" Josh's voice hovered over my racing thoughts. *What the fuck was she still doing here?*

"Earth to Hunter?"

I shoved my ice cream cup to Josh's chest and marched towards P&D's. Why in the hell Bambi was still in Aurora was a mystery to me, and a mystery I was going to solve, excavate and squash.

Fuck she made me angry. I couldn't even place why. She reminded me of everything I hated about the big city folk. The pearls, the dressy clothing, the silky hair and shit. All of that was a no for me. It was one thing to walk into my lane, demand we fix her car and gather sympathy. But now she was too close to home, and I wasn't about to let her rock my placidity.

Rebecca was just like her. She waltzed into my life about four years ago, and within six months waltzed right back out. She was visiting her sister at Iowa State where I played baseball for a year on scholarship, and we'd hooked up one night at a frat party. Fuck, I thought she was the darndest little thing I'd ever seen.

A graphic designer from Chicago, made the meanest little toy out of me when we were fooling around. We dated on and off for those few months and she played me like a fucking fiddle; cheating on me, pretending she didn't, wheeling me back in just to run me over. Over, and over, and over again.

I'd never trusted a big city girl before her, but now I'd never trust one again. If it walks like a duck and talks like a duck, it's probably a fucking duck. *And Bambi, baby, you're as identical to a duck as Rebecca.*

Payton and Bambi were heavily engaged in a conversation at the front of P&D's when I hastily interrupted.

"Payton," I acknowledged. That's all I ever really did.

Her blue eyes, so uncannily similar to mine, found my gaze. Sometimes I felt like the biggest asshole when I looked at my stepmom like this. Objectively, she was a sweet woman. I'd believe it any day. But she wasn't my fucking mom. She'd never be, and trying to replicate that love and energy was damn near impossible. Yet, she tried to. And over the last year, I guess she finally accepted her defeat cause she stayed out of my way *most* of the time.

Next to meet my eyes was Bambi. Her brown spheres roamed over me with curiosity. She was so short, God, so fucking short. Probably half my height and a quarter of my weight if that. Her cheekbones were high and an assortment of tiny freckles covered her nose.

In this light, she had an innocent glow to her. Like she was untouched by the world and was naïve to all duress. But I knew for a fact she had some type of ulterior motive. She wouldn't still be here if she didn't.

"Come with me for a sec, will ya Bambi?" I nudged my head over to the side of the store, walking away with the knowledge she'd follow.

"Are you always this demanding?" she bickered, flattening the creases on her white blouse.

I shook it off. "What are you still doing here?"

She clenched her jaw, looking back towards Payton who had her arms crossed throwing daggers my way. She didn't intervene though, *good woman.*

"Bambi," I rasped. "I asked you a question."

Her arms crossed in evident frustration. "I have a name and it isn't fucking Bambi, so I suggest if you want to speak with me you address me appropriately from now on."

I leaned in closer, amused by the fire radiating off this woman. "Remind me."

When she told me it was Marley, it didn't come as a shock because I already knew her name. Bambi just suited her better, I don't know. She looked like a fucking

Bambi so if she thought I'd be calling her Marley any time soon she was dead wrong.

"Well *Bambi*, now that we've got names out of the way," I smirked sensing her agitation, "can I get an answer to my question?"

She stared at me with an inscrutable expression before sighing heavily. "I'm going to help Payton with her business."

I couldn't pinpoint what I felt in that moment. I laughed, but I didn't know why. I didn't say anything for a few seconds, glancing at Payton, the store, then back to Bambi.

"Helping Payton with what exactly?" I questioned, eyeing her with suspicion. *What was she up to?*

"Oh my God, just talk to her about it. I'm tired of this conversation."

Hell no. "Bambi –"

"It's Marley!" She snapped, swinging her puny little American Girl doll arms at me. "M-A-R-L-E-Y. Marley! Is that so fucking hard to understand, Hunter?"

Before I could react she continued to rip me apart.

"I'm helping her with advertisements to increase her business sales, because unlike you, I actually care about helping others not just antagonizing them until they break!"

My immediate reaction was poor. Very fucking poor. *"What's in it for you"* almost slipped off my tongue before Josh interrupted, still holding my ice cream.

"Fuckin' hell I wasn't going to intervene but it was so entertaining I couldn't resist. Finished my ice cream just watching the two of you," he handed me back my cup and turned his attention to Bambi.

"Nice to meet ya little lady, I'm Josh. Hunter's best mate."

"Huh," she smiled so sweetly I could've contracted diabetes. "At least one of you has some manners." She extended a hand out to Josh and shook it politely. "I'm Marley. *Not* Bambi."

"Well Marley *Not* Bambi, Hunt and I are going to Cid's Pub tonight if you want to join?"

"No," we both said in unison.

I glanced at her quickly and she returned the gaze, her cheeks heating before she quickly paced backwards to meet Payton.

"Nice to meet you Josh!" She called back, completely ignoring my existence before escaping into the glass doors of P&D.

I caught myself staring at the empty space in front of me, the weight of her presence slowly fleeting away.

"Pretty girl," Josh poked. "Think she'll come?"

The store bells chimed and I half expected Bambi to come out and yell at me some more, but it was just an elderly couple holding a bag of tools and shit.

"I hope not." I grumbled, swallowing back the frog in my throat.

Yeah. I, uh.

I hope not.

Chapter Nine
Marley

Stupid Hunter.

Stupid freaking Hunter with his stupid nicknames and stupid questions. *God I could kill him. I could legitimately feed him to an apex predator and smile while his head was being ripped off.*

He didn't want me to go to the bar tonight, boo freaking hoo. I didn't want to go anyways. He knew that, I mean, why else did he scowl at me when I refused the invitation? Probably didn't want me around his friend, who was actually sort of cute now that I thought about it. *Ugh, Marley stop. He is NOT your problem, and neither is anyone he associates himself with.*

I was so deep in thought I barely registered Payton speaking to me. "And this is where you'll be settin' up shop, hun. The computer's old but it's still kickin' and all the ad info is on the table there –"

When her words trailed off I turned to her with an apologetic smile. *Apologetic because I couldn't focus on jack shit thanks to that bloody heathen.*

"I'm so sorry, Payton. So much has happened in one single day, my mind is all over the place. Please, continue, seriously. My attention is all yours." And I meant that. *Well, I'll be trying my best to mean that.*

Her gaze softened as she let out a hand, squeezing my fingers gently. "Want to talk about it?"

"Talk about what?"

"Hunter," she let out. "I don't know what in the hell was bein' said but Hunter's got a mouth on him sometimes. If he said anythin' that offended you, I'll talk —"

"No," I shook my head, "no need, Payton. I'm sure he was just in a bad mood." *Like always.*

A scoff escaped her throat as she moved towards the grey lockers in the corner of the office, decorated in stickers. She pulled out a crimson red vest with a name tag reading: **Payton Lane.**

Payton Lane. Huh. You know those names that just fit? Like, from the moment you hear them it clicks and you think, wow, that really suits you? That's exactly how I felt when I read her name tag, and my thoughts immediately drifted to the rest of the family. Dex Lane and... *Hunter Lane.*

"It'll be the day when Hunter's in a good mood, Marley."

I almost completely forgot what we'd been speaking about but then it came back to me and I chuckled, nodding my head in agreeance.

A soft knock alerted both Payton and I as we turned to the doorway, my eyes meeting a tall man with black hair and brown eyes.

He wore the same red vest as Payton with a name tag that read: *Cramer Hughes.*

"Hi, Payton, and..." He flashed me a cordial smile and extended a hand. "Payton's friend?"

"New hire," Payton corrected, slapping his fingers away. "I don't want no germs spreadin' around, Cramer. What ya need?"

Cramer smiled brighter, a dimple poking through his right cheek. My gaze trailed up his face once more, admiring the fact that his eyes seemed to smile with him. *Freaking precious.*

"A customer out front wants to know if we got more of those socket wrenches in stock."

Payton wiggled her nose and narrowed her eyes, seemingly in deep thought as she scurried towards the door.

"I'll check the storage, 'think we got a shipment a few days ago. Thanks Cramer."

And she was gone, leaving me alone with this tall, adorable man.

An awkward silence passed between the two of us which I'm pretty sure he noticed. He rubbed the back

of his neck and glanced behind him, waving at a
customer passing by.

When his attention returned to me I decided to
shake off the tension and extend a hand of my own.

"She isn't looking," I joked. "I'm Marley."

He laughed and shook my hand, keeping one
half of his body outside the doorway while the other half
leaned in.

"Cramer," he smiled, retreating to his standard
position. "So you're goin' to be helping out around
here?"

I nodded a yes before clearing my throat. "That's
the plan. But I'm going to be doing more behind the
scenes work, I think. Advertisements and stuff, you
know, garnering notice for the store."

He tilted his head in bewilderment, looking me
up and down with a curious stare. "Alright, where'd you
come from?"

I let out a chuckle. "What do you mean?"

"Like, where you from, Marley? Cause it sure
doesn't look like you're from around here."

I glanced down at my silk white dress shirt and
pearl necklace, playing with the golden ring on my
pointer from Piaget. It was my grandmother's before she
passed away and all her stuff came with a hefty price tag.
But no matter how much money I needed, I couldn't
bring myself to selling the possessions she left behind.
She was more a parental figure to me than my actual
mother, and I was going to remember her as such.

"What gave it away?" I teased, knowing damn well it was my choice in attire.

One thing I've come to learn about Nebraska was the difference in style. It wasn't a bad thing at all. In fact, I admired the way people didn't care much about what designer bag to wear on their Sunday strolls. I just always felt a little out of place walking around with my NYC getup, but in a way, my clothes were a little piece of home.

Todd travelled a lot when he won the million dollar jackpot three years ago so he never really spent time here by choice after the fact. That was up until he decided to sexually fraternize with his ex-girlfriend. *Yet another man I'd feed to an apex predator with no remorse.*

"You uh," Cramer voice pulled me back into reality. "You okay there? Lookin' a little flustered."

I felt my cheeks heat at the realization of my harboured anger, something I truly had to deal with. I'd purposely left my phone at Payton's to avoid any incoming messages from Todd. That man was the reason I was in this freaking – *No, no stop it Marley. If you want to turn your life around, you have to stop blaming other people. Take a deep breath.*

"Yeah, I'm all good. Sorry."

He curved his lips upward, running his fingers through the black locks of hair that hovered just above his cocoa coloured eyes.

"So you're from..."

"New York," I chimed. "The Big Apple. Very, very different from here."

"Got that right. Can I ask how you ended up in Aurora? I mean, not exactly the ideal vacation spot."

How much did I want to tell this guy? I mean, I'd known him for a total of ten minutes and I'd already dumped so much emotional damage on people I barely knew. But at the same time, if I was truly planning on staying here to help Payton with her business, then it might do me well to make some friends.

"It really is a long story, and I feel like I have to do some work for Payton and all. But, I'm sure in the next coming weeks of us working together, I'll definitely tell you all about it."

He smiled ardently and rapped the door frame. "Or I can take you out for drinks tonight and we don't need to waste any work hours?"

Drinks... I didn't even know where I was staying. That was something I definitely needed to sort out before anything else. Plus, where the hell was Payton? How long did it take to get wrenches? Ugh, *fuck.*

"Erhm..."

"C'mon Big Apple, you can even do a background check on me if you're worried."

What the hell was up with Nebraska people and their nicknames?

"You could've falsified the records," I quipped, stalling the urge to jump at this opportunity and branch out.

"Ha," he bubbled, stretching a grin across his face. "I can assure you I ain't that smart."

I couldn't help but smile back. This exchange was so... *normal.* And honestly, I wasn't even sure what normal meant anymore. My entire life was dictated by people trying to steer me in different directions while I ran them off the road. I didn't want that anymore, I didn't want to be that person. I needed some stability, something to keep me grounded while I couldn't do it myself.

Could I go for some drinks? Did I want to go with him? *I mean, it would definitely benefit me to speak with someone who didn't know my situation, or anything about the train wreck my life has become.*

It was in that moment that I remembered a specific someone who happened to also be going out for drinks tonight. Someone who didn't want me anywhere near them. And someone who I so desperately wanted to anger with every fiber of my being.

Yes, *that* is what I needed. A thrill, some excitement. A distraction to get me out of my heavy head because that's where I lived ninety percent of the time and I was exhausted. I didn't want to think about Todd, my parents, or my non-existent living situation. Not right now.

Fun. That was all I wanted, all I craved. It got me into trouble for years, but I had nothing to lose anymore. I knew I was a good worker, I knew I was fully capable of helping Payton out just as she did for me. A night out drinking with a new friend could be just the thing I needed to settle in this foreign environment, to allow me to plant some roots in this new Nebraska soil.

I wouldn't let Payton down, but I also couldn't die in the fatigue of my own mind. *Oh boy... is this the right decision? It's reckless. You shouldn't do this, Marley.*

"I'd love to get drinks with you." I said, completely ignoring the warnings of my brain.

And just to make matters worse, I worked against my coherent psyche, pushing me to the depths of hell once again.

"Meet me at Cid's Pub? Seven o'clock?" I suggested, burying my conscience six feet under. And that was that.

Screw you Hunter Lane.
Screw you.

Chapter Ten
Hunter

I soaked in the warm water dripping down my torso, lathering a layer of soap over my chest.

Wet fingers trickled down the center of my abdomen, finding their way to the tip of my dick as I thumbed the sensitive parts of my shaft.

"Fuck," I groaned, wrapping a firm hand around my cock, stroking gently.

My mind immediately went to Britt's tits, picturing them squished beneath me as I face-fucked her against the side of her mattress. I pictured her high-pitched moans, her mouth taking me in like a good girl. God, she fuckin' loved taking me in.

I pumped faster, feeling the climax approaching. *Her bare ass against my dick, her nipples raw in my fuckin' mouth, her big brown eyes staring up at me...*

I came before I could register what the hell pushed me over the edge. Because Britt had green eyes.

Or maybe they were blue. Fuck I don't fuckin' know, but they sure as shit weren't brown.

"Just in time!" Josh hollered, sliding two double shots my way as I slid into the booth.

Cid's was pretty packed for a Thursday night. Not that it wasn't always busy but tonight was a goddamn lion's den.

Josh lined up two shots of his own, sprinkling a little lime juice on top of the golden liquid. "Pound 'er back, Hunt, come on!"

We clinked glasses and tapped the table, downing both in a row. The familiar taste of rum and bitter apple coated my throat, sending me into a euphoric bliss. *This is where I fuckin' belong.*

"She workin' tonight?" Josh asked over the blaring music of Three Days Grace.

"Who?" I responded, looking around as if I knew who the hell he was referring to.

"Britt, ya dud."

My pulse stalled as I thought about my shower earlier, how I busted a nut to Britt. *Sort of.* Honestly, I'd hoped to fuck she was working so I could verify her eye colour. They had to be brown, they had to. Why the fuck else would I be thinking about those eyes if they weren't? It was her tits I thought of, her face I fucked. So why the hell did I think of a pair of brown eyes? *And why did they look so damn familiar?*

As if the angels above heard my prayers, Britt and her skin tight server fit strolled our way.

She winked at me upon arrival, pulling down her shirt to show more of what I wanted to see.

"Hey boys, hope you don't mind I stole your table from Gracie," she purred.

"No bother at all, baby. Can we get another round? Say, two Captain and two Bacardi Golds?" Josh ordered.

I stared at her in complete contemplation, arms crossed as I leaned back into the booth. The pub was dark and flashes of multicolored lights made it damn near impossible to see the correct colours of fucking anything. *Now if I can just get a closer look at those eyes.*

"C'mere for a second, will ya sweetheart?" I flirted, beckoning her with two fingers.

She obeyed and leaned in, giggling with amusement as I brushed away blonde locks from her forehead.

"*Fuck,*" I whispered, releasing her from my grasp. Fuckin' green. Her eyes were fuckin' green. *Then who the hell was I thinking about? Jesus Christ.*

Her girly titter pulled me out of my head as she fixed her hair and threw me a playful side eye. "What was all that about, Hunty?"

Hunty? Fuck no. Never say that again, was what I almost spat, but I deemed it rather inappropriate given the circumstance. I did sort of just stare at her face for like two minutes, trying to convince my brain that her eyes were in fact brown when they were as green as a spring fucking clover.

"Just wanted to get a better look at ya, darlin', no shame in that."

"No," she cooed. "No shame at all." She turned to Josh and rounded up the empty shot glasses. "Be back in a bit boys."

The weight of a barbell sat heavy on my chest as I watched her walk away, knowing damn well she wasn't the mystery woman who sent me over the edge earlier.

"Man, what was that about? But for real?" Josh poked, looking utterly perplexed.

"Nothin'. Just needed to confirm something."

"Oh yeah? What'd ya need to confirm, *Hunty*?" He imitated, letting out a loud snort.

"Shut the fuck up, just, no."

A moment of silence stretched between us as I scanned the surroundings of Cid's, shrugging off the thought of those brown eyes to some chick I probably saw in porn.

Vintage posters of Johnny Cash, Hank Williams and Jimmie Rodgers plastered one side of the venue while the other half was painted in classic rock records from Metallica to AC/DC.

Neon strobe lights hung from every corner of the ceiling, casting down laser beam lights at the grinding horde on the dance floor.

That's probably what made Cid's so appealing. It was a newer venue with an older feel. It had a wide booth selection for the calm drunks and the wild ones.

"Huh, look like she came after all." Josh chirped, motioning towards the entrance.

I followed his gaze to the front door and my breath halted in surprise. Bambi was chatting with the coat check lady, dressed in a tight red dress and some black heels that coiled around her ankles like a fucking shoelace.

Her dark hair was swept over one side of her shoulder, drawing more attention to the deep V pushing her tits together.

I clenched my jaw, attempting to steady my racing thoughts and just watched her. She looked nervous, holding a hand over her chest as if she didn't realize she looked like the sweetest goddamn cherry in this wreck of a ruin.

"Christ, she cleans up nice." Josh babbled behind me.

I didn't need to look his way to know where the hell his eyes were. Where the hell everyone's eyes were in this fucking pub.

My eyes shifted to the meat stick standing next to Bambi, swooning over her like a kid in a candy store. Crudder, I think his name was. Cracker? Fuck if I knew. He worked at P&D's with my dad and Payton, and as far as I was concerned he didn't cause any trouble. But I'd never seen him out before. *Probably cause he never had the fuckin' opportunity 'till now.*

"And here you boys are." Britt slid a tray of shots, way more than we'd ordered, in the center of the table. "I added a few extra just in case you wanted to thank me later."

"Oh I'll thank ya right now, sugar, come here."

Britt leaned towards Josh but he blocked her path with his forearm. "I was talking 'bout the shots, Britt but, I'll uh – I'll tip ya real good."

I would've laughed at that had my attention not been on Bambi and Cracker. A tenacious bitterness lodged itself in my chest. Why the hell was she here? Wearing *that*? And with him of all fuckin' people? Guy looked like a pool noodle with no pool.

"Anything else I can get for ya, Hunty?" Britt chimed, batting those emerald eyes at me. *Hunty. That will always be a thorn in my side.*

I stole one last glance at Bambi who was now sitting at the bar, Cracker's stool way too close for my liking. *Man, what is goin' on with me?*

"Actually, yeah." I uttered, nodding towards the two newbies of Cid's Pub. "Send the girl in red a whisky on the rocks, the guy in blue a tequila sunrise."

Britt turned to look at Bambi, craning her neck to the side before curling her lip in annoyance.

"Is that, *everything*, then?" Her tone was sharp, curt, but I was too wrapped up in my own thoughts to care.

"Make sure to add a ton of syrup, sweetheart. He likes himself a fruity drink."

She stormed off and I knocked my knuckles against the table, downing all three shots in one go before turning to Josh. "Be back in a minute."

"You're evil!" He called behind me, but I was already stalking towards Bambi and no one was getting in my path.

When I reached my destination, I planted a firm hand between the two lovebirds, leaning my weight towards her.

"I'm goin' to have to call you cherry from now on." I teased, my tone filled with disapproval.

Her big brown eyes met mine with – *No. No fuckin' way. No fucking WAY it was her.*

I swallowed hard, stepping back to regulate my laboured breaths. Those chocolate spheres, the ones I seen in my climax, the eyes that sent me over the edge... they were *Bambi's*? How in the literal fucking hell were they Bambi's?

"Cat got your tongue, Hunter?" Bambi scowled, wrapping her slender arms around the middle of her dress.

Get your head outta your ass, Hunter, Jesus fuck. It was just a coincidence.

The familiar buzz comforted me as I coughed out a response. "Nope, just a pretty girl in red."

When I regained my composure, I stepped forward, surveying her like it was my damn job. My eyes roamed over her collarbone that glistened with some sparkly shit. A little music note tattoo was stamped on her skin, the size of a pea. Her flesh was bronzed and glittered like she just stepped out of some award-winning movie. *I mean, to be expected. Rich brats always looked like they were polished and ready for a fuckin' photoshoot.*

All the sentiment I was feeling dissipated when I remembered who the hell she really was. A spoiled girl from a big city who stormed into my family's life, *my* life, and expected us to bend the knee. *Don't matter how shiny a ruby, Hunter. They always cut you.*

"*Pretty*?" Her voice was filled with disdain. "Are we playing nice, now?"

Before I could retort, Cracker cleared his throat, forcing me to his attention.

"Hunter, right?" I watched his Adam's apple rise and fall as he spoke again. "I'm Cramer Hughes, I work with your mom and dad."

"*Step*," I corrected, throwing him a jagged stare. "Stepmom."

He swallowed in response, fumbling with the two top buttons of his tacky blue shirt. "For the sake of tonight, let's just call her Payton?"

I couldn't have been less interested in a conversation.

Turning back to Bambi, I leaned in closer, inhaling the scent of lavender and honey.

"In need of a little rescue sweetheart, or are you trying to get a reaction out of me?"

Her mouth gaped open which amped me up even more. *Fuck she was easy to annoy.*

"Why the hell would I try and get a reaction out of you, Hunter? Not every girl lives to worship the ground you walk on."

"Why the hell not?" I stated, wounded at her comment.

"Because you're rude. And kind of a prick."

A red hue glowed in her eyes, resembling embers and flames. It brought a rush out of me as I leaned in closer to her ear and whispered, "you got a fire in your eyes, sweetheart. And lucky for you, I'm drawn to the heat."

I recognized the bearded bartender as Kenton, who regularly worked the shifts now that the other bartender was fired. He trotted over, passing two glasses out – the whisky to Bambi, and whatever the hell kind of cocktail I ordered to Cracker.

"Oh, I didn't order this." Bambi waved a manicured hand around the rummer, attempting to return it.

"A gentleman ordered it for you a few minutes back. I'd expect a lot more drinks comin' your way tonight."

I caught his eyes roving over her like a damn hawk so I decided to pay for the drink right then and there.

"I happen to be that gentleman," I shot, slamming a crisp twenty on the wood. "Payin' for his too."

He met my stare and snagged the twenty, moving away from my presence. *As he fuckin' should.*

"Thanks for the drink, Hunter. I can't say I'm into the sweet stuff." Said Cookie, Cracker, fucking what's his face.

"Really?" I jeered. "Thought you'd love that shit."

I turned right back to Bambi and slid the drink in her direction. "Drink up, buttercup. It's good for you."

She kept her arms crossed, alerting me to the most sinful part of her skin. "I don't like whisky."

"Well that is a damn shame." I cupped her glass and downed it in one gulp, revelling in the sweet taste of poison.

"You're gon' get a lot of attention tonight, bartender's right. So eyes on me sweetheart, you got that?" I commanded, wiping the remnants of whisky off my lip.

"What the fuck is your problem?"

Twice.

Twice now she's asked that.

And both times I couldn't give a sane answer.

What the fuck is wrong with me? Why was I acting like I gave a damn when I hated everything this girl stood for? Her attitude, definitely needed a fuckin' reality check. Her lifestyle, anything but humble. Everything about her... fuck everything about her.

"Enjoy the evening." I muttered, stealing Cracker's fruity cocktail as I turned away.

Waste of time.

I passed Kenton on the way back to my booth, his eyes planted on Bambi's seat as he strode towards the bar door.

I placed a firm hand on his chest, halting his movements instantly. "If you're lookin' where I think you're looking, we're goin' to have ourselves a problem."

And I walked my dumb ass away.

My dumb ass that lost control.

My dumb ass that just made a fucking fool of myself to Bambi.

And my dumb ass that hated her guts for a reason I couldn't explain.

Her walk, her talk, the way she smiled, the way she sat there like this was her home. Like she didn't just belong somewhere else twenty-four hours ago. A whole new life, surrounded by fancy cars and money and shiny shit. And now she was living in my town, helping Payton with her business, staying here for God knows how long and I'd just have to watch.

So that's what I did.

I watched her all night; flirting with Cracker, eyeing up strangers, making friends, while I drank myself to oblivion and stayed in my damn lane.

Chapter Eleven
Marley

I knew Hunter would be here but I didn't realize his presence would be so authoritative.

Eyes on me sweetheart... As if I'd be freaking staring at him.

But I was. Only because I could feel his heavy gaze on me the entire night.

You know, for someone who hated me so much I didn't understand his approach to conversation.

So Payton was his stepmom. That explained why she was so nice and he was literally the devil incarnate. They weren't actually related, not by blood anyway.

Within twenty-four hours, I'd seen at least three different sides to Hunter. One, being the obvious, he was a fucking douchebag. Two, he was a full grown man child who didn't know how to control his emotions and three, well, he was a clear spectacle to everyone in the room.

It was no secret that he was easy on the eyes, as much as it pained me to admit. He had this rough bravado about him that evidently shined through his style. Black leather jacket, a white t-shirt and dark jeans paired with brown combat boots. His blonde hair always looked rough up, probably because some girl was pawing her fingers through it all night. That scruff on his face that followed his jawline and those eyes... those crystal blue eyes that seared through me the first time we'd met. *God, why couldn't he have had some sort of defect? Like fins for hands or a zebra striped nose?*

"I think Winter is just outside, I'll go on and get her."

I can still feel you staring at me, asshat. Good God does he not have anything better to do?

"Marley?"

I shook my head, realizing I'd been zoned out the entire time Cramer had been speaking.

"Huh, Winter?" I posed, turning my attention to the man I'd come here with. "Who's Winter?"

He lifted his butt off the barstool and adjusted his shirt. He did that a lot. *Maybe a nervous twitch.*

"A friend from college. I assumed after the events of tonight you'd wan' to get shit faced with some company."

"But..." I shook my head in confusion. "You are company."

He laughed. "Yeah, but nothin' like a girls night, right? I got a sister. I know the way you's do it."

Before I could respond, he passed by me and placed a soft hand on my back. "I've only had one drink so I can drive y'all home."

Then he was gone, leaving me to the nervous anticipation of meeting yet another new person in the span of twenty-four hours.

I'd never been good at meeting people. It wasn't even my tendency to be quite shy, just, I never knew the right thing to say at the right time. Honestly, I didn't even understand why Payton took me under her wing all things considered.

But Cramer seemed like a nice guy and after he'd shown me all the sections of P&D's, we set up my office and workspace together. He even gave me my own personal pen and notepad. I figured it was definitely a product of the store but hey, a welcoming gift nonetheless.

Payton didn't mind me going out on my first work night. In fact, she encouraged it and drove me to Cid's knowing I'd be drinking. She even asked me to stay in their basement for as long as I needed but I refused. The woman already gave me a job, a *friendship*, how could I take more from her?

After many hours of heart to heart conversations, Payton helped me settle in to a residency hotel near The Square.

Surprisingly, it was very posh. Not that Nebraska was entirely rural, but this building looked like a few I'd seen back home in New York.

The Atlas Aurora was a twelve story building, covered by Newcastle brick and glass windows. The doors that led to the lobby were a rich mahogany wood and the front-desk lady might've been the sweetest little old woman I'd ever encountered.

I got the cheapest room that I could afford, with only twelve-thousand in my savings left and my space was more than enough. I had a kitchenette with a countertop burner, a queen-sized bed and dresser with an ensuite bathroom.

Because rent was only five-fifty a month, I was on the lower levels of the residency but I still got an amazing view of a gorgeous lake that was freezing over in the cool October climate. On top of that, I had my own underground parking space free of charge. I don't know how Payton managed to swing that but I guess she was friends with the co-owner of T.A.A. *I really owed that woman my life.*

I made a mental note that once Spring hit, I would venture off there and have a picnic. Maybe I would've made some friends by then. Or maybe I'd be alone. Only time would tell, but I was feeling rather optimistic of my new situation.

Even though I was still in Nebraska, I was hours away from Lincoln where Todd and I lived. I still hadn't checked my phone; mostly out of fear that he'd somehow track me if I opened his texts. But I didn't need to, not yet anyway.

I had a ride home, a new friend and a place to stay. Screw anyone that tried to bring down my mood. *Especially if that someone was a six-foot Greek God with rage issues.*

Cramer returned with a beautiful, Amazonian heartthrob on his arm. She had the silkiest bronzed skin and her curly hair was tied up in a bow, two loose locks framing her face. Her tan dress extenuated her curves, curves I envied on woman for so long and she was no exception to my jealousy. *Oh. My. God.*

"Winter, this is my friend Marley. Marley, Winter Camden." Cramer pushed the small of her back towards me, buzzing like a bee.

She instantly pulled me in for a hug, her vanilla perfume brushing my senses.

"How are you?" she asked, her tone taking me off guard completely.

"You're *British*?" I questioned, leaning out of her hug in awe. *I love British people. Well, the sound of their voices anyway.*

A crisp laugh rose from her throat, exposing pearly white teeth and a diamond gemstone embedded into her canine.

"And here I thought I lost my accent," she perked, taking a seat next to me. "I'm a transfer student from Leeds. I went to NU for criminal justice and that's where I met Cramer."

Huh. "NU, University of Nebraska? That's in Lincoln, right?"

"Actually, the Omaha campus! Are you from there?"

"No, no, I'm from Lincoln – New York, actually. I'm originally from New York City."

She crossed her arms and tilted her head downwards to analyze my red dress and heels.

"That explains why you look like an actress, in the best way possible."

Cramer pulled aside a server and asked if we could have a booth since we were now a party of three, and I couldn't be happier.

The entire night we sat together chatting, ordering various different drinks and shots, celebrating my first day as a new woman. *Or what felt like it.*

I learned that Winter and I actually had a lot more in common than I thought. She, too, had an overindulgent family who put so much pressure on her to pursue a medical degree when she was passionate about law. She actually lived in Columbus for a little while, tried her luck in Colorado, and eventually settled in Aurora after graduating from NU to work in family law.

Cramer actually graduated NU with the same degree, only he tried becoming a paralegal and hated his life so he moved back home to Aurora, working at his dad's construction site with part-time hours at P&D's.

When it came time to ask about me, I was hesitant at first. I didn't really know how to explain myself, why I was here, what I was doing, without sounding like a complete basket case who was one marble short of losing her shit. But as the night progressed, the words flowed out of my mouth like I'd known these people for ages.

They listened to every shitty story about my parents, about how Todd got so drunk one night he accidently shit his pants. They howled in laughter when I said I hadn't checked my phone in twenty-four hours because of him, and they didn't blame me for it. They didn't blame me for a single thing, in fact. They understood.

Eventually, I allowed the alcohol to consume me and relaxed my posture, sending all trifling anxiety to run off into the sunset. *Giddy up, bastards!*

I'd come to the conclusion that I liked this girl. I liked Winter Camden and Cramer Hughes. He was so right by inviting Winter, it was exactly what I needed. Maybe by Springtime I wouldn't be eating at my picnic alone. Maybe I'd have this company, these friends that have made me laugh harder than I had in ages, by my side.

It was in my elated bliss that I realized one thing:

I didn't look at Hunter Lane for the rest of the night.

Chapter Twelve
Hunter

Three weeks went by, Bambi free.

I chalked off my pathetic outburst at the bar as my emotions going haywire cause of the booze, which has happened in the past so it ain't my fault.

Halloween came and went, Beth and Josh deciding to call it quits.

"Didn't work out," he'd told me.

Nothin' ever does.

Britt became my personal pleasure port and I didn't mind. She'd been angry with me about buying a drink for another girl but after I explained that's all she was, Britt was back on my arm.

I cared about Britt, but I didn't want no relationship. Hell, I didn't know what I wanted in general. The only thing I was sure of was death. That inevitable, black hole we'd all reach someday and in my best efforts, I'd been hoping to expedite the process.

But here I was, still alive, still kicking, still breathing. Unlike my mom, who got the shortest end of the stick in this fucked up world. Well, maybe it was a blessing. What's life gon' do for us anyway? Pain, pain, pain. The moral of the goddamn story.

We'd just wrapped up harvest season so I was doing menial tasks around the farm to help my dad. Farmer by day, drinker by night. *Got a nice ring to it.*

Payton was out most of the time and I cursed knowing exactly where she was and who she was with. But I couldn't even be mad about it. From the reports, P&D's was beating out every hardware store competition in town.

Bambi had managed to get the shop in flyers, posters and even the newspaper ads. I'd actually seen the new slogan when I read the paper a few days back:

Every Project's a Breeze with the Tools of P&D's!

It was the cheesiest thing in the world but people ate that shit up, and it was rolling in the dough so I couldn't complain.

Actually, the business grew so much that my dad created the store's personal "handy-man" collection which he and Payton delivered to hardware shops all around Nebraska.

They have always been happy since they'd gotten together, but now, they'd turned their business runs into staycation honeymoons which made them look like cupid shot an arrow right through both their asses.

My mom passed away when I was twenty-one, and my dad n' Payton got together about a year later. I remember I hated my dad for it, thought he'd gotten over the death of his fucking wife like it was the easiest damn thing in the world.

When Payton came around, I never talked to her. Didn't want to. Sometimes, I still don't. But I can tolerate her now, knowing she treats my dad alright and he's happy.

But I wasn't.

Four years now she'd been gone. Four years of drinking my life away, testing fate, wondering when I'd finally crash my truck into a post or fall off a bridge. But life really loved to crucify me.

No matter how much I drank, how many bar fights I'd been in, drunk drives down the road, I came out without a scratch.

My mom on the other hand... I watched her get wheeled out of my truck. I'd seen the state of her body; the bloody clothes that stuck to the gashes in her chest, the glass glued to every part of her skin, coating her face to a point of unrecognizability. She was dead by the time the paramedics came, I knew it, they knew it. They fuckin' knew and they still tried their damn best to save a life.

Me, well, I was trying to end mine.

I was in the garage giving my truck a tune-up when Payton patted the hood.

"Come help me up front, will ya? I got some handy-man boxes I need hauled into the van."

"Where's Dad?" I asked, cleaning the throttle in my baby's engine.

"Pickin' up supplies." She said, turning on her heel.

I wiped my hands on an old rag and followed Payton to the driveaway, surveying about a dozen boxes lined up near the porch.

They really did have a good thing going on, and everyone seemed a lot brighter lately. My dad even smiled more, and Lord when I tell you it was the creepiest damn smile I'd ever seen. My dad was many things, but a smiler? That'd be the damn day. And that day came, a week after Bambi brought the shop's average sale count to fifteen-thousand a week.

I don't know what she got out of helping the family. I don't know why she stuck around, I didn't care. She did right by staying elsewhere and working from a distance, because that girl was trouble. And no matter how many customers she'd pull in for my family, I wanted no part of her being in my life.

"We're headin' over to Kearney today. A shop up there paid big money for these." Payton sniffed, drawing her coat tighter.

"Kearney?" I asked, lifting a toolkit into the back of my dad's work van. "Not much goin' on up there."

"No, that's why it came as a shock but hey, we ain't complain'. Business is business."

I nodded in agreeance, hauling boxes silently until there were none left on the ground.

It was mostly silence between us. I didn't mind it anymore, and I doubt she did as well. She quickly became accustomed to who I was and that was something I actually commended her for.

"Anythin' else?"

Her eyes roamed around the empty lawn before quickly shaking her head.

"Nothin' material but Hunter," she paused, "let me talk to you 'bout something quick."

I crossed my arms over my chest, spectating her little white hat and checkered jacket. Payton and I were never really alone and I'm positive my dad made sure of it. I knew he cared for her so he didn't want to make it awkward knowing my stance on everything, so I was curious as to what she had to say.

"I was thinkin' of asking Marley to come with us to Rivertown Bay."

I let out a laugh before my mind could process what she'd just said. I've heard a lot of dumb things in my life, but that took the cake.

Bringing Marley on our annual Thanksgiving trip? To the place where my mom used to take me sailing, where my dad and I hid seashells underneath our cottage in the Summertime? Fuck no. That was too close to home, she wasn't touching that, no fuckin' way.

"No." I responded, flatly, marching towards the garage.

"Hunter –"

"*Payton*," I snapped, barely containing my anger as I zipped back around. "I barely let you come on this damn trip. It's a *family* thing. So just be happy with the fact you're still invited."

I left her with that comment, refusing to turn around because I couldn't look at her. I couldn't believe my *step*mom would make that kind of suggestion when she wasn't even my own flesh n' blood. I mean, even if Dad asked that of me he'd sure as shit know the answer. But Payton? What the hell kind of crack was she snorting to think that was a good idea?

I slammed the hood of my truck into place, deciding I better not touch my baby in the state of mind I was in. *She deserved better than that.*

The warmth of the shed house heated my nerves as I locked the door, soaking in the peace and quiet of my space.

When Payton moved in, I was already twenty-two and should've been out on my own by that age anyway. After dropping the baseball scholarship, I couldn't leave my dad to tend to the farm by himself so I built a separate shed house out in the field and called it home.

It had everything I needed from a TV to a comfy couch, kitchen, bathroom, bedroom and enough booze to last me a lifetime. Only I rarely drank at home considering I went out every night. Driving drunk had become as much of a routine as drinking at the bar, and one day, if I was lucky, my mom and I would crack open the first bottle of scotch I'd ever bought for this damn place. Somewhere far away from here. A place where pain didn't prosper.

I stripped off my clothes and jumped in the shower, leaning my forehead against the wet tiles. I hadn't touched my own dick since I busted to the thought of Bam – *Britt*, Britt.

To be honest, I didn't fucking need to. Any hour of the day, any minute of any moment if I called Britt to swing by she'd be here unless she was working. And her job didn't even stop us. We'd fooled around in Cid's one-stall bathroom more times than I could count.

Now was a better time as any.

I turned off the water and grabbed a towel to dry my hair, picking up my phone to text Britt.

5:42pm – Hunter: Hey, sweetheart. Busy?

5:48pm – Britt: Not particularly. Need me to come over, Hunty?

I gotta have a talk with her about that fuckin' nickname.

6:01pm – Hunter: If you can. Would make a man real happy.

6:02pm – Britt: Be there in twenty 😊

I tossed my phone on the bed and grabbed a Truly from the fridge, placing it on the kitchen counter ready for grabs.

Good hospitality for good measure, my mom used to say. Even though Britt never drank it cause she was as eager for sex as I was, it was always laid out for her to take.

Now we wait.

We wait for another distraction, another temporary thing to ease my permanent pain.

We wait. *That's all we ever fuckin' do.*

Chapter Thirteen
Marley

The last three weeks went by in a flash of world renowned success. *Well, Nebraska renowned success.*

I wanted to prove to Payton that all it took were advertisements, getting the company name out there and having the right marketing scheme. Of course, confidence was the biggest factor of getting your foot through the door. *One of the only useful things my dad taught me.*

He'd always said, "if you aren't willing to fight for what you're after, you don't deserve it in the first place." And Payton deserved this, more than anything.

Her business had been struggling for a few months now. Not to the point of bankruptcy, but their method of sales marketing needed some work. I created Google Ads, Instagram Ads, any ad possible in the Aurora radius to hit the consumers next door.

In New York, branding was everything. The P&D logo was completely outdated, so I decided to give it a makeover... well, the entire store really. And what do you know? It was a huge hit.

After the first week of non stop ad campaigns, we had an influx of orders. Friends told friends who told friends about our shop, shooting our reach up almost seventy-five percent. In just two weeks, people all over the state drove to our hardware store to get their hands on merchandise unavailable to other shops.

Honestly, I completely underestimated my capabilities. I'd been out of the game for so long, I thought I would never be able to play again. But after securing several clients, networking and expanding P&D's services all over the state, I managed to garner more sales in three weeks than the shop had in two years.

We were in the process of moving to a bigger location, seeing as we needed more storage and supply space for the handy-man tool kit Dex put together. God, that thing was a hit.

Payton hired a few more people and promoted Cramer to manager and me, well, I was her right hand woman. If she got a coffee, she made sure I got one as well. If I needed a day off, she told me to take two. Before, I was hesitant to call this a friendship, but now I knew. Payton was the mother I truly never had, and me... I was a freakin' badass.

After discovering that Winter and I lived ten minutes away from each other, we got coffee together almost every morning. She introduced me to a few of her friends and we frequently ventured to different pubs around The Square on weekends.

I hadn't gone back to Cid's since the night I had last seen Hunter, and quite frankly, I was glad. From the second I met him, he made up his mind about hating me. And how does that saying go? *Why would you want to be friends with someone who doesn't want to be friends with you?*

I didn't want to be friends with Hunter. In fact, I wanted nothing to do with Hunter. He was a toxic, emotional mess and I saw it. I saw it because I was *it*. Well, not anymore. I was a new woman, and I was done with trying to please people whose sole purpose was to drag me down.

I was separating nuts and bolts, bagging them and placing them into an appropriate casing when Cramer approached me carrying a big moving box.

"I can't believe we're relocatin' to Cutter's Quarry. That space is huge."

"I know," I boasted. "I visited the site yesterday and the parking lot is two times bigger than the entire perimeter of this area alone."

Cramer chuckled almost dropping the package. "We've got you to thank for that, Marley. You know we wouldn't be headin' off there if it weren't for you."

I blushed, looking down at the screws in my hands before returning Cramer's smile.

"I'm glad I could help."

"A lot more than you know. Have you seen Payton, lately? She's been drinkin' that happy water I swear to you."

Just as he released the words, Payton emerged from the storage room wearing a flowy white top covered by her red work vest.

"I'll be thirsty for some angry water if you don't move that box along, Cramer. *Get.*"

He scurried past her and made his way outside, leaving me alone with Payton and my nuts and bolts.

"Leave it, deary. I got somethin' to ask you." She said, planting herself on a work stool.

"Okay." I stood up and dusted my jeans, making my way towards her. "What's up?"

"You doin' anything for Thanksgivin'?"

Was I doing anything for Thanksgiving? God, I hadn't even thought about it. With all the craziness at work, I was solely focused on P&D's sale growth that I hadn't really settled much. I mean, besides going out with Winter when I needed a breather, my mind was focused on growing this business to its full potential. Plus, there was no chance in hell I was going back to New York to visit my family. They'd throw a pumpkin pie in my face and call it a day.

I sighed at the thought, returning my attention to Payton. "I don't have anything going on, I mean, not as far as I know."

Which was true. As close as I was getting to Winter, I still wouldn't call her or Cramer my best friends. We'd only known each other for a few weeks and they had their separate lives as well. And Payton, well, she had a whole family. And one member in particular who would've rather watched me burn on the stake than spend a second in my presence.

"The Lanes got a family tradition of goin' up to Rivertown Bay on holidays and the least I could do is ask ya to come."

"The Lanes..." I trailed off. "Which includes you, Dex –"

" – and Hunter, yeah. Don't worry hun, I already talked to him 'bout it."

"And he said no, I presume?"

She pressed her lips to a downturn frown, shifting in her seat. "Hunter doesn't pay a damn cent to Dex's cabin, but I do. I may not be blood but I have just as much a right to that place as him."

A bladed tension filled the air as Payton exhaled a long breath, shaking her head tenaciously.

"I don't get that kid, I don't."

I'd never seen Payton so... so – pained? Was that even the right word? Her entire demeanour changed at the mention of him, but I didn't want to pry. I hadn't pried since I'd met her and she hadn't as much spoken about him in my presence but now... I wasn't about to stop her.

"His mama passed a few years ago," she began, bobbing her leg up and down. "That boy never been the same since, as far as Dex told me. I always met him on the wrong side of the bed; bags under his eyes, reeked of whisky and fumes.

"I don't know that he'll ever recover at the rate he's goin'. I mean, I put up with his shit cause I'd never understand the pain of losing my own mama right beside me. But Hunter's got a mouth, and sometimes I just wan' clock him in the jaw."

I stared at her in disbelief, processing my thoughts while absorbing a tidal wave of emotions all at once. I wanted to ask how she'd passed, but Payton gave me so much information already I wasn't sure I wanted to know.

Holy crap. Hunter's mother died... right beside him. Oh my God, that would traumatize even the strongest of people. That would probably traumatize... God? Fuck, I don't know? Holy shit. Poor Hunter. Wow. I didn't think I'd ever feel sorry for that asshole but that is all I felt. Pity. For a man who made it his conquest to hate me. I didn't have to like him, but I couldn't hate him, not with a loss like that.

"I didn't..." I swallowed, scratching my scalp nervously. "I didn't know."

She scoffed, standing erect and sliding the work stool underneath the counter.

"How could ya? That boy don't speak. He just drinks and sleeps and works on his damn boats, cussin' at anyone who gets in his way."

Boats. I remember seeing boats the first night I'd slept in their basement. Those cute, tiny little ship figurines that were displayed loud and proud on the bookshelf. *Those were his?*

"Look Marley, I don't want nobody – no boy, no Hunter, *no one*, tryna run you outta this town, makin' you feel upset about bein' here, you got that?"

I chewed on my bottom lip, staring into her blue eyes that hurt. And that's when it hit me. The reason I thought they were related was because of their eyes.

The first time I'd met them both, I compared the blueness, the shape. Only now I was seeing why they looked so similar.

It wasn't because they were family, it was because they shared the same sadness. The same pain. Their eyes looked haunted in ways I couldn't describe, only Payton masked hers most of the time while Hunter's was on full display.

"Come," she urged. "I'm not gon' ask you again."

I nodded a yes, forcing my most genuine of smiles while she retreated back to the storage room, rummaging through bins.

The crowd of empty boxes in front of me was all I could fixate on. Emptiness, hardship, sorrow. Pity for Hunter, his mom, whatever else happened to him that made him so numb and reckless.

His actions, his rudeness, everything I'd come to learn about him was distorted in a way I couldn't put into words and I'd realized that all this time I spent hating him, I should've been trying to understand him.

"When are we leaving?" I called out to Payton who was transferring supplies off the shelves.

"Friday, so two days time, deary."

Friday.

The first Friday I will attempt to see Hunter in a different light since grounding my roots in this Nebraska soil.

Chapter Fourteen
Hunter

The Friday before thanksgiving, I drove up to Rivertown Bay by my own damn self.

I couldn't for the life of me understand why Bambi was coming to our FAMILY fucking cottage. Really had high hopes for my dad backing me on this one, but as per usual, he succumbed to his bitch boy behaviour and sided with Payton. Something about "owing Marley for the success of their business."

Like? Okay? Give her a box of chocolates or some goddamn peach rings, not this.

Once again, Bambi had single handily weeded her way into my family's good graces but I was having none of that. No one saw through her fake smile and innocent demeanour, but I did. She had a plan brewing and I needed to figure out what it was.

After a three hour drive, I pulled up to the two-story wooden cabin that sat near the lake, taking in the fresh smell of fucking nothing cause Bambi was marching up the driveway right behind my truck.

My dad and Payton were still unloading the van when the scent of lavender and honey strangled me as I turned around to meet her for the first time in weeks.

Those big brown eyes peered up at me, only they wore a different expression this time. They were downturned, softer, like a real life deer in the headlights. *A Bambi.*

"Hi Hunter," she spoke, her voice levelled and... kind? "Happy Thanksgiving."

"It's tomorrow." I grumbled out, eyeing her with suspicion.

The only encounters I'd had with Bambi, she'd been quiet, then snappy, then bitchy, then quiet, and the cycle restarted like a goddamn carousel.

This... this *weird* side, this, whatever the fuck - I hadn't seen.

I didn't like the way I noticed her freckles more in the afternoon light. Or how the snowy ground brought out the darkness of her hair. Her eyes were still the prominent feature of her face, like miniature globes that contained the world and all its land within them.

"It's close enough." She smiled.

She fucking smiled.

And it wasn't a 'fuck you' sarcastic smile either. It was sort of... pleasant? Sweet? Pure? *Jesus Christ, stop reading into it.*

I gave her red puffer and black jean combo a look down before moving to the back of my truck and yanking out my duffel bag, shutting the door to carry it up the walkway.

The cobblestone path was covered by a fresh blanket of snow, the lake completely frozen over by ice. The sun's reflection on the stilled water made it look like a mirror; a mirror reflecting the sky where I knew my mom was smiling down at me.

I paused to take in that view, remembering where we'd sailed out on the marina and stargazed by the docks. *I'll see you soon, Mom,* I thought. *I'll see you soon.*

"Hunter!" my dad called from the bottom of the driveway. "Come help me out with the girls' bags, will ya?"

I turned to look at him, catching another glance of Bambi and Payton staring off into the lake, chatting as if they were the best of fucking friends. Her eyes met mine briefly before she quickly returned to her conversation. *What was this girl's damn motive?*

Throwing my duffle to the stone entrance, I jogged down the driveway to meet my dad.

"Christ, they pack for a month long vacation or what?" I blurted, surveying three different luggage's; one with an I <3 NYC keychain attached to the strap. *I knew she was a big city brat.*

"Let 'em be." My dad retorted, hauling out Payton's massive cargo.

I reluctantly grabbed the black luggage with the keychain, knowing it held Bambi's possessions and an odd feeling came over me that I quickly shrugged away. *Just get over it, Hunter. Can't do anythin' about her being here no more.*

"Why'd you let her come?" I prodded as my dad collected the last of the baggage.

"Payton asked."

"That doesn't answer my question."

He began wheeling up the baggage through the snow, looking out to the lake where he'd sailed with my mom many times.

I watched a hint of sadness contort his features but he tried his damn best not to show it. I knew he missed her, but fuck that man did not allow a single prick of pain to come through. Sometimes, all I wanted was to sit down with him, have a beer and talk about Mom. But God forbid the name Leslie ever came up in conversation.

The girls retreated inside the cabin but my dad still stood, looking out to the shadow of the mountains covered by a misty fog.

I took my place beside him and watched as well, accepting the cold air into my lungs before breathing out the frost.

"I miss her." I whispered, hoping, *praying* that he'd say something.

His chin quivered but of course, he didn't. He didn't say a damn thing about my mom, his *wife*. He just stood there like a fucking mannequin, studying the empty lake filled with dead memories.

"Don't be an ass this weekend, Hunter." He finally released, turning to me with a stoic expression.

"Dad –"

"No I mean it, boy. I get you don't like Marley, that's fine. Havin' a hard time myself adjusting to this new situation. But she's done some damn good work for us and as much as you don' like it, you've gotta respect it, you hear me?"

I forced my words down and nodded as he made his way towards the cabin, leaving me alone with the memory of my mom to hold on to by myself.

As per usual, *all by my self.*

"I'm goin' boarding, be back later."

I grabbed my helmet and jacket, stepping into my boots before snagging my snowboard in the hallway closet.

The intermediate hills at Rivertown Slopes were some of the best I'd ever experienced and I wasn't leaving this weekend without feeling that adrenaline rush again.

"Hunter," Payton called out from the opposite side of the wall. "Why not take Marley with ya?"

I turned the corner into the living room which was attached to the kitchen, throwing a glance over my shoulder to where Bambi was planted on the couch reading a book.

"Oh, I'm uh –" she stuttered, her face as red as a damn tomato. "I'm good here."

"Yep," I agreed, palming my wallet and keys from atop the kitchen island.

"You don't like boardin'?" My dad asked her, almost too pleasantly.

How the tables have fuckin' turned I guess.

"I don't really know how to..." She began, placing her book to the side. "I mean, I tried skiing once but that was definitely a mistake."

Payton chuckled and even my own father cracked a damn smile but I kept my jaw tight, itching to get out of this conversation.

"Hunt's been boardin' since he was a kid." My dad's attention was now on me, nodding Bambi's way. "Why don't you take her out on the kiddy hill, yah?"

"You're fuckin' hilarious."

I saluted a two finger wave at the rents before rotating on my heel out of the family room.

"Wait –"

Her voice called after me.

I stopped in my tracks and turned around, coming face-to-face with Bambi and her fuzzy grey turtleneck.

"Maybe I..." her voice was small, like the rest of her. "Maybe I can come with you, actually."

The fuck? "Why?"

She cleared her throat, pulling down the sleeves of her sweater so they hung over her knuckles. "It'd be nice to get some fresh air."

I scratched the back of my neck and peered to look at my dad who had his back turned to me, helping Payton cut some vegetables.

"Why don't you be a good little bunny and read your bedtime stories?"

"*Bunny*?" She huffed. "I thought I was Bambi."

I don't know why that did it for me but it did. My grin almost cracked. *Almost.* But fuck her for tryin' to bring one out of me in the first place.

My dad told me to play nice this weekend, so that's what I'll do, even if every fiber of my fucking being went against it. If she wanted to learn how to board, I'd teach her, but not on that damn kiddy hill. Something a little more... intense.

"Alright come on then, slopes close in three hours."

Her tiny physique disappeared into the living room before she emerged a minute later wearing her red puffer and a white beanie.

"I don't have a snowboard." She said, following me out the door.

"They got some there."

"In my shoe size?" She asked, her little legs struggling to keep my pace.

I shook my head, glancing at her in bewilderment. "You got size three feet or somethin'?"

"No," she sniffed, pulling on a pair of black mittens. "Size six."

I snorted as I walked to the passenger side door, opening it for her with a grunt. "Watch your step."

"He opens doors?" She joked, sinking into the black polyester cushion of my seat.

"He closes 'em too." I responded, slamming it shut.

The fifteen minute drive to the slopes was in complete silence until the very end, when I decided to pose the question that'd been picking my brain.

"Size six, really?" *That was damn fuckin' tiny.*

She shrugged. "My brother used to call me Minnie Mouse."

A quiet laugh escaped my throat before I could stuff it down and bury it with a hatchet.

Bambi.

Bunny.

Minnie Mouse.

God, this girl was every name in the book except for fuckin' Marley.

Chapter Fifteen
Marley

Rivertown slopes was a sight to see.

For a ski resort in a small town, I really wasn't expecting much. But the glistening snow, the sandy wooden lodges and the smiling faces encircling me brought out all the happiness this place could provide.

I'd only ever been to a ski resort once and it was a luxe chalet near New York for a Christmas retreat with my dad's coworkers. That was probably one of the only fond memories I shared with my mother because while my father was out making business deals, my mom actually taught me how to ski. Well, *attempted*.

I couldn't even count how many times I fell on my ass but my brother was a natural. As per usual, the polymath of the family who did no wrong, who my mom *adored*.

And once again, Marley Matthews didn't get it right. I couldn't even stand on my own two feet without crossing my skis and faceplanting into the snow.

Hunter carried his black snowboard as he walked us through an open path, halting in front of a square booth containing two workers on opposite ends.

"For fuck's sake Bernie, you haven't aged a day," he released, slapping a fifty dollar bill in front of a brawny bald man who couldn't be younger than sixty.

"Hunter!" The man replied, grasping hold of his hand. "Just the man I *didn't* want to see."

The two of them shared a laugh as Hunter scooped up a red and white wristband, handed it to me and looped the other one around his wrist.

"Who's the girl?" The bald man rapped, regarding me curiously.

"Friend of Payton's." Hunter released, like he couldn't give less of a shit.

"She looks like Little Bo Peep."

I raised my eyebrows, taken aback. *Little Bo Peep? Seriously?*

Hunter shrugged off the comment, shoving change in his wallet. "Yeah, she looks like a lot of things."

"Girl must be a good boarder if you're takin' her to Avalanche."

This remark, Hunter smirked at. "The best."

I stared at him suspiciously but he didn't meet my gaze, giving the bald man a firm handshake before walking through the fenced entrance.

Scurrying after him, I took in the aroma of hot chocolate and mulled wine, kids in snow pants and trinket stands.

Off in the distance, I watched a dozen ski lifts carrying people to the slopes; some big, some tiny and some so steep they blended into the mountains.

"Who was that?" I asked Hunter, finally maintaining his pace.

"Who?"

"The guy at the booth, the bald guy."

I swear he smiled, I swear. Or maybe it was my wishful thinking knowing what I knew about his past. I wasn't sure if Payton told him that I was aware of everything, but it didn't matter. Regardless of his knowledge, I had some of my own. And I wanted to be nice, for both our sakes.

"Bernie's been workin' here since I was a kid. Surprised he's still kickin'."

"His hair isn't." I teased, but he didn't look at me. He didn't even move a muscle. *Oookay then.*

After a few minutes of awkward silence, we reached a booth that read: *Board Rentals.*

A wide array of different snowboards hung behind the young teenager working the stand, his brown hair hidden beneath a bright orange beanie.

"Hi," I nodded at the boy, surveying the boards on the wall.

A bright red board caught my eyes, brimming with gold and silver stripes. *Ou, I love that.*

"It's gon' be forty-five for the day ma'am."

I zipped open my purse and pulled out my wallet, pointing to the red snowboard I had my eyes on.

"Can I get that one?" I asked.

He nodded, taking it off the wall and setting it to the side.

"Just tap here."

He clicked a few buttons then handed over the card reader. But just as I was about to lay my credit on the scanner, Hunter snagged the machine and paid with his own.

"Why the red?" He questioned, his eyes facing the screen.

"Um," I swallowed, squeezing my unused card in hand. "It matches my coat."

He glanced up at me, those icy eyes giving my red puffer a lookdown before handing over the machine to the boy.

"That it does."

Before I could respond, the worker asked me to come around the booth to adjust my bindings which we did while Hunter scoped out a scarf booth.

"You not from around here, are ya?" The boy asked, measuring the length of my boot.

I looked down at him in his dark blue parka and worn out gloves, pressing my lips into a smile.

"What's your name?" I asked.

"Tate."

"Well Tate, you're right," I chuckled. "I'm from New York."

He slid one knee to hold his position on my other boot before responding.

"It nice? I always wanted to go."

That question made me reflect for a minute. I think when people picture New York, they see all the glamourized aspects to the city; Central Park, Times Square, Statue of Liberty... the list goes on and on. But what people fail to realize is the business of it all. The non-stop action, the unaffordable living and the littered streets. Was New York nice? That was a hard question to answer. Because I believe that every city has its perks, but the downsides are always concealed.

I settled with the most conservative answer I could possibly give. "It has a lot of opportunity." *That wasn't a lie.*

There were ample opportunities to kiss a stranger at the New Year's Eve ball drop, stare down at ant-sized taxis atop the Empire State Building, and eat your bodyweight in street meat. But there was also the high chance of corruption, stealing, theft, or in my case, falling for a complete asshat who kidnapped my heart all the way to Nebraska before cheating on me.

A few minutes passed before Tate stood up and handed over the board. "All set."

I nodded a thanks and found Hunter at the booth, purchasing a black and red plaid scarf from a little old lady.

"Doesn't really seem like your style." I released, running my hands over the furry white throw underneath the selection of cloth. I acknowledged the lady before following Hunter out of the booth.

"Cause it ain't."

I ogled him strangely. "Then why'd you buy it?"

He let out an arm, handing me the soft material. "It matches your coat *and* mittens," he smirked, a sunken dimple poking through his cheek. "Two for one."

I glanced down at my black gloves and red puffer, reluctantly taking the scarf in my hands. *Did he know I knew about his mom? Was that why he bought me this? I mean, he was being a dick earlier... but he also paid for my snowboard? I am so confused.*

"You're really hot and cold, you know that?" I wrapped the scarf around my neck, lifting my hair out from beneath it.

He shrugged. "Makes things interesting."

We stopped in front of a trail crusted by snow that read: Avalanche.

My mind instantly returned to the conversation with the bald man earlier and I poked Hunter. "This isn't the beginners hill?"

He laughed, throwing down his snowboard and placing one foot inside of it. "Great observation, sweetheart."

The next thing I knew, his helmet was on and he was pushing himself towards the dip of the slope.

"Hunter wait –" I grabbed hold of his coat. "I can't do this, I barely know how to keep myself upright."

Through the visor covering his eyes I could make out an amused stare as he spat out a response.

"Tragic," he pouted. His two fingers saluted me in a wave as his board curved sideways and he let the slope sweep him away.

After finally getting the proper directions to lead me down the hill, I found Hunter sitting at the Avalanche bar with a girl on his arm.

My mouth gaped open when his tongue slid down her throat and her hands bunched into his collar.

She was a pretty blonde with her hair tied up in a pony tail and a fur white overcoat. I must've looked like a creep standing near the hostess table watching them but I was more concerned with the familiarity of that jacket.

And then it hit me.

My mom had that exact coat from Clabonita, a designer store in California and it was about the same price as a second-hand car.

She'd been shopping on Melrose for a business trip and stumbled into this store when she saw the coat on a mannequin. I guess the owner only set-up shop there and wasn't an online vendor. *So where was this girl from? Or was she – Oh my God, why are they going so hard in public? There are children in this freaking establishment.*

I marched over to Hunter's table and knocked hard on the wood, drawing both their attentions to me but I was only concerned about one.

"You left me up there." I pointed to the top of Avalanche slope.

He slowly wiped the gloss off his bottom lip and planted one swift kiss on the blonde's forehead. "Give me a second, darlin', will ya?"

She had an eager fuck-me-eye expression written on her face as she wiggled her fingers into a wave and met her friends at the bar.

I rolled my eyes, pulling out the chair across from him. "Why did you leave me up there? I thought you were teaching me how to snowboard?"

He let out a pathetic fucking laugh and I was fuming.

"I wouldn't have come if I'd known you were just going to abandon me!" My cheeks heated as I glanced around, lowering my tone to the best of my abilities. "There are kids in here Hunter, Jesus. There's a time and a place for hooking up."

He settled back into the seat and crossed his arms, looking so disinterested he could've fallen asleep.

"I never asked you to come, sweetheart. In fact, what'd I say? Read your damn book or some shit? Oh, and –" His fingers laced together as he leaned against the edge of the table. "Left side of the bar's for families, right side's for adults. As far as I'm concerned, I'm on the right side of the bar and I don't give a damn 'bout no kids watchin'."

And there it was. The douchebag, heartless, soulless Hunter Lane I'd met so many times in the past. I was trying to be nice. God, I was trying all day to change my opinion about him but no. He was never going to teach me how to snowboard. He was never going to give me the time of day. How could I be so stupid, thinking maybe he knew that I was aware of his loss and maybe he'd open up to me. I was so wrong, I was so undeniably wrong.

Tears burned in my waterline and I couldn't understand why. Maybe it was the defeat I felt for trying so hard, *yet again*, for someone who didn't deserve it. Maybe for the past three weeks I'd been doing so well without his presence hovering over me and now I was consumed by it.

As much resentment as I felt for the way my mother treated me, she was still my mom at the end of the day. Heaven forbid something happened, I would want to confide in someone, someone who understood, someone who cared. The fact that Hunter quite literally would rather saw his own arm off than be vulnerable was something I could never understand and at this point, I was sick of trying to.

I stood up in defeat, unwinding the scarf Hunter bought me and placed it on the table.

"Despite everything," I began, my lip quivering in regret, "I really tried to spend some time with you."

"I didn't want your time, Bambi." His voice was so levelled and unmoved, I could've punched him in the face and he wouldn't so much as flinch.

I glanced over at the blonde girl in the white fur coat and inhaled a breath. "Is she from here?"

"Why do you care?"

"Damnit Hunter, just answer the question."

His lips pressed into a thin line as he slowly shook his head. "L.A."

I knew it. I knew she wasn't from here. I fucking knew it. And yet, he was all over her, all over a *big city* girl. Everything he supposedly hated in me, he liked in other people.

"So what am I then?" I scolded, staring into those crystal eyes filled with anger and scorn. "Your personal punching bag?"

His face twisted in disgust. "What the hell are you on about?"

"Her." I nudged my head towards the blonde. "She's from Los Angeles. You hate me because I'm from New York but she's from Los Angeles. How does that work?"

His jaw clenched as he worked a hand over his stubble. "I like them better when they aren't yappin' in my damn ears."

I took a step back, forcing myself to turn around. But I couldn't do it, the words came out of my throat before I could catch them.

"You know what, Hunter? Losing your mom isn't an excuse for treating everyone around you like a waste of time. Fucking check yourself."

And I fled. I fled so freaking fast and I couldn't look back. I couldn't face the admission I'd just said to the man who lost his mother. And whatever part of me that felt bad for him, whatever part contained an ounce of pity, was numb and paralyzed.

Even if it was just for one minute, Hunter deserved to feel the way he made me feel since the moment I met him.

Unwanted.

Chapter Sixteen
Hunter

My fingers froze around the wheel of my truck as I drove Piper and I to her Airbnb.

We took a backroad away from the main street so she could give me head and she was delivering. Too bad I couldn't fuckin' focus on anything but Bambi's words.

Her blonde head bobbed up and down my dick as I tried to relish in the sweet pleasure of a blowjob, but I couldn't. I couldn't fuckin' do it.

Fuck. Fuck. Fuck. "Alright, ease 'er back. Need somethin' to look forward to when we get home, yah?"

She wrapped her fat lips around the tip of my dick, rolling her tongue around the head before sitting back in her seat.

For a split second I actually felt it. For a split second I enjoyed a pretty girl loving every second of my cock in her mouth. But only for a split second.

Because Bambi knew.

Bambi knew about my mom. *How the fuck did she know about my mom? Did she read about it in the papers? The journalist interview I did? How much did she fuckin' know?*

Payton.

That was the only explanation I had.

My dad wouldn't be dumb enough to open up to a girl he barely knew when he didn't even say a damn word about Mom to his own son.

Bambi fucked up my entire day and left me hanging like a shaved sheep at the slopes. She just walked off. Walked her little ass off into the sunset after dropping that goddamn bomb on me when that wasn't her story to share.

I was being a gentleman. Paid for her snowboard, tried to be nice, even bought her a damn scarf which was now stuffed in my glove compartment. I was never going on that kiddy hill, why the hell would I? She should've known better.

I didn't give a single shit if I provoked her. I didn't give one fucking shit about that bratty girl who waltzed into my life and tried to soften me up.

After her confession, every piece of the damn puzzle fit together. The reason she was being nice, offering to come with me at the slopes, all that fluffy marshmallow bullshit, that was just a ploy to get me soft. I placed there was something behind her deer-in-the-headlights exterior and I was right.

But now she knew. She knew the one thing that broke me apart and tore out my insides. The one thing that had any sort of power over me... She knew. She'd use it to her advantage just like my ex Rebecca.

The one time I opened up to a girl, I got close with someone who wasn't my damn family, she pulled out *that* card.

"Everyone's going to think you're fucked up, Hunter." She'd said. *"Losing your mom, being an alcoholic, driving drunk to chase a high. You're a ticking time bomb, and I'm the only one who understands you."*

Rage accelerated my pulse as I squeezed tighter on the wheel, resisting the urge to slam my brakes and send me flying through the windshield.

But I had company. And she didn't deserve to die. She was a nice girl, as far as I knew her to be. But I'd only known her for a total of four seconds. Still, this was my burden to bear, not hers. I was the one who was fucked up, not her. No one deserved this torment but me. *I let my mom die.*

When we reached Piper's Airbnb, I didn't get out of my seat. *And I wasn't going to.*

"You coming?" She stepped out of my truck, flashing me a polished smile but I shook my head.

"Change of plans, sweetheart. Text you later?"

I cranked the engine and locked the doors, shifting gears as she huffed in irritation.

"You don't even have my number!"

But I was gone. Driving down the road with only one thought in my head. The thought that nestled permanently in my skull, the thought of comfort, warmth and security.

I need a fuckin' drink.

Chapter Seventeen
Marley

Hunter missed dinner.

Of course he missed dinner, he was too busy hooking up with some L.A girl to spend time with his own family at their cottage.

God I hated him. I *hated* him – I hated him so much I could scream.

You know, if he wanted to be a polite asshole he could've just simply said: "No Marley, I don't want you to come with me," and left it at that.

But nope, that would've been too easy for him. He let me come, he paid for my rental snowboard AND bought me a scarf. I liked the scarf; it really did match my outfit but screw him. SCREW HIM and his fucking scarf.

Payton made spaghetti and meat sauce with a side of bread and I gobbled it up like tomorrow wasn't promised. If she made pasta taste like it was bathed in holy water, I could only imagine what tomorrow's Thanksgiving dinner would deliver.

Dex and Payton weren't surprised that Hunter wasn't home to eat with us, but they weren't happy that he let me call a cab alone in a foreign town.

"I know he's your son, Dex, but that boy is irresponsible." That was the only thing she said about Hunter the entire night and Dex grumbled in agreeance.

He and I didn't butt heads anymore, but we weren't exactly BFF's. Honestly, I preferred it that way. We worked well in the business side of things and he treated me fairly. There were no more harsh stares or rude side comments, and he actually addressed me in conversation which was a pleasant bonus.

Payton knocked on the bathroom door when I was brushing my teeth, leaning against the wall.

"Goin' to bed?"

I held out a finger to briefly pause any attempt at conversation while I spit out my toothpaste and rinsed my mouth.

"Sorry about that." I said, facing her tired eyes and polka dot pyjamas. "But most likely. I've had quite the day."

"About that..." She hovered for a moment before clearing her throat. "I'm sorry 'bout Hunter. Leavin' you an all that, that was low."

I played with the drawstring of my joggers, ruminating on today's events. I didn't want to think about it. I didn't want to think about him, where he was, why he acted so hot and cold. He wasn't my issue, but staying in his family's cottage... he became it. At least right now I wasn't a victim to his presence because he was off with blondie.

"You have nothing to apologize for, Payton."

"I do," she replied. "He's my son, in a way. I mean, I care for the kid. I do, a lot, Marley. With Thanksgivin' tomorrow... I dunno. I thought he'd do better than he did, is all."

I sighed, crossing my arms over my cream coloured tank top. "He knows I know about his mom's passing."

Her blue eyes met mine, guarded. "You told him?"

"He made me so angry I just... I guess I just snapped."

"Well, maybe that'll knock some sense into him for a change. Knowin' that someone else can be there for 'em when he's ready."

But would that day ever come? And if it did, would I even want to be there for him? I meant what I said earlier. His mom passing away was not an excuse to treat others like shit. But then again, the biggest part of me couldn't even begin to comprehend what type of demons were strangling him on the inside.

There were so many layers to Hunter, I was scared to peel them back. I figured that if I did, he'd snap even more at me for trying to help. But how could I help? He didn't want anyone, didn't need anyone. So my best course of action would be to just stay put and mind my own business this weekend.

"Anyways, g'night deary. Fresh sheets in the guest room."

I smiled in appreciation and watched her walk down the hallway, closing the door to the master bedroom and taking the light with her.

My feet padded against the wooden floor, as I stepped into my own quarters and settled into bed. The grey weighted blanket buried me in the mattress as I extended an arm to switch off the lamp.

Once I was consumed by darkness, I let my thoughts race. This was a lot of people's biggest fears I think, being overwhelmed by their mind and fighting off all the thoughts they'd tried to ignore throughout the day.

But not me. I made sure to think about every horrible thing in my life, every decision I made that pushed me to this point. Maybe I was a sadist who loved to punish myself. Or maybe the deepest part of my soul just wanted to reflect on what I could do better now that I've done it all – I tied an anchor around my ankle but I was still breathing.

There's got to be a reasonable explanation for that. Otherwise...

Why am I not drowning?

I tossed and turned in bed for a couple of hours before I gave up entirely and decided to stay awake.

Todd always used to complain about my insomnia saying I should go on sleeping pills or whatever, but I couldn't be bothered. Contrary to popular belief, I actually liked being awake before dawn. There was something about the complete and utter silence of the world, the onyx sky that was no longer polluted by the exhaust fumes of motor vehicles, that calmed me.

I enjoyed the quiet. New York, the city that never sleeps, was where my insomnia began. When I was younger, I used to hate it. I'd get on average maybe three, four hours of sleep if I was lucky. But when I left for college, I actually relished in my sleepless nights and channelled those moments into work.

If it wasn't for my insomnia, I honestly don't know if I would've graduated. During the day I would spend most of my time with friends because to me, that was the point of the day – *living*. But when night hit and everything fell still, I'd transform into a workaholic and just grind my dues until the sun was up. Caffeine was my fuel, and it never let me down for years. *Why stop now?*

I flung my legs out of bed and sucked back my tongue, cursing the one symptom of insomnia I absolutely hated: dry mouth.

Usually I kept a water bottle on my bedside table at all times, but I'd forgotten it back home so I threw on a sweater and made my way to the kitchen.

Immediately I was swept up by darkness, walking down the creaking staircase that had no railing. *This has to be some sort of hazard.*

A gust of wind rattled the window pane as I crossed the area rug towards the fridge, soaking in the silence.

My eyes glanced to the oven clock that read:
2:16am

"Penny for your thoughts, sweetheart?"

I jumped up and launched my entire body to the nearest wall, inhaling a sharp breath as I fumbled with the light switch.

When the dim brightness illuminated my surroundings, I found Hunter sitting on the arm chair with a glass of dark liquid in his hand, staring at me sharply.

"Or do those thoughts just lead back to me?" He poised, finishing off his drink in one swig.

His blonde hair was a disheveled mess atop his head, the points of his knuckles coated in a reddish brown substance.

"Hunter?" I tiptoed around the kitchen island, maintaining a fair distance between him and me. "What are you doing?"

He grumbled lowly. "Enjoyin' myself, by *myself.*"

Those diamond eyes were darker now, similar to sapphire gems that cut into my skin like glass. I crossed my arms over my middle, feeling more exposed in a sweater and joggers than if I was completely naked.

"Why are you looking at me like that?"

"You walked into my line of sight Bambi, I'll look where I want to."

With careful footing, I moved closer just to get a better view of his torn up knuckles.

"What happened to your hands?"

Immediately he shot up, placing the glass on top of the fireplace before making his way towards me.

"Let's talk about you, Bambi."

I stood glued in place as his chest made level to my eyes, forcing me to look up at his face.

"What's your story lookin' like? You seem to love pokin' in other people's lives so why don't we take a dip into yours."

"What are you –"

"New York, you said. What was that like, Bambi? Take a lotta drugs? *Fuck* a bunch of rich scumbags? Sell your soul to the mother fuckin' wolves of Wall Street?"

I held a hand out as he towered over me, stepping closer and closer until my back collided with the kitchen island.

"Hunter you're drunk..."

He bounced back and raised his voice, spitting out in anger. *"I'm always fuckin' drunk!"*

Before I could react he pointed in my face. "Who told you about *her*? Huh? Payton? Now that y'all are two peas in a damn pod, you sharin' secrets now? Secrets that aren't yours to fuckin' share!"

"I'm not..." I swallowed back any cuss word, any bad thing I could've said because I couldn't say it to him. I didn't want to set him off in this fragile state.

He was visibly so intoxicated, his eyes beady and bloodshot. Sweat painted his forehead and his knuckles... God, they were so bruised. *What the fuck happened to him?*

"I'm not having this conversation, Hunter. Not when you're like this."

"Not when I'm like *this*?" He scoffed. "So how d'you want me to be? What'll fit your fancy, Bambi?"

His legs carried him to that same loveseat where he sat erect, his back straight as board and he crossed his legs as if he was a lady-in-waiting.

"This better? If I sat here and listened to you tellin' me shit? Sit here listenin' to how you'll use me and tell me I'm fucked in the head for drinkin' and shit?"

"Use you? Hunter you need to drink some water –"

"*Fuck!*"

I swung my head around at the sound of broken glass, watching Hunter mutter curse words holding up his bleeding hand.

The glass he'd placed atop the fireplace was now a heap of shards on the floor beneath him.

"Oh my God." I released, grabbing a bunch of paper towels and rushing to his side.

Blood trickled down his forearm as he examined the cuts across his palm, his face grimacing in pain.

I tried to grab his hand but he pulled away, slicing me open with a daggered stare. "Don't."

"For fuck's sake, Hunter! Quit being a child and give me your hand." I snapped, wrapping my fingers around his forearm and yanking it towards me.

For the first time ever, he actually obeyed, allowing me to observe the wounds not only on his palm but on his knuckles.

His breath was erratic as I brushed over the dried scrapes and cuts crisscrossing over the rough bone. The callouses on his palm were slashed by broken glass, soaking the paper towel as I pressed it to the gash.

I felt his muscles soften as I tore off long strips of paper towel, wrapping them around his hand like makeshift gauze. As I folded them, I could feel his stare breathing down my neck.

He didn't want me near, I got that. But in the state Hunter was in there was absolutely no way he would've taken care of it himself. And judging by his lack of caution, I don't think he minded the pain at all.

"You got cold hands, Bambi." He whispered, his words sliding down my spine like water. "Need me to light a fire?"

I sucked in a breath, feeling his presence shift closer to me, his thigh brushing against mine with warmth.

"Your hand is bleeding." I let out, attempting to block out his closeness.

"I got another hand." He flexed his fingers, wiggling them about. "Works pretty damn well, too."

Rolling my eyes, I stepped back and released his palm. "What happened to your knuckles?"

That shut him up real quick as he held the paper towels in place, turning away from my gaze.

The lights switched on in the upstairs hallway as Payton and Dex bolted down the stairs; Dex completely shirtless with black shorts and Payton wearing her polka dot pjs.

"What's goin' on down here?" Payton complained, eyes wide at the broken glass on the floor. "The hell happened, Hunter?"

Dex didn't make a sound as he marched straight up to Hunter and grabbed him by the shirt, drawing him closer with one pull.

"You're a fuckin' mess, boy!" Dex shouted.

And Hunter smiled.

He smiled so brightly that the world could've fallen apart on his head and he would've rejoiced.

"For once..." He whispered, his voice breaking. "For once you noticed."

A slab of weight pressed itself against my chest as I watched Hunter carefully, taking in a second of vulnerability in his eyes. Those blue crystals that were filled with anger and hate dissipated into a cloud of sadness right before me. And I wanted to capture the moment forever just to show him that he was capable of feeling.

Whatever that emotion was, it faded the second Dex tossed him to the side, shoving him towards the staircase.

"Clean yourself up n' get your ass to bed."

Hunter didn't move for a moment, surveying the havoc he'd caused in a short time. His eyes moved from his father's, to Payton's, than mine, and that look returned... but only for a second before he made his way up the stairs and slammed a door shut.

Payton came to my side but I stood frozen, staring at the bottom of the staircase as Dex climbed up and he, too, slammed a door.

"Good God, deary, are you alright?" Payton asked, sweeping up the glass shards with a nearby broom.

I swallowed hard as I forced my eyes to meet Payton's, nodding once before returning my gaze to the base of the stairs.

It was then that I knew...

Hunter was carrying the weight of a thousand swords on his back, and he never let a single soul in. His entire persona was centered about being in control, but when he got drunk he let that mask slip and he was a wreck; a deeply, damaged individual who didn't have the first clue on how to love, *how to be loved*.

It was then, in the chaos of tonight that I realized I wasn't the one who was drowning...

It was Hunter.

Chapter Eighteen
Hunter

It took me a while to finally get some shut eye but once the liquor reached its peak, I was knocked down.

The sunlight poking through the shudders yanked me out of sleep, forcing me to recognize the severity of last night's events.

After I dropped Piper off at home, I found myself at the nearest bar which was a bummed out shithole but hey, two dollar highballs.

Didn't think anyone could beat my buzz but about half a dozen later, a fat fucking snowplough barged into my lane and knocked my glass over, hoping to start a fight probably. Guys like that had nothing better to do.

Next thing I knew, snowplough was shoving my chest and shit, making a scene and I lost it; drove my fist right into his jaw and then the other while he was still recovering.

I took my leave, slammed way too much money on the bar and jumped into my truck.

When I got back, I realized how peaceful the comfort of my own place was and I relaxed with a few more drinks of bourbon.

The rawness of my knuckles didn't feel too bad once the alcohol settled in my veins; I actually completely forgot it was there. That was until Bambi showed up.

God, I fucking lost it. I fucking lost it when I saw her and all the words she'd said to me earlier waterfalled through my brain.

I don't remember a damn thing that came out of my mouth, but I knew it was bad. Cause what I do remember was the way she looked at me. The way everyone fucking looked at me.

Like I was a goddamn monster.

A disappointment that couldn't be helped. A fuck up, a menace to society.

Dad told me to apologize to Bambi when I woke up, and I was planning on it already but not by his orders.

The look on his face when he sized me up, the anger on his features written in regret... fuck that.

Every time I drove drunk, every single time, I expected a reaction. But never once was it given. Never did he ever stop me to say, "son, you keep doin' that and you'll wound up like your mother," or "Hunt, I can't lose you too."

None of that shit. He let me suffer alone, while he had a new woman distracting him, feeding his urges while he set aside the sadness.

I didn't have the luxury of doing that, and he didn't give a fuck about who I was or who I became because of it all.

My eyes focused on my phone screen, a calendar reminder popping up that read: Thanksgiving Day.

Ha-ha. What a blessed start to the fucking event.

I found a few missed texts from Britt and Josh saying:

> 1:02am – Josh: Why'd you call me?
>
> 1:02am – Britt: Are you okay, Hunty? I missed your call.
>
> 1:16am – Britt: Miss me? *open image*

My dick hardened at her naked picture, making a mental note to call her over when I got back.

> 1:19am – Josh: Lemme know that you're alive, man.
>
> 8:32am – Britt: Happy Thanksgiving Hunty!!!

Checking my call log, I realized I'd dialled both of them a handful of times, probably out of my mind wasted cause there's no way I'd just talk for shits.

I got out of bed and pulled on a pair of black sweatpants and a grey thermal, combing back my blonde locks with my fingers.

It was only ten a.m. and I was wide awake for some reason. Probably the urge to get out of the house, as far away from my dad and Bambi as possible.

But not without an apology. As much as I didn't remember the night, I knew there were lines that had been stepped over. And I couldn't go on with my day knowing I'd crossed those boundaries; not just with her, but with anyone.

I stalked down the hallway, passing my dad and Payton's room and resisted the urge to slide up the middle finger.

Bambi was staying in the guest bedroom and before I could lift my bruised knuckles to knock, her quiet voice floated through the cracks of the door.

It was muffled, so I couldn't exactly point out what she was saying, but I heard enough.

"This is why I didn't tell you –"

"Mom, you're not listening to me."

"Please, just –"

And sobs. Tiny little Bambi sobs that glued me to the floor.

In that moment, I didn't know what to do. I'd nursed crying girls to good health before but definitely not in the ways Bambi would like to heal... not in the ways I could help her even if I tried.

She probably hated my guts and it was warranted. After the disaster of last night, I'd hate me too. Fuck, I already did.

Bambi sounded so... helpless. Like she'd had this conversation with her mom before or something.

Come to think of it, I never actually asked her about her family life in the city. And that's when it hit me, what I'd said last night... it all came back.

I was assuming she just screwed a bunch of rich pricks and sold her soul to the wolves of Wall Street? Who fucking says that? What was I thinking?

There really wasn't much I knew about Bambi other than her surprise appearance in my life, the fact she read books, was damn annoying and a wizard at growing the family business.

She also had this weird thing of greeting everyone who passed her. Like she sought out any single person who looked in her direction just so she could say hello.

The door flew open and Bambi appeared, red faced and puffy eyed. Her dark hair was wrapped into a wilted bun and she wore a white t-shirt and blue jeans.

"Hunter, oh my God –" she threw a hand over her heart, quickly turning away from me. Probably trying to hide the evidence of her tears.

"You scared me. What are you doing here?"

I swallowed back a snarky response and settled with what I came here to do in the first place. "I wanted to apologize."

She looked taken aback, as if I'd told her I murdered someone or ran a fifty mile marathon in seven minutes.

"It's um..." Her bottom lip quivered as she tried to conceal another wave of sadness. "It's fine – can I please get by?"

But she already scurried along, making a B-line to the bathroom next door.

What the fuck's happening right now?

I hung back near the wall, taking in the sound of more hushed weeping and sniffling. A pang of guilt flared in my chest. *Did I do this? Was I really that bad last night?*

I knew I was an asshole to her. She was right to think it was because of the big city nature she'd come from. Rebecca was a beauty and brains but also a manipulative bitch that captured my heart and let it burn.

A damn shame the city girls were always my go-to. The hookups were shameless knowing ninety percent of them were unattainable. Even if they wanted a relationship, I could chalk it off to the fact we lived in different states and it wouldn't work. It was easy, and there was no commitment.

But Bambi was a rover in my life. Just when I thought I'd never see her again, she pranced right back in. Knowing she held the knowledge of my mom's death, worked with Payton and Dad, fuck, she would be sticking around whether I liked it or not.

And right now, I didn't want to live in the confined space of my own actions. I needed air, and judging from her rough morning, Bambi did too.

I stood waiting in the hall until she finally emerged from the bathroom with a light sweep of makeup over her face and significantly less eye bags.

"You're still here," she released, looking everywhere but me.

"Mhm." I grumbled.

She forced the most painful smile I'd ever seen, attempting to move past me but I held an arm out, stopping her before she could hide again.

"How 'bout I teach you some snowboarding today?"

This time she faced me, looking up with a downcast expression. "I can't do those extreme hills, Hunter."

"No, none of that." I shook my head. "The kiddy hill."

A light glimmer of amusement twinkled in her eyes as she crossed her arms over her chest.

"You said you wouldn't be caught dead there."

I shrugged. "At the risk of lookin' like an idiot... could be fun."

Her expression remained contemplative for a moment before she nodded in response. "Okay then, I'll go get changed."

She hurried into the guest room and shut the door, leaving me to my hopes and prayers that today's snowboarding lesson wouldn't ridicule me.

Please, God, don't draw any little kids my way.

Chapter Nineteen
Marley

All the little kids were swarming around Hunter.

I don't know why they liked him so much, but a whole horde of children camped around him like he was a superstar.

His eyes were panicked trying to run away from all of them, but his feet were strapped into his snowboard, cementing him down.

"Why a big man on a little hill?" One girl asked her mom.

"I board better than you!" Another boy added.

I could tell Hunter wanted to bite their heads off but he maintained his cool for the majority of the day, eventually ending up teaching a few kids some tricks. *Only the cocky ones, though. Maybe he saw himself in them, God only knows. It was hilarious.*

After a few hours of lessons, I finally learned how to stand on the snowboard without literally dying, and even managed to ride down the beginner slope with ease.

"Not bad Bambi," he'd said. "Can the teacher take a quick drink break?"

We walked to a different bar near the kiddy hill called Baskin Slopes and grabbed a two-seater table near the back.

The waitress, a smiley redhead, placed water on the table while ogling Hunter as she took his order – a double whisky on the rocks, and before she could take mine, he ordered two.

"Why'd you do that?" I asked, removing my coat and placing it behind my chair.

"Do what?"

"You ordered two drinks. You know you have to drive us back, right?"

His jaw hardened as he looked away, but his features weren't tense. "Nobody tells me not to."

"Well that's a stupid excuse," I muttered. "You should know better."

He scoffed. "Thanks mommy."

A rigid silence stretched between the two of us before he cleared his throat.

"Are ya hungry?" he asked.

My throat sprung out a laugh. I don't know what came over me but Hunter asking me if I was hungry had to be the most normal, mundane thing in the world and I couldn't believe it.

I was so used to him barking at me all the time, I couldn't believe he could actually converse normally, let alone ask questions without spitting in disgust.

"What's so funny?"

I shook my head, playing with the straw in my water. "I've never heard you so calm."

He leaned back in his chair, raising his eyebrows. "Yeah well, the kids tired me out."

"Maybe you should volunteer at a daycare. It'll level your attitude."

His blue eyes held me tightly, speaking a thousand words yet none at all.

"What happened this mornin'?" he asked, his tone softer than normal.

My cheeks immediately heated as I thought back to my mother's phone call earlier on in the day.

I remember waking up to a few texts from Adam but before I could read them, Harlow Matthews' name flashed across my screen.

When I answered, my mom was angrier than I'd ever heard her.

"Our P.I found out where you're staying. Care to tell me why you're in Aurora and not Lincoln?"

I almost vomited at the thought of my family hiring a private investigator to track down my whereabouts after a year of no communication.

They'd known I fled to Lincoln, that's why they despised me. But to care enough to hire someone and hunt me down? That was not out of love, that was out of control.

They were so used to monitoring every single aspect of my life that finally, when they couldn't anymore, it drove them mad. That was the only reason I could place. So they could scrutinize me, make me feel like that young, sheltered minion that couldn't survive without them.

I confessed to Todd's infidelity and a pitchy laugh harped through the other line.

"What did you expect, Marley? A prince charming? You're a fool in feathers, so naive."

In all my best efforts, I fought off the tears as long as I could, listening to my mom berate me and play victim.

"You know, I *was* calling to wish my only daughter a happy Thanksgiving but that greeting was clearly misplaced."

And she hung up.

Cut the line without so much as a goodbye.

I let the tears run, then. Trying to hold them in would've killed me on the spot. And to make matters even more emotional, Adam's texts were a series of "I miss you's" and "please visit sometime."

When I found Hunter standing outside my door apologizing, I broke in half. I was already a ruined mess, having to relive the pain of losing my family all over again. I wanted to visit Adam so badly, and I thought maybe after one year of no contact, my mother would've realized that I ran off for a reason.

But once again, Harlow and Mike were always right. My dad didn't even bother to text me. After the phone call with my mom, she probably relayed all sorts of incriminating messages like I was living on the streets selling cocaine or something.

The waitress returned with a tray of drinks; two doubles for Hunter and a glass of Prosecco for me.

He took a swig from his cup and licked his bottom lip before questioning again. "Bambi?"

My thoughts were in shambles over this morning's ordeal that I completely forget he'd asked me what happened.

"Don't worry about it." I drawled, sipping the bubbly liquid.

His finger toured the rim of his drink as he exhaled, flexing the muscles in his jaw.

"You were cryin'."

"People cry all the time."

"Bambi –" he paused. "Look, we got off on the wrong foot."

I snorted. "You think?"

His fingers laced together as he set aside the liquor, pressing his lips into a thin line.

"I'm not gon' press you if you don't wanna talk about it. But I'm throwin' a line if you decide to."

He sounded sincere. Every part of him. From his downturned eyes, softer and less stressed with anger, to his calm features. I'd never seen him in this light, as a human being rather than a prisoner of his own mind.

I'm going to need a freaking drink for this.

In one gulp, I drained half my Prosecco, swallowing down the bubbly fizz that burned my throat.

His eyes widened but he didn't say a thing, letting me have the stage to talk.

"I'm going to start by saying that I'm not looking for sympathy. My situation pales in comparison to yours, and I –"

"Stop." He shook his head, gripping the crystal glass that housed his whisky. "Don't be comparin' nothing. Just talk. I'm listenin'."

I couldn't help it. But I obeyed and peppered the backstory.

"When I moved to Nebraska to be with my now *ex*-boyfriend, I left my entire life behind. The glamourous career, the ditzy groupies, my brother..." That one pained me to say.

"Anyway, I left it and I didn't look back. My mom and dad, they always had this image of what my life *should* look like... never taking into account what I wanted from it at all.

"You know, from an outsider's point of view, my life looked like a dream. Money, country clubs, all of that bullshit you see on T.V. But the pressure... the pressure to be everything my parents wanted, the way I had to maintain a level of credibility to be seen by them... I never found myself."

The rest of my drink was calling my name so I quickly downed the last half and averted my eyes from Hunter.

"When I met my ex, I didn't know who I was. Honestly, I still don't. But more so back then, I lived off inheritance money and his lottery winnings and –"

"How much did he win?" Hunter teased, but there was scrutiny in his tone.

I couldn't help but chuckle. "A million."

He gulped his drink in one go, finishing it off. "Lucky bastard."

"Yeah, but he spent it so carelessly and I did too. The entire year I was with him," I shook my head, "God, I learned nothing. And when I found out he was cheating on me, I realized I was more upset about what my family would think than leaving him behind.

"I blocked his number a few weeks ago and I didn't feel anything. Like, I was grieving the loss of my old life over the love I supposedly had for him.

"And when I met your mom – *step*mom," I corrected, "it was like this second chance for me. That life wasn't going to shoot me in the foot every turn I took. I don't know, I'm sorry for piling up all my baggage on you. I can't even begin to understand what you've been through."

When I finally found the courage to face him head on, his eyes were burning into mine with inscrutability. They held empathy, compassion and pity but also vexation and torment, the look I was used to.

He slid the second whisky towards me, untouched and full to the brim.

"My mom used to tell me *good hospitality for good measure*."

I tilted my head to the side, taking a moment to ponder before realizing what he'd meant.

"You were never going to drink that, were you?" I asked, wrapping my fingers around the cool crystal.

He shook his head. "I know you said you don't drink whisky, but you might find it handy in tryin' times."

Lifting the brim to my lips, I tipped back the brown liquid, allowing it to coat the inner linings of my throat with a bittersweet burn.

"Trying to make me an alcoholic?" I joked, swatting away the acrid scent from my nose.

A faint smile appeared on his lips as he eyed me with a rarity I could only imagine.

"No sweetheart, just doin' what I can to make up for lost time."

After a couple of hours at the bar, I learned a few things about Hunter.

One, he liked to build boat figurines because his mom would take him sailing when he was a kid.

Two, his favourite colour was green but not an emerald green, more like the mossy camo green that resembled dead grass. *Odd, I know.*

Three, his bruised knuckles were due to the fact he got into a bar fight last night, something he was supposedly used to.

And lastly, he actually was interesting to talk to, once you peeled back a layer and he actually held somewhat of a personality.

We didn't talk about me or his mom after my backstory admission and I appreciated it. When he wasn't inebriated beyond belief, he had this way of making you feel like no storm was ever strong enough to drag you down. Which was such a tragic irony considering he couldn't weather his own trauma.

The entire drive back to the cabin we discussed my snowboarding improvement and listened to classic rock.

I'd always been a fan of alternative, but his song choice was actually enjoyable, and I ended up adding a few songs to my playlist.

Payton's Thanksgiving meal was off the charts, and her expression when she saw Hunter alongside me was the best gift anyone could've asked for.

I could tell Payton just wanted him to be okay, even though she never knew how to get through to him. Though Dex was sort of quiet the entire time, avoiding eye contact with Hunter. *I wonder what that's about.* But I didn't ask.

After dinner, I was helping Payton with the dishes while the boys were watching a war documentary on T.V. *Classic.*

"He seems happier." Payton began, rinsing gravy off a plate. "Well, as happy as Hunter can be."

I smiled, glancing over my shoulder at the blonde hair swept up in a backwards baseball cap.

"Yeah, he wasn't a total asshole today."

Payton laughed, handing me the clean dish as I dried it off with a towel.

"He ain't a bad kid. Just needs someone to talk to, I think."

"And someone who's willing to listen."

She turned off the tap and piled up a stack of bowls, wiping off the wet edges hurriedly.

"You think you can be that for him?"

I put down the plate I was drying and sucked in a breath, reminiscing on the oddly pleasant and tranquil state of Hunter Lane today.

He never jibed once, he apologized for last night and he was attentive when I spoke about my past. As much as he hated the swarm of kids today, I saw a hint of merriment when he helped them snowboard.

There were traits to Hunter that I don't think he'd ever seen himself, that he suppressed to the point of invisibility but they were definitely present, waiting to be released.

I saw glimpses of what he could be had he tried to control his emotions and not let alcohol consume his grief. He held the door open for me every time, paid for everything like it was second nature, observed what I needed when I didn't know it myself and I admired him for that.

It didn't change the way he treated me in the past, or anyone for that matter. But if Hunter had the potential to be someone good, why not see it all the way through.

"I'll try my best."

Chapter Twenty
Hunter

We left Rivertown Bay at nine the following morning, and made it back to Aurora for lunch.

Payton invited Bambi to stay and eat but she said she had some stuff to do and thanked us for the invitation.

I remember before she got into my dad's van, she'd given me a sincere goodbye. It wasn't one of those cheesy 'oh I'll never see you again' goodbyes, but an actual salutation that implied she had fun. *For the most part.*

I don't know when the shift happened between us, or when I began to see her a little differently than I used to, but it was sort of a relief.

When Bambi opened up to me at the bar, I saw this defencelessness in her that I'd never seen before. I had a bad habit of assuming the worst in people and that's exactly what I did to her from the moment we met. It's not like I fully trusted her but I didn't exactly hate her either.

All the little quirks I chalked up as weird, were highlighted in such a polarizing light yesterday.

When those little fuckin' critters were storming around me at the kiddy hill, acting like they'd never seen a six foot twenty-five year old at a baby slope, she'd actually levelled my nerves.

It's the stupidest thing in the world, I'm the first to say, but seeing a girl good with kids pumped my heart a little.

Rebecca had a niece who we visited from time to time and she never bothered to say hello upon greeting. She just tossed whatever dollar store gift she'd bought her way and made an escape route to the family's alcohol supply.

Makes me wonder how I ever fell for someone like that. I mean, it was right around the time my mom passed away and I guess I needed to channel my pain into a distraction. And that distraction was a shrewd waste of my energy.

I always planned to get Bambi talking after hearing her cry yesterday morning, but I didn't realize she struggled with family so much. As irritable as my family was sometimes, I was grateful for the things they'd given me.

My dad, especially before Mom died, taught me everything a man could teach his son. Hunting, fishing, taking me out to the mountains for days on end to coach me on survival skills.

For a while there, he was my best friend. After the accident though, he closed himself up a lot. Didn't think he'd actually find someone ever again and a part of me didn't want him to. But Payton was as good a woman as they come. Even though we weren't that close, I could visibly see the change she brought out in my dad. At least in an affectionate sense. He didn't give a damn 'bout what I did no more.

Nonetheless, Bambi and I experienced losses in different ways. I don't think I realized how lonely she really must've been, even when she was dating that slimeball from Lincoln.

Loyalty was always a big thing for me. As promiscuous as I seemed, I'd never fuck around if I was committed. That's why I stayed single; cause I knew I wasn't ready and I wouldn't be caught dead telling someone I was.

Bambi's issues didn't change the way I felt about my own, but it adjusted my perspective on things. Fuck, I was hard on her. I was. I never really took much into account other than myself and my damn problems. To me, Bambi didn't have no feelings. She just... existed, I guess.

But I'd be the biggest dick in the world if I just sat there, listening to how she had no family to turn back to when things got tough and slap an insensitive remark while she opened up. *I'd already proven I could be an asshole, now I can prove that wasn't entirely me.*

I didn't know when I'd be seeing her again, but I definitely needed to wedge some distance for the time being. Yesterday honestly felt like two friends just hanging out, but a few good moments wouldn't change her opinion of me and I knew that.

Bambi had already seen the ugly wreck I'd become, and yet she still tried. She took a chance on me and that was more than a lot of people had ever done in years.

I found Payton digging through some old boxes in the garage when I called her attention.

"Hey," I said.

She stopped rummaging for a second to acknowledge me, then returned to her business. "Need somethin'?"

"Yeah, I wanted to ask you a question."

"Alright then."

"How did Bambi react when you told her about my mom?"

"Who?" She poked, confused.

"Marley." Fuck that sounded weird coming out of my mouth.

Payton removed an old rug from one of the boxes and threw it to the side, running fingers through her blonde hair.

"What the hell you callin' her Bambi for?"

I rolled my eyes. "It came to me, and it stuck. Now can you answer the question?"

"Well," she cleared her throat, standing erect. "She was pale like a ghost. Don't think she expected to hear that comin' out of my mouth, but she felt sorry for ya if that's what you're askin'."

I gritted my teeth. "I don't want her to feel sorry for me."

"Nah, Hunter. You don't want no sympathy from anyone." She kicked a box over and used some scissors to slice open another taped cardboard. "Tough as nails, right kid?"

"What's that supposed to mean?"

"It means," she snapped, staring me down, "you don't consider no possibilities for a better life. You ever just stop an think, Hunter, maybe people give a damn about you? Don't wan' see you wound up in the gutter?

"Cause Marley, *Bambi*, whatever the hell ya call her, she's a good kid. Works hard, compassionate, and she tried damn hard to see somethin' good in ya this weekend."

Her chocolate eyes flashed in my brain again, the looks she gave me when I paid for her drinks and held the door open for her, listened to the stories she had to say... those were all a given. But Bambi had stared at me like it was the first time anyone ever treated her with some fucking decency. And that said a lot coming from the man who practically spat in her face time and time again, making her feel like garbage with zero excuse behind it.

Fuck. "She is... *nice.*" I admitted, trying to shove down my pride.

Payton coughed out a laugh, carrying the dusty rug and a weaved basket, moving past me. "Now was that so hard to say?"

She made her way to the side entrance of the house before I called out to her. "She workin' today?"

"I ain't runnin' her schedule by you. Give the poor girl some time to breathe. One day ain't gon' make up for the past thirty."

And that's exactly what I'd said to myself. I just needed to confirm that, for a fact, I had fucked up and I needed to put a barrier between the two of us for now.

Time's got to make this situation better, otherwise I may have pushed an already fragile girl into a worse state.

That wasn't even a diss, anyone could tell from the look of her mannerisms how much she hid herself from the world seeing her.

Every time I'd look at her speaking, she'd avert eye contact almost instantly, hold it for a few seconds then turn away again. She wrapped her arms around her like it was a safety blanket every time someone eyed her body, which was a damn sight to see so I couldn't understand why.

I think she had a nervous twitch of scratching her nose which was the size of a peanut and as red as a cranberry.

But she shouldn't hide it. She shouldn't conceal anything about herself. And I wasn't about to be the man who confirmed her suspicions about everyone else.

Nah, anyone deserved better than that.

Especially Bambi.

Bless her fuckin' heart.

Chapter Twenty-One
Marley

I half expected to see Hunter in the weeks leading up to Christmas, but all those hopes were merely a waste of my time.

After Thanksgiving weekend, we hadn't so much as spoken since parting ways at the cabin.

I really thought we got somewhere, or at the very least, made progress towards a potential friendship. But it was evidently clear he didn't want one, otherwise I would've heard from him.

He had my number, I'd given it to him that day at the bar... the day I sliced open my past and laid it out on the table for him to examine.

Maybe that was his ploy. To get me to open up, and use my weaknesses against me. It wouldn't be a surprising outcome. He did say something about me using him when he was belligerent that weekend. *Well, who's the user now?*

I watched the heavy snowfall outside our warehouse window. We'd moved into the new space at

Cutter's Quarry a little over two weeks ago, and it was exactly what the business needed.

At this point, we were selling Dex's handy-man tool kit as a prime merchandise and even hired four other employees to run an online shop for local deliveries. P&D's had become everyone's go-to hardware store and I was ecstatic to be along for the ride.

Adam and I had been texting a lot more, even spent a few nights on Netflix party together, marathoning the Pirates of the Caribbean movies. Even though I couldn't physically see him, it felt good to have our relationship back.

It was slow, of course, considering my mom had in fact told him a bunch of bullshit about a life I was clearly not living. She somehow convinced him that I refused contact and renounced the family name which was absolutely ridiculous. Like always though, my brother had nothing but respect for me and my supposed wishes even though that was hardly the case, and stepped back from my life.

Although once I told him that Mom was spitting complete nonsense, he apologized profusely saying he would've never stayed away had he known. And to be fair, I never tried to reach out anyways. Whether it was fear or embarrassment of what he'd think of me, I, too, played a part in the detriment of our relationship.

But that was Harlow Matthews. If she didn't get her way, she'd make sure you paid. Didn't matter if I was her kin, I was as good as dead to her now that I wasn't a marketing executive in New York. But to hell with her. I had my brother back.

He informed me that he was expecting a baby with Michelle, his fancy chef wife, who was due for delivery in sixteen weeks. The joy I felt in that moment was unlike any other.

"*I'm going to be an aunt?*" I screamed, bouncing on my heels like a freaking rabbit.

I didn't care if I had to hide from my parents, wear a disguise or wiggle around like a secret spy to see Adam. I was going to be an aunt, and Satan himself couldn't stop me from seeing my baby niece.

Christmas was right around the corner and I'd been invited to Cramer's family dinner as well as Winter's holiday spectacle. But when Payton had asked me to spend Christmas at the Lanes, it was a no-brainer.

On the morning of the twenty-fifth, I secured all the gifts in the trunk of my Malibu and started my journey towards the farmhouse.

On the drive over, I kept running scenarios through my head, imaging what possible situations could arise between Hunter and I.

Did he go back to hating me? Was he even going to be there? I wouldn't have put it past him since he had a kink for reckless behaviour. Well, only time would tell.

The snow was coming down harder, practically covering my windshield with sleet as I parked my car in the driveway.

I unlocked my trunk, fishing for my window scraper when Dex's voice sounded from the side of the house.

"Don't worry 'bout that, I can clean it off for ya later." He said, walking towards me.

He was dressed in a heavy flannel jacket with a plaid button down underneath. His beard was trimmed nicely, giving him a more youthful look.

"You don't look so scary today, Dex." I teased. I never did that, but hey, I was in the Christmas spirit.

"Well, when the fur's catchin' scraps of food, something's gotta be done."

Was he... *did he just joke back with me?* Wow, this really was a Christmas miracle.

I laughed in response and carried out my bag of gifts: one for Dex, one for Payton and lastly, one for Hunter.

Payton was relatively easy to shop for since her and I shared so many common interests. Every time I bought a new skin care product, she'd ask me to review it and tell her if it was worth the money. So over the last few weeks, I'd collected a total of four beauty products for her to try out and wrapped them all in a cute pink basket.

Dex was a little bit tricky, since I barely spoke with him unless it was for business. But with Payton's help, I managed to figure out that he'd been itching to buy this electric four-blade razor that was exclusive to CleanMen's brand in New York.

Conveniently for me, I was in touch with my brother again so I asked him to go over to the store and ship me the razor while I transferred him the money.

Hunter... well, the idea came to me pretty quickly. Almost too quickly, actually. I wasn't sure where we stood but there was no way I was going to get his family gifts and not him. He didn't strike me as someone who enjoyed receiving presents, but it was Christmas and what was Christmas without giving?

After a few hours of tedious Etsy shop surfing, I managed to find a seller who made custom paint brushes. I practically screamed when I saw a bundle of six smaller tipped brushes, perfect for his boat figurine hobby, and added it to my cart. It was certainly something small, and he would probably laugh in my face for even purchasing it, but I was happy and I hoped he would be too.

Dex took my presents and unlocked the front door, leading me to the kitchen where I was greeted by the scent of peppermint and vanilla.

Payton was sitting next to a lady with similar blonde hair, wearing an orange Charlie Brown sweater, holding a can of green beans.

When Payton stood up, I saw that she too, was wearing a Charlie Brown sweater, only hers was in red.

"Marley! Merry Christmas, deary." She said, enveloping me in her arms.

"Hi," I laughed, squeezing her like I hadn't just seen her three days prior.

"Ah, Marley. Meet my sister Betty." Payton nudged me towards the blonde woman holding green beans. "Betty, this is the girl I was tellin' you about."

Up close, I could really see the similarities in their faces. Betty looked a bit younger than Payton, with bright blue eyes and deep smile lines. Her front teeth held a little gap which made her grin more endearing as she set her beans down and grabbed hold of my hand.

"My, my, you pretty thing!" She gripped tighter and pulled me down to sit. "Payton told me ya helped her shop out a ton. Thank you for that, she needed the confidence on that one."

"I'll tackle ya, don't think I won't." Payton retorted.

But Betty shrugged it off, praising me again before shovelling a tablespoon of green beans into her mouth.

I couldn't contain the grin stapled to my face as I watched them interact like two little kids, unironically on Christmas morning.

"Why the matching sweaters?" I asked, looking down at my own basic white knit. "I feel so out of place."

Betty piped up, pushing out of the booth and scurrying for the hallway. "I got an extra one for ya, Marley! Just wait here."

What have I done?

A trickle of laughter carried from the main entrance as a huge man dressed in lumberjack clothing emerged, followed by...

"Hunter," I let out before I could retain my words.

As if the breath caught in my lungs, I stilled completely. His ice blue eyes caught mine almost instantly, spiking my core with heated tension.

His muscles were confined in a black long sleeve and his blonde locks were swept back into a white baseball cap. He held a camel toned jacket in his hands as he stepped into the light of the kitchen, peering at me with intent.

"Ho-ho, what do we have here?"

My attention turned to the massive man in lumberjack clothing who grabbed Hunter's shoulder blades and shook him vigorously.

"Get your hands off me, Uncle Glen." Hunter laughed, swatting at him with force.

"I wasn't talkin' bout you, son." The man pointed a chubby finger at me, nodding my way. "Haven't seen you 'round here before."

I swallowed back the intimidation this man stored. Hunter had said *uncle*, which implied that this was Dex's brother, and honestly, it made sense. They had the same build and height, the same booming voice. The only difference was that this man, *Glen*, smiled... a lot.

I stood up, extending my hand out to the intense man in front of me and curved my lips upwards.

"I'm Marley, a friend of..." I looked to Hunter whose eyes were glued to my face. "A friend of Payton's."

"Marrrley... I heard of ya, actually! Dex, told me about 'cha, helpin' out with his business, makin' him a millionaire."

My cheeks heated. "Well, I'm not aware of his financial statements but..."

"*Dex!*" He called, but Payton's freshly made peppermint bark caught his attention right away as he sauntered over to her with two hands on his belly.

"Paws off, Glen!" Payton snapped.

"Yah, don't wan' look even more like a flabby pancake do ya, sugar?" Betty added, licking green bean juice off her spoon.

The racket of bickering relatives should've made me anxious but it had the total opposite effect. I stood in awe, watching this cheerful family come together in one room, arguing about the most normal things like Christmas treats and canned goods.

In New York, all the Christmases I'd spent were isolated in a room full of kids who belonged to my parent's co-workers while they had a separate table to talk future plans for their company.

Adam and I always found our own little corner to play with the Lego sets and Bratz dolls they'd gifted us, but when we got older we just skipped family Christmas parties altogether and spent it with our friends.

It really was a shame since Christmas was my favourite holiday. I loved driving through neighbourhoods to check out how each house was decorated. All the lights and love and unity of people circled around fir trees made my heart melt.

And this... this was as close to the merriment of Christmas that I could possibly wish for.

Gentle fingers grazed my wrist as I turned around to find Hunter pulling me away from the noise.

"Little loud, don't you think sweetheart?"

I blushed. I freaking blushed because I hadn't heard him call me that in so long that a fuzzy tingle ate me right up.

"It's a pleasant ruckus, I'd say."

His chuckle made my morning, afternoon and night. This entire time I thought he'd hated me or worse, went back to his old ways of being an inebriated asshat, but he was fully sober standing in front of me with a jovial expression.

"Well darlin' you're more than welcome to stay here, but I need a shower and I got quite the selection of Christmas mixers back at mine."

He stalked towards the side exit of the house, glancing back at me once before holding the door open.

As if he knew I'd follow, I rolled my eyes and passed him, keeping his steady pace as we crossed the crust of snow towards a massive green shed.

The flurries created a blanket of white fog that emanated far beyond the field, hindering my vision.

"Where are we going?" I asked.

"I told you, mine."

I furrowed my brows in confusion. "Your house is where exactly?"

He let out a laugh and continued in silence until we reached the door of the green shed and he unlocked it.

Warm air poured out from inside, drawing me into a cozy space that resembled a tiny home. *So this is what he was talking about.*

A T.V sat perched atop a black table that contained a row of medals and picture frames. A grey couch faced the television accompanied by a side table that served more of a bar-cart purpose, and a massive marina tapestry hung behind the sofa.

There was a small kitchen which filled the space in the back of the room that held all its necessities crammed together in one area. Next to it was a door that I could only presume was the bathroom, and the final door was fully open, containing a bed from what I could see.

"Wow," I stated. "This is... you built this?"

He nodded, setting his jacket on the couch before walking to the fridge. "All by my lonesome."

This was incredible. It looked like every mancave I'd ever seen from past flings, only more elevated and less... trashy.

I crouched down to glance over the countless medals and inspected the bronze, gold and silver awards.

"Which sport?"

"Baseball." He replied, taking a sip of his water. "I got a scholarship to play for college."

Huh. "Do you still play?"

"Got no reason to."

"But... you played it for school?"

"School's expensive, sweetheart. Iowa State offered me a free-ride, would've been dumb not to take it."

I couldn't argue that. To this day, I was still paying off my student debt and it felt never-ending. Heck, if I got a scholarship to play curling I wouldn't turn it down.

"Were you good?"

He shrugged. "Could've been. I dropped it after a year."

My mind circled around why that could be. If he got a free-ride, he would've had to have some skill. And from all these younger photos, he seemed... happy. *Drop it, Marley. Don't pry.*

"I'm gon' take a shower but, remote's on the table if you wanna watch Netflix or," he pointed to the array of liquor bottles near the couch, "*indulge.*"

A laugh escaped my throat as I moved towards the alcohol inspecting his wide selection.

"Just don't touch the Johnnie Walker at the bottom. I'm savin' that for somethin' important."

My eyes glanced to the unopened scotch that sat hidden behind a bunch of other bottles with mismatched caps and peeling labels.

"What are you saving it –"

But he had already disappeared behind the bathroom door.

"...for." *Alrighty then.*

My legs carried me back to the medals and picture frames, this time scanning the photos encased in the square shells.

There was a picture of a small blonde boy wearing elf ears, standing alongside a bearded man who I could already tell was younger Dex.

The next photo was a picture of Hunter in his baseball uniform, significantly older than the first picture.

But my eyes were cemented on the last frame that had a teenage Hunter wrapping his arms around a blonde woman who shared identical eyes.

It looked like a candid photograph where they sat atop a hill, the blonde woman wearing a tennis skirt and pink trainers while Hunter wore gym shorts and a blue t-shirt.

His smile was so bright. Brighter than I'd ever seen since knowing him. I thought the first time I saw him smile was the most precious thing in the world since he rarely did it, just like Dex. But in this picture he looked like a completely different person... like a boy whose world was complete.

This woman... she had to be his mom. They looked too similar for it not to be. The same eyes, the same smile, the same redness in their cheeks. Her hair was curled down past her collarbone and she held teenage Hunter like he was made of glass.

I felt my pulse quicken as a glossy hue swept over my eyes. This was Hunter's mother... a mother he lost, right beside him. I never asked about how she passed and quite honestly, seeing this now, I don't think I wanted to know. I didn't want him to relive that moment, even if he wanted to tell me which was highly unlikely but still.

Fuck, how did he keep this photo here? I mean, if it were me and I saw a picture of my late mom and I... God, I don't know what I'd do. I suppose it's better to have this memory of them, a happy recount on display, but wow. Talk about heartbreak.

I heard Hunter curse from inside the bathroom as the showerhead switched off.

"Bambi?" he called out, poking his head through the crack of the door.

I quickly stepped away from the picture frame and diverted my eyes to Hunter's red face and wet hair.

"Yeah?"

"Get me a clean towel, will ya? I forgot to put one here last night."

I zipped my eyes around the room, searching. "Where do you keep them?"

"There's a hamper in my bedroom, should be one just on top."

I met his eyes again and started to giggle. His neck was stretched out long, and all you could see was this bobble headed man and no body.

"What're ya laughin' at?"

I chuckled once more, passing by him to enter the bedroom. "Nothing, you just look like one of those long neck dinosaurs on animal planet."

He shut the door with a grunt. "I fuckin' am one."

Just as he instructed, a black towel was tangled in a heap of men's clothing in a white hamper. I scooped it up, doing a once over his room.

The closet doors were closed shut and a double bed was pushed in the corner of the wall, covered by a grey bedspread. Each wall was painted a different shade of green which made the room darker without the presence of a window.

I made my way back to the bathroom door which was opened slightly wider, giving me a sneak preview of Hunter's... *everything.*

Holy fucking shit.

I didn't want to stare. I mean, I did, but holy crap I shouldn't have. His lower half was covered by the kitchen sink *and thank God for that because I would've probably collapsed on the spot*, but his chest was entirely exposed.

His tan skin contrasted the curve of every muscle buried beneath his flesh, highlighting all the right parts of him. A paragraph of words was tattooed on his left peck with writing I couldn't read from here, but that was definitely not my main priority.

Those abs. Those freaking abs carved by gods above that were sopping wet, droplets of water trailing down his V-line all the way to his...

"Door's always open darlin', come in whenever you like." Hunter smirked in the reflection of the mirror, catching me staring.

I launched the towel through the gap of the door and hurried towards the entrance of the shed, hastily putting on my coat to return back to the farmhouse.

"Meet you back at the house!" I called, stepping from the heat of Hunter's shed into the snowy tundra outside.

My boots crunched against the crust, carrying me like a rabid wolf over the field. At this point, the snow had reached mid-calf and I was certain the bottom of my jeans were drenched.

But I needed to escape Hunter's place as quickly as possible because I couldn't face him or his family as red as a freaking tomato that was sunburnt two times over.

No way.

At least I had an excuse.

I could blame my crimson tint on the cold climate. But I'd still have the memory of his bare torso engrained in my brain as I ate Christmas lunch.

Happy freaking holidays.

Chapter Twenty-Two
Hunter

Catching Bambi checking me out had to be the highlight of my Christmas, and it hadn't even started yet.

I mean, I sort of did it on purpose but I didn't expect *that* reaction. Girl practically leaped out of her clothes and sprinted like her tail end was on fire.

For a second I caught myself feeling self conscious, but quickly shrugged it off knowing how hard I worked for my body.

If I wasn't working out at the gym, I was on a hike with Josh. And if I wasn't hiking with Josh, I was helping my dad on the farm. My entire lifestyle kept me active, which was my justification for drinking all the damn time. *Definitely not the healthiest thing to do, but who's gon' tell me not to?*

Payton told me to dress nice for the Christmas lunch but I wasn't about to suit up for a small family gathering, so I settled on a black button down and some jeans.

When I made it back to the house, everyone was already helping themselves to a buffet style feast, consisting of potatoes, turkey, stuffing, gravy, the whole fuckin' nine.

Payton's sister Betty was gobbling green beans like it was her only source of sustenance while Uncle Glen munched on a turkey leg in the corner of the booth.

My dad and Payton were already chowing down on their food while Bambi sat in a Charlie Brown sweater at the edge of the table, cutting open a baked potato with a knife.

I snagged a chair from beside the oven and pulled it towards the table, settling beside Bambi as I grabbed a plate and piled on the grub.

"What's with the getup?" I asked, giving her C.B sweater a look down.

She blushed. "Betty talked me into it."

And I didn't press any further. That woman was a force to be reckoned with.

The Christmas lunch was pleasant enough. Betty went on about her recent endeavours since living out of a van for the past six months, while Uncle Glen fought off indigestion silently.

Everyone was curious about Bambi's home life to which she shared very little. *Smart girl, Betty and Glen were a couple of yappers.*

"You don't like cranberries?" I asked Bambi, forking some into my mouth.

She glanced up at me and did that thing where she quickly looked away and scrunched her nose.

"Does it not look like organs?"

I almost spat out my food right then and there, choking on a laugh.

"Holy shit," I wiped my face, covering my mouth with a napkin. "You almost killed me."

She shrugged, completely unfazed as she returned her attention to the plate of food. "I'm just saying."

"They don't look like organs, Bambi. Not even close."

She spooned some stuffing into her mouth as she leaned in closer, whispering beneath the chatter of the family.

"What's with Betty and green beans?"

I averted my gaze to Betty's hand which held a freshly open can of those slimy vegetables.

"Don't know, she says they got mad health benefits or somethin'."

She chuckled, repositioning herself in her seat. "I mean, I think they do. But eating anything in excess can't be good for you."

In that moment, Payton returned from the kitchen carrying a tray of peppermint bark, placing it in the center of the table.

"Glen," she directed, "now you may try it."

Uncle Glen howled as he patted his stomach, rubbing up and down the buttons of his shirt. "Already did, darlin'. Snagged a couple bites when you weren't lookin."

My dad chuckled, shaking his head downwards as Payton threw Uncle Glen a death stare.

"If looks could kill." Bambi piped from my end of the table, baring her swan white teeth in laughter.

The whole table erupted in a series of cheerful agreements, Payton's features softening as she passed around the plate of peppermint bark.

I leaned back into my chair and looked around the crowd of five in front of me, smiling, giggling and sharing stories like they'd lived a thousand lives.

And for the first time in a long time, a bubble of something foreign floated through my mind, filling me with sunlight.

A feeling of hope.

After lunch we all gathered around the tree like a couple of happy campers and began the gift distribution.

I'd gotten my Uncle a gift card to P&D's as a gag gift cause I knew he'd fucking use it regardless, and Betty a flamingo hairbrush since she was obsessed with flamingos. *Flamingos and green beans... absolutely wild.*

After seeing Payton fishing out that old hallway rug a few weeks back, I decided to get her a new one with a brown and blue zig zag pattern to match the funky pillows she had on the couch.

My dad needed a new jacket since he'd been wearing the same flannel one for decades, and Lord knows he didn't ever buy clothing.

When Payton told me Bambi was coming for Christmas I was clueless as to what gift I'd get her. But when the idea came to me, I took it and ran. Even though it was the most embarrassing present on this planet, it was still something regardless.

After the oldies finished handing out their gifts, I ended up with a set of thermal socks from Betty, a twenty dollar voucher to fuckin' McDonalds from uncle Glen, and Payton n' my dad managed to cop me a signed vintage poster of The Rolling Stones, framed in black casing.

"How the hell d'you get this?" I gasped, examining the ragged paper and glossy finish.

"Found an authentic seller on eBay, guess he was a groupie back then and had a couple dozen posters lyin' around." Dad said.

The Rolling Stones was my mom's favourite band, and automatically became mine as I grew older. I learned the guitar because of Keith Richards, and had their hits on repeat every damn day. *Fuck, this would look mighty fine next to my T.V.*

"Thank you," I nodded at Payton and my dad, smiling like a goddamn fool.

When I turned to Bambi, she was already holding out her gift with a wishful twinkle in her eye.

"You didn't need to get me nothin', Bambi..."

"I thought you'd say that." She chuckled. "Open it."

The black box was long and rectangular, tied together by a bright purple bow. When I lifted the lid, I examined the contents before realizing what it was.

"Paintbrushes?" I asked, placing the box in my lap as I removed the slender sticks in my favourite shade of green. *Huh, she remembered.*

"For your boat figurines," she released, tucking a strand of hair behind her ear. "I know you have to be super precise when painting certain parts so... I don't know, I got them engraved if you want to turn them over and see."

I already felt my smile before my nerves could control it as I rolled over the paintbrushes and found the initials *H.L* carved into the stems.

"H.L," I whispered, running my fingers over the silver lettering. "For Hunter Lane?"

She dipped her head, averting eye contact once again but I wasn't having it, not this time. Like second nature, my hand cupped her chin, forcing her to meet my eyes.

"I fucking love it."

She blushed, fighting the urge to turn away again but she managed to see my look through.

"It's not much but –"

"Hey, none of that. Okay? My turn."

Her big brown eyes widened in surprise as I pulled out a box of my own, only it was wrapped like shit but it's the thought that fucking counts.

I placed the present in her lap as she delicately unwrapped the paper, lifting the lid of my gift.

She threw a hand over her mouth, giggling, when she spotted the scarf I'd bought her at Rivertown Bay, folded into a square.

"This is hilarious," she let out, petting the soft material.

I caught myself smiling at her smile, clearing my throat before I got too excited. "There's more um, I kind of shoved your other gift inside."

"Oh?"

Her tiny fingers worked their way around the stitching of the scarf until they latched onto my embarrassing little I <3 Nebraska keychain.

At first she looked confused, holding up the tiny metal trinket but her grin stretched across her face when I explained.

"I saw the I <3 NYC keychain when I carried your luggage up to the cabin an' I thought, well, New York ain't your home no more... maybe it's time for a replacement."

Without a word of warning, Bambi leapt into my lap and wrapped her arms around my neck, squeezing tightly.

I was completely frozen, holding my hands out like they were immobilized and fucking broken. But when the warmth of her frame settled into me, I let my hands touch the wool fabric of her sweater.

The familiar scent of lavender and honey emanated off her neck as I rested my head on her shoulder, holding her until she decided to let go.

When her gaze met mine, a lustrous sheen had lightened her pupils, making the brown in her eyes appear almost golden.

"I'm going to change the keychain as soon as I get home," she smiled, bright like a damn star.

I preserved it in my brain for as long as I could, realizing how much of an idiot I was for thinking this girl was like my ex, chalking her up to be a vicious viper when she had no malicious bone in her body.

Bambi was exactly that... a Bambi. A deer in the headlights who trusted the road so much she didn't think she'd get hit. She was a naïve, curious little thing who saw the world in colour, not black and white. A pure soul tainted by hardships of the past. And I wasn't proud to be one of them.

But if I could capture this moment, her sitting in my lap, smiling at me like the world was made of fireworks, then I would. I'd bottle it up forever cause no woman had ever looked at me the way Bambi had.

"Merry Christmas, Hunter."

I paused for a second, taking all of her in; the closeness of her body, the warmth of her proximity and I beamed. I beamed like a goddamn idiot.

"Merry Christmas, Bambi."

And a merry fuckin' Christmas it turned out to be.

Chapter Twenty-Three
Marley

The rest of the day was a complete and total blur.

The Lanes had a Christmas family tradition called "Down it for Derry" which was essentially a drinking game named after Hunter's great grandfather. Was there a point? Nope. I guess the man just loved to drink so when he passed away, they named a card game after him.

The objective of the game was to get drunk, naturally, so if you picked up any card under a ten, you took one shot and if you picked a face card, two shots.

Like I said, no significance, no purpose, only obliteration.

And that is exactly what happened until right around nine p.m.

"Holy dicks, it's bleedin' snow out there." Glen said, opening up a window shutter. "Still got that spare room, Dex?"

The rest of us flocked to the window, staring out at the icy tundra that swallowed our cars.

"Shit, that's gon' be a bitch to clean off in the mornin'." Betty gaped, running stressed fingers through her hair.

Payton began swatting us away from the window, shooing us to the kitchen. "Alright, alright, we got two spare bedrooms upstairs. Ain't nobody drivin' in this."

My eyes peeped to my white Malibu that was completely invisible, buried beneath the sheath of snow. *Shit.*

"Marley," Payton let out. "You got a bed downstairs, yah?"

"Um, well I guess –"

"*Hunter!*" Payton yelled, whipping her body around to find him standing a few feet away.

"Blow my ears out more, will ya? Christ." He scoffed, crossing his arms.

She paid no mind to his comment. "Bring some blankets down for Marley. There's a few in the laundry room."

He saluted a wave and led me away from everyone, snagging a dark blue blanket and some sheets.

"I don't know if Payton made the bed so just throw these aside if you don't need 'em."

I followed him down the basement stairs as the echoed voices of commotion slowly tuned out.

Hunter dropped the blanket and sheets on a fully made spread then proceeded to stalk straight to the fireplace.

The familiarity of this room made me reflect on the last couple months I'd spent in this small little town. So much happened, so much changed.

It felt like just yesterday that my entire life turned around, and I spent the night crying in this very room about Todd, my family, my lack of direction, everything under the sun.

Dex almost blew my head off with a shotgun, Payton fed me cinnamon rolls and Hunter well... Hunter hated my guts back then. Crazy how things play out when you have no expectations.

"Fireplace ain't workin'." Hunter released, rubbing the stubble on his jaw. "I'll go get you an extra blanket."

Before I could get a word out, he was already up and down the stairs within a minute, carrying a grey throw.

He laid it out on top of the duvet and set aside the clean sheets, rolling the blue blanket into a makeshift sausage pillow.

"You think you'll be warm enough?"

I walked over to the bookshelf that held Hunter's boat figurines and analyzed the craftsmanship of each one.

It was an odd hobby, not in the sense that it was weird but knowing Hunter's personality, I never expected him to enjoy such a... *calming*, task.

My pointer finger carefully grazed the little American flag glued to one of the ships as I joked in response.

"Are you offering to be my furnace?"

I didn't even realize how long it took him to respond before he grumbled out, "trust me, sweetheart. I've thought about it."

My head zipped around so fast I could've gotten whiplash. I found Hunter laying on the bed, *my* bed, with his head propped up against one of the pillows.

Heat scorched my cheeks as I turned my back to him, forcing my attention to the boats.

I counted about six mini ships, all painted in different colours and designs but the biggest ship in the center was the most complex.

Intricate carvings were engraved on the bottom of the boat, like angel wings that swirled off into tumbleweed. The sails on the boat were a rich yellow, dark blue glitter framing the outskirts. *This is freaking beautiful.*

"How long did this take you?" I asked, afraid to even stare at it in fear that it'd break.

I moved to the side to show Hunter what I was talking about, but he didn't even look, knowing exactly which one I was referring to.

"'Bout seven months I'd say. Needed to get it right."

My feet carried me away from the bookshelf of ships because frankly, I didn't trust myself any longer being around such fragile objects. I wasn't clumsy, but I definitely wasn't born with surgical hands.

"Why is it so much bigger than the rest of them?" I asked, sitting on the edge of the bed near Hunter's legs.

Ever since I hugged him when he gave me that adorable I <3 Nebraska keychain, I'd been fighting off the urge to feel his warmth again. I didn't exactly mean to jump on him, but when I saw the scarf he bought me in the box I couldn't hold in my affection.

Call it what you want, but Hunter truly was thoughtful in his own way. Most people would let something as silly as a keychain slip their mind, but he saw it and I guess it held some sort of significance for him to buy me an entirely new one. What had he said? *New York ain't your home no more... maybe it's time for a replacement...* My. Freaking. Heart.

"You really wan' talk boats with me right now?" He poked, eyeing me with that bright blue gaze.

I rolled my eyes and glanced away. "I mean... I did get you those paintbrushes."

He snorted. "I'm not talkin' bout boats, Bambi."

I perched on my elbows, repositioning myself on the bed. "Well, what do you want to talk about then?"

He sunk his head further into the pillow and shut his eyes. "The definition of silence, how 'bout we re-enact that right now?"

No freaking way he was sleeping. It was still Christmas. And then an idea hit me. I leapt off the bed

and made my way to the basement stairs before he
called after me.

"Where you goin'?"

"Stay put!" I commanded, hurrying to the
kitchen to snag two glasses and some whisky.

When I made my way back downstairs, he was
sat on the bed with his knees drawn up, eyeing the
liquor in my hand.

"What's all this?" He questioned.

I set the glasses down on the bed, pouring each
of us a generous shot of brown liquid.

"Let's play a game." I smiled, handing him the
cup.

His eyebrows raised in confusion taking the
alcohol without protest. "What kind of game?"

"It's called burning questions. I ask you
something, and if you don't want to answer it then you
take a shot and vice versa."

He let out a husky laugh, downing the glass
before the game even commenced. "You're playin' with
fire here, Bambi."

I swished the contents of my cup, frowning in
disgust. "Hunter, I hate whisky. So whatever you ask me,
I'll most likely answer to avoid drinking it. If *I'm* being
vulnerable, so are you."

He scanned my face before grabbing the liquor
bottle and refilling his drink. "Just for tonight, cause I'm
feelin' jolly."

A wide grin stretched across my mouth as I crossed my legs and faced him. "Who goes first?"

"Your idea, your play."

"Okay, hm..." I had so many questions, it was freaking impossible to pick one but I settled on something easier to start.

"How many girls have you slept with?"

He cocked on eyebrow, letting out the faintest laugh. "We in high school or somethin'?"

I swatted his knee. "Come on, I'm starting off light."

"God, fuck, I don't know. Like, twenty or some shit?"

My mouth flew open. "Twenty? That's it?"

"You expectin' more?" He chuckled.

"No, I mean, yes. Is that bad?"

"Depends on how you see it."

I stared at him for a moment before shaking my head. "It's not bad."

"Then there ya go." He lifted his lips to the brim of the glass but I pinched his leg.

"Quit doing that!"

His eyes flew open as he threw his hand up surrendering. "Force of habit."

"Mhm, your turn."

His fingers ticked the glass as he open and closed his mouth. "How many guys have you slept with?"

"You can't reuse my question," I frowned. "Be creative."

"Alright, alright."

After a few more moments he cleared his throat. "You miss your ex?"

Well oookay. "Just ripping off the band-aid right away, I guess?"

He shrugged. "Not askin' anything I don't care to know, sweetheart."

"No," I answered. "Not even a little."

"How long d'you date again?"

"A year and a bit, if you're counting that sort of talking period beforehand."

I unconsciously took a sip of the whisky and grimaced in revulsion. "I don't know why I just did that."

He clinked his glass to mine and drained it in one swig. "How 'bout after every question, we just drink, yeah? Loosens us up."

Ugh, why the hell not? It's Christmas after all.

I nodded in agreeance and filled up my cup. "Why did you hate me so much in the beginning?"

This time, I watched him stall as he too, poured more alcohol into his glass. In a state of heavy contemplation, he licked his bottom lip and took a sip of whisky.

"Hate's a strong word."

"Yeah, reserved for me." I teased.

He tapped the side of his drink, hesitating before clearing his throat.

"You reminded me of someone."

Are you serious? He literally berated me, hated me, cussed me out because I reminded him of someone he didn't like? Oh my God.

"But I'm not that someone." I replied, flabbergasted as all hell. "How is that a fair reason to hate someone?"

"You gon' make me regret answering that question, Bambi?"

"No, I just..." I trailed. "No, I'm glad you answered I'm just shocked. Who did I remind you of?"

He downed his drink and pressed his lips together, staring at me with a tight expression.

"You're not going to answer?"

"Take a drink with me and I just might."

Fair enough. We tapped glasses and down the bitter whisky went, burning the insides of my throat with ease.

"Go on," I encouraged, feeling the buzz of today reappear. *Or maybe it never left... God, I'm such a freakin' lightweight.*

His cheeks were a tad more flushed than before, so I could tell he was feeling it too. *Maybe now he'll start talking.*

"I dated a girl –"

"Hold on, hold on." I put a finger up. "I reminded you of your ex?"

"You want the story or not?"

I leaned back into the bed, giving him my full attention. "Sorry, sorry, continue."

"I dated a girl back when I played baseball in Iowa, an she was from Chicago – big city like you. Played me like a fuckin' fiddle that one. Always made me feel like I needed her to move forward in life, that she was the best damn thing that's ever happened to me."

An evident regret swept his features, those crystal eyes darkening by the second. I almost stopped him but he continued, downing his drink in one go.

"When I saw you, lookin' the way you do and that, I thought you were another one of 'em. Stuck up, fuckin' asking the most from people who didn't owe you nothin'. I just don't got that kind of sympathy for people."

My heart hammered in my chest as I tightened my fingers around the crystal cup, taking a large sip of whisky. "When did you start seeing me differently?"

The corner of his lips turned up a smidge as he met me with glossy eyes. "Bout the same time as you did."

I remembered the moment at Rivertown Bay, when he was drunk out of his mind and Dex practically shoved him away for breaking the glass. He'd called Hunter a mess and he responded with something that broke my heart in two. *For once you noticed.*

I think that's when it all changed for me. Even after Payton told me about his mom, I'd still harboured so much resentment for Hunter that my best efforts couldn't pull me out of my head. But when I saw the look in Hunter's eyes, the pleads of neglect he'd suffered since his mom past away... I'd never seen someone so broken.

"Do you still hate me?" he faltered, his voice hushed under his breath.

My mind began to swirl into a kaleidoscope of thoughts, brushing against one another in unison. But the answer to his question was definite.

"I wish I did," I admitted. "It would make things a lot easier for me..."

The air between us thickened, heavy with tension and warmth. That same warmth that I'd felt when I hugged him. *God I want to hug him so badly.*

I don't know if I imagined it, or if the alcohol was causing my brain to animate my desires, but I could've sworn his fingertips grazed my leg. *And if they didn't, I wanted them to.*

Before I could open my mouth to speak, I felt the bed shift and Hunter stood up, running his fingers through falling locks of hair.

"I'll uh," his Adams apple bobbed. "I'll take the whisky upstairs and let you get some sleep."

The words escaped my lips before I could capture them. "Stay."

My whole body was a caged inferno, staring at him in his god form with his muscly body and holy hotness. *Fuck, fuck, fuck.*

"Darlin'…" His voice, an echo, rattled against my brain. "If I stay, I ain't gon' wanna leave."

My head hit the pillow beneath me as I stretched out my limbs and yawned.

"Where's the issue?" I slurred, laughing harder as the soft fur of the blanket tickled my neck.

When the mix of ceaseless alcohol consumption and tiredness took over my senses, I faded into a dream land of Christmas bells and Christmas songs and cloudy white skies, reindeers dancing and singing and chirping my name…

"*Goodnight, Bambi.*" A low voice murmured.

"Goodnight Rudolph." I crooned.

And off I went, to the North Pole.

Chapter Twenty-Four
Hunter

I woke up to the sound of Betty and Uncle Glen rapping at my door, informing me that the snow had cleared up and they were heading off.

After minutes of cursing at the ceiling, I dragged myself out of bed and yanked open the shed entrance to find nothing but footprints.

They had already walked back towards the house when I called out, "thanks for the morning fuckin' alarm!" and slammed the door shut.

It wasn't Christmas no more, so I could go back to being the goddamn grinch. Though, it was good to see them, I just hated waking up early if I didn't need to.

I walked back to my bedroom after snagging a bottle of water and checked my phone, seeing a few missed calls from Josh and another nude from Britt.

The time stamp read: **11:32pm**

I'd fucked Britt a couple weeks back, thinking we were still on the same page but when she brought up becoming exclusive I pulled away so hard I could've broken my damn neck.

Like I said, I cared about her but not enough to commit. And that wasn't me being a dick, that was a preference I'd maintained for a while now and it did me well. No shame in casual sex, but it wasn't casual no more.

I didn't want to hurt her, so I hadn't been answering her. I guess some girls take you responding to their messages as a win, but I couldn't lead her into a direction I wasn't going to take.

After deciding against replying to Britt, I gave Josh a ring back.

"Hey Hunt."

"What'd you need?" I held the phone between my ear and shoulder as I carelessly tossed the covers over my bed.

"New Year's Eve plans, man. What we doin'?"

Fuckin' guy. Christmas quite literally just passed and he's already thinking about another social event filled with people. *I fucking hate people.*

"What'd we do last year?"

"Uh..." He took a minute before piping up. "Right, Cid's. They had them sparkler shots for two bucks."

"Cid's it is. See ya."

My finger hovered over the end call button but he was quick to speak.

"Wait Hunt, we still goin' out tonight?"

The banging in my head spoke against it, answering for me. "Nah, I got a rude hangover. Gon' see if Dad needs some help with new shipments."

He let out a low gasp as his dumb ass laugh escaped the phone. "Since when d'you say no to a drink?"

He's got a point there. But my stomach was turning and whatever taste coated my mouth was vile like venom so I said my goodbyes and headed to the bathroom.

I stared at the bags under my eyes, the scruff on my skin and decided I needed to trim it down a little. The entire time I shaved, I wondered if Bambi had already left since Betty and Uncle Glen got out early this morning. *Was she an early riser?* I never really asked. But I did ask if she still hated me last night.

Fuckin' dumb ass. As if I wanted to pour any more salt into the wound. We were still walking on thin ice, her and I, and I didn't want to jeopardize anything by saying the wrong thing. What if I reminded her of all the shitty things I've said and done and she left without me saying anything to her?

And that moment at the end there... when she asked me to stay, when she looked at me with those Bambi fuckin' eyes, I could've collapsed on that bed and fucked her without remorse.

Maybe that's what I needed. I needed to lay Bambi, needed to take out whatever mush I had stored inside of me and just fuck her raw.

On second thought, screw that. She'd told me about her braindead ex who cheated on her and made her feel like shit, and I didn't want that for her no more. Not that I ever did, I mean, sort of? *Holy fuck, straighten yourself out, man.*

My phone taunted me, calling me out to message Bambi and see if she was still around. I didn't know what I'd say to her, but I knew I wanted to say something. Maybe I could invite her out for New Year's with me and Josh? Was that pushing it? *No harm in asking.*

I put down the razor and clicked Bambi's name, typing out a text that read:

9:43am – Hunter: You up?

I didn't expect anything right away, so I went about shaving again. Then after a minute or two, my phone chimed with an incoming message.

9:45am – Bambi: Hey, yeah. Good morning 😊

I stared at the screen for a few seconds, my eyes hovering over the smiley face emoji she'd put.

God, I was so fucking wrong about her. I still didn't trust her, not as far as I could throw her but she wasn't the monster I painted her out to be.

When I really stopped to think about all the shit I'd said to her, the way she looked at me made sense. She'd been so used to the maltreatment of others, the way her family made her see herself like a walking insecurity. And I did the same damn thing when I met her. Treated her like trash, talked down to her like I had a right – I had no fuckin' right. No one had a right.

I shook away my irritation and typed back:

9:50am – Hunter: Have you left yet?

9:53am – Bambi: I'm having breakfast with Payton, then I'm going to head off. Why?

Throwing my phone aside, I jumped into the shower and rinsed off as fast as I could, tossing on a pair of black sweats, an old Green Bay Packers hoodie and my jacket then sprinted out the door.

When I reached the farmhouse, I found Bambi and Payton sitting at the kitchen table surrounded by coffee, bread and a plate of breakfast meats.

"Mornin'," I wiggled my fingers into a wave, snatching a piece of crisp bacon.

"How's your head?" Payton asked, taking a sip of her coffee.

I leaned back against the counter, ripping a paper towel off the holder. "Hurtin', yours?"

Payton's laugh filled the room along with a hushed chuckle from Bambi.

"Down it for Derry is a recipe for disaster," Bambi added, meeting my eyes tentatively before turning away.

I smirked. "Don't play if you can't keep up, sweetheart."

A moment of silence passed between us before Payton slammed her hands down on the table and stood up.

"Well, Hunter, you gon' eat?" She said, facing me.

"I might."

"Then you're doin' the dishes while I help your dad put together some tool kits."

She passed by Bambi, giving her shoulder a squeeze. "Your shift's at..."

"Nine, tomorrow." Bambi responded with a smile.

"Nine." Payton snapped her fingers, exiting the kitchen to the walkway. "Nine, nine, nine."

When I heard the backdoor shut, I took a seat across her at the table, piling a plate up with food.

"How's your head?" I asked.

"Fine. I don't get hangovers."

My eyes widened. "Don't you lie to me."

She laughed. "I'm not lying. I could drink an entire bottle of wine and be out for a morning jog the next day."

"Early riser?" I posed, pouring myself a cup of coffee.

"You could say that. I don't sleep much to begin with. Bad insomnia."

Huh. The more you know.

"What are you doin' for New Year's Eve?"

Fuckin' shit, this breakfast is good. Payton never made stuff like this before, EVER. Might need to invite Bambi over more often to soak up the benefits.

"I think Winter and I are going out with Cramer."

Cramer? Oh, Cookie. "The fuckwit from Cid's?"

Her face reddened as she took a sip from her cup, hiding behind the coffee mug. "That *fuckwit* is essential to your family's business."

I decided not to combat that since it was probably true. The few time I decided to read reviews on P&D, they always talked about how Cookie was a "stellar employee" and "made their shopping experience extra fun." *Like shopping at a hardware store is the highlight of people's damn days.*

"Why don't you bring 'em to Cid's? They got a special on drinks; don't know what but I could find out."

Her eyebrows raised like she was shocked that I invited her somewhere. No word of a lie, I was shocked myself. But I liked her company, not that it was daisies and fucking roses but I don't know, she was sort of... *pleasant*, to talk to. Like a breath of fresh air. Something new. *Yeah, that's it.*

"I don't think Cramer likes you very much, Hunter." Bambi let out, chuckling softly.

"I was drunk that night," I responded, leaning back into the bench.

"You were rowdy."

"I'll apologize." *No the fuck I won't.*

I managed to capture her chocolate eyes for a moment before she snatched them away, twirling the tip of her hair.

"I'll talk to them."

I gathered the used plates and stepped out of the bench, walking away in victory.

"I better see you, Bambi. Or so help me God."

She stood up, pulling on her coat and snagging her car keys. "We'll see what ends up happening."

I'll take that. "Let me walk you out."

As we reached her Malibu, I studied her outfit; the wool coat, her white sweater and jeans, a red beanie but no...

She had already settled in her car when I tapped the window, urging her to roll down the glass.

"Where's your scarf?" I asked, searching the space.

She pointed to the back seat. "It's in the box you gave me."

I frowned, rubbing the light stubble on my jaw. "And where's it meant to be, darlin'?"

Her eyes rolled and I couldn't hold back a laugh.

"Around my neck?" She guessed, curving her lips into a smile.

I beamed. "Good girl," then tapped the hood of the white Malibu, sending her off onto the snowy road.

The sunlight danced over my face as I made my way back to the farmhouse, scanning the transparent icicles that hung from the gutter.

Water droplets slid down the sharp picks as the sun penetrated their hard shells, melting away the form

of what they once were, and turning them into
something new.

> *I feel that, icicle.*
> *I fucking feel that.*

Chapter Twenty-Five
Marley

"I think you should wear the blue dress, Mar."

Winter and I were getting ready at my place since it was a closer Uber and I couldn't decide on an outfit for the life of me.

After talking to Cramer about Hunter's behaviour, he decided to let it go and agreed to come with us to Cid's.

Actually, Winter was thrilled when I suggested it since she was trying to get out of a bummy New Year's Eve party her friend had invited her to.

I stood in front of my full length mirror, pulling down one of the flashy pink dresses Winter brought over from her place.

Her style was definitely out there; wild, patterned, and borderline manic. But I loved it. It matched her flamboyant personality and everything looked good on her.

Me on the other hand, well... I looked like a parrot had thrown up on a feather scarf and dumped it all over my body.

"Okay, can you toss me the blue dress, please?"

She sifted through a pile of clothing spread out on my bed and finally pulled out the cyan blue fabric, handing it over.

"So..." Winter chimed, thumbing through her phone as I got changed. "Think he'll kiss you tonight?"

I kicked out of the parade dress and stepped into the new. "Who?"

"Who else, love? Hunter."

I coughed out a laugh, pulling the thin straps over my freshly tanned shoulders. "Hard no, and I do NOT want him to."

First lie of the evening, last lie of the year. It's not that I didn't want him to, it was the fact that I DID and I couldn't let myself fall into that fantasy.

Just a few days ago, I'd been so unsure about him, about us. We'd been harbouring resentment for so long, despite being wrong about each other, it was odd to just jump into... well, whatever the hell this was. *Nothing. Marley. Nothing. This is nothing.*

"So you mean to tell me that if Hunter leaned in to kiss you, you'd pull away?" Winter stared at me intently, waiting for another lie.

I crunched my bottom lip, figuring out the possibility of such an event occurring and no outcome registered so, why would I even waste my time thinking about it?

"We just started over, Winter. There's no way that's going to happen."

Her finger twirled in the air. "But if he did..."

"Then, fuck, I don't know! I'll kiss him back? Maybe?" My face reddened as I zipped up the back of my dress, turning to my reflection.

"How do I look?" I asked, blinking back at the girl in the mirror.

Winter stood up, throwing a hand over her mouth as she looked me up and down. "Marley! Stop it, you look absolutely phenomenal. Turn around, turn around, babe!"

I did as I was told, laughing as she spun me in a circle and flattened out the bottom creases of my dress.

"You're glowing, love, just radiant. This is the one, this is what you're wearing."

When I faced myself in the mirror, I tried so hard to see what Winter saw. My legs looked long even though I was short, but that was probably just the silver heels. The blue contrasted against my skin, but it made me look orange and splotchy, like a pumpkin. My breasts were pushed together by the deep dip of boning on either side of the middle, making me self conscious about the exposure.

"I don't know, Winter..." I swallowed. "It's really showy."

"Babe, it's New Year's Eve. You're supposed to be showy."

"I know but..."

"Marley, look at me. I'm wearing two strips that cover my tits and a skirt that could be a baby bib. Embrace yourself, love yourself. You are stunning."

I giggled, pulling Winter into a hug as I let my fragility shine through once again. When I was in high school, I was well aware of the attention I received. From boys, from girls, everyone. But when the curtains were drawn and I faced Harlow Matthews, I was never good enough.

She told me to use my looks to my advantage, but to her that was all her fabrication and good work. If she thought I grew a size, she'd shrink me two. If I was on her arm, I had to embody her, dress like her, look like her. But at the end of the day, I didn't. I got my father's sharp jaw and thicker eyebrows. My mom thought I looked masculine, so she booked me monthly microblading sessions to keep them in check.

I'd always been self conscious about my appearance, even though I tried my best to regulate my diet and exercise. But I couldn't stop the thoughts, the judgment I'd put on myself whenever I wore something daring.

"If Hunter doesn't kiss you, I will." Winter teased, plumping her glossy lips my way.

"Well looks like I'll be kissing you tonight, then."

She winked at me and ran her manicured nails through my hair, fluffing it up before squeezing my collarbone.

"Ready to make some memories?" She smirked, moving towards the front door.

I took one last look at myself in the mirror, breathing out all the insecurity and embracing all the praise. *You look good, Marley. You're hot. You're pretty. You look good.*

Let's end the year right. "Ready."

The flashing lights of Cid's Pub were a combination of blue and white strobes.

Silver disco balls hung from the ceiling with water refreshment tables lining the dance floor.

Flocks of people bumped and grinded to the old throwback playlist blaring through the enormous wall speakers, making it nearly impossible to hear anyone speaking unless they were right next to you.

We met Cramer inside the bar. He totally looked like a fairy-tale prince charming, dressed in a brown and white vest combo with taupe slacks.

"You girls look amazin'!" He yelled, drawing us into an empty booth further away from the dancers.

When the sound fazed out, an echo of noise rang through my ears before I comfortably settled against the hard wood.

"Shall we order some drinks?" Winter asked, bobbing her head from side to side.

Cramer called over one of the waitresses working, a pretty redhead wearing a black long sleeve and leggings.

"Hey all, what is everyone havin' tonight?" She perked, taking out her notepad.

"Can I get nine tequila shots to the table?" Cramer asked, grinning at us widely.

"*Nine*? Cramer are you insane?" I laughed, shocked and yet, not at all.

"It's New Year's Eve, Marley. Night's young!" He shot back.

The waitress took our order and left us to converse, which went on for a few minutes before two men approached our table, silencing our discourse.

I didn't even need to look into those sea blue spheres to tell who it was. My gaze trailed from his dark jeans to his black dress shirt, cuffed at the sleeves. The top two buttons of his shirt were undone and I almost died right then and there.

"We had a table, but yours is better." Hunter released, addressing me and me only.

I swallowed hard, looking to my company but they were already making room for the guys to slip in.

"Order any drinks yet?" The man beside Hunter said, as he slid into the spot next to Winter.

I recognized him as Hunter's best friend, Josh I think. God, he really was a cutie too. His brown hair was short and shaved at the sides, and he sported that porn stache girls went feral for. *Including me.*

He, too, wore a black dress shirt with grey jeans to match. They looked like two dark knights in the midst of chaos, and I was soaking in every second of it.

"Care to trade places with me, man?" Hunter addressed, staring at Cramer dead in the face.

When Cramer finally clued in to where he was looking, he got up and sat beside Josh who quickly engaged him in conversation about football.

"Hi, sweetheart." Hunter released, taking his place next to me.

I inhaled the scent of his cologne, trying to tame every fiber of my being but it was almost impossible. *Like fighting off a tiger with a spoon.*

"You look nice." I smiled. *More than nice, holy crap.*

"Stole the words right outta my mouth, Bambi."

I blushed and there was nothing stopping me anymore. I couldn't contain the attraction I felt, that I always felt. *Maybe he may actually kiss me tonight...*

"Hunty, I was hoping I'd see you here." A blonde waitress approached our table, boobs out on full display. *Hunty?*

He shifted to the side, wrapped an arm around her as she leaned down to kiss him on the cheek.

Oh. My. God. Red hot fury, that was all I felt. Fuck! I wasn't jealous, no *I'm not.* But... really? She looked just like the girl he was hooking up with at

Rivertown Bay. The L.A blondie with big lips and long blonde hair. Clearly he's got a type.

"How you doin', Britt?" His voice was levelled, calm.

She tapped her black acrylic nails on the wooden table and ogled him, completely ignoring the presence of the entire freaking table.

"You haven't answered me in a while, I was worried 'bout you."

Hunter turned to face Josh who had a hard time holding in laughter as he whispered something into Winter's ear.

After a few moments, Hunter turned his attention back to *Britt.* "Doin' just fine, darlin'."

"Well how's about we get you started on a free drink, my treat?"

I watched his eyebrows raise in content. "Not gon' say no to that."

"Whisky on ice?" She perked, bouncing on her heels.

"You got it."

Again, she paid zero mind to anyone else and scurried through the crowd of people, fleeing into the kitchen quarters by the bar.

"Kitty's persistent, I give her that." Josh joked, his eyes following a group of girls that walked by.

Hunter didn't respond and turned to me as if that entire interaction with blonde number two didn't happen.

"What'd you get to drink, sweet cheeks?"

I folded my arms over my chest, suddenly extremely hyper aware of the way he was looking at me.

"Cramer ordered us some."

"Oh yeah?" Hunter licked the bottom of his lip. "And what did Cookie order?"

Before I could respond, the redhead returned with a tray of shots and some limes, laying them all in a straight line, ready for the taking.

"Goddamn party, ain't it, Hunt?" Josh chimed, passing out the tequila.

"I ordered those for us three..." Cramer butt in softly.

But Josh slapped him on the back and downed a shot. "Easy fix, man."

He called over a server wearing a bow tie with a name tag and shouted over the music, "I want six tequila shots, this booth, three minutes!"

Winter and I exchanged a look before taking one of our own, clinking the glasses together and downing the clear liquid.

I wiped the residue off my lip before handing one of my shots to Hunter.

"No trainin' wheels?" He asked, pulling the small plate of limes over to me.

But I pushed them back, urging him to take the shot. "Training wheels are for pussies."

A crisp, tender laugh emanated from his throat as he held his stomach, shaking his head.

"Say it again, darlin'. Please, just say that again."

I couldn't help my own chuckle and repeated my words. "Training wheels are for pussies?"

He flung his head back, barely missing the hard wooden headboard of the booth and drained the shot, flinging a muscular arm around my shoulders.

"Not bad for a New York City brat, Bambi. Not fuckin' bad."

As midnight approached, I could barely stand without the assistance of another human being. Winter and I decided to brave the dance floor, swaying our hips in a crowd of drunken people.

My mind raced, my skin dripping with sweat as I laced my fingers around Winter's arm and followed her back to our booth.

I found Hunter laughing beside Josh, actually sharing a drink with Cramer as I snuggled in next to him. *Totally blaming this affection on being drunk.*

"Any more drinks?" I slurred, grinning like the freaking Cheshire cat when Alice dropped down the rabbit hole.

"Yep," Hunter let out, pushing a cup of clear liquid to my hand.

I took a massive swig, frowning when I realized it was water. "You're no fun."

"Hear that Josh?" Hunter shouldered his best friend. "I'm no fun."

Josh put a hand over his heart, throwing me a wounded expression. "How dare ya, love bug? He's got a brittle heart."

"Or no heart at all," I teased, rolling my eyes.

He placed a strong hand over mine, forcing me to face him. "Now, you don't really believe that, do you Bambi?"

The longer I focused on his features, those pretty, pretty features, I felt the buzz being drawn out of me, orbiting around my head but no longer overpowering my thoughts.

"I don't."

He kept me in his hold for a little longer before a crowd of people began calling out the New Year's Eve countdown.

"Ten!"

"Nine!"

Our entire booth shook as Winter, Cramer, Josh, Hunter and I bounced out of our seats and made our way to the flat screen T.V at the bar, watching the ball drop at Times Square. *My home. Where my brother was probably sipping hot chocolate with his pregnant wife. Where my dad and mom were off playing poker with a team of businessmen. Where I didn't belong. Where I never belonged.*

Hunter gripped my hand, glancing at me with shimmering eyes before engaging in the countdown chant.

"Six!"

"Five!"

Winter and Cramer were shoulder to shoulder, cheering on the horde around us as Josh swooped his arm around a raven haired woman.

"Three!"

"Two!"

This was my home now. These people. This life. *Goodbye past, cheers to a new beginning.*

"Happy New Year!"

The bar howled in celebration, kissing and embracing everyone around them. Tons of people chugged their drinks, jumping up and down once they'd finished.

Winter and Cramer hugged, swaying in each other's arms while Josh was fully making out with the raven haired girl.

How was I seeing this you may ask? How was I observing everyone's intimate actions so well as the clock struck midnight? Well, no one was kissing me, I was sure about that.

I was too afraid to look at Hunter, too embarrassed. I couldn't tell you what I was doing in that moment. Probably standing there like an awkward, single, bozo who expected something that didn't happen. Of course, once again, I let my clouded desires fog the truth of my relationship with Hunter.

There wasn't one.

And I couldn't be upset about it. I couldn't be, because what did I expect? That we'd go from hating each other, to tolerating each other, to kissing on New Year's Eve. *Delusional, Marley. That's what you are.*

I took in the blur of motions around me, a glossy sheen sweeping over my eyes when a firm arm wrapped around my waist, drawing me towards them.

"Happy New Year's, sweetheart." Hunter's cologne infiltrated my senses as I leaned into him, craving his touch even if he didn't want it.

But as the music restarted and the crowd of people began to disperse, I stood there, in his arms, holding onto the fabric of his shirt.

A gentle press of soft lips touched my forehead as Hunter pulled me in closer, leaning down to my ear.

"Not yet, Bambi." He whispered. "We got time."

Chapter Twenty-Six
Hunter

A month and a half since New Year's.

A month and a half since P&D's was voted the number one hardware store in the state. At the end of January, my dad and Payton got in touch with some old friends across Nebraska, asking if they wanted to open a few branches in their areas. Obviously they agreed, who wouldn't want to manage a six figure business?

So now, P&D's was a chain? Sorta? Fuck if I knew how that worked but we were selling.

A month and a half since that goddamn ball dropped on T.V and the start of new opportunities, new life, new *everything* breathed into me.

And forty-five days since Bambi and I officially became friends; no strings attached, no snarky remarks... just a raw, honest, *friendship*.

Unexpected, of course. But I had the time of my fucking life at Cid's with her by my side. She looked like a dream, and with all the bitterness that blossomed between us, it was somewhat hard to admit that out loud. But that night, all I wanted to do was claim her. In what way? Fuck if I knew. But when she was close, I wanted to be closer. And that settles that.

So I did. I stuck by and loved every second of this friendship I dismissed for so long.

We spent almost every weekend together with Josh and her little crew of Winter and Cook – *Cramer*, fuckin' Cramer. He was good shit, I liked him. Yet another unexpected turn of events.

I showed her the nice hiking trails around here, we went out for ice cream, she spent a lot of mornings at ours before her shift with Payton. It was... Christ, it was the most perfect normal any man could ask for.

Don't get me wrong, there were nights I'd spend with Bambi that drove me wild. Sometimes she'd wear something a little too nice and my mind would combust. She had a killer bod, and the more I got to know her, the less that became important.

She opened up to me a lot more than I ever thought she could. Not in an overbearing way, but she kicked those shy mannerisms to the curb and was branching out.

Bambi, a deer *outside* the headlights.

It was crazy to think I ever questioned this girl, ever thought she'd twist my heart and snap it in two. She held it, yeah, carefully, with those tiny little elf hands she had.

Despite the attraction, I didn't want to fuck up the dynamic. We were no longer treading on rocky waters, but we had something good going on and I wanted to keep it that way. Commitment wasn't a specialty of mine, and I wasn't about to start now.

I'd popped into P&D's to get some fertilizer for the soil when Bambi was on her way out.

"Hey, darlin'," I said. "We still meeting at Cid's tonight?"

She nodded her head in a hurry and forced out a smile, shielding her eyes from me.

The fuck? "Whoa, whoa, hey. C'mere."

I held her wrist in one hand, cupping her cheek in the other as I scanned the puffiness of her face, evidence that she'd been crying.

"What happened?" I asked, keeping her in lock.

"It's nothing."

"Bambi."

I watched her lip quiver as a tear rolled down her cheek.

"My mom won't get rid of the P.I. she hired when I moved out of Lincoln. She keeps texting me saying that I shouldn't be spending all my time at bars, and I should be doing more useful things and... *fuck!*"

She swivelled out of my grasp and took a step back, placing a hand over her mouth as she tried so damn hard to contain herself.

I let her. I let her hammer out her emotions cause I didn't know what the hell I'd do if I had some rando creeping down my neck every hour of the day and I couldn't do nothin' about it.

"You know, a little part of me hoped that she'd come around. That she'd want to be involved in my life again. This... this is not at all what I meant."

The cold air slapped my face as I surveyed the area, spying out anyone who looked like they could be a fucking private investigator... as if I had the qualifications of seeking that out.

"There's got to be somethin' you can do 'bout this, Bambi. That's a hundred percent an invasion of privacy, no?"

"Oh it totally is. It totally is but my mom doesn't care. She just wants to have the rundown on every single part of my life without actually being in it. *God*! I can't stand her, I can't."

I clicked my tongue, siffling through a variety of words I could say, but probably would do no good in this situation. What her mom was doing was just bonkers and I couldn't comprehend how that was even legal. But from what Bambi told me about her parents, they had a ton of money and a lot of connections, so. How could you fight fire with the devil?

"Hunter, I will see you tonight." Bambi let out, exhaling a deep breath and shutting her eyes.

"Yeah?" I almost laughed but it was definitely not the time. Couldn't help myself, though. She was a puny human with the strength of a bull. It was hysterical.

"Yes. But right now, I need to walk to my car peacefully, drive home and make some chamomile tea so I don't capsize any sanity I have left."

I held my hands up and let her pass, watching her practically squeeze the life out of her palm as she got behind the wheel, waved, and drove off.

That fuckin' girl. A trojan horse she was. *Now what the hell am I doin' here again?*

Chapter Twenty-Seven
Marley

I plopped down on my mattress, fingers knotted in my hair as I screamed into a pillow.

Screw her! Screw her! Fuck, she's unbelievable!

After finishing up some work in P&D's office, I checked my texts to find numerous pictures of me standing in front of Cid's Pub with Hunter and Josh, a few coffee outing dates with Winter, and Cramer and I sharing a pizza at Berandino's last Thursday.

My mom had attached the images saying I wasn't taking my life seriously, that I didn't learn from any past mistakes and I was going in circles. It went on and on and on, to the point where I couldn't handle the verbal harassment from my own freaking mother, that I blocked her number.

I blocked my own mother.

Tears of insanity flowed down my face as I laughed in hysterics, alternating between sobs, then feral laughter once more.

Holy crap, what the hell is my life?

No, I couldn't keep sitting here like a lamb waiting for slaughter. I still had a few more hours before I was meeting Hunter at Cid's so I could call up my phone provider and have my number changed. Or maybe get a burner phone? Screw it, whatever it'll take to get Harlow Matthews off my back.

God, that feels good to say.

After heading to Verizon, I finally got a new number and they'd actually upgraded me to the newest iPhone for twenty dollars cheaper. Something about being a loyal member for the past few years, so it was an added perk. *I wasn't complaining.*

I met Hunter at half past eight, where I found him sitting at one of the back booths wearing his black leather jacket and a dark sleeve to match.

His arm was linked around the headboard peak when he noticed me coming, smiling with sunken dimples.

It still blew my mind how good we became in just under two short months. So much had happened with the business, I never really stopped to think about who I was spending my time destressing with.

In a way, he had become an important part of my relaxation periods; showing me around, hiking a few times a week, getting drunk on Fridays much like tonight.

Crazy to think that once upon a time, I never saw Hunter smile. And now, I saw it more than I saw him frown. At least around me, and that made me proud.

"Hey," I let out, scooting in next to him.

His eyes drifted from my face to my lips, something he'd commonly do when we were speaking. At first, I was really self conscious about it. I thought I had something on my face or whatever, but after accepting the obvious truth that both he and I were clearly shoving down levels of attraction, I relished in it. *Hunter Lane checked me out. A lot.*

"Feelin' better, sweetheart?" He asked, pushing a martini glass in front of me.

"I am now," I beamed, taking a sip of the cold appletini. "My favourite."

He chuckled, peeling off his jacket and stretched out his long arms.

"Did you figure somethin' out?"

My eyes widened as I cleared my throat, taking out my new phone from my purse.

"Not exactly, but I changed my number and got a new phone." I handed it to him and tapped his contact name. "Can you add your number in, please?"

Quick fingers moved this way and that then he returned my phone back to me. "Smart move, actually. Don't think it's a long term solution, though."

"Definitely not, but in the meantime my mom will most likely think I'm ignoring her and keep trying the old number until she realizes it isn't in service anymore. So it'll buy me a few days of peace."

He smirked, clinking his glass of what I assumed to be whisky against my martini rim.

"Cheers to peace, Bambi."

I giggled, taking a proper swig of my drink and smiled through the burn.

"Amen to that."

"You cannot tell me that's not the grossest thing ever," I released, showing him a picture of small circles bunched together.

He stared at the picture for a minute too longer than I felt comfortable with as I gasped in disbelief.

"Hunter, look away! It's literally disgusting."

"Bambi," he choked out a laugh, "it's just holes."

I placed a hand over my eye as I struggled to delete the photo, clearing my internet search history.

"I have trypophobia."

He wiped imaginary tears from his waterline as he downed the rest of his whisky. "That ain't real, sweetheart."

"I hate you." I crossed my arms, draining the fourth martini I'd ordered.

"Cause I don't believe you got *tippytopia*?"

"Try-po-phobia."

He shook his head, rounding up both our glasses as he attempted to escape the booth. "Want another?"

But I beat him to it, pushing my legs closer together as I wiggled out into the open area. "I'll do it. I have to pee. Whisky?"

He nodded as I stepped away and changed course to the bathroom. The music drained out of my ears when the door shut closed, allowing me a moment of silence to breathe and compose myself.

My brown eyes were darker, coated by a lustrous sheen of liquor sparkle and my white top had a few dotted stains from when Hunter accidently spilt his whisky earlier.

The redness in my face looked like I'd braved an Alaskan storm but I didn't mind it. *Who needs blush when I have the wonderful effects of alcohol?*

The music returned to its original level as I finished up my business in the bathroom and stood at the bar, waiting for Kenton to take my order.

I'd made friends with him the first night I'd been to Cid's and he truly was a lovely man. Divorced with two kids, but still worked every single night to provide for them since his wife cheated on him with their plumber. *Some freaking people.*

Right on cue, Kenton strode towards me, throwing a white towel over his left shoulder. "What can I get ya, Marley? Same as before?"

I opened my mouth to respond when I froze at the sound of a man speaking.

The familiar voice of a man I knew all too well.

The same voice of the man I'd run away from.

Don't look, Marley. Don't look. Oh my God, please for the love of fuck do not be him.

My mouth gaped open as I examined the snake-green eyes, the dark scruff and brown curls of the man I'd left my life behind for.

Todd was sitting on the barstool directly across from me, twirling a toothpick in an empty glass as he eyed me with a humoured expression.

"Appletini, right baby?"

I almost hurled. I swear I almost hurled right then and there, on his fucking smug face and white turtleneck and corduroy jacket.

Kenton looked to me but I swallowed in response as he moved away, making the drink that my ex-boyfriend just ordered me.

"How the fuck..." I shook my head, refusing to move out of place. "How are you here right now, Todd?"

He stood up but I extended five shaky fingers in front of me, creating a barrier of distance with whatever courage I could muster up.

He put his hands up and eased back down, cocking a grin my way.

"Your mom tipped me off, actually."

In that moment, my entire world shattered at the seams. My mom never even liked Todd, and now she was suddenly buddy-buddy with him, sharing my location? How the hell did she even know I'd be here? *Holy crap the P.I. THE FREAKING P.I.*

I glanced around the room, finding no one but a crowd of drunk individuals head-banging to Mötley Crüe.

"Marley, I've tried calling you so many times. Not once did you care to talk to me."

Fire filled my veins as I erupted into a volcano of seething fury. "You cheated on me, Todd! For months! With your fucking ex-girlfriend and you expect me to stay with you?"

He was too calm, too relaxed as he responded to my outburst. "No, but I expected you to hear me out."

"You're fucking insane, Todd."

"Oh I'm insane?" This time, he got up, marching towards me with strong strides. "You dropped everything to be with a guy you don't know, a guy who could've beat you and left you on the street with no where to turn. But I spent months providing for us like the good man I am. I was raised with integrity, you know that."

Tears waterfalled down my cheeks as I stood cemented in place, unable to move, unable to react. All I could focus on were his eyes, his terrible eyes filled with torment and anger, anger fuelled for me.

"And what are you doing in this shit hole town? Huh? Still running away from your problems, Marley, like a lost little bit –"

The metallic taste of blood splattered onto my tongue as Hunter slammed his head down against the bar, punching him repeatedly.

It took me a few seconds to register what was happening when a horde of people made their way around Hunter and Todd, videoing the fight with excitement.

"Fuck him up, Hunter!" One person yelled.

"What the hell's happening?" Another said.

Kenton jumped over the bar and attempted to break up the fight but it was no use. Hunter bodied Todd onto the ground, coming down on him with heavy throws.

"Stop!" I yelled, finally escaping the chains of my paralysis and wrapped my arms around Hunter's shoulders. "Hunter, stop!"

His breathing was hoarse, sporadic, like an untamed lion who was ripping at its prey. Todd's body was flayed onto the floor, his nose bent to the side, his face covered by thick gore.

I managed to pull Hunter back, shoving him away as I knelt to the ground beside Todd who coughed out a clot of blood.

"I need an ambulance!" I yelled, wrapping my hand around the back of his neck.

I didn't like Todd, I didn't love Todd, but he was still a human being who needed some fucking help. The entirety of his outfit was painted red, my hands were painted red... *Everything was. Everything was coated in his blood.*

"Oh my God," I covered my mouth with blood soaked fingers as Hunter tried to leap out from behind me again, grabbing at his ankles.

I whipped around and shoved myself in between them. "Are you fucking crazy!"

Hunter had a dead look in his eyes, bloodshot and beady as he zeroed in on Todd's limp body behind me.

"Look at me, fucking look at me!" I commanded, grabbing his face in my palms.

He did, but only because he had no choice. If the decision was his, he'd be on top of Todd killing him with broken glass, I could bet my life on it.

My hands trembled as I cupped his jaw, terrified at the look in his eyes when those crystal blue gems faded into a hollow pit.

"*Move*, Bambi." He demanded, locking his jaw tight.

"Hunter –"

"Let me fuckin' at him!"

"You're acting like a fucking monster!" I scolded, darting my eyes between Todd's injuries and Hunter's scowl.

He took a step back with a pained expression, tilting his head to one side as he surveyed the mess he created.

"After all this time..." he muttered, barely a whisper. "You still don't see it."

Hunter parted the crowd of curious bodies and stomped through, slamming the front door open violently.

I ran after him, finding him stepping into his truck and shutting the door.

"Hunter, stop." I banged on the windows repeatedly, but he just glared at me with an icy stare, cranking the ignition.

"Hunter, please don't drive like this!" I screamed, begged, pleaded.

But it was no use.

Once he tore his eyes away from mine, he backed out of the parking lot, forcing me to fumble backwards onto the gravel.

I watched the back of his truck turn onto the road, disappearing into the night's fog.

The commotion coming from inside Cid's was no match to the clanging breaths escaping my mouth. It was all I could hear. The sound of my pulse, the patter of my heart, my ear drums ringing and ringing and ringing.

I can't... I can't do this to him. Fuck! *I have to do this.* With tentative movements, I pulled out my phone from my back pocket, dialling 9-1-1.

I swallowed the bullets cascading down my throat as an officer announced a hello.

"I'd like to report a drunk driver down Tintsy Road..." Tears flowed down my face as I released a hushed sob, knowing there was no miracle in the world that could fix what I was about to do. "Black truck, licence plate 923 – N72."

Chapter Twenty-Eight
Hunter

I didn't even try to fight off the drunk as I zoomed down the backroad going 75mph.

Bambi's fuckwit of an ex had the balls to show his face at Cid's Pub and I just so happen to have overheard most of what that bastard had to say.

I didn't do nothin' wrong. I didn't do shit! *Fuck!* He was provoking her, egging her on, making her feel like a goddamn fool and I took it upon myself to change his fucking diapers and wipe that grin clean off his face.

But Bambi, no, to her I was a mother fucking monster. I was the villain, I was the piece of shit who tried to protect her but no, *NO! Ha-ha, I'd done nothing right, clearly not there, not anywhere.*

I blasted *Sympathy For The Devil,* pressing harder on the gas as the tears stung my eyes.

This road. This very road I was with you, ma. Four years ago, I watched you suffer. I watched you take your last breath. Now it's my turn.

The wind pushed against my truck but I carried on, driving until the black trees morphed into one big mountain.

"Pleased to meet you, hope you guess my name..." I sang, tapping my fingers against the wheel.

Why'd she look at me like that? Like I was a psychopath that was going to kill him? I wasn't going to kill him, fuck, he just needed a little rough up.

"Ah, what's puzzling you, is the nature of my game, oh yeah..." The sound of the radio tuned in and out as I screamed the lyrics.

"I watched with glee, while your kings and queens, fought for ten decades, for the gods they made!"

A barrage of sirens wailed out of nowhere as a trail of blue and red lights followed my truck, honking their horns to pull me over.

"The fuck?" I squinted, adjusting my vision to my rear-view mirror.

I pulled my ram to the side of the road and cut the ignition, slapping myself to try and stabilize my buzz. *Sober up, damnit, fuck!*

When two cops rapped on my window, I rolled down the glass, flashing a saccharine smile at the officers.

"Evenin' fellas. How can I help you?" *Levelled breaths, man. Steady.*

The dark haired cop flashed a light in my truck, aiming it directly in my eyes. "Step out of the vehicle, sir."

"I can assure you there's got to be some sort of –"

"Out! Now!" The other cop ripped.

I held my hands up in surrender as I unlocked my baby, planting my feet down on the cement as I rounded the hood.

"We got word that you're driving under the influence, that true?" The dark haired cop demanded, eyeing me up and down.

"Wrong." I spat, coughing out the congested air in my lungs. *Who the fuck ratted on me?*

"Can you confirm that your licence plate number is," he looked down at a piece of paper, "923 – N72?"

I swallowed hard, thankful that the night sky blocked out the evident redness in my cheeks.

"That's right, but I'm not –"

"Take him." The officer said to his partner, a scrawny blonde man who I could've easily pounded with one fist to the jaw.

But obeying my better judgment, I understood that the charge I'd be receiving would be lighter in comparison to aggravated assault on an officer.

As they escorted me to the cop car and guided me into the backseat, I sat in silence as my brain screamed.

An influx of questions accumulated in my skull, thoughts and concerns of the worst possible outcome. I'd never been to jail, fuck I'd avoided this for years and never got caught.

I swear to fuck if someone from Cid's ratted on me cause of that fight, some goddamn bystander who didn't know the half of what I'd been through – but how... how did anyone know my licence plate number? Who the fuck would've paid any attention to...

Flashes of painful reminders bore into my brain; Bambi helping me tune up my truck, loading tool kits into the bed, laughing in my passenger seat as she reorganized my glove compartment.

Bambi.

She knew my licence plate. She was the only one. She tried to stop me from driving off.

She...

The metallic taste of blood filled my mouth as I clipped the tip of my tongue, my nails digging into the creases of my palm.

A sharp pain lodged itself in my chest at the realization of what I knew was true.

Bambi was responsible for my current position.

Bambi put me in the back of a cop car.

Bambi...

She was exactly what I knew her to be.

And now, she was a memory to burn.

My chest heaved as I rested my head against the cold concrete walls of the holding cell.

I'd been sitting in this damn block for nearly two hours until a commotion broke out in the hallway and my dad plowed through the door.

"I paid the damn bail, now get him out Pat."

The bald cop in a blue and grey uniform took out a set of jangly keys and clicked open the bars, allowing me to pass.

As we walked through the sheriff's office, a few whispers floated through the cramped space, fading off as I exited the building.

My dad's truck was parked smack dab in the center of the lot, still running as he stepped inside and slammed the door.

Fuck, this isn't going to be good.

I followed suit and slumped down into the passenger seat, my buzz completely exiled from my brain as I stared forward.

My dad's stare bled into my skull as he turned onto the dark road, grunting in agitation.

Let's just get this over with. "Dad –"

"No." He interrupted curtly. "Not a word outta your mouth, boy."

I cracked my jaw, forcing my head forward as he unleashed his fuckin' wrath on me.

"You know what I did for you back there? I paid your five hundred dollar fine to get you out of a goddamn jail cell! You hear that?

"What the fuck is with you? You hit your head or somethin'? Think you can just go around getting arrested without it tainting my name? Payton's?"

"I talked down Sherriff Cordon to a sixty day licence suspension and four demerit points. But you're workin' off that five hundred dollars and your keys stay with me, Hunter. You hear me?"

I clenched my fists in attempt to keep my cool as I grumbled out in response. "Yeah, got it."

My dad's head hung low as he drove, glaring at me occasionally before he snapped once more.

"You're lucky that boy at Cid's didn't press charges. Marley vouched for you, sayin' he was harassing her and if it wasn't for you she would've socked him herself."

"*Don't,*" I spat. "Don't say her fuckin' name to me again."

His bemused laugh filled my ears, painting a real pretty picture of death in my goddamn mind.

"She ain't to blame and you fuckin' know it."

"I've been driving drunk for years! Never been caught for fuck's sake and she strides into my life and now I don't got a license!"

His hand slammed against the wheel. "Are you fucked in the head, boy? What the hell is wrong with you? You're lucky I didn't tell Cordon 'bout your dumb ass stunts cause you'd be rottin' with the rest of the low lives in prison right now!"

Anger. Heat. Rage, that's all I fucking felt. All I allowed myself to feel. I got no truck, nowhere to go, a prisoner of my own home and a disappointment to my family once more.

All the progress I'd made, the smiles I'd shared, the laughs I let out, all of that – six feet under. Fed to the worms.

All because of her.

I tuned out my dad's incessant beratement as I shut my eyes and allowed the darkest parts of my mind to consume me once more. I lived in the shallow end of the water, but slowly, slowly I dove deeper. Deeper, and deeper until I hit the bottom of the sea and I couldn't be pulled up. Unsalvageable, wrecked and ruined.

Marley, you're fucking dead to me.

Chapter Twenty-Nine
Adam

The congested New York City air polluted my lungs as I stepped into the front garden of Darlington Circuit, where my parents resided.

I debated whether or not to leave my car running, praying to the gods above that this meeting wouldn't be long, but all the rational parts of me assumed the worst.

A shame to declare dinner with your parents a meeting, though there was no other way to call it. Everything was a meeting to the Matthews. Brunch, lunch, tea-time, boating, barbecues... endless opportunities to talk business, no room for updates on the wellbeing of their children.

When I found out my mother was fabricating the real reason Marley ran off, I was beside myself with frustration. Had she truly abandoned her life here to live with another man in a different state, I'd have no qualms with the fact. Would I have approved of her life choices? Probably not considering it was so sporadic and quite honestly, random.

But my mother, *our* mother spewed lies to make her seem less than the human she was... the irony in that. And where was my dad in all this? Gone, probably off in a separate area of New York dealing cards with the higher ups of every company he somehow managed to co-own.

I checked my watch: **5:32pm**, and rang the doorbell which alerted a series of chimes and jingles.

Not a moment too soon, my mother appeared dressed in an egg-white dress with matching heels, her brown hair puffed and curled to her shoulders.

"You're early, Adam." She released, kissing me on the cheek.

"Better early than late. You taught me that."

She wore a prideful simper as she shut the door behind her, leading me into the dining room with large glass windows and a crystal chandelier.

I hadn't been back to my parents' place since Marley left. The biggest parts of me were devastated that she'd fled, but more than anything it felt wrong being back here without my baby sister.

The memories we'd created in this home, only us in the absence of our parents, were spectacular. We managed to cut corners, hide in vents, create our own little world amongst the snoots and riches.

"Will Michelle be joining us later?" She asked, taking her usual seat at the table with a glass of wine.

"Will dad?" I combatted.

She placed down her drink and threw me a side-eye. "What kind of question is that, Adam?"

"An honest one. He's never here."

"*Never* is a strong word."

I rolled my eyes and folded my jacket over the back of my seat, cuffing my sleeves as I sat down across my mom.

"Is he here then? I have some things I want to discuss with you both."

She twirled the diamond rock on her ring finger as she looked through me, never at me. I don't remember a time where she did.

A part of me always envied Marley for diversifying herself to the wonders of life, even more so now that she was miles and miles away from this atrocity of a family. To my parents, I'd always been the golden boy. And for that, they put even more pressure on Marley to maintain my interests.

But that was just the issue they could never comprehend. Her interests and mine were never aligned. Marley and I were two peas in a pod growing up, though we were always different flavours, different colours.

Did she make mistakes? Of course. Was I here to condemn her for them? No. That has never been my place and would never be. I understood the choices she made, even more so now with the new information I was given.

I worked on Wall Street as a credit analyst, and where I loved my job and the perks it came with, a part of me was never content with myself at the end of the day. It was such a 'woe is me' mentality to have, considering the life I possessed was wonderful.

My beautiful wife was pregnant with our first baby girl, we were both successful in our own fields, living in a city bursting with potential, and yet... I was incomplete.

Marley was the yin to my yang, the more wild and eccentric counterpart to my personality. I'd take joy out of living vicariously through the untameable stories she'd tell me about.

Although the goal for me was never to live in the wealth and prosperity of my parents' approval, no, I always wanted a rural life. I thrived by myself, in the silence and serenity of my tiny corners and hidden offices.

That's why I loved Michelle so much. She understood how much quiet time I needed, and that alone was a huge reason I married her.

When you grow up, you find that the people you meet are considerably different. Sometimes, you take it personally when those people fail to understand who you are when in reality, they have no reason to. They owe you nothing.

Michelle was the first person that saw my quietness, and mirrored it even with her busy lifestyle.

My parents on the other hand? Well, there was a valid reason why I rarely visited them.

The sharp taps of my dad's oxfords bounced out of the hall and into the dining room as he took a seat opposite my mom and me, pouring himself a glass of red.

"Hello Adam."

My father, Mike Matthews was as shiny as a polished shoe. To say he got a rise out of me was an understatement. He practically threw me into finance without my say, and took me under his wing against my will.

"Dad." I responded, flatly.

"The chicken should be ready in just a few minutes, dear." My mother said, placing her hand over his.

I scoffed in disbelief, adjusting my tie to keep me from losing my temper. "I don't eat meat, Mom, I told you this."

"I beg your pardon?" She questioned.

"When did you decide this?" My dad added, baffled.

"Since Michelle and I got together two years ago?"

It always amazed me when they did this. It was as if everything that didn't directly concern them was a waste of memory, and they'd continue to do it and blame the fact that it was never brought to their attention. Heaven forbid they had any fault.

My dad's features soured as he took another sip of wine. "If she wasn't carrying our grandchild, I'd call her a menace. Who converts their husband to vegetarianism?"

"*Our* grandchild? You mean *my* daughter? Does it always have to be you before everyone else?"

His knuckles whitened as he eyed me with distaste, but I interrupted him before he could erupt.

"Don't bother with a plate, I'm not staying for dinner." I pushed out of my seat and dressed myself once again. "My reason for coming has to do with Marley entirely."

My mother looked to my father with disgust, sharpening her grin as she jeered. "What of her?"

I turned to my dad who shared a similar expression. "Are you not going to say anything?"

"I'm withholding my comments." He steamed, crossing his suited arms over his chest.

Enough of this. "You had no right to tip off Todd Sherman. You know he has a broken nose because of the stunt you pulled?"

My dad cracked a smile, amused at the thought of a defenceless person being attacked. "That must have been the most pivotal moment of that man's life."

"Your daughter dated him."

"And she was not bright in doing so." He snapped.

Rage boiled within my veins as I analyzed the two robots sitting before me, surrounded by gold with iron hearts.

"Call off the P.I. now. It's wrong and you have no right to be doing this to her."

My mother stood up, baring her teeth. "I gave birth to her, she'd have no life if it weren't for me and I will do as I please."

I took a step back, realizing how corrupt and inhumane my parents turned out to be and made my way for the front door.

"Then I'll do as I please, Mom."

Pulling out my phone, I rang Killian Gladstone, Michelle's brother who worked as an officer for the NYPD and put in a report.

"Adam?" He answered, surprised. "I don't have a lot of time but –"

"It won't take long. I need you to look into a private investigator hired by Harlow and Mike Matthews."

"Your... parents?" He asked, seemingly confused.

"Hang up the phone, right now, Adam!" My mother stormed, attempting to swat it out of my hands.

"Just do it, Killian. I'll explain later."

I hung up and shoved the cell in my back pocket, stepping up to her frail stature with intimidation.

"You lied to me, Mom. You told me Marley wanted nothing to do with this family, that she was living out on the streets by choice. You lied to me, and you didn't bat an eyelash doing it."

I turned my attention to my dad and held out a pointed finger. "And you, Dad, you should be ashamed of yourself. You don't prioritize anything but your work and your money, never us. Never once did I see a piece of your kindness."

He glared at me with hostility, his nostrils flaring as he contorted with rage. "You're cut from your inheritance."

And in that moment, I let out a laugh of sheer and utter madness as I flipped off my own father and stepped out of the manor.

I settled behind the wheel of my Mercedes as my dad bolted out of the house in a state of delirium, breathless and savage. "You aren't getting a penny out of me! You garbage, waste of a son! *You are the –*"

But I pressed on the gas and drove. I veered out of the gated garden with a pang in my chest, a feeling of despondency but most of all... peaceful anticipation. Anticipation that my baby sister would somehow feel at ease after I mentioned the news, because I sure did.

I burned the final bridge between me and my parents, something I should've done from the second they put me on that godforsaken paleo diet.

Took me long enough.

Chapter Thirty
Marley

"And just to finalize, you would like to add a fifteen percent discount to any customers driving more than one hour to their nearest P&D location?"

I wonder what Hunter's doing with all his spare time. Payton told me he got his license taken away for the next two months so at least he isn't driving drunk anymore. But she wouldn't tell me anything else. Probably for the best. His new favourite hobby most definitely included throwing darts at a picture of my face.

"Ms. Matthews?"

My head raised in attention as I focused on our client supervisor in charge of several P&D branches across the state. "Finalize... um, yeah. Fifteen percent off regular price and ten off sale, Mr. Dexond."

His lips pressed into a thin line as he signed off on a paper and pushed another towards me.

"Ms. Matthews, I'm an old friend of Mr. Lane and I would highly appreciate that next time you agree to a meeting, should you appear as their representative, to come less *preoccupied.*"

I forced out a sugary smile and slid the agreement papers into my orange file folder, stepping out of Garett Dexond's home office and retreated to my car.

He definitely wasn't my favourite person to work with, but he did the job right. Everything was kept in line; he handled payment transfers, returns, inventory, all of the daunting tasks none of us really wanted to do ourselves.

Plus, him and Dex used to be neighbours growing up and they'd stayed in touch all throughout their lives. Dex was a hard cookie to crack so if he trusted someone, I did too.

I pulled out of the freshly paved driveway and started for my place, ruminating on the last two months of my life; all the moments I'd shared with Hunter that were tainted by my decision.

Three days ago I decided to call the police on him. Three days ago I wept in my room about it, worried for him, for others driving on that road. I sat by my bed all night until Payton gave me an update that he was okay, and the charges weren't as severe as they could have been.

When the cops questioned me about Todd and Hunter's violent outburst, I blatantly explained the situation from the start of our relationship to the end.

My own mother was stalking me through a private investigator I had no idea about, which alone was an infringement of my rights and privacy so that was noted down. I defended Hunter not just for his sake, but for mine as well. Had he not intervened when he did, I most likely would've slapped the shit out of Todd and I admitted that to the authorities. He was harassing me when he shouldn't have even known my whereabouts, and that alone was enough for Todd to run scared back to Lincoln without pressing charges.

As I pulled into my parking spot at The Atlas Aurora, I settled on the fact that all intentions were pure that night. At least on my part. What Hunter did was wrong, and maybe even Todd deserved to be taught a lesson, but not by Hunter's fist.

Todd showing up at Cid's was completely uncalled for, and the things that were spewing out of his mouth were demeaning and horrible, but Hunter didn't have the cleanest track record with me either.

I could've handled Todd, once I snapped out of my paralysis and actually regained my composure. But Hunter didn't even give me a chance. To him, violence was the answer, and quite honestly, the last place I wanted to be that night was beside either of them.

But when I looked into Hunter's eyes, there was nothing. It's like a demon possessed his soul or something and I knew by the way he looked at me that he didn't care. Not about me, or anyone, especially himself.

So when he got into that truck and drove off after six glasses of whisky, I knew what I had to do. Punching in those three little numbers scarred me, turning in someone I cared for... God, he had every reason to be upset at me. But he couldn't hate me for this, he couldn't.

Did he not realize how much of a hazard he was to the rest of the town? What if someone was driving along that backroad and he swerved into them? What if he killed innocent people because of his reckless behaviour? Did he even give a shit about that? Did he even *think*?

I focused on my breathing, rubbing my temples together as I leaned against my seat. "You did the right thing, Marley. You did the right thing."

Now I just have to believe that before I show up with a fruit basket begging for his forgiveness.

"Hey Mar, I'm on break so I can't talk too long. What's up?" Adam answered, his soothing voice filling the line as I cozied into bed.

"I just wanted to thank you for confronting Mom. I don't think I properly expressed my gratitude over text."

"It's the least I could do, Mar. They aren't right in the head. I mean, I don't think they ever were but our parents got a screw loose somewhere, I swear."

We both shared a laugh as I bit the tip of my fingernail, exhaling an admission.

"I think I'm going insane."

"Well, you aren't."

"No, Adam, tell me honestly." I sat up from my position and adjusted my posture against the headboard. "Did I do the right thing? Calling the cops on Hunter?"

He sighed. "Marley, the guy went ballistic on Todd. I don't care if he's Jesus reincarnated, that man should be locked up."

I felt my temperature rising at his poor assessment, but I shoved it down low due to the fact Adam didn't know Hunter like I did.

"He has a lot going on, Adam..."

His scoff was apparent as he cleared his throat. "That doesn't excuse him for beating someone senseless. You should know that."

"I do." *I knew that.* "You're right."

"Listen, you did the right thing. Todd's out of your life, hopefully for good now. Hunter's hopefully going to learn from this and stay out of your hair as well. And Mom and Dad are taken care of."

Hunter's hopefully going to learn from this and stay out of your hair as well... Did I want that? After everything that happened between us, did I really want this friendship gone? I didn't, I knew it couldn't end with him hating me because of the choice I made. It was for the good of everyone else, especially him. No, it couldn't end like this. I wouldn't let it.

"He isn't a bad guy, you know. Hunter." I faltered, feeling a pang of guilt residing in my chest.

"Why do you care about this guy so much, Marley? From everything you told me, he never made you feel welcome at all. You said from the second you got to Aurora, he was arrogant and selfish."

I opened my mouth to speak but quiet chatter rang through Adam's end of the phone, forcing me to zip my lips.

"Mar, I got to get back to work. Text you later, okay? I love you."

He hung up just as I released those three words, filling my room with silence once again. Me and my thoughts, me and my regrets, me and my wrong freaking doings.

God, why couldn't he react like a normal person? Why couldn't he just talk to me about the way he was feeling in the moment and we could have hashed it out. Why was he so aggressive when things went wrong? What went down between me and Todd didn't even involve him for goodness sakes. And why, WHY did he think it was a good idea to get into his truck and drive drunk?

I sat in my emotions for a little while until curiosity got the best of me and I pulled open my laptop. Hunter never mentioned what caused the death of his mom, and I never wanted to ask. Honestly, I was afraid to find out and I didn't trust myself to hold it together the next time he mentioned her. So I held off, until now.

When the Google search bar popped up, I typed in the name: Hunter Lane, clicking enter to find over a hundred results with articles and photos.

My eyes widened as I scrolled through countless headlines that read: TRAGIC CAR CRASH. THREE SURVIVORS, ONE DEAD.

And another: WIFE AND MOTHER, LESLIE LANE, AGED 46, FOUND DECEASED IN COLLISION.

And another, and another: TINTSY ROAD TRAGEDY. THE LOSS OF A LOVED ONE.

My heart hammered in my chest as I circled through images of the woman I'd seen in Hunter's picture frame, her smiling face that was once alive and beautiful, to an obituary sharing that exact same image.

As I read along the articles, I found a written interview between a journalist and Hunter a few weeks after the crash.

Q: **"How is your family coping with the loss of your mother, Hunter?"**

H: "It's tough."

Q: **"You're only twenty-one years old, a promising young athlete drafted to play baseball for Iowa State. Do you think this will hinder your ability to participate this season?"**

H: "I think my mom would want me to keep moving forward. She wouldn't want me to stay stuck in her loss. She always used to say that pain was a necessity to life, and to keep your head up when it was falling down."

Q: "**What amazing advice. Leslie will be missed, as such a prominent part of this community. I cannot even imagine what you and your father must be going through. Is it just you two remaining?**"

H: "Yeah. Me and my dad."

I shut my laptop closed, feeling the anchor in my chest sinking deeper and deeper into the most fragile parts of my soul. Tears blurred my vision as I recounted all of the times Hunter mentioned his mom, all in the most heart-warming ways and I allowed the sadness to break.

This was four years ago. Four years ago he was involved in the crash of his mother, and from the articles it said he only withstood minor injuries while his mother died right then and there.

A drunk driver lost control of his wheel and smashed into their truck, sending it rolling over the ditch on Tintsy road.

And Hunter... he managed to call the paramedics while his mother was bleeding out inches away from him. He saw it all, he was a direct witness to the loss of his own mother. Saw her take her last breaths, mouth her last words... all towards him.

My heart broke for Hunter, my *everything* broke for him. I couldn't imagine what he went through in that moment, what thoughts were racing through his head. And now I understood, I understood why he became this cold, broken person.

No one, at any age, should ever experience seeing their parent die in such a horrendous way. Not even the strongest warriors could battle that pain and come out unscathed. Hunter was reckless, drank himself into oblivion, jeopardized the relationships around him because a part of him already died with his mother.

And now I understood.

Why he got behind the wheel of his truck that night without question. Why he was rash and careless and incautious. He didn't care about life, he blamed it. His soul wasn't redeemable because he deemed himself irreparable.

But the one thing I couldn't grasp, the only thing that weighed heavy in my brain was the reason behind his drunk driving. Why would he want to re-enact the exact scene that killed his mother, by being the driver himself? What the hell was the purpose of that? Did he want to torture himself more? Why would he jeopardize other people when he knew the possibilities of a deadly outcome?

God he was broken. Hunter Lane was so broken.

He was a jumbled mess, living inside a labyrinth he created, and he only found peace in a few things: Josh, his dad, painting his boats, drinking and... me. *Not anymore.*

Now I knew why he valued the people in his life so much. He lost someone so important to him, he didn't want to go through that again. He didn't take those closest to him for granted even though he was a pain in the ass sometimes. He wanted his dad to care the way he used to before his mother passed away. He wanted to accept Payton but he couldn't, because anyone he let in was a chance at loss.

But he let me in.

And only now did I realize the severity of my own actions.

He chose to let me in, and I fucked it up.

How the hell am I going to fix something completely beyond repair?

Chapter Thirty-One
Hunter

I unlocked my front door for Britt six times in the past two weeks.

Six times she's come in here, letting me fuck out my frustration, playing with her as I pleased.

Tonight was no exception, and the good hospitality could go fuck itself. I was half a bottle of Jack down, craving something pretty to entertain me. And that blonde haired bombshell standing in my living room was just the thing.

She dropped her black coat to the ground, revealing a matching set of silk panties and a bright red bra that exposed her perky pink nipples.

I sat back in my bed, stroking my cock as she smirked, unclasping her bra so I could revel at the sight of her tits.

My breathing hitched as my dick hardened to Britt's rounded breasts, making me ache and angry all at once.

I growled in frustration. "Walk over here right fuckin' now sweetheart, don't make me ask again."

"Ask nicely," she toyed.

Fucking woman. "I come in you, on you, or by myself. Don't fuck with me, not now."

And like the good girl she was, she obeyed and sauntered over, straddling me as I pulled her down for a kiss.

As soon as my tongue slid into her mouth, I tasted the mint she'd been sucking on and drew it into mine.

"Want to do me a favour while I finish this for you, darlin'?" I smirked, trailing a light finger down her spine.

Without protest, she planted a path of kisses down my abdomen until her juicy lips reached the head of my cock.

I groaned in pleasure as she enveloped me into her mouth, bobbing her head up and down with ease.

"Fuck, baby..." I gripped her hair in my hands, lifting my hips to push further into her mouth.

She gripped my ass and continued to suck, her moans doing unthinkable things to my mind.

When I felt my climax getting closer, I yanked her off my dick and cupped her chin, lacing my tongue against hers as I pushed her onto my bed and tore her thong in two.

"Hunt –"

But I didn't let her finish that fucking sentence. My tongue dove inside of her as I pushed the tip of my finger into her ass, penetrating both holes with all the might I fuckin' had.

She cried out in pleasure, grabbing onto my hair as I sucked on her clit, using my other hand to wiggle two fingers in and out of her pussy.

"Don't call me *Hunty*. Ever. Again." I spat, positioning myself on top of her as I reached for the condom atop my bedside table, pulled it on and thrusted my cock into her.

Her heavy pants filled the air as she cooed my name, properly this fucking time. Lifting her legs over my shoulders, I rolled my hips into her, thumbing her clit as I watched her tits bounce.

"I'm coming, baby!" She whined.

One step ahead of you. My dick had one more pump left before I swiped it out and busted in the dome.

I leaned down to kiss her, holding a finger up so she stayed put as I fetched a ball of tissue paper and wiped up my remaining cum.

As I made my way to the bathroom, I heard her high-pitched voice calling. "Come to bed, Hunter, I already miss you!"

A fuckin' trade off this situation was. When I agreed to fuck Britt again, I made myself entirely clear. No relationship, no goodnight texts, none of that shit. After sex, she always got snuggly and I wasn't about it.

No, I'd never shove her off but I wanted my damn peace and quiet. She was anything but.

Though she was a beautiful distraction, and it felt nice to have someone around now that I was always by myself.

My dad couldn't tolerate my presence for more than five minutes and Payton didn't know how to look at me without mentioning Marley's fuckin' name. Why? I wish I knew. It'd save me a lot of wasted thoughts and energy on that bratty brunette who messed with my life.

Just a month and a half left and I could regain my place out in the world. Mind you I'd be banned from Cid's until I had the time to hash it out with Sheldon, Cid's son who took over the business when he retired.

Sheldon was never around anyways since he settled in Omaha. He collected his payout, heard stories through the grapevine and returned back to his little world without ever saying a damn thing.

Kenton, the bartender, he was usually in charge when Sheldon wasn't around but he would totally vouch for me. I mean, he heard that fucking moron talking to Marley. If he had any balls, he would've done the same thing I'd done.

No, there was no way in hell I was going to let her take away my spot. The spot I'd been to for years before she came to Aurora. She fucked up my life in such a short amount of time; who knew that such a miniscule being could carry a stage five shitstorm inside her.

I took a sweep of my appearance in the bathroom mirror, admiring the way my physical strength was building since I had all the free time in the world to workout.

After brushing my teeth and splashing cold water on my face, I settled into bed beside Britt who was luckily out cold, the smell of sex floating through the air.

My palms pressed against the cold wall as I inhaled a breath, drifting off to the thought of big brown eyes. Only this time they weren't looking up at me...

They were looking down.

After my hike with Josh, we decided to hit up Blu's ice cream parlor for some half priced shakes. Wednesdays were always discounted menu items, and I was craving something cold.

"Can I try yours?" Josh asked, sipping some light pink foam out of his straw.

"Fuck no, you got your own."

He pouted, staring at the strawberry cotton candy toothache in his cup. "Yours is better, Hunt. It's always better."

I smirked with pride. "You're damn right about that."

The Square wasn't usually this busy in the afternoon, but they had some flea market thing going on downtown so the streets were bustling with people. *The worst outcome imaginable.*

"You know how many kids I gotta dodge when this fruity bullshit goes on?" I cursed, pointing to the pack of tents conglomerated in a circle.

"Lighten up, man. It's all for fun and –" his words cut abruptly as he drew my arm and spun me around.

I yanked out of his grasp and continued my original pace, walking the path I had been earlier. "The fuck's your problem, man?"

"Hunt," he chastised. "Don't make a scene."

"What are you –"

Ha-ha. Oh fuck. Oh fuckin' fuck now I got it.

Walking towards the flea market was Marley and Winter, arms linked with a gleeful grin on their faces. My jaw tightened as they came nearer, and she halted her movements at my recognition.

I swallowed hard, attempting to control the rage boiling inside of me as her brown eyes met mine, pleading and innocent but hidden with malice. Malice she concealed so well that it blindsided me for months.

"Hunter, if you're gon' walk, just walk." Josh dragged my arm once more but I shrugged off his hold.

"I'll walk on my own, damnit." I snapped.

Winter huddled closer to Marley as if I were a gunman on the loose and she needed protection. No, Marley was the fuckin' villain here, not me. Guess she got Winter wrapped around her finger too.

We were close now, close enough where I caught a whiff of lavender and honey, the scent I used to soak in when she was near. But now, it was a tainted reminder of all the bullshit she had on me. The memories I wish I could ravage and destroy, all because of her.

I was passing her now. *Just keep walking, Hunter. Head up, eyes straight. Walk on, walk on, walk –*

"Hunter..."

Her voice. Her fucking innocent Bambi voice; it caught me like a deer in the headlights when that was supposed to be her. Not me, *HER.*

"Hunt," Josh gripped my sleeve and I broke.

"See that bin, Josh? Yeah, the bin next to Cleaver's? I'll throw ya in that fuckin' bin if you put your hands on me one more time."

"Man, you need to fucking relax." He shot, turning his attention to Marley as she stood now inches away from me. "Babe, now's not a good time to be talkin' to him, alright? Just go on off, enjoy your day."

But like usual, Marley didn't listen and proceeded against Josh's warning.

"Hunter, can we talk? Please? I have so much to say and I –"

Bite your tongue. Bite your fuckin' tongue. "Are you fucked?" *Well, there goes that.*

Her eyes widened as she scorned me with chocolate eyes. "Excuse me?"

I took a step closer, towering over her baby carrot physique and let out a husky laugh. "You really think you can talk to me after the shit you pulled?"

"She was doing the right thing." Winter combatted, lodging herself between Marley and me.

My gaze shifted to the firecracker in front of me, fighting Marley's battles, covering up the coward behind her.

"With all due respect, Winter, I'm not fuckin' talkin' to you."

"Buddy –" Josh tried.

"Back up, Josh."

Marley placed a hand over Winter's shoulder and faced me head on, glaring at me with daggers. The look she first gave me when I met her. *There she is.*

"This is between you and I, so don't talk to her that way."

I shrugged, unfazed. "She addressed me, I addressed her. No harm done."

"You don't understand, do you? Why I called the cops on you that night?"

I clenched my fist, remembering my dad ripping me a new one in the car, Payton's uneasy stares and the bottles and bottles of alcohol I'd devoured in the past fourteen days because of her. Nowhere to go, nowhere to run. Stuck. Stuck. Stuck.

"What I understand, *Marley*, is that you were exactly the girl I always knew you to be. And I'm to blame, *me*." I placed a twitchy palm over my heart. "Because I was dumb enough to think any different."

A glossy sheen covered her eyes as her lip quivered in response. "*Marley*."

That was all she said. All she said before she turned right around without her friend by her side, and walked away.

She left. She fucking left.

Winter flipped me the bird as she jogged after her, but Marley continued to walk like a ghost without a head. An empty shell, shoulders hung low, as she disappeared into the crowd.

I was up to my neck in emotion, heat, anger, pain. A lot of fucking pain as I stood in my spot and watched, waited for her to re-emerge from the crowd but she never did. She never showed her face again, as if her face was never there at all.

My eyes aimlessly searched the throng of people. What for? What the fuck for? She was the one who fucking destroyed me! Played with my emotions, got close to me just to crush me, and ruin me and fucking wreck me!

I wanted to scream at the top of my lungs, I wanted to bury something, hit something, drive off a cliff and land on a goddamn spike because this feeling was shit. It was shit and I needed to get out of here.

"I don't give a rat's ass if you're listenin' to me right now, Hunt. But whatever hope that girl had, just now, you crushed. And whether you're happy with that decision, not mine to speak on. But that was outta line."

I turned my back to the horde at the flea market and stalked away, shutting out the sound of laughter and happiness emanating from The Square.

"She deserved it." I said to myself. I convinced myself. I tortured myself.

"She deserved it."

"She put me in this position."

"She fucked me up."

"She fucked me up!"

I said it again, and again, and again until the anger seeped through my veins and infiltrated my skull. *Comfort at last.*

I had to say something.

I needed to.

Otherwise my heart would take control, and I'd go running back into that crowd to find *Bambi* in a heartbeat.

Chapter Thirty-Two
Marley

Words couldn't describe how badly that hurt.

It sounded absolutely ridiculous; the fact that I spent every night this past week thinking about how Hunter called me by my real name, instead of Bambi.

At first, I thought the nickname was freaking irritating. But after a while, I almost caught myself smiling every time it left his lips.

Marley just didn't sound right coming from him. From the day we met, he'd branded me with something personal, something entirely his. And now it was nothing. He was done with me, and that much I knew.

When I saw Hunter that day, exactly seven days ago, Winter and I were actually talking about him on the way to the flea market. And clearly, my mind had manifested him popping up because there he was with Josh, sprightly as ever.

That was until he saw me.

Hunter had been cold before, stand-offish and intimidating but this... this was an entirely different case. He was ruthless, cruel, impossible. There was nothing I could've done differently that would have gotten through to him.

Looking back on it now, it was a complete waste of an altercation. My words carried zero merit and I just had to accept that he wouldn't listen to me... well, not verbally anyway.

I'd been sitting on this idea for the past forty-eight hours. Was it a good one? No, probably not. Once again, it would most likely be a complete waste of my time but I couldn't drop it. I couldn't drop him.

After finding out about his mother, I just wanted to help him. Maybe I was the bitter apple in all of this, but I was positive that if I got through to him one last time, I wouldn't let him slip. He was deeply troubled, and he needed someone. I don't know why I wanted to be that person but I did, and I wasn't apologizing for it.

Growing up, I always wanted to change the discomfort in my life. My parents, friends, all of my toxic ex's; I felt like I could bring something to the table. I fell in love with the idea of love and they just happened to be the accessory I was using. So naturally, I made them something special even if they weren't.

Hunter wasn't like this. I despised him at first, everything about him. I didn't want to get to know him, didn't want to be in the same room as him. But after months of grovelling and painstakingly horrid interactions, we'd managed to build something substantial.

Through it all, I wouldn't have changed a thing. I saw the bad parts of him and I accepted them. Only that was the problem – he didn't. To Hunter, everything human about him was an issue to be solved, but he didn't know how to move forward. Truthfully, I don't know that he even wanted to.

But I wanted him to. I couldn't see this fall. So I decided to put my plan in action, and I sat on my bed. Tearing out a sheet of paper from my notebook, I grabbed my pen and I began to write. *If he won't listen to my voice, maybe he'll listen to my words.*

Dear Hunter Lane,

This is weird, I know. I don't really know what to say all things considered. But I just... I need to talk to you. I know technically by me writing this letter we aren't actually having a conversation, but this is the closest thing to it so here I am.

I just wanted to start off by saying I'm sorry. Not sorry for calling the police, but sorry for what happened to you and your mother. I did it, Hunter. I caved and I researched what happened the night of your mom's death and my heart breaks for you in every single way.

I don't blame you for the things that you've done, or whatever bad habits you currently do. I will however say that I am never going to apologize for reporting your drunk driving because what you did was dangerous and callous. But I feel like with each passing day, I start to see your layers unravel.

I'm not scared of you, Hunter. I know you try and conceal all the best parts of you, but I don't know why you do. These past two months have been sunlight in my freaking soul and you smiled and laughed and you showed me ~~weakness~~ vulnerability and I think that's why you hate me so much right now.

You think I betrayed you, you think I purposely ruined our ~~relationship~~ friendship for the gain of something. I don't understand why you think everyone is out to get you, or intentionally tries to sabotage the good you have in your life.

That was never the case with me, Hunter. I don't want you to feel ashamed of shining. I don't want you to believe you aren't worthy of love or light or happiness. I want you to free yourself from the chains holding you back.

I read in one interview that your mom used to say that pain is a part of life, and she wouldn't want you to stay stuck in her loss. She'd want you to keep moving forward. What happened to the man that wanted that for himself?

Where did you go, Hunter?

Anyway, I'm not writing you this letter to make you feel like shit or hurt you further. I just want you to realize that people care about you and I ~~cared~~ care about you. You can talk to me whenever you want. However long it takes, I'll be here.

P.S: Find it in your heart to start calling me Bambi again. I hate the way you say Marley, it's icky.

Bambi

Chapter Thirty-Three
Hunter

Payton brought me six letters over the past two months. Six all from Marley.

The first four times she was optimistic, knocking at my front door with a wide smile on her face.

"Marley sent another one." She'd said, gripping tightly of the tiny white envelopes, hope flooding her eyes.

All four times I'd taken them, crumpled them up right in front of her and shut the door.

I wasn't trying to take my anger out on Payton, but she was a direct link to the NYC brat who condemned me to a shallow life for two months, so I needed to send a message.

But tonight, tonight was the night I'd be free of the shackles and could reintegrate into society. Society being Cid's Pub, that is.

After speaking to Kenton over the phone, he said he did in fact hear what that fuck face said to Marley and scratched me off the bar ban. *Bartenders weren't made for fighting, Hunters on the other hand...*

Josh and I got to Cid's at nine, scoring the last table available on a Friday night.

"Happy to be back?" He asked, stretching out his arms.

I glanced around the crowded room, spying all the drunks back and better than ever. Or they were always the same and I never took in the moment like I should've. *That's what happens when you take advantage of things; you never appreciate the beauty of 'em when they're right in front of you.* And Cid's, my oh my was she fuckin' fine.

"The happiest," I replied.

I began updating Josh on the approaching harvest season when a waitress came up to our table, dressed in a white tank top and black leggings. Her face was a bit forgettable but her red hair wasn't, and that's when I instantly recognized her as the server who brought us drinks on New Year's Eve.

I remember that night like it was yesterday. Bambi, fuck – *Marley*, Marley was in my fuckin' head again. She'd only been here six months and everywhere I went was a goddamn reminder.

"Haven't seen ya in a while, Hunter." She smiled, sliding out her notepad.

"How d'you know me?" I poised, scanning her head to toe.

She threw me an *'are you serious'* expression and shook her head as I shrugged.

"You beat a guy up once and all of a sudden you're the talk of the town."

Josh bubbled in laughter as the waitress chuckled to herself.

"I wasn't workin' that night, but Kenton gave me the run down. Don't blame ya, sugar."

The corner of my lips curved into a smile as I scooted closer to the edge of the booth. "I kinda like you."

She pet my shoulder and threw me a golden grin. "I got a boyfriend over seas, and Britt claimed ya. Good effort though, Hunter. Drinks?"

I grumbled in annoyance as Josh ordered two whiskey's and four shots of Jager.

The waitress tapped the table with her long acrylics and headed off to the staff quarters. I didn't mean to flirt, it just came out of me. And hey, if she decided to give me a go I wouldn't have refused but I respected the loyalty.

"Jager tastes like tar, man." I released, taking a glance around the room. I couldn't shake the feeling that someone was watching me, or following me or some shit. It was weirding me out.

"Tastes like liquorice to me." Josh combatted. "When you gettin' your truck back?"

"I just got to change my tires then I'm good to get the baby on the road."

Josh slapped my back, pushing my shoulder forward. "You know the saying '*April showers brings May flowers?*' Well, April showers brings Hunter Lane back – man of the fuckin' hour!"

I glared at him like he'd killed my hamster with a thumbtack. "That's was the dumbest shit I've ever heard."

"I couldn't think of a rhyme to save my damn life."

"Well if it really was life or death, you'd be dead." I bantered.

Zipping my head around, I surveyed the faces of the room, illuminated by the neon lights. *Man, who the fuck is staring at me?*

"Josh, I'm gon' get up right now and head to the bathroom. Text me if ya see someone following."

I didn't give him a chance to object as I stepped out of the booth and stalked towards the restroom hall.

When I reached the corridor, I leaned my back against the wall and unlocked my phone to find a text from Josh that read –

"Hunter."

My eyes met the girl named down in Josh's response. She was dressed in a beige dress, tight at the waist that flowed down her legs. Her dark hair was swooped up into a ponytail, exposing every contour of her bone structure.

"You've gotta be kiddin' me." I released, ready to retreat but she grabbed my hand.

I hadn't seen her since the day of the flea market, and while she did resemble herself, she didn't at all.

Every part of me wanted to stand and analyze the change I could see, but it wasn't physical, it was just... there was *something*.

Those tiny, bony fingers curled around my pinky as she begged me to stay even one second. In her right hand, she held an envelope, similar to the ones Payton had given me only this one was longer.

"I'm not goin' to read it, Marley." I started. "I haven't read the others, and I'm not gon' read this one."

After I crumpled each of her letters, I tossed it in my recycling box waiting to throw it out. But for some reason, I couldn't do it. I didn't have to read the damn things, but I'd be lying if I said it didn't pique my interest.

A single tear dripped down her cheek, leaving a white stain residue that separated her face makeup. *Christ.*

"If you do decide to read any of them, please read this one."

She let go of my hand and replaced it with the envelope, staring up at me with glossy chocolate eyes before moving out of the corridor.

I stood immobile for a few seconds before I snapped out of the goddamn spell I was under and shoved the envelope in my back pocket.

When I made it back to the booth, all our drinks were spread out on the table and Josh was full of fucking questions.

"Did you talk to her?"

"Yep."

"What did she say?" He pried.

"Nothin' important."

He stared in confusion, looking me up and down with squinted eyes.

"What the hell are you checkin' me out for? Let's drink." I tipped back a shot of dark liquid and scowled. "It's fuckin' tar, man. Try it."

But he didn't move a muscle. He just continued to glare at me with that dumb ass expression.

"Go on." I pushed.

"What'd she say to you, Hunt?"

"Damn it, Josh!" I slammed my palm on the table, rattling the glasses up top. "I don't want to fuckin' talk about her. I've talked about her enough, I've thought about her enough, I've had enough! I've had fuckin' enough."

My whisky was down in two seconds, and another shot, and another.

My first night of freedom, out at my favourite place and she showed up. Probably wanted to call the cops on my ass again, try and get me barred. *Damn woman.*

"She stormed outta here cryin', that's why I'm askin'."

"Let them tears fall, Josh." I grabbed his drink and drained it too. "Let 'em fall."

He scoffed, adjusting his position in the booth and pulled out his wallet, slapping two twenties on the table.

"Where the fuck are you goin'?" I ripped, strangling the glass in my hands.

He shook his head. "I get why she did what she did, and call me a piece of shit, call me nuts, call me whatever the fuck you want, Hunt. But that girl don't deserve to be cryin' over you."

My chest heaved with frustration as I watched Josh, my best friend, leave me to drink by myself on my first night out in two months.

I'd never felt so much anger towards one person, one girl before. Rebecca manipulated me, played with me, screwed with my emotions but this girl... *Marley*, she was a whole different ballgame.

She'd managed to turn my best friend, my stepmom and my own flesh and blood against me. My dad wouldn't even glance my way unless he was telling me what to do, where to put things, and how to fix shit up.

Somehow, I'd let her fall through my fingers and weed her way into my brain. She was lodged there, like a malignant tumor ready to kill me off. And she was winning. Winning by each second that I let out a breath.

No, she can't take this night away from me.

I drained the last remaining shot on the table and launched out of my booth, stalking towards the dance floor with my mission on lock.

Two beautiful women stood by the speaker next to a Billy Talent poster, ogling me from head to toe. I approached them both, twirling my fingers into theirs and dragged them to the dance floor.

Beauty number one grinded against my dick, shoving her perfect little ass in just the right spot. Beauty number two was tangled in her friend, leaning over her to plant sticky lips against my neck.

The blazing sound of club music scarfed the air, wrapping me in the euphoric pleasure of drunk fucking freedom. Just for one second, I let go and shoved the weight off my shoulders. For one second, I embraced the pain and burned it to ash, gripping beauty number one to my chest and kissing her with longing.

Finally.

For one goddamn second...

I was alive.

Chapter Thirty-Four
Marley

Tears waterfalled down my cheeks as I hugged Payton tightly.

I hadn't stopped crying for three days when I made the decision to move back home.

After sitting with myself, taking in all the events over the past few months, I realized that I needed to be with my brother.

Adam's wife Michelle just gave birth to their daughter, my *niece,* and I wanted to be as involved as I could in her life.

The majority of the work I did for P&D's was online, so after a heart wrenching conversation with Payton, we figured it would be absolutely possible to continue working in a different state.

Yes, I wouldn't be able to do run-in meetings, but the company had grown immensely since October last year and there were several employees who could fill that position.

Payton begged me to stay, and the biggest part of me wanted to for her. But I'd fixed things with my brother, Winter and Cramer were determined to make regular visits to NYC, and Dex was never my number one fan. Though when I did tell him I was leaving, his usual stone face softened just a tad, and that alone made the upset worse.

"Does..." I swallowed, choking on a sob. "Does Hunter know?"

Payton wiped her crusted, red nose and blew into a tissue. "I don't give a damn 'bout Hunter right now, Marley. I told you once before, I don't want no boy drivin' you outta this town and he did."

"Payton..."

He didn't. Hunter wasn't the reason why I was leaving Aurora. Did he contribute to my decision? Partially, yes... scratch that. *Big time.* But there were bigger things at stake and it was time I put myself first.

"No, I know, I know deary. I know why you're leavin', I just wish you weren't." Payton sniffed, pressing her lips into a sad smile.

I wasn't moving back to New York without a plan. My brother said I could stay with him and Michelle until I found my own apartment, but I did take it upon myself to call back the old company I worked for. After showing the results and sales increases on my behalf working for P&D's, they took me back in. Mind you, it was a different position and I needed to work my way back up but it was still reliable income.

"What time you leavin' tomorrow?" She asked, wiping mascara fibers off her lower lash line.

I squeezed her hand and struggled against tears. "I'm hoping to be on the road by noon."

"Noon, yah. Good time."

Gale, one of our newer employees knocked on the office door. "Hey, sorry to be a bother but a customer up front wants to talk about a return with ya, Payton."

Payton waved off Gale who quickly left the room and took languid steps towards the door before turning back to me and saying, "I'll see you before ya leave tomorrow. Don't you dare go without sayin' goodbye."

I nodded a promise and watched her exit the room, taking in the space we created and let the tears run free.

After a tearful ten minutes, I decided to head back to my car and finish the rest of my packing at home. But as I was crossing the parking lot, a familiar face made his way towards me.

"Josh?" I questioned, stopping in my tracks. *No Hunter in sight. Huh.*

He threw me a genial half smile, clearing his throat. "How you doin', Marley?"

My eyebrows furrowed in confusion, looking around the area to see if there was another Marley in sight but obviously not.

"I'm okay, Josh... are you okay?"

"Why wouldn't I be?" He chuckled.

"Well, I mean. I've never spoken to you without Hunter around, so I don't know... is there something you need?"

I realized that came across as kind of rude so I retracted my comment. "I didn't mean it like that, just, you came out of nowhere so."

"Yeah, kinda did."

We stood there awkwardly, saying nothing for a few moments before he spoke up again.

"Dex told me you're movin' back to New York?"

Dex told him that? Did that mean Hunter knew? Out of all people, why was Josh coming here to talk to me about that?

"I am, tomorrow. You've been around Dex?"

"Hunter's been... *busy*. So, Dex rang me up n' asked me to help out with the harvest. We got to talkin' and yah, mentioned you were leavin'."

A pinch of pain pierced my heart knowing that Hunter didn't care I was moving back home and he was off doing God knows what with God knows who.

"Hunter doesn't know, by the way. That you're leavin' and shit." Josh added, swiping his heel on the cement. "I kinda figured that you told him in the letter but when I went over to his place, I saw a stack of 'em unread."

Wow. Holy crap, wow. After I nagged Payton to tell me where I could find Hunter that night, went out of my way to write him countless notes apologizing and admitting how I felt... he still didn't care enough to read them. After begging him to open the one envelope that was most important, he didn't. He really was a lost freaking cause.

"Maybe it's good that he doesn't know." I released, passing Josh as I started the walk to my car.

"Marley –"

"Josh," I turned, "it was really good to meet you. And you are a great person, and I think you keep Hunter in check… for the most part. But there's no getting through to him, and I'm sick of trying so. Farewell? I guess?"

Tears pilled in my waterline as I spun back around and unlocked the door to my Malibu.

Josh's shadow caught up to me as he placed his hand on the hood of my car and eyed me solemnly.

"I can't get inside with you standing there, Josh."

He inhaled a breath and hung his head low. "Marley, Hunter's been through it. You know it, I know it, he fuckin' knows it. I rarely ever saw that kid smile, y'know? A handful of times in the past four years, I saw him smile. You were here, not even a year, and he smiled when he was angry at ya, laughin' at ya, and fuckin' happy with ya."

I stood paralyzed, watching him as he dragged two hands down his face.

"Look, my point is he smiled. And *you* brought that outta him. That means a hell of a lot more than ya think."

At this point, my waterworks were on full display, staining my shirt with wet dribbles.

"God," I choked out a laugh, sniffling. "He's such an asshole. But I cared… I *care*, a lot about him and I don't know why."

He leaned forward and brushed a tear from my cheek. "You wanna fix him, babe. Lotta people do. That's why I get why you did what ya did, callin' the cops and that."

"You do?"

He nodded. "Are ya kiddin' me? You did what we've all wanted to do for years, but shame on us. We were too scared to let him slip, y'know, finish the job he wanted to do every time he got behind that damn wheel."

My arms cradled me in place, running over the goosebumps surfacing on my skin. "I know that a drunk driver killed his mom... so why does he do exactly that? Why would he do that, Josh?"

"I don't know." His lips pressed into a firm line as he ran stressed fingers through his hair. "I don't think he thinks 'bout anyone else when he's drivin'."

"That's stupid. And reckless."

"That's Hunter."

Not an excuse. Fuck that. Before I let any more tears fall, I opened my car door and settled in the drivers seat.

Rolling down the window, I held out my hand for Josh to take. "Please watch him from now on. And please remember, Josh, better him safe behind bars than a handful of casualties."

The engine roared to life as I made my way out of the parking lot, staring at Josh's still form in the rear-view mirror.

Don't cry, Marley, don't cry. You've cried enough...

Damnit.

Chapter Thirty-Five
Hunter

I stepped onto my driveway after a three-day bender with Tabitha and Zetty.

Tabitha was a college student in Omaha, visiting home for the Summer while Zetty, her roommate, was an exchange student from Japan. Wildcats they were... *fuckin' wildcats.*

The sun pissed on my face as I approached the farmhouse, spotting my dad and Payton out in front shovelling some shit looking dirt into a hole they dug up.

"I'm sober, cross my heart." I joked, but I was entirely serious.

Ever since Marley put me on the feds' radar, I'd kept the drunk driving to a minimum. I'm sure there'd be other ways to kill me softly, but my truck was taking a back seat in the bliss from now on.

No one reacted to my remark, completely ignoring my presence like usual. But I was in the mood for a little confrontation, now that I had my baby back and could escape the scene if I wanted to.

"Buryin' a dead body or somethin'?"

Again, no response.

The birds tweeted in the branches, amused by my joke so I decided to speak again.

"Beautiful day for some ice cream, don't ya think?"

My dad threw his shovel aside and stared at me with harsh eyes. "You on drugs, boy?"

I scoffed, turning to Payton who also shelved her task and glared my way.

"No." I replied.

"Then why you actin' like your brain got tased?"

Ah, big old Dex Lane. Scary bear, brute man got his fuckin' period again. This is why I was out every chance I could get. Marley fucked us up even more than we already were. *I'm done with this conversation.*

I stepped around the dirt and started the journey towards my peaceful sanctuary when Payton called after me.

"You say goodbye to Marley, yet?"

Huh? Did I hear that right? My feet refused to move any further, no matter how much I willed them to. *And I didn't will them much, that was for damn sure.*

"Goodbye?" I spun around, facing her. "What for?"

"She's movin' back, Hunter."

"Movin' back where?"

Payton dabbed the sweat on her brow as she peeled off her gloves. "New York."

I caught my breathing in a chokehold as I stared at Payton in disbelief. My tone was unsteady, hard as rocks when I asked, "why?"

"If you actually gave her the chance to tell ya, you'd know. Instead, you been doin' everythin' in your power to run her outta Aurora."

My eyes travelled from her to my dad as I locked my jaw, clenching my fists with force. *Why didn't she tell me? Why didn't she just spit it out and fuckin' tell me?*

"I didn't run her..." I choked on my words, knowing damn well I did. I fuckin' did. But she deserved... *she deserved -*

"Save it, Hunter." Payton combatted, throwing a hand up. "Y'know that girl, the one you hate for savin' your ass and everyone else in this fuckin' town. Yah, that girl? She spent days cryin' over you. She wrote letters that she didn't even give to me, that I found in the damn storage bin torn n' tossed. Bout ten, maybe twelve.

"You know why? You didn't even give her the time of day to explain why she ratted on your dumb ass. Ya just pushed, n' pushed, until she decided she'd had enough of your shit and waved bye bye to the life she made for herself over here."

I opened my mouth to retort, to say something that would help my case but there was absolutely nothing. I had nothing.

"So you die, Hunter, what then?" She took a few steps closer to me, red faced and furious.

"What then? You gon' join your mama, right? You gon' leave your dad here to lose someone else?"

"Payton." My dad's voice boomed, halting her movements.

Ice coated my veins but I couldn't melt it. I'd bitten so hard on my bottom teeth my head began to scream in agony, commanding me to close my eyes and lay the fuck down so I could think. *I needed to fucking think!*

"She leaves at noon tomorrow." Payton spat, turning away from my sight before stepping onto the porch and heading inside.

My eyes burned a hole in the grass beneath me before I found the courage to lift them and meet my dad's.

"Dad –"

"You made a mess of your life, Hunter..." he shook his head, following the trail of embers Payton left behind. "Bless that girl's fuckin' heart."

I flinched as my dad slammed the farmhouse door shut, leaving me alone with the sunlight and the birds. Only they were no longer tweeting, there was no sound... there wasn't much of anything no more.

And there was about to be even less.

The moon took its place in the night sky, shining through the living room window of my shed. I clicked my phone open, reading the time: **12:42am**

A bottle of Jack sat half empty on my side table, taunting me to drink it. But for once, I couldn't stomach the thought. My mind wouldn't silence unless I confronted my feelings head on. *Bambi's leavin', and I drove her away.*

"Fuck." I cursed, gripping the back of my hair.

Every five seconds I'd stare at the bin filled with Marley's letters. They buzzed at me, called to me, begged me to read them and I almost caved. *Almost.*

It was like diving into Pandora's Box. If I decided to rip open one envelope, I'd tear open another, and another until I read them all and crumbled to pieces.

Did I forgive her? No. Could I forgive her? Did I miss her?

Screw it.

I bent down and snagged all the white envelopes, laying them out in front of me. My heart hammered in my chest as I inspected the dainty little swirls of her cursive, reading my name plastered on the front of each envelope: *Hunter Lane.*

My eyes tore away from the letters, spying the label of Jack. *Goddamn it.*

I flicked off the cap and downed a generous amount of dark liquor, shoving it away before I lost control.

It'll take one second to rip this open. One second to hear her out. One second to have some heart and listen.

I didn't have to forgive her to open them. This is what I wanted, right? I wanted her gone and she was leaving, so what did I have to lose?

Nothing. I lose nothing. I told myself. *Fucking nothing.*

And I read.

I didn't let myself break until I read the last letter. The letter she gave me at Cid's. The letter she pleaded for me to read. *The letter... Where's that fucking letter!*

My jeans from that night were buried in my hamper as I tore and tore away a mountain of fabric before I found it lodged in the back pocket, tearing the last envelope.

It was heavier than the rest of them, and the second I opened it I discovered why.

The I <3 Nebraska keychain I'd given her for Christmas was lodged between the page, burning my eyes as I stared at the shimmering heart before reading the letter frantically.

Dear Hunter Lane,

I'm embarrassed to say that the only thing that held me back from leaving was you. For months, I'd been contemplating going back to New York, since Rosy (my brother's daughter) was going to be born. But now, she's finally here Hunter... in this world, my niece.

I'm going to be an aunt! Not like you care, but I'm happy and I know I can't tell you that because you hate my guts. But it makes me happy sharing these things with you. These little moments... I just wish you'd listen to.

Hunter, I'm going to move back home. Nebraska, Aurora, Lincoln, all of this... it was a journey. An experience I'll never forget. To stop myself from crying, I tell myself that not every stop is a destination and the people you meet on the road have their own memories to create.

God, Hunter, I wanted to create those memories with you. I don't know how to put my feelings into words, but I really really ~~really~~ liked you. And I sound like a pre-schooler saying this but I don't know how else to word it.

I'm not madly in love with you, I don't think our relationship qualifies for that sort of thing. There are so many layers I never had the chance to pick apart, and now, I never will. But just know, when we were good, I felt incredible. All the insecurities, they faded away. All the laughs, they stayed with me, knocking in my brain when I was sad. I loved spending time with you, hiking with you, watching you fix your truck even though big vehicles intimidate me.

Before I end this letter, I just want you to understand why I did what I did.

That night, when you got behind the wheel of your truck and drove off drunk, I saw this look in your eyes that wanted death. Craved it, in fact. I'd never seen someone look so defeated, so broken before. But I saw it in your eyes at the cottage when Dex finally acknowledged the chaos you created.

You wanted someone to care. You wanted someone to notice. And I did.

But Hunter, noticing someone's faults doesn't mean you condemn them. It means you care. I ~~cared~~ care about you. Do you hear me? I care about you, and it's possible that you are capable of caring too. Your mother knows it. And you know it, even if it's buried so far down you can't seem to reach it. It's there. And every time you think about getting behind the wheel, think about this letter. Think about the people who are still alive to tell you they love you.

Please don't stop yourself from living, even when you don't feel alive.

P.S: You were my favourite rest stop.

                                        Bambi

1:53amand I was banging on Marley's front door with an active battle in my damn mind.

Noon. She was leaving at noon. She was here. She was still here.

I rapped and rapped until my knuckles were white and swollen, cursing under my breath until the

locks clicked and Bambi, bare faced and fuckin'
beautiful, eyed me with shock.

My gaze was glued to those big chocolate
spheres, puffy from sleep loss and probably tears. Tears
that I forced out of her.

"Hunter –" She whispered, her voice breaking.

"No." I shot, swallowing hard as I gripped the
doorframe. "You're not fuckin' going anywhere cause of
my dumb ass decisions. Unless you really want to, then
I'll make some more to drive you back."

My mind was racing a mile a minute, taking all
her in, acting on the adrenaline and fear of losing
something that made me feel alive for one goddamn
second in four years.

I was an asshole. I didn't see anything clearly. I
didn't let my own damn self accept the kindness she
gave out to everyone so freely. Everything I'd done to
her, all the torment and crudeness... I was sabotaging
myself of happiness.

When my mom left the world, I thought she'd
bagged up all my contentment, all the joy from my life
and she took it with her. But that wasn't true. I'd starved
myself too long. I'd become used to the pleasure of pain
and dejection that I let things fall through my fucking
fingers time and time again.

But from the second I met Bambi, I'd known she
was trouble. Not for the reasons I once believed, but
because she could've easily split my heart in two and
repaired it just the same.

"I'm so sorry." I admitted, out loud and finally, to
my fucking self.

Her chin quivered as she took a step forward, filling me with heat and lust and... fuck! *Her! Filling me with her!*

"For what?"

The golden specs that dusted her pupils, warm like honey and inviting me in sent a wave of impatience through my veins. Impatience for this moment, letting down all the walls I'd built up just to bring me here... to her.

Fuck the barrier. "For fighting against my heart since I met you."

I drew her in swiftly, grabbing her waist with two hands and kissed her. I fucking kissed her sweet, soft lips with all my anger and fury and might. All the sensitive parts of me, all the weak parts of me, every single part of me that lived in the shadows... it was hers.

She was hesitant for a moment before she fully gave in, melting in my arms as her lips parted. A soft groan escaped her mouth as I hoisted her puny little Bambi frame and kicked the door shut, securing us in the privacy of her space.

My back hit the door as I held her against me, wrapping both her legs around my middle. Her tongue found mine, twirling in sinful bliss as I sunk my teeth into her bottom lip.

Another gracious fuckin' moan escaped her when I cupped her ass, retreating breathlessly as I took her in.

"What..." She murmured, panting softly. "Why did you stop?"

I surveyed her face, the freckles across her nose like a starry constellation, the doe like glaze that covered her bright brown eyes and gripped her tighter.

I'd spent countless nights lost, sleeping in different beds, waking up next to all these women, drowning myself in despicable amounts of liquor to feel a rush. It became survival, to chase ecstasy in its purest form. An elation that came from something, somewhere, only I never found it... until now.

"This..." I stuttered, searching for the right words. "This is what I needed all this time. This makes me feel alive."

I planted a gentle kiss on her lips, leaning my forehead against hers. "You, sweetheart... You make me feel alive."

A single tear escaped her eye as she wrapped her arms around my neck, just... holding me.

The warmth of her body, her chest against mine, the scent of lavender and honey transferring onto my skin. This is what it felt like. *This is life.*

"Do you like me?" She whispered, both arms still secure around my neck as she leaned back to address me. "I mean... do you still hate me?"

I shook my head, smiling like a fuckin' kid on Christmas morning and walked us to the bed. "I like you, Bambi."

Normally, I'd take in my surroundings, see what kind of atmosphere I was working with but all my attention was focused on the girl right in front of me. Christ, she was a tease without even trying; her white tank top tight as tack, those tiny booty shorts and her radiant shiny skin, drawing me in.

I planted her on the bed, bringing my lips to hers once again. Her fingers sifted through my hair, scratching my skull as they made their way down my back. *Fuck this is Heaven.*

I trailed my lips across her cheek, planting soft kisses all the way down her neck to her collarbone. Every part of her enticed me, tempted me to move further but I didn't know what she wanted and this was more than I could've asked for.

Once her fingers reached the hem of my shirt, she scraped long nails against my bare flesh, sending a jolt of pleasure up my spine.

"Yeah, baby..." I muttered, "I really fuckin' like you."

She snickered, balling my shirt in her hands and lifting it over my head, leaving my torso exposed and flushed against her thin tank top.

A soft hand cupped my cheek as her eyes trailed over the tattoo on my chest, reading the inked bible verse I'd gotten for my mom.

"What's this from?" She queried, tracing over the lettering.

"Romans twelve. *Love must be sincere. Hate what is evil; cling to what is good...*" I chuckled, balancing on my elbows as I lifted some weight off of her. "You read the rest. My mom wasn't religious, but my grandma was. She loved that quote and my mom had it framed on my wall when I was growin' up."

The corner of her mouth turned up, her full, red lips urging me to kiss them. "Are you a sincere lover, Hunter Lane?"

Oh, she's tryin' to get the devil outta me. "How bout I prove you that one, darlin'."

I ran my tongue up her throat, nibbling on the silk flesh behind her ear as I gripped her waist, finding my way to her breasts. My thumb circled her nipple over the fabric separating me from sweet skin.

"How far do you want to take this, Bambi?" I released, letting my fingers dance all over her stomach.

A breathy response left her lips. "As far as you're willing to go."

"That's pretty fuckin' far, baby."

Her eyes flicked with desire as she pulled me down to her. "Take me there."

Ask and you shall receive. My mouth slammed against hers, hungry for her flavour. She fumbled with my belt but I stood up before my button came undone.

I spied her like my prey, watching her needlessly as she flayed out on the bed.

"Take off your shorts." I commanded, resisting the urge to do it my fuckin' self.

Brown eyes were gleaming with longing as she fiddled with the pink silk and slid it down her legs.

My cock was rock solid, begging to be released from my jeans as I took in her perfect pink pussy, waiting to be toyed with.

I almost didn't notice her lifting her top but I threw a hand up in protest. "Leave something on for me,

darlin'." My feet carried me towards the edge of the bed
as I tugged her ankles down and spread her legs apart.

Her nipples pebbled underneath her tank top,
pursing out from beneath the fabric. "Let me wonder
what I can do to the parts I can't see."

I pet her thigh with the back of my hand,
watching her wait and tremble, silenced by her
anticipation.

"Don't you move." I ordered, stalking to the
kitchen freezer and fishing out a cube of ice.

Walking back to the bedroom, I plopped the ice
in my mouth and spotted her unmoving, being the good
girl I asked her to be.

I knelt in between her parted legs and lifted one
over my shoulder, holding the softened ice between my
teeth and letting it graze along her inner thigh.

"Oh my God..." she cooed, grabbing a fist full of
her comforter.

Changing legs, I did the same thing until the
cube of ice was a slick pod in my mouth and gently held
it over her clit, allowing it to melt over her pleasure
point.

She moaned out her gratitude, releasing a gasp
as it fully dissolved into water and I licked it up her
center. "I was thirsty," I whispered, smirking.

Fuck she tasted like a dream. Every part of her
trembled as I dove my tongue deep inside of her,
pressing one hand over her lower stomach and the other
secured tightly around her thigh.

Her breaths were loud, ragged and pleading for
more. "Hunter... *Fuck*, Hunter."

I pulled her closer towards me, removing my mouth from her as I sunk two fingers deep inside her pussy, using my thumb to rub her clit.

"Don't be shy, sweetheart..." I rasped. "*Speak up.*"

And that she fuckin' did.

"I need you inside of me, Hunter." She begged, squirming beneath my hand. "Please."

I wanted to prolong her personal gratification as much as I could, satiating myself just by watching. But if I didn't stick my dick inside of her right fuckin' now, I'd explode without having ever done so.

My belt was off within a matter of seconds as I shoved down my jeans and boxers, ogling her beautiful features as I positioned myself above her.

"Are you sure, Bambi?" I asked.

The last thing I wanted was for her to regret this. Fuck, if roles were reversed and she was as horrible to me as I was to her, I'd be screamin' at my dumb ass to run for the hills. But I didn't want this to end. I needed this moment. I needed her.

She wiggled to her bedside table and pulled out a condom, handing it to me with urgency. From the look in her eyes, she pleaded for me to come down on her, to fill her with everything I had and to fuck her like no one ever could.

As soon as my dick was secure in the latex, I slid inside of her, gasping in pleasure as her tight pussy hugged my cock.

"Baby..." I groaned, gripping her thighs. "Baby you feel so good."

"Good." She pulled me down closer, wrapping her legs around me once more as we moaned in unison, kissing each other like this moment was indestructible.

This was happening. I was inside of the girl I'd hated, the girl I'd tolerated, and now... the girl who drove me wild. It felt complete, *I* felt complete. No one came close in comparison to her, not the feeling she brought me or the way she smiled or laughed or kissed. She was it, *this was it.*

It took a solid twenty minutes of mind blowing fucking sensation to feel my cum begging to shoot out. *FUCK!* Fuck! I couldn't help it, I couldn't help *her* being so goddamn fucking hot.

"Bambi..." I rocked into her slowly, planting gentle kisses on her neck. "Baby, I'm goin' to come."

Her candied giggle brought a blush to my cheeks as she whispered in my ear. "Beat you to it."

In that second, I let out a husky growl as I busted in the condom, taking all of her in as my tongue slid against hers with each thrust.

Sweat dripped all over my body as I set one last kiss on those rosy lips and pulled out of her. I felt her smile against mine as I relished in the moment of her lips, completely content.

"Kiss me, baby." I pleaded, trailing a finger down her soft cheek. "Just kiss me for a second... I need to savour how good it feels just to kiss you like this."

And we stayed in that moment until my lips were bruised and my saliva was drained. I booped her nose and made way for the bathroom to dispose of the condom and shut off the lights.

I didn't even care to look at myself before I huddled into bed, nestling against Bambi's half naked body, imprinted by yours fuckin' truly.

Her hand wrapped around my forearm as she pulled me tightly towards her, turning over to meet my eyes.

"Are you leaving?" She asked, her chocolate spheres brimming with concern.

I let out a laugh of irony, kissing the tip of her nose. "I should be askin' you that, miss New York City."

She slid her fingers up my chest, poking my skin a few times like she'd never seen a body before.

"What're you doin' there, darlin'?"

"I just... I need to make sure this is real."

I chuckled. "Real as rain, sweetheart."

Bambi hugged me closer, burying her face against me as she drifted off to sleep. "Please don't hate me anymore."

For a couple of minutes, I laid still, staring outside her window as the moonlight illuminated her skin. She was a fucking treasure, something I lost for so long when I didn't realize I had it.

How long had she wanted me? How long had I wanted her? None of that... none of that mattered, not in this moment because we had each other. And for the first time since we met, there was nothing getting in between that.

All of the poor decisions I'd made in my life, I never bat an eyelash towards. Nothing concerned me after my mom passed away; nothing fazed me or shook me or rattled me. But her, this girl holding on to me like

I was her knight and shining armour... I couldn't fuck it up no more. I didn't want to.

I blamed life for constantly shitting on my head, taking things away and burying me until I broke. Bambi was one of those things; the nuisances I'd rang true for so long, another piece of the problem brought onto me by the gods above.

But she wasn't the problem at all. I was. And I'd been so blind to see that, when she was trying to show it to me this whole time.

For once, I stared at the sleeping girl in my arms and I didn't blame life.

For once, I thanked it.

Chapter Thirty-Six
Marley

When I was younger, my dad used to say that we should always hang on to the things we fight for even if they're out of reach.

Mind you, he said it from a business perspective; that if you dig your claws into an outstanding offer, to see it through no matter the obstacles.

But in my case, waking up in the arms of someone you fought with and fought for, that advice remained steadfast.

My entire room was in boxes; all the clothes I'd bought over the past six months, food stored in a cooler, everything I'd taken with me from my past life, to the new.

I averted my eyes to the wall clock that read: 11:32am but time was sprinting by every second I remained locked in Hunter's grasp.

All the memories from earlier this morning vibrated in my brain, filling me with butterflies and pleasure. The way he touched me, held me, *handled* me... God, it was like nothing I'd ever experienced.

317

Before Todd, I'd only slept with a handful of people. Two of which were unmemorable drunken hookups and the rest were toxic flings.

Todd never went down on me unless he got something in return, and even that was a stretch. I'd utilized my vibrator more than we'd have actual sex and that was saying something. Why I ever fell for that man was above my comprehension, but we all make mistakes, don't we?

Besides, that mistake led me here, to this moment, with Hunter Lane.

Throughout all the volatility that we'd endured, I never expected this moment. His strong arm securing me against his core, his head atop of mine, the soft breathing that came with every rise and fall of his chest.

I was so sure New York was the right decision for me after my brother told me he was expecting a baby girl. Every night I contemplated going back, since he practically shunned my parents just as they shunned me and we were siblings again.

I missed him, I missed him so freaking much. Seeing my baby niece grow up would be a dream, as well as pursuing my potential, considering I'd proven myself in a rural town was exceptional experience on my resume. And yet...

Yet I was holding on to the man who held on just as tight. And right here, right now... this is where I wanted to be.

I craned my neck upwards to examine his sleeping features. I'd never seen him like this; peaceful, quiet, serene in his own head without the damage and defeat he'd masked throughout his day to day.

Unconsciously, I ran my finger down his cheek and grazed the stubble along his jaw, blushing at the touch of him so close to me.

He stirred, flexing his arm while slowly opening his eyes. Those crystal diamonds were soft, calm like waves and inscrutable. His eyelashes fluttered as he blinked a couple of times before leaning down to press a gentle kiss on my lips.

"G'mornin', sweetheart."

If I woke up every day to this, I'd die happy. My heart beat faster as he cupped the back of my head, running his thumb over my cheekbone.

Everything about his touch felt ethereal, magnetic. As if I couldn't get enough the more I took in; I wanted all of him again.

Before I could move, he shifted behind him, leaning over the side of the bed to his jeans on the floor.

That's when the closeness of his naked body hit me all at once, reminiscing on the muscular frame of his core commanding me to take off my shorts, the fullness of his penis crashing inside of me. *If there was a name perfectly suited for him, it would be Hunter.*

When he returned to his original position, he held something in his hands... something silver and red.

"You've got to stop returning my gifts, Bambi. It's twice now." He laughed, wrapping my fingers around the I <3 Nebraska keychain I'd given back in the letter.

I pressed my lips together, chuckling softly. "You have to stop pissing me off."

"No can do, sweetheart. Take it or leave it."

"I don't have a choice then, do I?"

His smile faded as he pondered for a moment, glancing behind him at the wall clock.

"You still leavin'?" He swallowed, barely meeting my gaze.

My eyes flicked to the only remaining thing on the bare beige wall; my P&D's schedule, reminding me that I had work in twenty minutes if I chose to stay.

A brick lodged itself in my throat. "This shouldn't change anything..."

He scanned my face, pressing his hand into the arch of my back. "But does it?"

It did. I hated to admit it but it really freaking did. What an embarrassment it was, for the second time in two years, that I decided to shift my life because of a man. When would I learn? This was my chance. I had a reason to go. I had something calling for me.

"I'm an aunt now, Hunter. My brother had his daughter a week ago."

His silence lingered as he blew out a breath, pressing his lips into a thin smile. "That's amazin', Bambi."

"Hunter –"

"No, I know it don't seem it. But I understand why you're leavin'. You got a job up there? Do you need help movin' things into your car?" He pushed out of the sheets and pulled on his jeans, flipping open some boxes.

"Hunter, stop."

"This is heavy." He pointed to my cooler. "I can lift it for ya."

"Hunter..."

"*What*? Marley?" He spun around, his breath hitching as he stared at me with sorrow.

Two hands slid down his face as he turned away again. "It's the *least*... it's the least I could do for drivin' you away."

At this point, I staggered out of bed, carrying the sheets draped around me. "You didn't do anything."

"Then tell me. Would you have left if I wasn't such an asshole? I don't doubt you would've considered it. But packin' up your shit like this? Would you have?"

"I haven't..." I placed my palm against his cheek, soaking up his worry and frustration. "I haven't left yet."

He took a step closer, grabbing my face with two hands and pressed his forehead against mine. "Then don't."

Soft lips crashed against my mouth as he threw the cloth off my body and hoisted me up, squeezing my bare ass tightly.

The tank top he ordered me to keep on last night rubbed against his naked torso, hindering the warmth I so desperately craved.

As if we shared the same mind, he slid off the lace straps and yanked it down so it gathered at my waist, exposing my breasts for him to see.

"*Fuck*, baby." He growled, eyeing me with hunger, lowering me onto the bed as he sucked on my nipple.

His teeth grazed my sensitive flesh as he slid a featherlight hand down my middle and slipped two fingers inside of me.

I raised my hips in response, moaning as he pulsed in and out of me. The rawness of last night filled me with painful bliss as he licked his fingers and slapped my outer thigh.

"You're gon' be the death of me, sweetheart."

"Better me than you." I retorted.

The blaring sound of my ringtone interrupted the moment as Adam's name repeated an incoming call.

I looked to Hunter who had already gotten off the bed, nudging me to answer.

Poor freaking timing, Adam. Jesus. After letting it ring another three seconds, I cleared my throat and announced a hello.

"Marley, hey. Are you on the road yet?" He asked, classical music sifting through the line.

My attention turned to Hunter as I wrapped the sheets around me once more and blushed. "Um, no, I'm... I'm not."

"It's a day's worth of driving, Mar. You planning to be here by the fourth of July?"

Fuck, fuck, fuck. God, I wish I had more time to choose. Yesterday it was so easy for me. I had everything ready and packed and waiting to go but now... Hunter came and changed everything.

If I left today, without ever knowing what potential lingered between us, then I'd forever regret what could've been. But if I didn't leave, I'd be missing out on the opportunity to watch my niece grow up, to get my job back in Manhattan.

"You're not coming, are you?" My brother let out, calmer than I'd expected.

"What? Why would you say that?"

"Because you're the most impulsive person I know, Marley." He laughed. "If it takes you longer than three seconds to make a decision, I know it's not happening."

My head hung low as I rubbed my forehead. "Adam... *something* came up."

When Adam and I were apart in college, we'd call each other every night to catch up. It was in those few years that we'd developed an act for sensing each other's demeanours over the phone. And in this very moment, I knew he wasn't upset with me.

"Something always does. How about we come visit sometime? The doctor said we should wait at least three months before flying, but we can try and make it for your birthday in August?"

My eyes began to water in appreciation. *WHY DO I ALWAYS CRY IN EVERY SITUATION POSSIBLE?*

"Are you serious, Adam? You'd come out here?"

Michelle's voice poked through the call. "Hi Marley, how are you?"

Wow. You underestimate how much you miss the people you never see, until you hear their voice and speak to them again. "Michelle! Congratulations on your baby, I'm over the moon for you."

"Thank you so much, she came out absolutely perfect. Four kilograms and just... yes, absolute perfection." She chuckled.

My heart exploded out of my chest. "Can you send some more pictures over the next few weeks?"

"Of course! And I hear Adam wants to visit for your birthday? I'm sure we can manage. It's been a long time and I've never been to Aurora before."

A vociferous shrill interrupted the conversation, the sound of my baby niece.

Adam cursed. "Marley, we got to go. But I'll Facetime you tonight okay? I love you a lot."

This time, I managed to say it back before he ended the call and I sprung onto Hunter, wrapping my arms around his neck.

"I tried to tune it out as much as I could, but are you stayin', baby?" He piped, the dimples in his cheeks deepening.

My lips slapped against his as I kissed and kissed and squeezed him tighter with a python's grip.

"I'll take that as a yes." He sat on the bed, gripping my thigh as he maneuvered me into a straddling position.

My eyes zipped away from his as he continued planting soft kisses down my neck, nibbling my skin.

"If I'm staying, that means I have to get to work in five minutes." I teased, allowing him to grip me in whichever way he pleased.

With one swift movement, he had my back pinned against the bed and his torso pressed against my chest.

"Spread your legs for me darlin' and I'll get you there in two."

Chapter Thirty-Seven
Hunter

As promised, I got Bambi to work three minutes earlier than expected.

When I kissed her goodbye, Cramer and Payton practically shit their pants but I didn't care. That was one of the best nights of my fuckin' life, and half the weight I was carrying fell off my back.

Damn, it really is true when they say it's harder to hate someone than it is to show heart. For a long time, I'd been living by the opposite philosophy, but the second I let my walls down I'd never felt more free.

It was nothing like I'd ever experienced before; that ecstasy just being encompassed in her presence. Definitely a weird feeling, I'll tell ya that. But a good one nonetheless.

After parking my truck in the driveway, I found my dad in the barn starting up the tractor when he saw me.

"Need help?" I asked.

He pulled down his cap. "I assumed that's why you came here."

"Yep, just doin' my civil duty as a son."

I hopped onto the combine but he slapped me off. "I can handle the corn harvest. There's some tool kits that need preparin' on the table there. Get started on that will ya?"

Before I headed off, I took in the sight of my dad. His eyes were covered by the front of his hat, but I could see an evident puffiness in his face that was usually covered by a strong visage.

"You alright?" I posed, eyeing his sluggish movements.

Again, he waved me off and grunted. "Go do your shit, Hunter."

Nah, not now. "Dad, I can do the harvest it's no problem –"

"I told you what to do, damnit, now go do it!"

My face felt like it'd been slapped. I know the past little bit was tense, but he was acting outta spite for something. Man, did I ever catch a break of peace? *Fuck, I missed Bambi even more now comin' home to this shit.*

It was in that moment that the arm sleeve of his flannel rose up, and I noticed the white beaded bracelet around his wrist... the one he'd gotten himself and Mom for their last anniversary together.

I almost crumbled on the spot, completely forgetting that today was the day she died now five years ago. *How the fuck... How the fuck did that slip my mind? How the fuck could I have forgotten this day? I mean, every year since she passed, I'd gotten drunk from morning to night so I wouldn't have to live in the memory but... I was dead sober. Completely coherent. And I... I forgot.*

My jaw locked as tears sprung to my eyes, gluing me to the ground.

"You saw Marley last night." My dad looked to the floor as he spoke.

There was the answer. The answer to why I spaced out on this day of all fucking days. I'd been so caught up in the high of what happened between us, soaking in the one shed of light I had in years that I neglected my own mother's death. *I'm going to fuckin' hell.*

"I didn't remember, Dad." I admitted, shaking my head in a state of shock. "I didn't fuckin' remember."

He toyed with the beads on his wrist, sniffing in response. "I'm glad ya didn't, son."

Son. I could've died right there and had a nice trip. He rarely called me that, rarely called me anything anymore. But acknowledging the fact I was his flesh and blood, that we were family... my mom brought that outta him. Today, she was still watching over us.

"It went well?" He questioned, his dark blue eyes meeting mine underneath his ballcap.

This was the softest my dad could ever be, and it was always on this day. When he actually showed a different side of him that wasn't uncommunicative or unresponsive. I've seen him show it to Payton, but to me? I'll be damned.

"Well enough that I fuckin' forgot." I replied, planting my ass on the ground.

I wasn't mad at Bambi, I didn't blame her. Fuck, I thanked her in a sense for making me block out all the trauma I'd endured from that day. It still haunted me every night... every fuckin' night I'd see her, my beautiful mother, and then... a ghost. A shell, a casket, and me. Standing erect, breathin', still alive. While she was feasting with the worms in a land unbeknownst to me.

"She stickin' around?"

I nodded. "For now. Unless I fuck it up again."

He snorted. "I'm countin' down the minutes, boy."

This was as normal as it got. Once a year, I'd tally my blessings and accept him as the dad he was supposed to be, the dad he *used* to be before my mom passed. And with what little conversation we exchanged, it still meant more to me than a thousand presents.

"April 22nd, 2017. The day it all changed." My dad mumbled, twisting his neck. "The day it all went to shit."

"Damn straight." I scoffed, drawing up my knees.

"Y'know, a year after your mom died, I met Payton, yah? Every time I thought about her, I'd shut down. Get sad, push her away. A true asshole, Hunt. Kinda like you."

I flipped him the bird as I chuckled, waiting for him to continue. *Begging him to.*

"At first, I'd beat myself up about it. I was hurtin', then I'd hurt Payton, it just wasn't fair. But slowly, I realized that I was killin' myself. Ain't ever let myself feel the happiness your mom brought to my life. But it was possible, it was damn possible.

"I don't talk 'bout your mom, not cause I don't miss her, but cause her and I talk enough. Every mornin', I come out here, I look outside and I say hey, g'mornin' Leslie."

Upon hearing her name, the image of her kind, loving features popped into my brain, as if she'd been there the whole time waiting for me to say hello.

"Look Hunt, my point is I'm real glad that you forget 'bout today. For the first time in years, I finally saw that smilin' kid out on the boats with his mama. So go thank Marley for me, will ya?"

I inhaled a breath of air while I hung my head low, shielding my bloodshot eyes from my dad. A tear flowed down my face, dropping onto the ground beneath me as I choked on a laugh.

"You talk a lot, old man." I joked, sniffling through the bittersweet pain.

He blew out a chuckle. "I talk once a year boy, grab your fill."

This. This is more than I could've asked for. These small moments, the tender ones that rarely happened but existed all the same.

I'd become so used to numbness, building up barriers to block out emotion but when I heard my dad speaking, opening up for the first time in years, it brought me closer to him.

My mom used to say that you can't love a stone. You can admire it, the outer detail, the display, but once you crack it open is when you relish in the diamonds. The beauty hidden beneath a hard exterior.

I used to think that shutting down was the only way to move forward. Pretending you don't feel until you convince yourself you don't. But feeling, vulnerability, that shit wasn't as weak as I thought it was. Cause my dad was sitting before me, laying his heart on the line and I could've never been more proud of that.

"So where you takin' Marley, tonight?" He probed, bringing me out of my head.

"I'm takin' her somewhere?"

His laugh was low and rugged. "Oh boy, you already fucked up."

I furrowed my brows in confusion, standing up. "How?"

"Son, you want a fresh start? Ask her on a date."

Huh. A date... Fuck, I hadn't been on a date in a long time. And why the hell was I taking dating advice from my old man?

"You'd been outta the game for a while there, pops." I teased, making my way over to the tool boxes.

"I kept Payton around, didn't I?"

I flicked a pointer up at the sky as he booted up the combine and drove out of the barn.

As I sat at the table, placing tools in their designated areas, I pondered the date idea a little more.

Bambi and I had been out so many times on little hangouts, but I wouldn't call them dates. We were friends at the time, and I guess we still kind of are? *Fuck, this is why I can't be bothered with the relationship shit.*

Friends can sleep together... Nah, fuck that, I ain't bein' her friend and I sure as shit wouldn't be watching her *friendliness* with another guy.

I slid out my phone and crafted a text, sending it to Bambi immediately:

2:09pm – Hunter: Be ready by seven. I'm picking you up.

A half an hour went by before I received a message back, and I smirked at her response:

2:40pm – Bambi: Okay, Mr. Bossy. Want anything else?

The thought of her perfect tits, her perfect body and pleasuring her was enough to give me a semi at the fucking work table. But tonight wasn't about sex, no. Tonight I'd show Bambi what I should've showed her since the second I met her.

The real Hunter Lane.

Chapter Thirty-Eight
Marley

"Why are you staring at me like that?"

I knew why. I knew exactly why Payton and Cramer huddled around me in the staff office as I scooped a spoonful of blueberry yogurt into my mouth.

"Quite the show back there." Cramer let out.

My cheeks heated as I bit down on the cold silverware, glancing at Payton who remained still with arms crossed.

"I changed my mind?" I squeaked, throwing an innocent smile her way.

Again, she did nothing but glare at me, her blue eyes intense and intimidating.

"Aren't you glad I'm staying?"

"I am," she muttered. "But I wan' know why."

She wanted the truth. Because I told her why I was leaving, which wasn't a lie. I did want to see my baby niece and that was fact. Watching her grow up would make me the happiest girl ever, but after what happened with Hunter... I couldn't bring myself to going through with it. Whether it was the right or wrong choice, it was the decision I was sticking with... at least for now.

"Don't make me say it, Payton." I fiddled with my fingers, bobbing my knee up and down.

"Say it." She imposed.

Ugh. "Okay! Okay, Hunter apologized. He came over and he apologized last night and I know I told you that I was leaving on my own accord but I really care for him and –"

"I'm just teasin'." Her face softened as she tapped the wooden desk and made her way for the door. "You watch your heart though, deary. He ain't easy to manage."

And she was off, leaving me alone with Cramer's unreadable aura. He tapped his chin, sucking in a breath as if he was about to speak but then quickly closed his mouth.

"Are you going to scold me?" I teased, but not really. I couldn't get a lock on his emotions, what he was feeling.

"No, no, Marley. I'm glad you're stayin'." He finally replied.

"Then why are you being so quiet?"

His long legs paced around the tiny area before the doorway as he stopped to face me. "Are you sure 'bout this? Him?"

I wanted to roll my eyes, because this entire situation felt like it was taken out of a ridiculous soap opera. But an overwhelming sensation of appreciation floated through me upon realizing I'd never had people in my life who cared so much about my wellbeing.

People who wanted to vocalize their concerns because they wanted me in good hands.

"I'm not sure of anything." *And that was true.* "But I want to see it through. He really opened up, Cramer."

And with a snarky snicker, he turned the point of his toe to the door and threw me a side smile. "I bet he did."

Oh my God! I balled up a piece of scribbled paper and chucked it at his head, which he dodged easily and left the room with a prideful simper.

"You're a fiend!" I called after him, blushing myself.

It was then that my cell chimed with a text from Hunter, telling me to be ready for seven tonight.

A dozen butterflies swirled in my stomach as I agreed in response, shutting off my phone before I exploded some more.

Could this really be the beginning of something good? Something substantial? Was this a fresh start? Hunter was so unpredictable. The second I thought I could figure him out, life threw a curve ball my way and I'd wound up back to square one. He wasn't easy, Payton was right about that. But the easiest things were never worth it.

Maybe that's why it took years of mistakes to find the missing puzzle pieces of my life... because the wait for something good always leads to something great.

I just finished pulling on my red short sleeve when a series of knocks alerted me to the entrance.

"Coming!" I called, spritzing some honey lavender perfume on my skin.

When I opened the door, Hunter was leaning against the frame with a bouquet of white roses and a pack of... *starbursts?*

My words drowned in my throat as I averted my eyes from the items he was holding to scan his attire. Grey trousers were fitted around his muscular legs and rolled up at the ankles, while his white t-shirt contrasted against his tan skin. His blonde hair was a disgustingly sexy mess, tempting me to rough it up even more.

"Red's your colour, Bambi." He smirked, drooping his eyes to survey my outfit.

I couldn't hold back a smile as I let him into my place, shutting the door. "Flowers and candy, Hunter? Didn't peg you as a cliché."

"Ain't a cliché red roses?" He combatted, placing the bouquet down on the kitchen counter.

We stood a few feet apart, in an air conditioned room, but I was scorching hot. Hot like I was tanning on the Sahara desert sand, hot like I wanted to rip off all my clothes and melt into the blue lagoon of his eyes.

But I didn't know what we were, if we even were anything. We barely spoke about what happened between us and I didn't want to be the first to initiate it. What if he just came over in a heated moment and he regretted it? *Marley, stop. He asked you out. He wants to be here.* God, how I wish I could turn off my brain sometimes and just enjoy the moment.

I walked over to the counter and picked up the roses, running a finger over the soft petals. "I didn't know guys still did this."

He turned his body to face me, leaning against the wall. "Did what?"

"Brought girls flowers on a first date... I mean, if this is a date." I blushed, unsure of our current situation.

The one and only time someone ever got me flowers was my brother when I graduated from college. But my brother was always a gentleman like that and the only guy I knew that actually enjoyed rom-coms and dramas. Maybe he got the idea from those films, but I definitely didn't peg Hunter as the romantic type.

I brought the roses to my nose as Hunter's footsteps stopped directly behind me. Nimble fingers lightly grazed the skin above my hip as he wrapped two arms around my waist, drawing my back to his chest.

"It's a date, sweetheart."

I could barely contain my breathing as he lowered his lips to my neck, brushing them against my ear. "The first of many."

"Where are we going?" I asked, sitting in Hunter's passenger seat as we drove along the highway exiting Aurora.

He held the plans for tonight securely, shooting me a glance before returning his eyes to the road. "It's a surprise."

I didn't press any further as he turned up the radio and rested a strong hand on my thigh. Squeezing his fingers tighter, I rolled down the window and peered up to the cotton candy sky above, taking in the moment with all that I had.

The feeling that Hunter gave me, the bliss and butterflies that knotted in my stomach, was incomparable to anything I'd ever felt before.

If someone were to ask me six months ago if I saw myself sitting in Hunter's truck, hand in hand with a feeling of pure elation, I would've called bullshit. But it all made sense, in some twisted, incomprehensible way... *we* made sense.

A lot of people say that you can only meet your match once you're fully ready; when everything is aligned and there's an affordance to settle. But that's not entirely true. I honestly think it's equally possible to find something magical within the ruin.

Though Hunter and I had a rocky start, it didn't define us. Call it fate or chance, even coincidence, we found each other for a reason. And whatever that reason was, I was happy for it.

After an hour of driving, the sun had completely set as Hunter pulled into a parking lot lit by the illumination of a gorgeous glass building. A crystal fountain sat in the center of a circular roundabout, emanating tri-coloured lights from beneath the waterfall.

"Wow," I released in awe, poking my head out the window to inhale the scent of open air and luxury.

Dozens upon dozens of cars lined the outer perimeter of the establishment as Hunter nestled between two sports cars and killed the engine.

"Don't you dare try n' get out, Bambi." He commanded, hopping onto the gravel and jogged to open my door.

"You're really giving me the princess treatment tonight, huh?" I teased, stepping onto the pavement as we crossed the parking lot.

He snorted. "A door I can open, but I ain't gon' kiss the ground you walk on, your highness."

I swatted his arm as we walked through a silver arch with marble stepstones, leading all the way to a gigantic black desk occupying a handful of workers. *What the hell is this place?*

Hunter took the reins as he approached the table, throwing a charming smile at a lady working the front-desk.

"Good evening, sir." She released, almost robotic. *Huh, first time I see someone not melting at the sight of him.*

"Hi," he responded, calling me to his side. "I made a reservation earlier for two at Empire Point."

After a couple of clicks on the keyboard, she pepped up and slid over a shiny gold card, pointing down the hall to some elevator doors.

"You're going to take the blue tagged elevator to floor twelve, sir. Enjoy your dinner." And she was back to facing her computer screen.

As if Hunter had been here a million times, he laced our fingers together and headed down the hallway where a line of elevators stood. Atop each metal door was a coloured rectangle that held an up and down symbol within it.

For the life of me, I still couldn't figure out what this place was, where we were going and how the hell Hunter, the most unposh person I'd ever met, managed to take us here.

I frowned, surveying the bare walls. "There aren't any buttons."

"That's what the card's for, sweetheart." He smirked, sliding it down a scanner that was concealed by the outer lining of the elevator.

Almost immediately, the door dinged and slid open for us. I followed quickly after Hunter who swivelled his pointer across a row of flashing buttons and selected number twelve.

As the elevator ascended, I took in the dimly lit atmosphere of the glass box we were encased in. There was relatively nothing in here but a wall of buttons and each other. No cameras, no handlebars, just the soft sound of smooth mechanics hoisting us up higher and higher.

"I'm so confused." I blurted, halfway to laughter before I closed my mouth. "Where are we? What is this place?"

"You ask a lot of questions, Bambi."

I rolled my eyes. "Well, I'm concerned for my well-being."

"You're in good hands." He retorted, cryptic as always.

A sharp ding vibrated through a speaker *somewhere* as the elevator doors slid open, revealing a sight I did not expect to see.

Rows and rows of white tables were packed with people chattering and laughing underneath lantern lights. The entire room was made of glass – floor to ceiling, transparent glass.

My eyes followed my feet as I marvelled at the ground beneath me, revealing a vat of darkness and a million bright dots, the size of ants.

I quickly averted my gaze to the ceiling which shared the same unending darkness, only it resembled a night sky filled with a constellation of stars, winking down at the tables below.

Hunter flipped the gold card around and nudged me to follow. "We're at table ten, darlin'. Come on."

As if my movements weren't my own, I followed with a cloudy mind overflowing with absolute admiration, unable to get over the sheer beauty of my surroundings.

"Hunter," I whispered, sliding into the cushioned seat of our table. "Am I allowed to take pictures? Or is that not allowed?"

He laughed, filling our glasses with a water basin that was already present. "I don't see why not. But why d'you want to?"

I audibly gasped. "Are you serious? Look at where we are! It's like space, but better."

"Definitely better." He chuckled.

A waiter dressed in an all black ensemble approached our table, carrying a bottle of champagne and two flutes.

"Good evening," he said, pouring a generous amount of bubbly liquid into our glasses. "My name is Pierre and I will be waiting your table tonight. You ordered the three tier experience so the entrée will be as follows..."

I completely zoned out as I gawked at Hunter in disbelief while the server spewed the names of two dishes I'd never heard of. This place was ultra fancy, and that was saying something from someone who grew up in Hudson Yards.

When Hunter caught me staring, he gave me a slow, deliberate wink as I caught the waiter's last words.

"... and a cerise crème brûlée for desert. Any disputes or shall I alert the kitchen to begin your order?"

"No disputes here." Hunter responded, holding up two hands. "Alert away."

Pierre bowed... he literally *bowed*, then scurried away like a mouse who smelt a cheese platter.

I took a moment of silence for my brain to register the fact I was in some type of affluent simulation and questioned Hunter. "Okay, where did you find this place?"

"Craigs list." He joked, sipping the fizzy liquid. "Go on, Bambi. Try your five hundred dollar champagne."

WHAT? I almost fainted on the spot. "No way, Hunter! There is no way this was five hundred dollars."

"You're damn right there's no way. Fuck that. I give it forty dollars at best."

We both shared a laugh as I eased my shoulders and took a sip of the drink. As far as champagne went, this was actually super pleasant. It was smooth and sweet, but not intolerably sweet which I liked.

"I'd say it's worth fifty."

But Hunter didn't mind my comment as he pulled out the package of starbursts I thought he left at my place. Slowly, he began to unwrap the pink paper and took out a red square, laying it flat on the white tablecloth.

Umm... "What are you doing?"

The corner of his lip turned up as he pushed the starburst towards me. "You know why I got you candy, Bambi?"

I was so confused. So. Freaking. Confused. "Because you're nice?" *That was clearly not it.*

"Because you feel guilty eating it."

Whoa. Okay. Not the answer I was expecting. I remember when Hunter and I became friends after New Year's, we went on a hike and he asked me why I only ever ordered the low-fat frozen yogurt at Blu's.

"There's like a million options, Bambi, and you go for the plainest damn one." He'd said at the register.

I admitted it was because my mom put me on a super strict diet when I was a teenager and I became obsessed with looking a certain way to fit the image she wished for me. So in turn, I avoided sweets at all costs unless it was a function or someone was offering and I felt bad refusing. *Like Payton the night I showed up at the farmhouse.*

"Let's play a game, darlin'." Hunter interrupted my thoughts, leaning back against his chair.

This is so weird. "What kind of game?"

"You always ask me questions, Bambi, I never answer 'em. But I think I owe ya some now. So every question you ask me, I'll answer honestly, and you eat a starburst."

"And what if I don't want to eat a starburst?"

He crossed his arms, chuckling softly. "Then question time's over, sweetheart. Don't nag me till you got a sweet tooth."

Interesting. I didn't understand why Hunter went through all of this just to get me to eat a starburst, but then again, there was not a word on this planet that could describe this man.

But he was right in his admission of never answering questions. So if I needed to eat some chew candy to get the honesty out of him, then I was all about it.

"Fair enough, Hunter." I raised my glass, clinking it to his. "Game on."

Chapter Thirty-Nine
Hunter

When she opened her mouth to ask the first question, it didn't come as a shock since she'd been bothering me about it all night.

"Where'd you actually find this place? And why did you take me here? I could be wrong but you really strike me as the type to avoid fancy places at all costs."

I cleared my throat and took of swig of champagne, attempting to savour every miniscule sip I had with one glass since I was driving. Yeah, there was no way in fucking hell I'd risk my life tonight, especially if Bambi was beside me.

"Google does wonderful things, sweetheart." I began, catching the buzz her smile always gave me. "But I promised you honesty, so. When you decided to stay, I was happy, but the more I thought about it, the more I felt kinda bad. New York was your home, besides your shitty parents bein' there but ya loved it. And your brother havin' a baby an all.

"So, I wanted to bring New York to you." *Fuck this feels awkward. Bambi better enjoy that starburst cause this is killing me.*

"I googled fancy restaurants out of Aurora cause God fuckin' knows we don't got none of that around there. Found Empire Point and thought it was a perfect fit."

Before she could react, I waved my pointer up and down. "I guess the floor is supposed to mimic the feeling of lookin' down a tall building to see taxis or people or some shit. And the ceiling's supposed to look like you're in the stars."

When I finally finished, I met her eyes that looked like they were going to melt onto the tablecloth and turn into lava. Her chin quivered as she placed her tiny fingers over my hand and squeezed.

"I'm really trying hard not to cry." She admitted, though I could already tell so I laughed.

"You won't be the only one cryin' if you don't eat that damn starburst, Bambi, we had a deal."

Like an obedient little dove, she unwrapped the red candy and popped it into her mouth, grimacing at first before relaxing her jaw.

"I haven't had one of these in forever."

"Is it good?" I asked, trying to think about the time I last had one myself. *Probably when I was six and trick or treating for Halloween.*

Pierre marched up to our table before Bambi could answer, carrying two small plates with a goo-like substance in the center.

"Pea soup with white truffle for you both. The chef is just finishing up the Wagyu steak."

And he was off just as fast as he came.

I stared at the Shrek shit in front of me, unsure whether I was supposed to eat it or wash my hands in it.

When my eyes found Bambi, she had already dug in, shovelling a spoonful of green glop into her mouth.

"Christ, Bambi. Hungry?" I grimaced down at the bowl.

She dabbed the corner of her mouth with a napkin. "Hunter, try it. I know it looks kind of yucky, but it's actually good."

Fuck. I'm not meant for this life. I spooned a little soup into my mouth and expected my taste buds to disintegrate but it wasn't actually that bad. *Who would've thought?*

"Well I'll be damned." I let out, downing more and more until all that was left was green residue.

As Bambi finished her final bites, Pierre returned as promised with two triangular plates of meat. "Enjoy."

And I did. Holy fuck I did.

It was like cutting into butter, melted butter but not really. Soft and tender and fucking hell. This dinner really was worth the money I dropped, and let me tell you, it was a fuck ton.

"I'm glad it's small portions, but I'm also sad because it tastes so good." Bambi let out, groaning in pleasure as she forked the last bit of steak into her mouth.

"Why're you glad it's small portions, then?"

"Because I have more room for starbursts." She pepped, holding her hand out so I could give her another.

I chose an orange one and placed it in her palm as she pondered for a moment, fiddling with her fingers.

"I'm kind of afraid to ask this because I don't want to ruin the mood."

"I gave you free reign, sweetheart. Go ahead."

Even though the lighting was dim, I could see the redness of her cheeks as she hesitated to speak up.

"Why do you drive drunk if that's how your mom passed away?"

I figured a question like this would be coming, but today of all days, when she passed five years ago, I dunno... it hit harder. Then again, it was reflective, because I asked myself the exact same thing every time I got behind the damn wheel.

It was hard to explain. A part of me wanted to feel what the guy on the other end was feeling; the rush, the adrenaline, the risk of driving under the influence and breaking laws. We've all got a dark side in us, always crave a high that we have to create. And I wanted to see if that high was worth killing my mom.

But it wasn't. Of course it fucking wasn't.
Nothing would ever warrant that. But Donny Deblin did
it, and he got three years in jail for stealin' my flesh and
blood away from my life. Three years for killing a
woman. Manslaughter they said... fucking hell.
Manslaughter for taking a life.

An accidental tragedy. A fucking joke that was. I
remember the first year after it happened, all I could
think about was his decision to drive that killed my
mom. I remember calling up the sheriff's office, asking
what the verdict was for Deblin's trial and when they'd
told me, I lost my shit. I thought, if I were the judge,
he'd be rotting in prison or I'd tie a noose around his
neck myself.

But that was back then. About two years ago, I
found out that Donny Deblin got laid off and his wife
got diagnosed with cancer so he had no way of paying
the bills to help her out. Apparently it was too much for
him so he got shit faced at the bar and ended up hitting
us on his way home.

I was drivin' that night. Lost control of the wheel
when his headlights blinded me and the collision threw
me off the road. Mom's side hit the tree and...

"Hunter?" Bambi murmured, squeezing my
fingers. "Please don't answer. I'm sorry for asking."

It was then that I realized my grip was strangling
the tablecloth. My nails sunk into the callouses of my
palm, opening the scars.

We had a deal, and I keep my word. "I drive drunk, Bambi, because in some fucked up way, I'm with my mom. Like she's right there, sittin' in my passenger seat, alive. And a drunk man can't tell the difference between a memory and a moment. That's why, Bambi. Ain't nothin' more to it."

This time, she didn't hold back the tears when they fell. And fuck did it cut me deep to watch that. "I haven't driven like that since you turned me in. And I don't plan on it again. It was fuckin' stupid, I was stupid."

"I'm sorry, Hunter. I just..." She inhaled a shallow breath and shook her head. "Can we go? I really want to be close to you right now and I can't and it's killing me because I just want to hug you and –"

"Bambi," I stopped her, cracking the hardest damn smile I could muster up. "Eat your damn starburst."

She patted her under eyes and plopped the candy into her mouth, crooking her finger with an open hand. "Give me another one, that answer deserves two starbursts."

I chuckled lowly. "Dessert's gon' be here soon, darlin'. No need."

The starburst idea sounded ridiculous at first, but when I thought about it more, I realized I was a fucking genius. Bambi's parents really did fuck her up to the point where she thought having a bite of something sweet was equivalent to drinking bleach. Damn disgusting, I'll say that.

I could tell she wanted to. Every time we'd go out for ice cream, her eyes practically slurped up my cookie dough cup before I'd even take a bite. It wasn't fair that she felt the need to restrict herself based off what her parents trained her to be as a teenager. And the one thing I hated most in this fucking world was being vulnerable so if she was having a hard time, I was too. Some things needed to be done though, and I was damn glad it was on my terms.

After eating the crème brûlée, Bambi never asked another question. I didn't blame her either. It didn't offend me that she was curious about my mom, but it also left a blade of tension that was impossible to cut. Though the date wasn't over, and I was stoked to get outta this Buckingham Palace. *No five star pea soup could ever rope me back here.*

As we walked out of Empire Point and made our way to my truck, I did what I was dying to do all fucking night and pulled Bambi against me.

Her back was secure against the passenger side door as I caged her in my arms, leaning my head down to inhale the scent I'd been itching to smell from across the table.

"Somethin' about you, sweetheart..." I whispered, cupping her chin in my hand. "The things I'd do."

Her breathing hitched as I trailed my lips along her soft skin, pressing a featherlight kiss against her lips. "I'm takin' you somewhere you're gonna love."

She giggled against my mouth, wrapping her arms around my neck. "Somewhere I'm going to love? Or somewhere *you're* going to love?"

I moved her behind me as I held the passenger door open, slapping her ass playfully and closed it shut.

When I got inside, I settled into my seat and started the truck, heading out of the parking lot I knew I'd never see again.

"Bambi, I spent an absurd amount of money on toddler portions tonight. I'm makin' some sacrifices to see that smile on your face, so if I fuck this up, I'm throwin' in the towel."

She bubbled in amusement. "You can't tell me the food was bad, though. Come on."

I shrugged. "Nah, you're right. An I do miss Pierre a little."

"Shut up," she laughed, covering her mouth.

"Did ya see his quads?"

She tittered some more and went to swat my arm, but I caught hold of her hand and placed it in my lap. Her fingers were swallowed in my grip as I rubbed my thumb over her skin, soaking in the feeling of this fucking girl beside me.

"Thank you for tonight." Her words laced around me like silk ribbon.

And as I drove, my mind was clear. Clearer than it's been in a while, with Bambi by my side, a head absent of liquor buzz and a skip in my heartbeat.

"Thank me later, sweetheart. We aren't finished yet."

Chapter Forty
Marley

About twenty minutes later, Hunter pulled into a much smaller parking lot than Empire Point, and cut the engine.

When the truck headlights dimmed, I focused on the tiny bookshop in front of me that held a wooden sign in curvy lettering: **Clara's Corner.**

"A bookstore?" I asked, clicking out of my seatbelt. "Do you even read?"

"Nah," Hunter grinned, "but you do."

My heart practically exploded out of my chest. This entire night had been unworldly, magical, *insane*, I don't know... I really don't know how to describe it.

When Hunter told me he specifically sought out a restaurant that would remind me of New York, I almost jumped his bones right then and there.

Never in my life had someone gone through the trouble to make a date personal, let alone ask me on one to begin with. I really didn't expect much from him, given the circumstances that we still hadn't spoken about... *Making a mental note to eat another starburst later and ask what's going on between us.*

Even that, the starburst thing alone was enough to turn me in a mound of cotton candy. It was like he paid attention to every single thing I told him about a few months ago and stored it in his brain, waiting for the opportunity to use it. Only know I knew he was never going to hold it against me, he was keeping it close to him for the day this date would happen.

Every single layer I'd been so afraid to see was slowly dissipating, shedding off his body with an open heart. When Hunter told me why he used to drink and drive, I went through all those stages with him. The anger I saw in his eyes, the feeling of regret he must've harboured for so long... guilt, so much guilt. And then a tundra of sadness, an overflow of pain. I felt it with him, and I needed him to know he wasn't alone.

This... this bookstore, the idea of him even taking me here triggered all the serotonin in my brain and I would've kissed him if he wasn't already around the truck, holding the door open for me.

"Come on, then. Let's check it out."

He laced our fingers together and guided me into the store, where the immediate smell of coffee beans and old books slapped me in the face.

My eyes roamed around the place which looked small on the outside but mega huge on the inside. There were rows and rows of books, shelves from floor to ceiling and a staircase that led to a basement of more novels.

In the corner was a beverage stand, and two women were standing behind it, serving white cups to an elderly couple.

"Okay, please tell me where you actually found this place Hunter." I gaped, running my fingers along a display of contemporary literature.

"Craig's list, darlin'. They got some good date suggestions." He shrugged, checking out a wall of car magazines.

"Liar."

His lips upturned as he flipped through the pages of a truck leaflet. "Caught me."

I shook my head with a smile and turned my attention to the aisles. This place was truly a crossbreed between a library and a Barnes and Noble, but homier. Even though it had an enormous selection, for some odd reason, I still felt like I was in my grandma's house checking out her old storage.

"What d'you like to read, Bambi?" Hunter asked behind me.

The list. "I like fantasy, mystery, psychological thrillers... you name it. But romance is my number one."

"Is it now?" He smirked, his eyes rolling to the different headers atop the book sections. "How 'bout we find you some good romance, then."

I followed his step as he led us towards the back corner where a large pink sign hung from the ceiling, reading: FOR THE LOVERS.

"Take your pick." He said, ushering me into the hollow aisle.

Since the shelves were from floor to ceiling, the books were shaded by the main lights. Though tiny pot lamps were positioned underneath the shelves to create a spotlight affect over the bevy of novels. *My God, this place really thought of it all.*

My eyes filtered through a bunch of authors I'd never heard of, as well as some familiar ones when a bright orange book stole my attention: *Caught Red-Handed.*

I was a sucker for cartoon covers and this one did it for me, so I tucked it underneath my arm before waving for Hunter to come over.

"Can I recommend you something?" I asked, batting my eyelashes. "I have good taste."

Assuming we were enclosed by books, I thought Hunter would be checking out some titles but he kept an eager simper, his eyes stamped to my face.

"You do have good taste, Bambi." He began, clearing his throat. "Have you checked the bottom shelf? Sometimes the best novels are kept secret."

I watched as he crouched down slowly, turning his head to look out the aisle before running a light hand around the back of my calf.

His other hand hovered over the novels as he slid calculated fingers higher and higher until he reached the bottom hem of my skirt.

I completely froze, gripping tightly of the book sandwiched between my bicep and swallowed. "Hunter... we're in public."

There were tiny slits at the back of the shelves that allowed me to see how many people were roaming in the bookstore, and although no one was around us, I wasn't about to take the risk of getting caught.

He pulled out a book, removing his grasp on my leg and turned to a random page. "Come down here for a second, sweetheart. Can't seem to read this line, forgot my glasses."

Glasses my ass. I rolled my eyes, squatting down beside him as he placed a deliberate finger in his mouth and licked his thumb.

"What um," *fuck.* "What line, Hunter?"

Those blue spheres didn't leave my eyes as he gripped the book in his left hand while guiding the other underneath my skirt, toying with the thin fabric separating him from entering me.

My beathing hitched as he carefully slipped one finger inside of me, causing me to fumble against the shelf.

"Hunter –"

"Baby," he let out, handing me the book he was holding. "Maybe it'll be better if you read it to me."

"You can't possible expect me to –"

His thumb circled my clit as he pushed another finger in, forcing a moan out of my mouth.

"Hush up for me, sweetheart. We don't want to draw any attention to ourselves now, do we?"

My head fell limp against the shelf as he continued, pumping his fingers in and out of me as I faded into a state of pure bliss, trying to stabilize my breathing.

"Read, Bambi." He commanded.

How... My eyes trailed up and down the page. "Before the sun set that morni..." *Oh my God.* I couldn't focus on any word or any line or fuck – *I can't see straight...*

"Hunter, I'm – I'm close..." I groaned in pleasure, my adrenaline pushing me further and further to my climax.

He wore a devilish smirk as he quickened his pace, pulsing his fingers in just the right places. "Pull that pretty lace to the side for me, sweetheart. I need to fill you properly."

I did as I was told and he placed a swift kiss on my cheek before I came apart on his fingers, throwing a hand over my mouth to silence my moans.

Slowly he lowered my knees, straightening them out so they fell parallel to the grey carpeting. I watched as one by one, he slid two fingers into his mouth, licking *me* off of him then stood up, holding out a hand for me to take.

There is no way that just happened. No way. I couldn't even move, still trying to recover from the orgasm he just gave me in PUBLIC while attempting to regulate the dampness in my underwear.

As if Hunter didn't just finger blast me against a bookshelf, he took the novel out of my hands and surveyed the cover. "This all or do ya want to look around some more?"

My jaw dropped as he snorted and nudged me forward, placing a firm hand on my back to exit out of the aisle.

"Is that normal for you?" I posed, keeping up his pace to the register. I couldn't believe how calm and composed he was after having done, well... *me.*

"Is what normal?" He furrowed his brows so sarcastically I could've ripped them right off his forehead.

"What you did back there?"

With a sly grin, he shrugged his shoulders. "I guess I was still hungry for somethin' sweet."

My legs turned to jelly as he placed the book down at the register, paying the cashier before I could even grab my purse.

On our walk back to his truck, I inhaled the fresh air and stored it in my lungs, feeling like I could breathe for the first time without Hunter's demanding presence on top of me... and yet, that is exactly where I wanted him to be.

"Why did you do that?" I murmured, pressing my legs together as I strapped into the passenger seat.

With one line he cracked me open. With one line he stabbed his Hunter Lane charm inside my heart, and watched me bleed.

"You said you liked romance, didn't you Bambi?"

Chapter Forty-One
Hunter

Since our first date three and a half months ago, Bambi and I didn't let each other go.

Three and a half months of pure fucking heaven.

We attended Josh's Fourth of July party down at Cabbelforg Beach, a pristine location on the opposite side of Rivertown Bay. My old buddy Carter came down from Boston, so we had the boys back together for the weekend while Bambi brought up Winter and Cramer who rounded up a few of their friends as well.

I'd never watched the fireworks with any girl before, besides my mom when we'd go sailing during the show. But this was a different feeling, incomparable to anything I'd ever felt in my entire damn life.

It was during the show that I asked Bambi to be my girlfriend. Having her wrapped up in a blanket against me, huddled together like a bunch of cuddly koalas, it was the right time and I knew it. Truly a concoction of pure happiness – nah, fuck that...

It was *home*.

In an interesting turn of events, after the first night of our festivities, I knocked on Josh's door to find him tangled up with none other than Winter fucking Camden.

"Holy shit!" I exclaimed, unsure whether or not I should close the door or slap his meaty arms with congratulations.

Josh hadn't hooked up with anyone since the broad on New Year's Eve; for some reason, he just didn't have the lucky streak he normally had so when I saw him balls deep in Winter I could've welded him a trophy.

When I told Bambi about it, she said she already expected it, which brought more confusion outta me.

"Am I just out of loop or somethin'?" I'd asked.

And of course, she laughed. That cute fuckin' laugh and told me Winter had been eyeing up Josh on our weekend outings and was planning on hooking up with him soon enough. *Good for him, Winter was awesome.*

Since then, Bambi and I had just spent more alone time together. We were in peak corn harvest season so I was busier than usual helping my dad out, but Bambi insisted she wanted to learn so I took her out onto the field.

"I want to drive." She beamed, hopping into the main combine seat while I slid in beside her.

"Go slow," I urged, unable to contain the joy I felt watching her do the work she'd never do in New York.

She changed a lot since being around the Nebraska folk. Not like I spent the first little bit trying to get to know her, but now that I did, I noticed all the small things that made her unique.

That averting eye contact thing she did? Yeah, long gone. She was an open book with me now, no walls to shut me out.

I always thought she looked hot in her city girl style, but she kind of tossed that out the rag too after her and I got together.

She sported a lot of basics, and half of my plaid shirts were hung up in her closet waiting to be worn... not by me, though – by her.

I'd be lying if I said I didn't like the idea of her prancing around in my shit. When I dated Rebecca, she'd practically drag me to the mall to buy athletic clothing.

"I ain't no hockey, boy, Bec." I used to say when she picked out spandex and windbreaker materials.

"You dress like a farmer." She replied.

Fuck it grinded my gears. Every. Single. One. I wanted to yell in her face, "just let me be me!" But that would've gone over very poorly, so I always shut my trap.

With Bambi, it was easy. I think from the very beginning she accepted me the way that I was, even when I didn't have the slightest clue as to what that man entailed.

Day by day, I was still trying to figure that out. But having her right there beside me, that alone was motivation.

"Just press on the gas lightly, sweetheart. Straight line, got it?" I said, pulling on some sunglasses to shield my eyes from the rays.

"God, this is so boring. Do you not have a radio or something?" She groaned in frustration.

"Service is always shit out on the field. You wanted to drive, don't you complain."

"Well, yeah. I want to live like you. A big, husky man-child who works on the farm. Can I wear your shoes?"

I threw my head back in laughter. "Can you wear *my shoes*?"

She chuckled as well, flashing those chocolate brown eyes at me that always got me going. "Can I?"

Fuck she's beautiful. She's so fucking beautiful. "I have to kiss you."

And I did. I kissed her neck, her cheek, her shoulder, her fucking arm because I couldn't get enough. There wasn't a time where another woman made me this happy, where I felt like I could be myself and laugh and just relax without expectations.

Bambi was closer than ever with my family now. Hell, my dad was inviting her over for pork chops last weekend and pouted when she said she had business to attend to.

In fact, he told Payton she was working her too much and Payton swatted him like a fly on the damn wall.

Everything was good. Everyone was happy. Bambi brought the sunlight, and I lifted up my glasses just to see her shine.

Instinctively, I ran my hand up and down her inner thigh, squeezing the tender flesh beneath her shorts. "Focus on the task at hand, baby."

The combine came to an abrupt halt which shot me forward, forcing me to look at Bambi who was red in the fucking face.

"You always find a way to distract me." She blushed, shyly looking away.

As much as I wanted to play, I could feel my dad throwing daggers at me from all the way at the barn.

"Switch places with me, sweetheart. We won't get anythin' done with you drivin' like a granny."

She cursed in protest but eventually planted her ass onto my lap as I pulled her to the passenger seat, trading her place.

"You can't just tease me like that, Hunter." She joked. But she was dead serious. And so was I.

"I got my right hand for a reason, Bambi. Now c'mere."

So what if we fucked like a couple of cats in heat? We weren't harming nobody.

After we'd finished up harvesting for the day, I took her against my shower wall then had her nestled in the corner of my couch, watching some hospital drama show.

"What's it even about?" I asked, painting my boat figurines at the new workstation in my shed.

Bambi helped me set it up last month when my dad's handy-man tool kit supply needed the garage space. It actually made more sense considering I had it now in the comfort of my own place, rather than always strutting off to the farmhouse.

"Grey's Anatomy?" She gaped, actin' like I was the dumbest motherfucker on this planet.

I finished off a few more brush strokes before I coughed back. "Grey's Anatomy, Bambi."

"Do you not watch T.V?"

"I got shit to do."

I could tell she rolled her eyes and when my neck craned to look back, she did. *Readin' my girl like a damn book at this point.*

"It's so complex."

"Medicine always is." I quipped, gripping onto the back-end of the stem as I finished off the silver railing.

Bambi's paintbrushes were the only things I felt comfortable using now. Every other one felt like a betrayal, like I didn't like her gift or some shit even thought that sounded like the dumbest thing. *I guess that's what you get for fallin' in...*

"My brother's coming down next week." She said, blasting me out of my brain. *And thank fuck for that because what the hell was I just about to say?*

I kept my head down to wipe my brush, clearing the croak in my throat. "Oh yeah? Am I meetin' him?"

"Well duh, I was thinking we can do a double date. Maybe to Berandino's or something for my birth..." but she cut herself off as I bobbed my head up quickly.

"Your birthday?" I urged. "Your birthday's next week?"

The light of the T.V screen concealed the colour in her face, but it was poking through.

"The second of August, yeah. I didn't want to make a big deal out of it."

"It's not a big deal, baby." I huffed casually, slugging my arm around the back of my chair.

She frowned, half insulted and I cracked a fuckin' laugh.

"I'm kiddin' Bambi, it's a huge deal. Why didn't ya tell me?"

"I hate when you do that."

"I do a lot of things that you like so it evens it out, sweetheart."

August second. August second. What to do for August second. I had a few ideas come to mind, but I didn't want to get all flowery on her when I, myself, really wasn't that type of guy.

Everything I did up until this point had been genuinely from the heart. But now, being her boyfriend and shit, I was kind of nervous to fuck it up. Screw the title and that, I just wanted to make her happy. A year ago, I hadn't even known she existed, and now... well, now she's all I know.

"Oh my God!" Bambi gasped, kicking out of the blanket she was wrapped in. "You're never going to believe who just messaged me."

I pushed out of my chair and made my way beside her, dragging her legs up so they sat in my lap. "Who?"

She shook her phone in front of my face, throwing a hand over her mouth. My eyes zeroed in on a Snapchat conversation with the name Todd Sherman at the top of the screen.

10:32pm – Todd: Marley, u and I know that u and I fucked up so let's try this again. *image attachment*

10:33pm – Todd: U miss that, babe. U miss my dick, don't you, babe. Babe. Babe answer me.

10:34pm – Todd: Marley!!!!!!!!! !

I saw his dick. I was literally staring at Bambi's ex-boyfriend's shlong right in front of me, unshaven might I fuckin' add.

"First of all," I nudged her wrist away. "Why the hell d'you still got Snapchat for?"

She locked her phone and shrugged. "It's easier for Adam to send me videos of the baby. I don't know, Hunter! I didn't even realize I still had Todd on Snap."

I really fucking hated that guy. All the bad blood I felt towards him the day I knocked his face into Cid's floor was still there; hearing him speak to Bambi that way, the fact he was comfortable talking to any woman like that was beyond me.

"You gon' reply?"

"I was just planning on blocking him but –"

"Turn your ass around, sweetheart." I ordered, grabbing her waist and heaving her to a doggy-style position.

"What are you doing?" She chuckled, waving her booty shorts in my face, tempting my growing cock some more. But right now I had one mission in mind, and I wanted to give Todd fucking Sherman one final send off.

"Phone, Bambi. Hand it over."

She did as she was told and I pulled down the silk fabric of her shorts, sinking my teeth into her soft ass-cheek as I snapped a pic of me doing so.

With eager fingers, I typed out the message:

10:42pm – Marley. Next time you expect a response from her, here's a pleasant reminder of what you lost and what I've gained.

"Permission to send?" I asked, my chest heaving with frustration. *This guy was a fucking prick.*

371

Her eyes quickly scanned over the picture and message as she nodded with approval, planting a kiss on the corner of my lips before sending the damn thing herself.

Almost immediately after, Todd's dumb ass bitmoji popped into the chat which showed he viewed the text and Bambi quickly blocked his ass, silencing those bitch-boy screams forever.

"I don't know who's the bigger jackass, Bambi." I smirked, cradling her like the deer she was.

"You," she purred into my ear, running her nails against my scalp. "Always you."

And I took her right there, on the couch, against my fridge, on the counter. I took her everywhere, painting my place with memories of us – memories I needed to remember until the day I fuckin' died because she killed me. She was the highest high, the strongest buzz, my intoxication, my ecstasy.

My goddamn everything.

Chapter Forty-Two
Marley

I booked a reservation for five at Berandino's, pacing around my kitchen, waiting for my brother's arrival one week later.

When I offered to pick them up at the airport, they declined and said they'd much rather rent a car since it was my birthday and didn't want to bother me. It was definitely Adam who made that call, but I wasn't really complaining since the closest airport was a few hours away.

Originally, I thought of inviting Winter and Cramer, but my brother managed to get four days off so I knew they'd have plenty of time to meet.

For my birthday, I just wanted something small – Hunter, Michelle, Adam, myself, and baby Rosy. *Ah!!* My niece, my baby niece was coming and I couldn't even contain my excitement.

I pulled out my phone for the thirtieth time in ten minutes and crafted a text:

4:09pm – Marley: Michelle, please tell me you're pulling into The Atlas now?

4:15pm – Michelle: Just got here. Are you sure we can park in your spot?

4:16pm – Marley: Yes! Hunter said I could leave my car at his place since he knew you guys were coming.

4:19pm – Michelle: Perf. Just getting out our bags. Floor two, room seven, right?

I replied with an excitable *yes!* and did one final sweep of my tiny place that would definitely be too snug for three adults and a baby. They knew it too, so they booked a room ahead of time in the same residency.

Hunter offered for me to stay at his for the duration of my brother's visit, but I liked my alone time even though I was with him often enough.

I'd always been that way, though. With Todd, there were numerous nights that I preferred the couch over sleeping next to someone. Of course, our relationship paled in comparison to mine and Hunter's, but the habit remained intact.

The best thing about Hunter was that he and I shared the same outlook on relationships; being with someone every second of every day doesn't give you time to figure your own self out. And today wasn't an exception to that rule.

Hunter had to run some stock out of town this morning, so he sent a bouquet of orange tulips to my door with a card that wrote:

Happy birthday my baby fuckin' dear. Little Bambi ain't so little no more. Red roses will always be a cliché, so I got you orange flowers to match that book you liked three months ago. If you want, we can re-enact our first date tonight?

Always,
Hunter

How did I get so lucky? Seriously? How? Every second I spent with Hunter over the past few months was a dream I never wanted to wake up from.

Never did I ever think someone sweet, someone so kind-hearted was underneath all the rough and gruff, but he was there, and he just needed someone to bring it out of him.

A knock sounded at my door and I just about twisted my ankle running to unlock it. When I did, a group of two people, two people who I hadn't seen in over a year and a half stood holding a baby carrier with my baby niece cooing inside.

Tears sprung out of my eyes as I pulled them both into a hug, trying with all my might to control the waterworks but there was absolutely no way.

"Geez, Mar. You look so different." Adam's levelled laugh chimed in my ears as I hurried them inside, closing the door behind us.

"I could say the same about you."

And boy did that ever ring true.

Facetime will never be the same as seeing someone in real life. I mean, I knew what my brother looked like, obviously I did. But seeing him, all 5'11 of him with his dark brown hair and stern jaw, the scar over his eyebrow that he got playing beer pong and ran into a cupboard... God, I missed him. I missed him so freaking much.

"It's so good to see you," I released, rubbing the tears off my face. "Both of you," I turned to Michelle, "and can I please say hi to little Rosy..."

As soon as she nodded a yes, I booked it straight to the baby carrier and dropped to my knees, scanning the features of the most precious little girl I had ever seen.

"She has your eyes, Adam." I whispered, placing my pointer over her tiny little baby bib. *Oh my God, I'm going to literally explode.*

Her soft fingers wrapped around mine as she chortled out a giggle, squirming around beneath a plush purple blanket.

"Hi Rosy," I smiled, "I'm Marley, I'm your auntie. You're so cute!" I turned to Michelle, mouthing, "*she's freaking adorable,*" before returning to the baby.

"She was phenomenal on the plane. We didn't even hear a peep from her." Adam said, placing a hand on my shoulder.

"She's beautiful, she's so beautiful and perfect and small." I gawked, forcing myself to stand because

Lord knows I'd stay staring at this gorgeous specimen for eternity.

Michelle pulled out a tiny giftbox from her bag and handed it to me. "Happy birthday, Marley. It's from both of us."

Her calm, green eyes sparkled at me with delight as I took hold of the gold package and shook my head. "Michelle, you really didn't need to get me anything. Seriously, the only thing I would accept are those cupcakes you made for Halloween two years ago."

"I'd be happy to make those for you instead of a cake. If I can remember, you only like –"

"Red velvet," my brother finished her sentence. "The only sweet Mom could never get you off of."

I returned his smile and slowly unwrapped the box in my hand, finding a gold Cartier ring and bracelet set hidden beneath the lid.

"Shut up!" I gasped, averting my gaze between the two robbers in my apartment. "You stole this, right? I cannot believe you got me this!"

"Marley, I work on Wall Street –"

"And you don't let me forget it," I beamed, dragging him into a bear hug and pulling Michelle's hand towards me.

"Thank you, thank you, thank you a million times. I'm not material but any girl would go feral for a Cartier set." I pulled away, gripping Michelle's hand. "Please tell me you have one too."

She shook her head. "No, but only because I can't wear jewelry while working in the kitchen. I don't even wear my wedding ring." She pulled out a dainty silver chain with a diamond band holstered on it. "I keep it with me underneath my apron."

Smart woman. "Well, thank you again. You both really didn't need to get me anything. But I'm sure you're hungry?"

Adam was already walking to my fridge, pulling open the door handle with a frown. "Famished, and you got nothing, sis. You sure you're crushing it at your job? All I see are yogurt cups and kombucha."

A grim look clouded his visage as he threw his shoulders back. "You're not still on that horrible paleo diet, are you?"

"No! I have some chips in the pantry if you want to have a snack. Help yourself, too Michelle."

"What time's the reservation?" He asked, already scavenging my shelves.

I made my way to the bathroom, calling out before I shut the door. "In half an hour and I purposely didn't wear makeup because I knew I'd cry so I need a few minutes!"

Their chuckles made me giddy as I absorbed the hushed chatter of their familiar voices in the next room, voices I hadn't heard in so long and voices I honestly thought I wouldn't hear again.

My waterline cupped a few more tears before I slapped my face and pulled myself together. *Stop crying, Marley. Stop crying.*

But they were happy tears, the happiest tears that could ever fall. Because it was my birthday, and for the first time in twenty-four years... I felt complete.

I'd been a regular at Berandino's for a few months now since Payton loved to throw her staff parties in the lounge.

The manager, Derek, actually lived in Brooklyn for a few years and tried to make his restaurant dream work there but it didn't. *Sad but expected. If you couldn't afford to rent a unit for three thousand a month, you were getting no where.*

But he made the smart move and he up and fled to a small town where he knew his business would thrive. He liked the quaintness of Aurora, and I didn't blame him. It grew on me more than I ever thought possible, and at this point, I couldn't see myself ever leaving. From New York City to Nebraska... who would've thought.

"Where's Hunter?" Adam asked, plopping an olive into his mouth.

We sat at the half-moon booth towards the back area of the restaurant which was the quieter part of

Berandino's. It wasn't a huge space, but it was always busier near the bar.

I swiped out my phone to check the time: 5:13pm "He should be here any minute."

"I'm excited to meet him," said Michelle.

"I'm not." Adam declared, flatly.

"Adam –"

"No, Mar. I am curious, don't get me wrong. I'd love to meet the reason you chose to stay back. But from everything you told me, he seemed like such an –"

"Asshole?" Hunter's voice popped out of the blue, startling everyone at the table, including me.

How the hell does he always pull that Batman stunt?

"Sorry I'm late." He kissed the side of my head, sliding in next to me with a pack of starbursts. "I was pickin' up some candy for the birthday girl."

I blushed, fully knowing the intent behind the treat. After the last few months, we learned so much more about each other that I would have never guessed. The funny part was he never actually forced me to eat any more starbursts, and fully answered any question I had willingly.

Hunter was the most closed off person I'd ever met, and for good reason. Facing life with an impenetrable forcefield was as easy as breathing to him, but I took great pride in being the first one to break through. Though, there was still so much to learn, and I was craving some sugar.

"She doesn't like candy." Adam retorted, eyeing him suspiciously.

"Surprisingly enough, they just happen to be my new favourite snack." I beamed brightly, shoving the starbursts into my purse.

A slice of silence cut the table as Michelle placed a hold on Adam's shoulder, offering her hand out to Hunter. "I'm Michelle, Adam's wife."

Hunter returned the greeting with a firm hand and his million dollar smile. "Hunter Lane, pleasure to meet ya."

His gaze turned to my brother's who had an elbow propped up onto the table, scratching the stubble across his jaw.

"I've heard a lot 'bout you, Adam. Marley's been dancin' around all week."

"Dancing, candy..." He huffed. "All news to me."

"Adam," I muttered but he was quick to interrupt.

"What do you do for work, Hunter? Marley told me you work for your father, if I remember?"

"I do. It's good pay, actually. Between the hardware store growin' thanks to your sister," he winked at me, "and sellin' our crop to the locals, we got a good thing goin' on over here."

"I see." Adam leaned back into his seat. "So you and Marley are happy together?"

Hunter gave my thigh a nice slap, causing me to bubble in laughter.

"Happy as a clam." He smirked.

My brother gave my blushed features a once over then proceeded to lean over the table and extend a hand out to the blonde Greek god who stole my heart.

"Well welcome to the family, Hunter Lane. I'm Adam."

We gobbled up our pastas like a pack of wild turkeys and settled on a decadent chocolate cake for dessert, free of charge since it was my birthday.

"Does everythin' taste like ass to you, Michelle? Y'know, since you're a five star chef." Hunter joked, forking a sliver of icing into his mouth.

God, why am I attracted to literally everything he does? He could watch paint dry and I'd take pleasure in watching HIM watch paint dry.

Michelle laughed. "I got a wide palette. It's good to try new things."

"Even though nothing will ever beat your cooking, babe." Adam jested, giving Rosy a scoop of bottled banana purée.

I agreed. "You should really try her cupcakes, Hunter. They're amazing."

"You guys are stickin' around for some time though, yah?"

"Until Monday. I have to fly back for a meeting but we have a good four days to sit and do nothing." My brother placed a hand over Michelle's. "A much needed break."

The server returned with our checks, handing one out to Adam and one to Hunter as one by one, they tapped their cards.

"I got some scenic areas to show ya if you're up for it? Don't know if hiking's somethin' you like to do, but I got Bambi on it and I don't think she'd mind watchin' the kid for an hour or two?"

He turned to me with those sparking blue eyes, showing me that he truly wanted to bond with my brother; not to get into any good graces, but because he cared about what I cared about and I loved him for that.

Besides, I was dying for an excuse to bond with my baby niece. And Hunter just gave me the best reason in the world.

"Adam, the trails are stunning here. I'll swing by tomorrow morning and watch her." I insisted.

"Wait, wait –" Adam raised a hand. "What did you just call my sister?"

My cheeks heated as Hunter said, "Bambi. Like the deer."

"That's adorable," Michelle piped, sliding out of the booth with Rosy fastened in the baby carrier.

As we headed out of Berandino's with full stomachs, my brother stopped to pat Hunter on the back. "How does eight a.m. sound?"

"Call it nine and I'll buy breakfast." Hunter countered, knowing he'd get his way.

Of course he did and we parted ways as I settled into the passenger seat of Hunter's truck.

"Today couldn't have been more perfect," I smiled, relaxing into the headrest.

He cranked the engine and grabbed my fingers, kissing my knuckles carefully before pulling out of the parking lot. "It's about to get a hell of a lot better, sweetheart."

Chapter Forty-Three
Hunter

Call me Cupid and tattoo my fuckin' name on your wrist cause I really sprinkled rose petals around my living room and lit a couple candles to set the mood.

Bambi insisted she didn't want anything for her birthday, but me being me, I managed to get her something I knew she'd appreciate.

There were so many things she loved, after all she really savoured the little things. That was a quality I really admired about her, and found myself taking habit of it subconsciously.

She really did make me a better person in more ways than I could count, ways that I never thought possible. I realized that over the course of the last few years, my drinking and driving really was the worst way I could've dealt with the loss of my mom. A part of me knew that all along, but no one ever pulled that realization out of me until her.

At the front door of my shed, I stopped her before she could enter. "Put this on," I ordered, taking out a black blindfold from my pocket.

Her chocolate spheres narrowed before she turned her back to me and let me tie it around her head.

When her eyes were covered, I led her inside, inhaling the vanilla bean candle I lit a few minutes prior to letting her in.

"It smells good in here." She chirped. "Is this the candle I got you from the market?"

I nodded even though she was blind like a bat underneath the cloth. "Yep, now sit here baby."

She planted her ass on the chair I used for painting, sitting quietly as I snagged the red gift box that housed my present and placed it on her lap, unravelling the blindfold.

Her head tilted to the side as she surveyed the room before even realizing there was an object in her hands. *Classic Bambi.*

"Rose petals?" She gawked, her jaw sweeping the goddamn floor.

"Petals of roses, sweetheart."

"You..." She poked a puny pointer at me. "You are a romantic, Hunter Lane, don't you ever deny it."

Even though the lights were dim, I could still see that effortless gleam that sparkled in her eyes. The happiness that was always present, vibrant inside of her. She was a drug, and I was her addict. Yeah, there was no way in hell I'd be going to rehab.

"Open your damn present, Bambi." I pushed, pressing my lips into a smile.

Her eyes finally dropped to the gift in her lap as she lifted the lid and furrowed her brows in confusion.

I chuckled as she picked up the odd looking silver tool with a gigantic circle welded to the end of the curved handle.

"I love it..." She began, drifting into thought. "What is it?"

Bubbling in laughter, I knelt down to her position as I reached over to a random book on my T.V stand and clamped the mechanism between two pages.

Holding it in place for a few seconds, I eased my fingers back to reveal a spherical stamp that read: Property of Bambi's Bookstore.

"It's an embosser for your books." I began, hovering my phone flashlight over the custom monogram. "I know ya didn't want anything, but it's your birthday and I know you love to read so –"

Her lips were on mine before I could even get another word out, tugging at my shirt with impatience.

Don't get me wrong, kissing her was fuckin' heaven, but I searched high and low for that damn thing so I needed to know it made her happy.

"Baby, baby..." I chuckled against her smooth lips. "Do you like it?"

"Hunter," she swallowed, unbuckling the belt loop of my jeans. "Can I show you much I like it?"

Well I'll be damned. *My. Fucking. Girl.*

I let her do her thing as we switched places, positioning myself onto the chair while she slid my jeans down my legs.

Fuck, she was hot. She was so fucking hot with her dark hair, her beautiful body and that smile... that smile that held an ungodly amount of perfection. Perfection I didn't think existed.

"I love it..." She whispered, gripping the back of my calves as she trailed baby kisses up my leg. "I love it more than anything."

My dick had been hard all night, sitting next to Bambi in her skin tight dress and heels. She smelt like sweet sin and I was ready to devour her, but if she wanted me now she could have me in any fucking way she pleased. After all, it was her birthday. *Who am I to go against her wishes?*

Juicy lips cupped the head of my cock as I dove my length into her mouth, strangling the groan pursing through my lips.

She took me in, all of me and I... fuck, *fuck* my God she was doing everything right. Her tongue twisted around the sensitive parts of my shaft, alternating hands as she sucked me like a damn lollipop.

My fingers tangled in her dark hair as she bobbed up and down, bringing forth my climax faster than I cared to admit.

"Bambi," I breathed, savouring one last second of those wet lips around my dick.

Her eyes were watery, hungry and waiting as she slowly sucked down my length and plopped me out of her mouth. "Yes, Hunter?"

My girl had the fuck-me eyes. The best damn fuck me eyes I ever did see. A list of naughty things popped into my brain, all things I wanted to do to her right in this very second but above all else, I just wanted to feel her.

The hand that had been wrapped in her hair cupped her soft cheek as I caressed that bottom lip with my thumb, watching her look up at me on her knees.

"Take it in," I whispered, pushing two fingers into her mouth, feeling the softness of her tongue winding through my fingers.

My dick was aching, missing the warmth of her pussy even though I could have it all right now had I asked her to spread her legs and give it to me. But I loved to torture myself, especially if it would prolong these moments with the girl I fuckin' adored.

My Bambi had a firm grip on my wrist as I pulled my fingers out of her mouth and slid the wetness down to her neck. "Come sit on my lap, sweetheart."

Obediently, she planted her ass on my left thigh and caged me in her arms.

The hot pink panties she was wearing made an appearance as her cream dress hiked higher, urging me to lower that lace and have her ride my face. But not before I made her crave me, beg for me.

"Do you see what you're doing to me?" I groaned, placing my fingers once more in her mouth before trailing it down her chest and underneath her dress.

"Look at my dick, baby." I commanded, tearing her thong away.

Once her eyes followed my order, I slipped two fingers inside her, soaking in the sweet moisture of her wetness as I pumped slowly, in and out... in and out of her perfect little cunt.

My soaked fingers manoeuvred inside her, watching my beautiful girlfriend get fucked by my hand. I gripped the back of her neck, pressing my fingers into her pressure points as she moaned in pleasure.

"Don't stop," she pleaded, those chocolate eyes rolling back into her skull.

In one swoop, I lifted her craving body up and wrapped her legs around my middle, carrying her over to the bathroom mirror.

When I set her down, she was in complete distortion, panting and pawing at me for more. And fuck was she ever going to get it.

"If you come any closer to me, Hunter... I'll fall apart. And I want to make this last. I want you to –"

Perching a gentle kiss on her forehead, then her upturned nose, I spun her around so her back was against me, the hard length of my cock digging into her spine.

"Can you feel me, Bambi?" I asked, the sight of her staring pulling me into full large once more. "Look at what you do to me."

Her breathing hitched as I slowly pulled the straps off her dress, unzipping the material until it was a puddle of fabric on the floor.

Ah, God, fuck. My fucking Bambi. Those rounded breasts and pebbled nipples left me impatient and demanding for more of her, more of her and *now*.

"Stare at yourself, sweetheart," I swallowed, knotting her long hair around my fist, "and watch what I'm about to do to you."

With one thrust I lodged myself inside her, bending her over as I gripped her waist and replicated my movements. Over and fucking over did I fuck this girl, relishing in the sight of her bouncing bare tits as I rocked in and out of her doggy style.

Her legs began to cross as she cried out, "Hunter, fuck! Fuck me!"

And I did. Her moans were music to my ears and her glistening body was mine to keep, cherish, protect and worship as much as I wanted.

"Look at you..." I growled, yanking her by the ends of her hair so her sweaty body was against mine. "How fuckin' beautiful you are, sweetheart."

"Hunter..."

I secured her wrist in my hand as I guided it down to her pussy, egging her to finish herself in all her beauty, staring at the sight of her coming apart as we watched together.

"You kill me," I kissed her neck, guiding a finger inside of her as she let out a gasp. "You bring me to life..." one more kiss behind the ear as she began to pick up rhythm, squirming in my grip. "All at once."

We fucked her own cunt as one, the friction of her spine against my cock pushing me into a state of stars.

"Hunt... Hunter," she whimpered, falling into my body. "Hunter I'm coming."

I continued to kiss my way up and down her neck as she came apart in my arms, releasing the chorus of fuckin' angels into my ears while her wetness dampened my fingers.

While she was still riding that high, I shoved her back down into a few more thrusts while I let myself break inside of her.

I didn't let her go, I fucking couldn't let her go. My back hit the wall as I shielded her away from the rest of the world, sinking to the ground to rest against the cold tiles.

She lay nestled in my arms; my princess, my golden girl. The sun in my fuckin' heart, clinging on to me like this was all we had left – each other, the moment of us, forever.

"I love you..." she whispered, refusing to meet my gaze as she pulled me closer to her.

I love you.

I love you.

I love you.

I thought it a million times. Her sweet words, her Bambi voice, all of my girl replaying in my mind like a broken jukebox.

I love you. I love you, I love you. She said to me. She said it and I heard it clearly, unmistakeably so.

Gripping her as close to me as humanly possible, I spoke the words I'd fought off for so long. "I love you, Bambi."

With whatever love I had left.

Chapter Forty-Four
Adam

I waiting outside Atlas Aurora with a backpack of two waters and a pair of socks, glancing at my watch that read: 9:02am

My job taught me how to be more punctual, though that was never really an issue for me. Dad slapped me senseless if I was ever late to any of his business training courses, so naturally I credited my on-timeliness to him.

Hunter pulled up in a monster black truck about ten minutes later, unlocking the passenger door while I stepped inside.

"Sorry 'bout that, man. I was doin'..."

"My sister, I presume."

I bit my tongue, realizing what just slipped my lips. *That certainly didn't come out right. Not. At. All.*

He cranked the engine and powered down the road, chuckling in response. "That escalated."

"That was not how I wanted to –" The thought of my sister doing anything with anyone brought a hurl to my mouth that I nearly regurgitated. "That was poorly phrased."

"Ya think?" He teased, rolling down the window. "Nah, it's fine. I just wanted to get her some breakfast before I left. Speakin' of which, you wan' walk off the grub or celebrate later?"

Huh? *I was clearly not versed in Hunter lingo because I really had no idea what he was saying.* "Walk off or celebrate what exactly?"

He gave me a look down and turned off onto a winding road. "Breakfast. Want it now or after the hike?"

"Oh, right. Later would work best."

We drove silently for a few more minutes before I ignited the conversation once more. "Sorry, in New York we have a very different way of speaking. Especially in my job, I'm surrounded by very... *calculated,* people, I should say."

"Well, Adam, I ain't no calculator I'll tell ya that."

I respected that, surveying the basic white t-shirt he wore and sport shorts, his hair roughed up underneath a black baseball cap.

When I first saw Hunter, he wasn't anything like I expected. My sister always went for the pretty boys, the Lacoste guys that weren't innately awful, but definitely not marriage material. It wasn't as if she was searching for a soulmate when we were growing up, but for the love of all things good was she ever naïve in her type.

I blame my parents for that, always setting her up with the sons of their country club business mates. Out of all the people I'd circulated around, those were by far the worst.

Hunter was the type of guy that those men would make fun of behind his back, but never to his face. No, they'd quake in fear because even I could admit... Hunter was a tank.

He was a little taller than me and carried himself with zero regret. Though from what Marley told me, he didn't have the easiest time.

I knew about his mom's passing, but I would never bring that up. We barely knew each other and I believed Hunter only asked me to come hiking as a common courtesy since he was dating my sister. But all the same, I appreciated the attempt.

We pulled into a gravel lot just below a forest entrance, parking between two sedans. He killed the engine and unlocked the doors, stepping out of the truck as we started towards the open fence.

"How long's the hike?" I asked, keeping up with Hunter's pace as we set course uphill.

"How ever long you want it to be."

One thing I noted about him, even throughout the dinner was his lack of substantive communication. Not that he was horrible at conversation, no, he was actually quite good at questioning. But when it came to him, he was very cut and dry. To the point, centered and no bullshit.

Honestly, I liked that. I'd met a few of Marley's past flings and they all tried way too hard to win some sort of approval. For my parents, it took two things – money and status. For me, I just wanted to see that look in Marley's eyes that told me she was happy.

The second Hunter walked in to the restaurant and they looked at each other, both lighting up like a Christmas tree, I just knew... they had something good and that's all I could ever want for my little sister.

After a tedious trek through mud and sharp branches, we finally exited the woodland area into an open path. I breathed in the fresh air, realizing that we were atop a hill that overlooked acres of greenery and flowers.

"Wow," I released, gazing at the vast plain that seemed never-ending.

"Gorgeous, huh?" Hunter chimed, stopping beside me.

"You come here a lot?"

"Yeah," he took a seat on a patch of overgrown grass and stretched out his legs. "Best place in the world."

I remained standing, stretching out my limbs. "For a place so pretty I assumed there'd be more people."

"Nah, we didn't take a common route." He pointed towards another trail that rested near a creek below. "Most people like covering lower ground. They got no idea what kind of sight they're missin' up here."

397

"Can't argue with that. It really is something."

That wasn't a lie. In New York, I was so used to the smell of toxic fumes polluting the air that breathing in something so fresh was unnatural.

When Michelle's parents retired, they moved to a small town near Maine with little population. Their house was situated near the lake with a private backyard, hidden by patches of trees on either side.

It only took one visit for me to miss a lifestyle I never lived. What an odd thing to say, I know, but it held merit. Something about a simple, quiet life that provided peace in a way I could never fully grasp. Peace that had been so out of my reach since the day I was born.

"Got any trails like this back home?" Hunter asked, playing with grass hairs.

"Not that I know of." I took my place beside him, resting an elbow on my knee. "Lots of gyms, though."

He snorted. "I bet. God, I could never live somewhere like New York."

"To be fair, I don't think New York would welcome you either." I joked, returning my gaze to the ethereal setting in front of my eyes.

We sat in silence for a moment, but it wasn't awkward. From the beginning, Hunter's presence never felt threatening. Sure, I sized him up to my best ability when I first met him, but I had to do that for Marley. I wanted a reaction, and he didn't give me one. That alone was grounds for respect.

"I'm sure Bambi's told you how awful I was to her in the beginning."

Bambi. Ha-ha, don't think I'll ever get used to hearing that. "Once or twice."

He cleared his throat, looking ahead. "I've apologized to her plenty of times, but I gotta say sorry to you."

"What for?"

"You're her brother, Adam. I misjudged her, treated her like shit, pushed her away cause of my own damn problems. In turn, I hurt her when she was already hurtin' and I didn't know.

"I didn't know how bad the family dynamic was. I didn't know you guys didn't talk for a period of time, I knew nothin'. Thought I did," he shook his head, "*nothin'.*"

All the times Marley told me about Hunter before they became what they were, she talked out of anger. I didn't blame her for it, hell, a part of me resented him for the way she'd spoken about his nature. Though after meeting him, there was a level I didn't fully understand. A part of him that was desolate and sad, and call me an asshole, but I'm glad I wasn't in his shoes.

"She cares about you," I began, "she's happy and she cares. That's enough for me."

His head hung low as he spoke. "I don't know if it'll ever be enough for me."

"What do you mean?"

"She's just..." he trailed. "She's so good, and pure and kind. I'm scared I'm gonna fuck it up even more than I did before. That one of these days, I'll snap and I'll lose her again. I don't know, I'm sorry for dumpin' all this on ya."

"You sound like Marley." I rolled my eyes, thinking back to numerous times she'd apologized when she called during work hours.

"I never used to, I can assure you that." Hunter scraped the stubble along his jaw as he turned to face me. "I love her."

Judging by the hesitation in his speech, his demeanour didn't strike me in a way that told untruth, rather, a vulnerable realization he was just coming to terms to.

"I knew that already," I snorted, slapping him on the back as I hopped up. "Don't go making babies with her, though. I love my daughter but I'm thinking of hiring a nanny to prevent stress-induced hair loss."

A laugh escaped his throat as he sprung to his feet and maintained my pace down the hill. "Wall-Street power dad."

Holding my head high, I smiled at the one guy I finally thought Marley got right.

"I'm getting that written on a t-shirt."

After the torturous hike, I realized I was completely out of shape and beside myself with hunger. Hunter delivered his promise and bought bagel sandwiches for breakfast, grabbing a few more to go.

When I walked back into our hotel room, Marley was holding Rosy while Michelle reheated some leftovers from Berandino's last night.

"Hi boys," my wife said, planting a swift kiss on my cheek. "How'd it go?"

Chugging down the water bottle in my hand, I wiped sweat off my brow. "I need recovery time and a massage."

"That's the most New York thing I've ever heard you say," Marley piped from the loveseat.

I shrugged, unable to protest my needs.

"Michelle, I got some bagels if you want 'em." Hunter passed me the brown bag, strutting towards Marley with a smile. "C'mere, sweetheart."

She looked so happy when he leaned down to kiss her, greeting my daughter with a gentle squeeze of the cheek. When I made my way over there to retrieve Rosy from Mar, she placed a finger over her lip.

"She's sleeping, don't disturb her."

"You don't want a break from carrying her?"

She shook her head. "Never, this is good practice for my future self."

Both Hunter and I exchanged a glance as he held his hands up in a joking fashion. "We aren't expectin' any kids, cross my heart."

But I wouldn't have been mad if they were. Marley was only twenty-four, but she always had a maternal instinct in her to care for someone, *anyone* rather than herself.

I had no doubt in my mind that she would be an amazing mother, and Hunter, though I knew very little of him, seemed to be completely taken by her. If he really was the real deal, I would not be opposed.

"So what's next on the agenda?" Marley asked, rocking Rosy back and forth. "Water rafting? Mountain climbing? Or maybe snorkeling in the Mariana's Trench?"

Fuck the ocean. Pardon my language but *fuck the ocean.* That's one hundred percent why Marley suggested it, and when she threw me a fairy-like wink, it confirmed my suspicions.

"Trying to get me killed?" I narrowed my eyes at her, chuckling.

And in the oddest, most comforting turn of events, Hunter placed a firm hand on my shoulder and smiled. "Nah, I always wanted a brother."

Chapter Forty-Five
Marley

I love Hunter Lane.

I love him so much. I love him with everything in me. Never did I ever think that four months ago, when I first told him I loved him on my birthday, that I could possibly fall even harder.

But I had.

I had, and I was over the moon, drunk in love with Hunter Lane.

Call me a sap, call me obsessed, but if you had a man like him, you would be too.

On the eighteenth of September, Hunter's twenty-sixth birthday, I made sure to plan out everything that he loved to do; shooting range, axe-throwing, four-wheeling... and do you know what he did? On *his* birthday? He bought *me* a Tiffany bracelet with our initials engraved in the silver heart. ME. HIS birthday. *My freaking heart.*

I didn't love him because of the gifts, though. I didn't love him because of his looks, even though he was a sight to see every time I saw him. I loved him because of who he was, to the core. The man that had been buried for so long, the man I swore never to give up on... he resurfaced, he was in shallow water. *He was no longer drowning.*

But even still, there were some things that took getting used to. I was as affectionate as a snuggle bug, but Hunter wasn't the touchy-feely type unless he wanted to. I chalked it off to some untouched corner in his brain that associated affection to loss, two opposite feelings that intersected within him.

It's a fascinating thing, your mind. How something could feel so good but hurt like hell, all at once. I think that was just it – Hunter didn't know which emotion to feel. And that only made me love him more.

A little under a month ago, Hunter and I had been laying in bed, and I popped a starburst into my mouth to ask him a question. *Yes, we still kept that tradition and I would never break it.*

I'd asked him, "when did you fall in love with me?"

And he replied, "the second I believed the smallest part of me deserved you."

I was stunned, baffled, confused. I shot up immediately after that and said, "you don't think you deserve me?"

"No." Short and simple.

My heart broke for him. I didn't know what to do, how to help him, so naturally... I cried. Sobbed like a freaking baby. Mixing my period and boyfriend who felt undeserving of genuine love... yeah, I was bound to be a complete wreck.

After that night, we never talked about it again. I didn't overcompensate for the love he didn't have for himself, but I made damn sure to prove to him he was worthy of it.

Months and months of dates, family gatherings and opening up to each other led us to this precious moment, right now, surrounded by the Lanes, Uncle Glen and Betty around the Christmas tree.

"Can I make a toast?" Payton said, standing up with a wine glass in hand. "I'm gon' make a toast."

The room chuckled as she carried on her speech, pointing to each person as she spoke.

"To Glen, for bein' such a stick in my ass."

Glen shrugged. "Sticks are fun."

"To Betty, the best and worst sister alive."

"Love ya, sis." She raised her can of green beans and grinned with sparkly wide eyes.

Payton bent down to plant a kiss on Dex's cheek, squeezing his shoulder. "I love you, Dex. Thanks for being the better half of me."

I blushed as Dex's stoic expression turned soft, an emotion he only reserved for Payton.

"Hunter," she addressed.

"Yeah, yeah, Merry Christmas Payton." He took a swig of his beer, smirking with full knowledge that he'd pissed her off.

And that he did. When I turned to Payton, she was red in the face, downing all her wine in one gulp.

"I'm jolly today, I ain't no grinch. But sometimes, Hunter..."

"Try again next year, will ya?" He pushed, but just as she was about to snap, he got up and did the most unexpected thing I had ever seen.

He hugged her.

Hunter Lane literally hugged Payton.

The whole room was silent, and I didn't blame them. In all the years Payton had lived with them, Hunter told me he never even shook hands with Payton, let alone wrap his arms around her.

Payton was white as a sheet and I burst into laughter, checking Dex who was stunned as well.

"Would ya look at that?" Uncle Glen slapped his knee, pointing over to his brother. "Your boy ain't no grinch either."

"I guess not." Dex released.

Hunter moved back to his spot, draping his left arm around my shoulder and raised a hand.

"Continue your toast, Payton. You left out Bambi."

When Payton was finally mobile again, she cleared her throat and broke a smile.

"And to Marley..." she shook her head, eyeing me with crystal blue eyes. "For bein' at the right place, at the right time, and blessin' our lives as each day comes."

Before I could react, the whole family brought their glasses to the middle and began clinking each other's, repeating "cheers" over and over until everyone was spread out across the room once again.

Hunter placed a gentle kiss on my cheek, pulling me closer. "To many more Christmases with you, Bambi."

... and the butterflies are back. Truthfully, I don't think they ever left. How could they? Every single thing Hunter said sent a rush through my spine and pierced my heart.

"So many more." I responded, leaning my forehead against his.

"I hate to break up this moment," Dex interjected, standing a few feet away from the couch. "But Hunter, can ya head on over to the store and get some more eggnog and Brandy? Glen's callin' for it."

Hunter rolled his eyes, keeping a firm hand over mine. "Can't go yourself?"

"Had too much to drink, son. Glen's shitfaced."

I raised a hand. "I'll go, I only had half a glass of wine."

But Hunter was already on his feet, yanking me upright. "That ain't a task for you, sweetheart. Grab my jacket over there and walk me out?"

It never occurred to me that guys like Hunter actually existed. When I first met him, I didn't think he would ever be capable of being a gentleman. Even at Rivertown Bay, when I saw a side of him I hadn't seen before, I didn't think it could get better... but it did. *He* did.

I snagged his coat and followed him to the door where he was already slipping into his boots.

"You okay to drive?" I asked, handing over the black flannel.

"Course, baby. I limit myself to one beer during these things."

The cold air slapped me in the face as he opened the door, hooking his truck keys off the wall rack.

"Forgetting somethin', Bambi?" He cooed, pointing towards a mistletoe hanging above the door frame.

Rolling my eyes, I grabbed hold of the collar of his coat and pulled his lips to mine.

"Tastes like fuckin' candy." He placed another gentle kiss on my nose and stepped outside. "You been eatin' those starbursts without me?"

"Never." I lied.

"Liar." He guessed.

I shrugged my shoulders, waving him off as he got into his truck and blew me a kiss. "I'll pick some up on the way back. Love you, baby!"

And I watched him go, pulling out of the driveway and disappearing onto the narrow road.

My man, my whole heart, my happily ever after.

Chapter Forty-Six
Hunter

Fuck was it ever icy.

The snow painted the grass like fluffy marshmallow icing, but the roads were coated in a thin layer of black ice patches, undetectable and slick.

I had my winter tires on so I wasn't totally freaking out, but had Bambi been out here with those tiny Malibu wheels, I'd lose my goddamn mind.

Oh well, the liquor store and grocery were just five miles down the road so I'd be back in no time.

Porn Star Dancing by My Darkest Days came on the radio and I turned it up louder, blasting my national fuckin' anthem on this festive holiday. *Sure as shit ain't no Christmas tune, but it was a bop nonetheless.*

I pulled into the general parking lot and snagged my wallet from the cupholder, stalking into the sliding door's of the liquor store when a twiggy, dishevelled man shouldered through.

"Watch it." He ordered, his filthy fuckin' breath splitting my senses in half.

My first instinct was to knock his yellow teeth out, then give 'em a quick brush right after. But I decided against it, holding my breath as I followed behind him. *Not today, Hunt. Not today.*

I found the brandy rather quickly and made my way to the festive drink aisle where I spotted some peppermint flavoured eggnog with scotch mixed in.

"Why the hell not?" I shrugged, swiping that in my hand.

On the way to the cash, I found some peach rings set on display, an orange label written above: Use me for a chaser!

Like, an alcohol chaser? Fuck it. It was no starburst but Bambi needed to expand her candy horizons. When she told me she'd only ever eaten gummy bears, I almost threw a fit.

"You've never had any other candy?" I'd gasped, in a state of complete and utter shock.

"Yeah, the gluten free ones from –"

"No, no, no. I won't hear anythin' more, Bambi."

Needless to say, I was in utter dismay over the fact she hadn't lived at all, having only eaten fuckin' gummy bears. Maybe this peach ring thing made a good chase, but it sure as hell made an even better redemption treat.

"Hiya." I smiled at the woman behind the register. "They really use candy as a chaser?"

She scanned all my items and said, "don't knock it 'till you try it."

Hm. "First I hear of this." I swiped my card on the reader, inhaling the putrid scent of that fart-bag standing way too close to me.

"Quit chattin'. People got places to be." The guy from earlier spat, clutching hold of an open J.D bottle.

"Sir, you gotta buy that before you drink it." The cashier said.

"I'm payin', aren't I?" He turned to me with beady eyes, beady *drunk* eyes and snarled. "Walk along, pretty boy. It's Christmas after all."

I wanted to kill him, I wanted to fucking kill him and stuff his body in the mud. All the flashbacks of my drunken bar fights with Josh surfaced to the forefront of my brain.

There was a reason why I came back with bloody knuckles so often. One wasted bastard after another, pestering me, taunting me to the point of blinding rage and I'd snap. Mind you, since Bambi I'd barely gone back to any bar for that matter, but those memories were still there. And so was that anger.

Just walk away, Hunter. Walk away. For once, my movements obeyed my commands and I grabbed hold of my items and mumbled a low *"merry Christmas"* and stepped out of the store.

"What's so merry about it?" I heard the drunk man say, but I shrugged it off and locked myself in my truck.

Inhaling a deep breath of private air, I turned on the radio and ripped open the bag of peach rings.

They were stale like dried wood, but I got a kick out of it. Thinking about Bambi eating those with a sour face but saying she loved them anyway would be a sight for sore eyes, and I was ready to see those chocolate beauties again.

Cranking the engine, I stepped on the gas and made my way out of the lot, tapping my fingers against the wheel.

The guitar riffs of AC/DC blared through the speakers as I hummed along to Thunderstruck, getting lost in my own world.

Fuck I loved music. I loved singing even though my voice sounded like my throat had been stepped on. I loved Christmas time even though I hated the goddamn snow. I loved it all. I loved Bambi. I loved her so much and she made me fall back in love with the things I forgot to feel for.

I don't know what it was about this time of year, but it put me in my damn feels. Last year, Bambi and I had spent Christmas together, but we weren't a couple. Did I like her then? Of course I did. Did my dumb ass admit it? Nope.

Realizing how much of my time I spent hating her, ignoring the feelings that were clearly there, God... I beat myself up about that every day.

There could've been months where I had the opportunity to hold her had I made the admission. But I didn't, I didn't and I was stupid. But now that I had her, there was not a damn thing on planet Earth that would get in the way of that.

Dim lights flickered behind me as I glanced to my rear-view mirror, seeing a beat-up Buick tailing me. When I narrowed my eyes to get a closer look, I could see that it was the drunk from the liquor store, right on my ass.

"The fuck?" I muttered, switching my eyes from mirror to road, mirror to road.

I felt the boot of my truck nudge forward, the metal screeching as the Buick kissed my licence plate. Fury bubbled inside of me and in my best efforts, I tried to confront it but it was too late.

Rolling my window down, I launched an arm out and threw up the middle finger, increasing my speed down the winding road.

"Drive faster!" His voice travelled in the winds, but I was beside myself in vexation.

I took care of this truck for years. There was never a scratch, never a fuckin' hairline fracture on my baby since I bought it after my mom passed.

Throwing my old Ford in to the junk yard was the best damn thing I could've ever done. Living with the guilt that my mom died right beside me, and I didn't have the ability to save her... fuck that haunted me. And no matter how hard I tried to fight it off, it tormented me still.

"Faster, asshole!"

He hit the back of my truck again, sure enough making a dent as I floored it, zooming at sixty miles per hour. The icy wind paralyzed my body, but the rush was blazing inside of me. The chase, the drifting, the driving... this adrenaline I'd been victim to for so long.

The trees raced by as I checked one more time at my rear-view mirror, seeing nothing but the projected shadows of hills and evergreen.

"Lost him." I laughed, doing a shoulder check with a prideful simper. "Fuckin' lost h –

Chapter Forty-Seven
Marley

"I'm going to try calling again."

Straight to voicemail. I rang Hunter twelve times in the past hour, baffled as to why it took this long to get alcohol and some freaking eggnog.

Worry began to set in as Dex, his own father, phoned him too.

"Voicemail." He grunted, a hard line cementing over his forehead.

"Where are you..." I whispered, biting on a hangnail as I paced around the living room.

By now, the buzz of the Lanes completely dissipated as we waited for Hunter's call. A call that never came.

"To hell with this, I'm goin' out lookin' for him." Dex said, snagging his keys off the side table.

"I'm coming." I insisted, trailing right behind him.

Dex didn't protest as I secured the buttons of my coat and followed him to his truck. For the life of me, I couldn't settle down. I had a nervous twitch that would manifest into my fingers when I had a horrible gut feeling. And for some reason, I couldn't shake it off. That was the worst part.

We drove for a couple of minutes, taking turns calling Hunter only to be redirected to his voicemail again. "Go for Hunter. *Beep.*"

"Oh, for God's sake." I snapped, locking my phone in frustration. *Where the hell was he? Was this a sick prank he was playing? No. He wouldn't. Not on Christmas.*

"This ain't like him." Dex muttered, driving down the winding road at forty miles per hour.

The sun was setting over the mountains, cascading feathers of light onto the black ice shining on the cement. That sinking gut feeling returned as we turned the corner, and my stomach sank.

Scratch that.

It freaking drowned.

Blue and red. Blue and red.

Police cars, police officers, they were everywhere.

They surrounded a truck lodged in between the trees, completely flipped on its head. A black truck. His truck –

Hunter's truck.

"No! No!"

I don't even think Dex stopped driving when I jumped out of the passenger door. My legs were carrying me, but they felt severed from my body. Like somehow I was floating and time stopped and everything was spinning and I was... I was out of control.

My heart ached as I ran passed the caution tape, barreling towards Hunter's truck seeing no sign of him.

Smoke, smoke was everywhere. Broken glass scattered the terrain.

Hunter. *Where's my Hunter!*

Strong arms wrapped themselves around my waist, dragging me away from the scene. Whose arms? Fuck if I knew. Fuck if I cared. *They weren't Hunter's. They weren't Hunter's.*

I came face to face with a cop dressed in a black and beige ensemble, mouthing words in my direction but they weren't meant for me. How could they be? How could he be talking to me when he should be finding Hunter?

"This is bullshit! Go look for him!" I completely lost it, ignoring everything vocal that came out of his mouth.

Dex's hand was wrapped around my forearm, gripping me backwards as he lowered his mouth to my ear.

"Marley, d'you hear what the deputy said?" His voice shook, but he wore a brave face. How could he wear a brave face. His son was missing!

"Let me go, Dex." I ordered, inching away from him but he yanked me back.

"Damnit, Marley, Hunter's at the hospital! He got into an accident."

Accident.

Hunter got into an accident.

I laughed. I laughed in disbelief. "No he didn't."

Ha-ha. Tears sprung to my eyes. *Why am I crying? I shouldn't be crying. He's fine. He's okay.*

"Let's..." my mouth was dry. So very dry. "Let's go see him. Let's go Dex. Keys, Dex. Come on."

I started for the truck, forcing my eyes away from the smoke emanating from Hunter's truck. Hunter's truck that was flipped, squashed between trees and giant stones, laid out like a corpse on the cold snow.

"Marley."

The way he said my name halted my movements. Pain. So much pain. Anger. Guilt.

Pain.

Pain.

Pain.

When I finally had the courage to look into Dex's dark blue eyes, they were covered by a blanket of gloss. Evident tears stamped his cheek as he sucked in a jagged breath.

"He got admitted to the ICU. It's fuckin' serious."

ICU. Intensive care. Why would he need intensive care? Why would he need any care? He was okay. I could take care of him. I could fix him, I could help, I could...

My knees hit the ground before I even realized I was falling. The frost penetrated my jeans, tickling my skin and numbing my body. But I was already numb before it could puncture any other part of me. I was already frail, and weak and cut open by razor blades as I looked upon the crash.

"Get up. Let's go." Dex ordered, sniffing as he lifted me to his side and secured me under his arm.

We walked and walked and walked. I dragged my feet across the ice until I fumbled with the passenger handle and locked myself away in Dex's truck. I was here not too long ago, before I knew what was to come. Maybe I can find that place again. Maybe if I settle in the same position, I'll find that blind comfort I lost.

But as we drove towards the direction of the hospital, my thoughts spiralled out of control.

Is he dead?

Is he breathing?

Is my Hunter still with me?

He has to be. I can't lose him. He can't lose me.

We can't lose us.

My dad's words replayed in my mind as I gripped Dex's arm, the skin of a Lane, and repeated, "if you aren't willing to fight for what you're after, you don't deserve it in the first place."

Well, I deserve you Hunter Lane.

And you deserve me.

"I'm sorry ma'am, he's in surgery right now. You can't see him."

The nurse had spoken to the paramedics who informed her of what happened at the scene. Apparently Hunter had slid on a patch of black ice while he was turning and flipped his truck over. For the life of me, I couldn't understand how that was possible because his truck was huge and he drove safe for the most part... at least now he did.

"Surgery for what?" Dex pried, a grovelling mess next to me.

"Hunter sustained life-threatening injuries, Mr. Lane. I don't know if you want to hear the –"

"Spit it out, goddamnit!"

Normally, I would've sided with any health care worker and defended their position to carry professional composure, but my mind was a bees nest of anxiety and fear. All I needed to know was one thing.

"Is he alive?" I whimpered, rubbing my eyes for the hundredth time in thirty minutes.

She nodded. "He is. But Hunter is suffering from multiple bone fractures and cerebral edema."

"Cerebral edema?" Dex questioned.

"Brain swelling. There's a significant amount of fluid build up in his brain from the trauma of the crash, and we are doing everything we can to –"

"You better be. You fuckin' better be." He threw up a finger and pointed directly in the nurses' face. "If my boy dies on a metal table, without me, I'm going to sue this fuckin' hospital."

"Dex, they're..." I needed to fight this pain, I needed to. I couldn't drop down to the ground again, not with the reality settling into Dex's mind. "They're going to patch him up. He'll be okay."

The nurse smiled sadly before mumbling a soft "I'm sorry" and returned back into the staff quarters.

"Dex..."

"I need a minute." He walked towards the seating area and took a spot near the window, burying his face in his hands.

There were a few others, sitting down reading newspapers and magazines, unaware that my boyfriend, Dex's son, was in surgery to drain fluid from his brain.

He was unconscious, being operated on.

He was alone.

He was alone when he crashed. Scared. Vulnerable.

Alone.

I couldn't fight the tears as I made my way to Dex, planting myself onto the cushioned seat next to him.

We sat in silence. What could I have said? Was there any hope in making this situation better? Was there even a solution? *Stop it, Marley. Stop it. You're making this worse. He's okay. He's okay. He's getting the help he needs. Stop running inside your head. Just breathe.*

"I told him to do it." Dex stirred, uttering under his breath. "I told Hunter to go to the store. He's on that operating table right now cause of me."

"Dex –"

"Don't, Marley. I have failed that boy one too many times, and I just did it again."

"You didn't fail him. This wasn't your fault."

"Leslie, my wife. She got into an accident, too. Couldn't save her. Couldn't save my damn self. And Hunter," he shook his head, releasing a slated breath, "Hunter fuckin' died and I had none of it. And now he could be dead, for all I know the boy could be fuckin' dead –"

I acted on instinct and wrapped my arms around Dex's shoulders, pulling his large frame against mine as he choked on tears. It squeezed more out of me, seeing him grieve the loss of his wife, accepting the tragedy of what had happened and what could happen to Hunter... *No! NO! He's in good hands. He's alive. He's freaking alive.*

A swarm of bodies entered through Gate Three of the ICU as Payton, Betty, Uncle Glen, Cramer, Josh and Winter barged in, making a B-line towards us.

Payton knocked twice on the front desk, practically yelling out, "Hunter Lane. What's the news on Hunter Lane?"

Winter and Cramer pulled me into a hug as Josh, Hunter's best friend stood back with puffy eyes.

"I saw on the news, babe." Winter rubbed dried mascara fibers off my cheeks. "Do we have any information?"

"The nurse said brain swelling and multiple bone fractures."

Josh cursed and threw his hands into the air. "That fuckin' guy! What was he, drunk? Was he drunk again?"

I was on my feet in seconds, yanking his disturbed presence into reality. "His truck slipped on ice."

"You mean to tell me Hunter's monster truck soared through the fuckin' wind cause of some black ice? Nah. I don't believe it for a damn second."

"Josh," Winter placed a gentle hand over his shoulder. "We have to put our trust in the doctors. We don't have any control in this situation."

"He's my best friend." Josh stuttered.

"He's my boyfriend." I contested, pulling back my quivering lip.

"He's my fuckin' son." Dex's voice sounded behind me, tainted with agony.

Payton's blonde hair bobbed against her neck as she stomped towards our circle with broken eyes. "*Our* fuckin' son."

Her words drained the life out of me, begging me to lay my head against her shoulder and sway into her maternal arms. I hadn't had this unity in so long. In fact, I never had it.

Since the day I was born, my parents never made me feel appreciated. I wasn't a human, I never was. A display, some spitting image of Harlow Matthews that she kept around until I was a bag of sticks to be tossed away.

These people, *my* people, they were a bundle of love. Warmth. Warmth that resurfaced into my life the second Hunter Lane walked in.

I refused to let him walk out. There was no chance in hell I was leaving him. None of us were.

The clock read: **9:54pm**

Everyone formed a square, sitting huddled against each other in the corner of the hospital. We didn't speak. We didn't look at each other. We were lost in our own minds, and I was a prisoner of mine.

But so was Hunter, my poor Hunter. My love. My heart. He needed to know he wasn't alone, that we were here. Fuck. Fuck. Fuck.

What I would give to know what he's thinking right now.

Chapter Forty-Eight
Hunter

April 22nd, 2017

"Don't those beaded bracelets tug at your arm hair?"

I drove down Tintsy road, blaring The Rolling Stones with my mom riding shotgun. She had a habit of twirling those damn stones around her wrist ever since my dad bought them matching bracelets for their anniversary. Call it cute? I call it cringe. And painful. Probably fuckin' painful.

"A bit. But I love it. Dad's got good taste."

"Or no taste at all." I rebutted, rolling down the window.

The crisp night air caressed my features as it filled the truck with a gentle breeze, sweeping underneath my ballcap.

"What would you get a girl then, huh? And don't tell me a deconstructed boat figurine."

I laughed. "Why the hell not? It's an interactive activity."

"Smart boy."

Picking up my mom from her evening spin classes was always the highlight of my day. It sounded dumb as hell, driving fifteen minutes down the road to get her when she was fully capable of drivin' herself, but we talked a lot on these trips.

She was always helping my dad out on the farm and I was practicing baseball with my coach almost every day of the week. We hiked a lot, but the trek was tough and talking made it impossible to breathe up in the hills. This was our time, and I adored it.

"Uncle Glen got a new dog, d'you hear? Teddy. Big malamute."

"At least he'll have company." *I joked, thinking back to all of his failed relationships.*

Honestly, it wasn't a mean thing to say cause he even acknowledged the fact. He tried many different women out, but he was never the sharpest shooter. Always attracted the ones who wanted to settle down, he said, and for some reason, that saggy ball-sack thought he still got the tiger in him. Delusional, I'll tell ya.

"You excited to play for Iowa?" *My mother beamed, placing a hand on my shoulder.*

I shrugged. "Sorta. It'll be a change. Not like I wan' go pro or anythin' but, we'll see how it plays out."

"You love baseball."

"I love home."

I did. More than anything, it was my comfort, my safe zone. I had Josh, my family, a guaranteed job for my future on the farm. Everything was planned out for me, and disrupting that peace wasn't something I jumped at the chance to do.

"Home's never gon' leave you, Hunt. Not even when you're a million miles away."

"Yeah?" I queried, throwing her a side eye. "You gon' lift the farm all the way to Iowa when I miss home?"

A soft chuckle escaped her lips. "Home ain't always a house, baby."

It happened before I could stop it.

It happened before my foot could slam the break and halt the movement of my truck.

The lights blinded my eyes, the speed was too fast.

We were spinning.

We kept spinning and spinning.

Spinning.

The force of another car pushed against my side door, throwing me off the road and into the ditch as my head slammed against the side window and immobilized my instincts.

My head. My fucking head.

My... my stoma –

The foul stench of vomit soaked back into my skin as I hurled all over myself, choking on bile.

"Mom," I coughed. "Mom, Mom... Mom."

I couldn't see her, I couldn't feel her. My hands were knotted around my seatbelt, the airbag and puke shoving against my face.

A shooting pain pierced my arm as I managed to push away from my seat and spit out all the saliva out of my mouth.

I tried to move.

I tried. I tried so hard but I couldn't.

I couldn't get to her.

A tree log had split and penetrated the glass window, separating me from my mom.

My mom who wasn't moving. My mom who sat still, lifeless.

"Mom!" I tried, reaching out my right arm to her, cutting the tips of my fingers along the sharp bark.

"Fuck!" I grunted, pulling harder against my seatbelt but the blood flow in my arm was cut off, weak and limp.

Sirens wailed in the distance as I took a deep breath and tried again.

Her blonde hair was a mess over her face, those blue eyes buried beneath her lids. They wouldn't open.

Why wouldn't they open?

"Move! Mom, move!"

The sirens grew closer, louder. "Mom, there's help coming, please..."

I managed to wiggle my fingers through a small opening beneath the tree, grabbing hold of a rough material that I recognized as her sweatpants.

A wet substance weeded through my fingers as I pressed down hard, collecting more of the gloop. When I yanked my fingers back out, bile rose to the front of my throat again when I realized they were covered in blood. My mom's blood.

  This can't be happening.

  This can't be happening.

  This isn't real.

  This isn't fucking real!

  This... this doesn't happen to people like me. This doesn't exist in my world.

  My hand shook violently, attempting one more time to reach out to my mom but she was unresponsive. She didn't move. She was... she was a fuckin' mannequin.

  "Over here!" Said a muffled voice from outside.

  She wasn't moving.

  She wasn't moving.

  It was cold, but there were no breaths.

  Why weren't there any breaths?

  Is she... I didn't have the strength to say it out loud.

  I would never say those words out loud.

  They weren't true.

  They weren't true.

  A strong light winded me as I craned my neck away from the beam, tuning to the sounds of frantic chatter and movement outside my truck.

  Help her.

  Save her.

  Save my mom.

  Shut up, Hunter. Why would she need saving? She's alive.

She's alive.

She's ali...

The passenger door flew open and two men grabbed hold of my mom, pulling her into their arms.

That's when I saw it.

The shard of glass lodged in her chest.

Speckles of it tainting her skin.

Blood.

So much blood.

And my mom... her face, her beautiful face...

White as stone.

My hands frantically searched for a piece of glass, a piece of anything sharp to slit my throat with.

I needed to die, I needed to die, I couldn't – I couldn't be here, not with her.

I killed her.

I KILLED MY MOM!

Strong arms gripped the back of my neck but I fought it, I fought it with every ounce of energy I had left.

"She's not dead!" I combatted, flailing my free arm at the officer. "She's not fuckin' dead! You fix her! You fix her, you hear me!"

My eyes were ringing, my vision was blurred. A pain so acute, so heavy pushed down on my chest.

I'm having a heart attack.

"Let it happen!" I shouted. "Let me go!"

I screamed for her, begged for her while they dragged me out of the car.

My injuries were kind.

Hers killed her.
I killed her.
I killed her.
I watched my mom die.
And I killed her.
"Let me go! I'm dying, I'm dying! Let me fuckin'
go!"
They didn't.
They wanted to save me.
They couldn't save my mom, but they wanted to
save me.
A shame that was. A waste of supplies –
To save a man who was already dead.

Chapter Forty-Nine
Dex

My brain was a mess.

I was a goddamn mess.

My wife, now my boy. How could I be so unlucky? So many times I watched Hunter drain a bottle or two in my presence, blaming himself for Leslie's death when he got nothin' to do with it.

And I let him.

I let him think he was the cause, the worst son, undeserving of happiness and love. Hell, I trained him that way. I didn't want no emotions on my lawn, not from him, no. He looked too much like her.

What a sick fuckin' twisted menace life was.

Couldn't quench the satisfaction of takin' my wife, now they were takin' my son in the exact same way.

God fuckin' damn life. Damn life and whoever wants to live it.

"Surgery." I muttered, running on no hours of sleep.

Payton and Marley had been the only ones who stayed back, though Marley had the good graces of falling asleep. Maybe out of exhaustion, but I couldn't do it. Fuck did I ever wish I could, though.

"Hm?" Payton stirred beside me, falling in and out of her scattered naps.

I surveyed the wall clock that read: 4:09am

We'd been here for so long, yet it felt like no time had passed. Probably cause I just kept trickin' myself into thinking the worst.

"You think he's dead?"

"Dex!" Payton whipped, slapping my shoulder. "Don't wan' hear that again."

My whole body fell forward, defeated, ready for the worst. If I prepped for it, maybe it wouldn't be so bad. "Do you?"

"They would've told us if there were any complications, don't you dare say that again."

Maybe they forgot. Maybe results got lost in translation and he was already at the morgue.

Tears burned my eyes. Fuck this. Fuck this goddamn situation. Fuck the cars. Fuck the streets. I'm never leavin' my damn house again, neither is Payton, or Marley, or anyone close to me cause this is bullshit.

I couldn't do it. I couldn't sit here and wait for them to tell me my boy had joined his mother, my wife.

If they told me that, I'd run myself into the river no doubt. Might as well lock me away now.

But as I stood up to collect my coat, a man wearing a bright blue coat with a paper bandana strode towards us, removing his gloves.

Payton kicked Marley's shoe as she stumbled away, wiping a trail of drool off the corner of her mouth.

"Mr. Lane?" The man asked, directing his attention towards me.

His tone was impossible to read. It was calm, but not overly calm and not overly enthusiastic. *Jesus Christ if he's about to tell me...*

"I'm Dr. Brinstead. Hunter just got out of surgery."

"And?" Marley piped, on her feet within seconds. "Can we see him? Is he okay?"

The doctor pressed his lips into a fine line and pulled out a clipboard, flipping over a few pages before he cleared his throat.

"Tell me he's fuckin' alive." I ordered. I needed to hear it. I didn't give a damn shit about any autopsy or labs or anythin'. My boy was alive. I had to know it.

With a slow nod of the head, he replied, "Hunter will be okay."

The salty liquid busted through the walls of my eyes before I had time to stop it as I yanked the doctor in for a hug and submerged myself in the relief.

Had I lost Hunter, I was ready to go. I was about damn ready to fall off a cliff and dive headfirst onto those rocks. I was the one who told him to go to the store. Me.

All those years, I never knew what Hunter felt. I didn't understand why he blamed himself. But there I was, guilting myself into oblivion cause I pushed my boy into leavin' and then he got hurt.

But he was okay. He was going to be okay. My boy was still breathin'. That was good enough for me.

Payton's arms wrapped around my waist as she tugged me back, drawing me closer to her side.

Before the doc could open his mouth again, Marley jumped onto him and sobbed like I knew she would. That girl loved my boy more than anything, and knowing that she could see Hunter again softened my heart.

She brought the best outta him. Never had I ever seen him as happy as Marley made him. They were total opposites, don't get that fuckin' twisted. But I saw Leslie in her. That light in the darkness, the precious, innocent spirit that could yank out all the bad in ya and turn you into somethin' sweet.

My boy deserved that.

They both deserved that.

"I'm sorry, Dr. Brinstead. Carry on. We're all just..." Marley turned to us with a quivering lip. "We're just emotional, and happy. Happy that's he okay."

He nodded in understanding, returning his gaze to the clipboard. "He is. Though he needs to stay in recovery for at least three weeks. That doesn't include the physio treatments which will be an extension of six months, regular weekly sessions."

The fuck?

"Three weeks? Physio? " Payton gasped. "What the hell happened?"

"Did the nurse discuss cerebral edema?"

"Yeah, yes." I responded.

His finger traced along a sheet of paper as he continued to speak. "Well, Hunter endured blunt force trauma from hitting his head on impact. Luckily we didn't have to perform a decompressive craniectomy... removing part of his skull, in other words. But we drained the fluid that caused the swelling in his brain and he is currently undergoing oxygen therapy."

I couldn't even find the words. I didn't have any. I mean, I had to. There was so much to say. But –

"One more thing. There was an injury to his left leg that ruptured his nerves. This can happen when a leg is bent in a certain way for a long period of time, but the muscles were strained and his joints need reparation. We need to monitor him, just as a precaution for the after-effects of surgery and for physio."

Marley's soft sobs sounded beside me as she wrapped her arms around her middle and let her head hang low. Payton made it to her side as I stood frozen, clenching my fist.

My boy endured that. My boy went through all that fucking pain because I sent him to the goddamn grocery store. Anger filled my veins but I kept it at bay. I could blame myself later. Right now, I needed to know he was in good hands.

"You keep close watch of him, Doc. You hear me?"

He flipped the loose papers back into place and nodded. "He's very lucky. Some people aren't."

And as he walked away, that final statement rang through.

Some people aren't.

My wife.

Had she not been lucky? Did life really hate her that much that they were unable to spare her life?

Shake it off, Dex. You can't change the past. Hunter's here now. He's going to be fine. Just in rough shape. But he's breathing.

Before the doc could get any further, I chased after him in a hurry. "Wait – hold on."

"Yes, Mr. Lane?"

I sucked in a breath, and broke my walls. "Thank you. Thank you for saving my son."

The crease in his forehead softened as he released a breath. "Mr. Lane, I have treated hundreds of patients in my day. Many of which give up the second they're wheeled in to my hospital. But your son, he had a will to live. Maybe the strongest I'd ever seen."

A glossy sheen covered my vision as I choked out, "you mean that?"

His smile said it all. "Hunter chose life."

Chapter Fifty
Marley

I visited Hunter every day for three months until he could finally manage without one of those walker things.

He was allowed to come home at the end of the first month, but I didn't want to spend all of my time smothering him with all my pent up affection. No matter how much he wanted it, I needed to make sure I wasn't disturbing any healing processes that were necessary.

About two weeks after Hunter had been admitted to the hospital, the sheriff informed Dex about what really happened that day. Turns out a drunk man had been tailing Hunter for a few miles, pushing up on his truck.

I broke down when I heard that. Knowing Hunter wasn't the one to have caused this because of reckless driving, but reacted to the man who provoked it... I was a mess. I wanted to track him down and spew fire onto his hands and feet. The fingers that gripped the steering wheel that turned him off the road... the foot that pressed on the gas to torment him.

But then I realized, harbouring hate in my heart for someone who was just a shattered shell, someone who was already being dealt with by law enforcement – well, that wasn't my place and I only cared about one thing.

Hunter.

When the doctor told us he was going to be okay, I think I stopped breathing for a second. My world fell apart when I found out there was a chance I could've lost him. But I didn't.

He was alive.

And the man I loved was sitting beside me, on this warm March afternoon, on a picnic blanket by the lake.

"You don't understand how much I hate the fuckin' walker, Bambi. You don't."

He shovelled a turkey sandwich into his mouth, gripping a handful of chips as he layered them on top of the meat.

I'd come up with the classic date spread; red-checkered blanket, a basket of wine and homemade sandwiches and some chocolate covered strawberries. *Yep, I finally got my picnic date after all. And I had the best company in the entire world.*

Sure, I was playing classic rom-com Hallmark movie, but I didn't care. Every single second I spent with Hunter was precious, valuable. I couldn't even think about the first day we met, those months that followed of agonizing tension between us.

But now here we were. Holding hands, laughing, cuddled together under the tree shade. We were together. This is what mattered.

All of the little moments in life make up the big ones. We can't pick which minute matters because they all do. And if you let one of those moments slip, you regret the time you lost when you could've had it.

I wasted my minutes hating the Hunter I thought I knew. And I cherished the seconds I spent loving every part of him.

"I quite like the walker," I teased, biting into a strawberry. "It's edgy."

He let out a laugh. It was so good to see him laugh. To watch those dimples, and the creases underneath those crystal eyes. The happiness. *Happiness I gave him.*

"If ya like edgy, darlin', I'll start wearing eyeliner and pierce my ears."

"You won't." I challenged.

"I totally would if –"

His sandwich dropped in his hands, the contents spilling onto his jeans as he muttered in curses, gripping his calf.

On instinct, I placed one hand over his and the other over his knee. "What can I do? Can I help?"

"No, baby." He eased back, grimacing. "No it's okay. It flares up sometimes."

Before I could meet his eyes, I forced down the feelings of pain and sadness. I don't know why I was always consumed with it. Every time I saw Hunter struggling to walk, or hurting in general, a part of me broke in half. *If only we could trade places...*

"Don't cry," he released, turning my chin to face him.

"I'm sorry this happened to you, Hunter. I'm sorry that guy aggravated you into reckless driving. I'm sorry that you fell into that old habit when you tried so hard to get out of it... God, I'm so sorry. You don't deserve this."

His soft lips pressed against my forehead as he snuggled in closer, pulling me onto his shoulder.

"Did I ever tell you about the first time I woke up after the surgery?"

My hand gripped his thigh, playing with loose strings on his ripped jeans. "Nope, please share."

He chuckled. "The nurses told me I was laughin' my ass off. I remember that. Realizing I manifested my almost-death in the same way my mom went."

"Hunter..."

"Nah, listen. I cried after that. A lot. At first, I didn't think it was fair but I was waiting for those feelings of guilt to come back. Y'know, the ones cursin' the world for letting me live and not Mom.

"They never did. And I realized it was cause I wanted to live. God, I've been trying to end it all for years. Four years that's all I thought about, all I wanted...

because I haven't felt alive since. But here you are, baby." He leaned his chin atop my head and planted a gentle kiss on my temple. "My lifeline."

My heart swelled as I pulled him down for a kiss. To consume myself in all of him. To relish in this moment for the rest of my life because he was here with me, completely intact, all mine. Forever.

Never in my life did I think I could find something substantial. I fought off tthe tyrants, the fake love, the horseshit image of affection my parents crafted for me. I hated myself for years, I didn't have a place. I couldn't find my purpose, what I wanted... I was a mess.

But when I met Hunter, that all changed.

I channelled my emotions into hating him, into indifference, into friendship then love. Love I suppressed.

Love I deserved.

And more than anything, he deserved this. This sunlight. These breaths. The pounding of his heartbeat thumping in his chest.

There was hope.

We healed each other.

And for the rest of my life, I would spend forever chasing after the high he brought me with one single smile. One soft kiss. One breath as long as he was breathing.

"I love you, Hunter." I promised. With everything in me, I solidified the emotion branded in my heart.

And he smiled. The smile I saw when he looked upon his mom. The smile he shared with very few people, but belonged to me.

"Till my heart stops beating."

Epilogue
Three Years Later

Bambi and I spent the first five months of my recovery travelling to the places we wanted to go most. At first she thought I was fucking insane, asking how I'd be able to sight-see with the pain in my leg, but I'll tell ya, Advil works wonders and so does a cane.

Actually, I took more pride in my appearance now that I had one. Personally, I felt like a James Bond assassin or some shit, and that cane became my ride or die.

Bambi's place of choice was Italy, so for three months we took it upon ourselves to get an Airbnb there where not only did I propose to her in Rome, but I also got her pregnant. Funny that.

It was towards the end of our stay there that we found out, so I swept us off to New Zealand for sixty-four days before returning back to ours in Nebraska.

When we checked in with our doctor, he informed us that there were two little babies inside of my Bambi, and out popped the fraternal twins: Wren and Luke.

Wren, our beautiful baby girl was born five minutes ahead of Luke, the wrestler who rocked out at eight pounds. Who would've thought that a boat-ride in Italy would've got me so horned up that I pumped two of the most amazin' critters I ever did see in my whole damn life. My fuckin' children. My world.

Adam ended up being promoted to the official manager of his financial advisory unit on Wall Street, so he bought a vacation home in Aurora where he spent most Summers.

I was glad to have him around. He became a brother to me, never looked at me like I had some sort of defect or anything and pushed me to exercise with whatever might I could. Those hikes were mighty hard, but I'll be damned if they were impossible.

Rosy, his daughter, was the best playmate our kids could ask for. They loved the shit out of her and seeing them play together made my life complete. Everything was complete. No matter what happened.

You see, life, it's a bitch. If someone told ya different, they were livin' in La La Land high on shrooms. The one thing people never tell you, though, is how important every part of your body is. How much you should cherish the things you often forget.

My leg could've been gone, clean off from the impact. I could be sleeping six feet under or a bundle of ash floating off in the river.

But I wasn't. I was here. I was here, I was breathing, I was alive.

Fuck all the times I wished for death, invited it. What a mistake that is, to believe life isn't worth living just cause something bad happens to you.

I was moving some stuff out of my old shed to take to our new apartment when the bottle of unopened scotch caught my eye, collecting dust in the back corner of my bar cart.

"Damn, been a while since I've seen you." I sighed, thinking back to my old self shelving that for the day I got to drink it with my mom.

Only it was never for a good reason, and for years I'd been trying to end it all just to share a glass with her. *Fuck, Mom, if you saw me now.*

Bambi's laugh rang through the air, flooding through my opened door as she pranced in with my baby Wren by her side.

"Dex needs you to help him lift an old box to the yard sale. Wren wanted to say hi to her daddy, so I let her tag along."

"Daddy!" Her chubby little arms jumped into mine as she gripped my leg, holding tightly.

I pressed my lips against her silky brown hair and shooed them off. "I'll be there in a minute, baby."

They walked across the field, disappearing behind the farmhouse as I quickly snagged the unopened Johnnie-Walker and followed suit.

After helping my dad lift an old box of toys out to the front, I planted my ass down on the steps, watching the kids run around with my girl by my side.

We sat, hand in hand on the porch, inhaling the fresh smell of blossoming flowers and clean air. Her head lay nestled in the crook of my neck as she huddled in closer.

"You know what's weird, Hunter?" She murmured.

"Hm?"

Her arm extended out as she pointed to the white sign up in front of the farmhouse. "2204."

I let out a low laugh cause I had zero idea what she was hinting at. "Yeah? What of it, Bambi?"

"2204." She repeated, meeting my eyes with a softened gaze. "April 22nd."

She didn't need to say another word for me to fully understand the coincidence of our address. "April 22nd..." I huffed, utterly flabbergasted.

My mind wandered to that day, the day she passed. The 22nd of April eight years ago. Jesus Christ, that was fuckin' something wasn't it.

All these years, living on this land, I hadn't even noticed it. That never clued into me, not ever. But seeing the sun shine down onto that sign, the breeze drifting this way and that like a wave from the wind, I knew it was no coincidence.

My heart pumped faster as I pressed my lips to Bambi's forehead, taking in the breath of being alive as I looked up into the sky to see a cloud shaped like a sailboat.

In that moment I knew. I knew she was there. She was always there, and I didn't need to be gone to feel her presence. My fingers wrapped around the stem of the unopened scotch as I took in a breath, and flicked off the cap.

Lifting the liquor up in the air, I nodded forward and pressed my lips to the brim. "Here's to you," I smiled, taking in the moment belonging only to us. "Cheers, Mom."

The End

Acknowledgements

For starters, I need to thank the real life Hunter Lane. Thank you for being the muse to my story, for providing me with a different perspective on life and every situation that comes with it.

Next, my family. Mom, thank you for all your support even when I know the content of this book is too raunchy for your eyes to read. My brother, for giving me the time to vent out all my frustrations and my best friends, Rachel and Mariah who constantly lift me up and believe in me with all that they have. Steph, my aunt and editor, you are the biggest help when it comes to my writing process. Without you, I'd be nothing but a girl with a dream.

Grand-Pa, well, you won't understand a damn thing I write but thank you all the same for being my biggest fan.

The real Winter Camden? You know who you are. Summer, I just need to thank you for the endless FaceTime calls you allow me to bore you with. You hype me up more than I deserve, and for that, bless your fuckin' heart.

And lastly, I need to thank you. The readers. The people who gave me this platform and interacted with me along this journey.

Always remember your place in this world comes with purpose, hope and love. Don't ever forget to live while you're still alive.

Author Note:

Reviews mean everything to me! I love talking to my readers so please do not hesitate to shoot me a DM on any of the following platforms:

- Instagram - @mariefranceleger
- TikTok - @maariefraance

I highly encourage you to leave a review on Amazon or Goodreads. It really helps small authors out (like myself) to garner notice and build a readership community.

Again, thank you all so much for reading "2204 Hunter Lane." Out of all the pieces I've written, this has been my favourite and something very near and dear to my heart.

Always remember, without you I would not have a platform and a bunch of friends that I can talk about my love for reading and writing with.

Thank you, thank you, thank you.
I love you all and I am looking forward to our next adventure together.

Xo,
Mar

Marie-France Leger

...

Manufactured by Amazon.ca
Bolton, ON

26582410R00266